RESURRECTION

....

STEVE ALTEN

....

FORGE®

A TOM DOHERTY ASSOCIATES BOOK
NEW YORK

This is a work of fiction. All the characters and events portrayed in this book are either products of the author's imagination or are used fictitiously.

RESURRECTION

A Forge Book
Published by Tom Doherty Associates, LLC
175 Fifth Avenue
New York, NY 10010

www.tor-forge.com

Forge® is a registered trademark of Tom Doherty Associates, LLC.

ISBN 978-0-8125-7957-4

First Edition: February 2004
First Mass Market Edition: June 2006

Printed in the United States of America

0 9 8 7 6 5 4 3 2

For Kim . . .

. . . and to the courageous Men and Women of the
363rd Expeditionary Airborne Air Control Squadron
and the Pacific Forces AEF 7

And there was war in heaven:
Michael and his angels fought against the dragon;
and the dragon fought and his angels,
And prevailed not; neither was their place found any more in heaven.
And the great dragon was cast out,
that old serpent called the Devil and Satan,
which deceiveth the whole world:
He was cast out into the earth,
and his angels were cast out with him.

—REVELATION 12:7

None of those who were born in the light,
Begotten in the light
Will be yours . . .

—THE HERO TWINS, TO THE LORDS OF THE UNDERWORLD

EXCERPT FROM THE MAYAN POPOL VUH

The Universe is not only stranger than we know,
it is stranger than we can even imagine.

—J.B.S. HALDANE

Acknowledgments

As a writer, I have found the experience of penning the novels of the Domain series to be both mentally exhausting and creatively exhilarating . . . *exhilarating* in that the research often required to flesh out the story line has been as fascinating as it is frightening, exhausting in that the backdrop takes place in humanity's past and future—an uncertain future, to be sure. One small futuristic detail can have a domino effect on dozens more, and at times, I felt as if I were consuming an iceberg from the tip down—the more I thought I had digested, the more it seemed was waiting for me below. Fortunately, I have come to know a growing circle of talented readers whose own intelligence and experience far surpass mine, and their contributions to keeping my work "in line" from a scientific perspective was invaluable.

And so, my heartfelt thanks to the Resurrection team: "Interstellar Bill" Parkyn (science and mythology), Dr. Lowell Krawitz (meteorology), Dr. David Mohr (rocket science), Bill McDonald of Argonaut-Grey Wolf Productions/ Web site: www.AlienUFOart.com (paranormal science and mythology, as well as the MAJESTIC documents, and images of the *Balam* and Nazca whale), Professor Barry Perlman (physics), Professor Stephen Davis (chemistry), Barbara Esmedina (research), Konstantin Leskov and Pat Weiler (science), Bill Raby (story editor), Rabbi Richard

Agler, and Kevin Williams, whose afterlife studies and Web site (www.near-death.com) provided valuable insight into near-death experiences and the spiritual realm.

As always, many thanks to my literary manager and editor, Ken Atchity, AEI creative executive, Brian Fagan, and the rest of the team at Atchity Editorial/Entertainment International for their hard work and perseverance, as well as Danny Baror of Baror International. Appreciation to Tom Doherty and the great people at TOR/FORGE Books, especially editors Bob Gleason and Greg Cox, as well as Heather Drucker in publicity. Special thanks to Ed Stackler at Stackler Editorial, who is always there when I need him, and copy editors Bob and Sara Schwager.

My appreciation to Matt Herrmann for his amazing original cover design and to Leisa Cotner Cobbs for the www.SteveAlten.com Web site, enhancing the reading experience for my fans, and for her enthusiasm and tireless efforts in the Adopt-An-Author Program (www.Adopt AnAuthor.com).

To my wife and soul mate, Kim, for all her support, and, as always, to my readers. Thank you for your correspondence and contributions. Your comments are always a welcome treat, your input means so much, and you remain this author's greatest asset.

—STEVE ALTEN

To personally contact the author or learn more
about his novels, click on www.SteveAlten.com

Resurrection is part of Adopt-An-Author,
a Free Program designed to excite
Middle and High School students to READ.
For more information, click on www.AdoptAnAuthor.com

A wisp of thought, in the consciousness of existence

I am anger.
A black hole of rage.
Lost in eternity.
God's abandoned child.
Seething with the mortar of indignation, imprisoned
within its invisible walls.
The confluence of bitterness ferments my soul.

I am the product of injustice, and self-servitude, and
greed.
I am the void that tasted love and lost it forever.
Loathing existence.
Set adrift in my own ocean of hatred.

I am the end of humanity and its beginning.
I am One Hunahpu and the universe laughs at me.
I am . . . Michael Gabriel.

PROLOGUE

THE JOURNAL OF JULIUS GABRIEL

Excerpt taken from video recording at
Harvard symposium*

AUGUST 24, 2001

*T*he End of Humanity. Who has time to contemplate such folly? Job security, the falling Dow, overdue bills, our diminishing retirement funds—these are the daily burdens that occupy our minds, not humanity's extinction.

"My name is Julius Gabriel. I am an archaeologist, a scientist who hunts humanity's past in search of the truth. For the last 32 years, my family and I have been searching for the truth behind the Mayan calendar, a 2000-year-old instrument of time and space more accurate than its latter-day European counterpart. Believed

---

*Footnote:
Professor Gabriel suffered a fatal heart attack moments after delivering his speech.

All grants supporting archaeological investigations into the Mayan calendar were suspended three weeks later following the terrorist attacks of September 11, 2001.

to have been created by the mysterious Mayan wise man, Kukulcán, the calendar abruptly ends with humanity's demise on a date equating to December 21 in the year 2012. As if to remind us of the event, the shadow of a giant serpent will again appear on Kukulcán's pyramid in Chichén Itzá in 29 days, just as it has each autumn and spring equinox for over 1,000 years. Let me assure you, this baffling special effect was not intended as a tourist attraction.

"Who was the great Kukulcán? The Mayans describe him as a tall, Caucasian man with long, flowing white hair and beard and blazing aqua blue eyes. Quite the mystery, considering the first white men didn't arrive in Mesoamerica until the early 1500s . . . 500 years after Kukulcán's passing! Adding to this mystery is the fact that, in every successful ancient culture, there has been a great teacher whose description is almost identical to Kukulcán's. In Giza, Egyptians worshiped this wise man as Osiris, at Stonehenge he was Merlin. In Nazca and Sacsayahuman, the Incas revered him as Virococha, and among the Aztecs he was Quetzalcoatl.

"Mysterious wise men . . . each introducing science and civilization to their assigned peoples. The Bible describes them as giants, men of reknown. I've identified them as extraterrestrials, humans from another time, another place. And they came here to save us from the cataclysm that will arrive on the winter solstice of 2012.

"I am not here to debate the existence of ETs and UFOs with Mr. Borgia. As archaeologists, we know real doomsday events have overwhelmed our planet's inhabitants throughout its history. As scientists, we know our Earth lies within a cosmic shooting gallery of asteroids and comets. We know that 65 million years ago, an asteroid, seven miles in diameter, struck our world at the same ground zero that would eventually become the Mayan homeland, ending the dinosaurs 200-million-year reign. Was it predestined or an accident? Could such an event happen again? It's been estimated that 2,000 such civilization killers continue to cross Earth's orbit, though to date, we've only accounted for one in ten.

"The Mayan calendar was left to us 2,000 years ago as a warning. Should we heed it, then perhaps we can save ourselves from whatever cataclysm lies ahead.

"Or, as is the nature of our species, we could simply ignore the warning signs until something terrible happens . . ."

PART 1

CONCEPTION

Time is not at all what it seems.
It does not flow in only one direction,
and the future exists simultaneously with the past.

—ALBERT EINSTEIN

We cannot change anything until we accept it.

—CARL JUNG

1

The *Dojo* is sixty feet long and thirty feet wide, its walls covered in mirrors, its floor made of polished wood. Master Gustafu Pope, fifth-degree black belt and former karate champion of Argentina, turns to his "Bushi" warriors, all seated along one wall in a lotus position. "Richard Rappaport. Andrea Smith."

Hearing her alias, thirty-one-year-old Dominique Vazquez jumps to her feet. Like the rest of Master Pope's students, the ebony-haired, Hispanic beauty is dressed in full *Bogu*—protective armor. Her chest and stomach is covered by the *Do*, her waist in the *Tare,* her hands and wrists by the *Kote* gloves. She slips the headpiece known as the *Men* over her long ponytail, the heavily padded base protecting her face, throat, and the sides of her skull.

In her hand is the *Shinai*, a sword consisting of four staves of bamboo, joined together at the handle and tip by leather straps. Designed to flex as it strikes an object, the *Shinai*, though infinitely safer than its predecessors, the *Fukurojinai* and *Bokuto*, is still a weapon that can kill.

She takes her place across from her opponent. Rich Rappaport is bigger, stronger, and more experienced than Dominique, but lacks her tenacity.

Master Pope calls out, *Rei.*"

The two student combatants face each other and bow.

"On your marks."

Bracing their bamboo swords, each moves into a crouching posture.

"Begin!"

Dominique attacks, shouting out, "*Men!*" as she launches an overhead blow to her opponent's head. Rappaport blocks the strike, but the woman's furious barrage continues, her *Shinai* a blur as it lashes out at the man's forearms and chest. Dominique calls out body part names before each strike, her brown eyes focused intently on her fellow Kendo student through the bars of her headpiece.

"Oosh!" Master Pope awards Dominique a point for a strike to the top of the head.

The two students return to their spots.

"One to zero. On your marks . . . begin!"

"*Kote!*" Dominique prances ahead, her *Shinai* raised to strike Rappaport's forearms—

"*Men!*" as the tip of her opponent's sword strikes her in the throat.

"Oosh!"

Dominique drops to one knee, swallowing hard against the throbbing pain.

Master Pope bends to her. "Can you continue, Ms. Smith?"

She nods.

"One to one. Back to your marks."

She hustles back to her place, her blood pressure seething.

"And . . . begin!"

Dominique is an erupting volcano, her anger raging, her arm and shoulder muscles bulging beneath her armor as she whirls the *Shinai* at the retreating Rappaport—

—who deftly blocks each of her strikes, then slices her across the midsection.

"Oosh!" Master Pope signals to Rappaport. "Two to one, point and match. *Rei* to me, to each other . . . and shake hands."

Rappaport offers his hand, his face expressionless in victory.

Dominique shakes his hand, averting the eyes of the senior student.

"Ms. Smith, may I see you?"

Dominique tucks her headpiece into her gym bag and joins Master Pope in his office. "Yes, sir?"

"How's your throat?"

"Fine."

Master Pope smiles. "It's good you were wearing *Bogu* or you'd be speaking out of a second mouth."

She nods politely, her cheeks flushing beneath her Hispanic complexion.

"Andrea, you're an excellent student, truthfully, I've never met anyone who trains so hard as you. But in battle, technique is not everything. Kendo teaches us to observe our opponent and devise the appropriate strategy in order to achieve victory. You fight with anger, you fight to kill, and in doing so, you reveal your weaknesses to your opponent."

"Yes, sir."

"The Way of the Sword is the moral teaching of the Samurai. The art of Zen must go hand in hand with the art of war. Enlightenment is the realization of the nature of ordinary life."

Ordinary life? Ha. I'd give my right tit to have an ordinary life . . .

Master Pope stares at her as if reading her mind. "The teaching of *Ai Uchi* is to cut your opponent just as he cuts you, to train without anger, to abandon your life or throw away your fear."

"Do I seem afraid to you?"

"What I perceive is not important. Each of us has his demons, Andrea. I hope Kendo will help you to one day face yours."

* * *

Dominique changes into an old Florida State tee shirt, shorts, and her cross-training shoes, then stuffs her equipment bag into a locker and heads for the weight room.

Chris Adair, her personal trainer, is waiting for her by the rack of dumbbells, his dreaded clipboard in hand. "How was Kendo?"

"Good," she lies.

"Then it's time for a little pain." He sets the bench press at an incline, then hands her the two thirty-five-pound dumbbells. "I want twenty reps out of you, then we jump to the forty-fives."

Dominique emerges from the gym two hours later, her freshly showered and massaged body still trembling with fatigue. The gym bag filled with wet clothes and equipment causes her right shoulder to ache, and she leans on the heavy bamboo cane for support.

The older woman with the burnt orange hair pulled into a bun is standing by her Jeep, the grin of a cultist pasted on her face. Her eyes are shielded behind the wide wrap-around sunglasses preferred by seniors.

Dominique approaches warily, gripping the handle of the bamboo cane tightly in her right hand. Concealed within its false bamboo outer casing is a *Katana*, the double-edged carbon steel blade of the Japanese sword deadly sharp.

"Hello, Dominique."

"I'm sorry, you must have me confused with someone else."

"Relax, my dear, I'm not going to hurt you."

Dominique remains at sword-striking distance from the older woman. "Is there something you want?"

"Simply to talk, but not here. Perhaps you could follow me to my home in St. Augustine."

"St. Augustine? Lady, I don't even know you. Now if you'll excuse me—"

"I'm not a reporter, Dominique. I'm more of a messenger."

"Okay, I'll bite. Who's the message from?"

"Maria Gabriel. Michael's mother."

In her peripheral vision, Dominique notices the two Homeland Security agents approaching, one from each end of the parking lot. "Sorry, I don't know anyone named Michael, now I have to go." She turns and walks away.

"Maria knows you carry her unborn grandsons in your womb."

Dominique freezes, the blood draining from her face.

"Maria's energy force reaches out across the spiritual world to contact you. You are in grave danger, my dear. Let us help."

"Who are you?" she whispers. "Why should I trust you?"

"My name is Evelyn Strongin." The older woman removes her sunglasses, revealing bright azure blue irises. "Maria Rosen-Gabriel was my sister."

Dallas, Texas

The three-thousand-seat arena is standing room only, as it has been every evening over the last four weeks. The television cameras and Internet videocams are manned and ready, the studio audience prepped.

Houselights dim, igniting a fresh buzz of energy.

The candy-apple red curtains flutter, then part, revealing center stage and a charred, seven-foot-high cross.

Mirroring the symbol, his arms outstretched, is the televangelist.

Peter Mabus is a heavyset Caucasian in his early fifties. His Alabama accent is thick, his thinning black hair slicked back and combed over. His pasty pale complexion matches his suit and tie and shoes.

The flock grows silent as he raises his head to speak.

"I'm going to tell you a story, ladies and gentlemen, a story about a man whose existence was riddled with disease, a disease that affects the mind and the body and the spirit. A disease that contaminates the soul. A disease that nearly destroyed society. Yes, my friends, I'm talk'n 'bout that disease known as Greed. This man had all the symptoms. Selfishness. Dishonesty. Malice. Jealousy. Envy. He was a liar and a cheat, and he was corrupt as corrupt can be. He was CEO of one of the largest defense contractors in the world, and he was heavily invested in oil. He was a man who treated women as objects, and bathed in the nectar of their sex until their flower withered and died. And then one day, ladies and gentlemen, as this despicable wretch of a human being lay in his mahogany four-poster bed in his fourteen-thousand-square-foot mansion, an Angel appeared before him. And the Angel brought with it a vision. And the man saw this vision, and in it was the Rapture. And he saw devastation and pestilence and death. And he saw the end of humanity, charred and ruined, buried beneath smoldering rubble. And then he saw the Lord."

Peter Mabus looks up as an overhead light casts its heavenly beam upon his face.

"And the Lord said to the man, 'My son, see what your sinful ways have brought? My children have forsaken me, allowing the serpent to take root in their garden.' And the man became frightened, and he dropped to his knees and repented. And the Lord said, 'Because you have asked my forgiveness, I will spare humanity, but only if you rise to lead the flock.' And the man bowed his head, and the Lord touched his heart.

"Gone were the greed and hatred that had corrupted the man for so long. Gone were the lies and the deceit. And the man rose from his knees and was embraced by the light, and the covenant was made."

Mabus steps away from the crucifix.

"I was that man, ladies and gentlemen, and that vision came to me four months ago, ninety days before the winter solstice of 2012. From that day forward, I have served the Lord as his humble servant, carrying His word to the flock. And when the Rapture arrived, and the bombs fell, the Lord kept His word to me, and spared our people."

A chorus of Amens.

"And when the serpent showed his face, that wily Devil, the Lord smote him with His light and saved us again."

"Amen, amen."

"Divine intervention, children, it was divine intervention. And now, as I stand before you, a changed man, a servant of the Lord, I ask for your support. It was our leadership in Washington that brought the Rapture, it was the policies of Clinton and Bush and Maller and Chaney that nearly destroyed us. God has given me a vision, my friends, and the vision is to carry his word to Washington, then to the rest of the world. America's strength as a Christian nation has been compromised, along with our values as human beings. The Lord Jesus Christ has blessed us with a second chance, one we cannot forsake. Support us now. Rise with me, rise up—"

Small sections of preseated worshipers rise, encouraging others to do the same.

"—take your neighbor's hand, children. Go on. Hold your hands high to the heavens and praise God. Will you praise Him with me?"

"Yes!"

"Will you rise above your sins with me?"

"Yes!"

"Will you support my campaign to restore goodness to our nation, so that we may never face our annihilation again?"

"Yes . . . praise God."

"Because there's so much work to be done, so much good to be spread around the globe, so that we may finally conquer the diseases that still plague mankind."

A small army of men in white suits appear in the aisles, their empty buckets aimed at the chanting crowd.

Mabus looks directly into the camera lens. "It's time to

go forth and spread the word, ladies and gentlemen. Call
tonight and pledge your tax-deductible donation. Call tonight and join God's party, so that together we can create a
groundswell of love that will sweep us into the White
House. This is the vision our Lord and Savior gave unto
me, it is the covenant He made when He spared us from
death. Remember back to that day, then reach deep into
your wallets and show the Man upstairs that you deserve
this second chance. Stand tall with me, my children, support the Lord so that we can walk together, hand in hand in
the spirit of Jesus Christ, our Savior, into the Ever-After.

"Amen."

The makeup artist touches up the last bit of shine beneath
Richard K. Phillips's eyes as the host of the political forum
takes his place opposite Peter Mabus.

The television producer pauses as instructions are re-
layed from his producer over his earpiece. "All right, gentlemen, we're rolling in three . . . two . . ."

Richard Phillips looks into camera one. "Good evening.
Tonight, *World News* speaks with Peter J. Mabus, former
CEO of Mabus Enterprises, and presidential candidate for
the 2016 election."

"Good evening, Richard, and good evening to all our
supporters. God loves you."

"Mr. Mabus, let's get right to it. The next presidential
election isn't for another three years, why begin campaigning so early?"

"Richard, the message I carry knows no political
timetable. Now is the time for sweeping changes, and even
though we're not in office yet, we believe the current administration needs to feel the will of the American people.
Ennis Chaney has failed to restore faith in the United
States government, and without faith, this administration
will collapse, America with it. We simply cannot wait four
years to make a difference."

"To be fair, President Chaney's only held office for little over a month."

"You either have the faith of the people or you don't. Chaney doesn't."

"Mr. Mabus, you've openly blamed society's near demise on the previous administration's policies that led to global isolation. And yet, your own company profited heavily from the new regimes that rose to power in the Middle East, as well as Asia."

"And Richard, who better to institute change than one who knows what it's like to walk down society's dark path? Having been there, I know what it will take to root out the evil that shadows our society. More than anything, I believe this is why God chose me to lead postapocalyptic America."

"Interesting. However, isn't it also possible, as your critics are quick to point out, that your sudden foray into politics has more to do with simply reading the writing on the wall. Chaney's already talking about canceling the Space Defense Initiative that's been blamed for fueling nuclear buildups in Russia and China, and your company was its main supplier."

"You mean my former company. I resigned weeks ago."

"Still, you walked away with almost $200 million dollars."

"Those were stock options I had coming to me. George Bush's vice president received $20 million from Haliburton when he left, and they lost money under his leadership. The money I received was earned. God has no problem with that, especially when I'm investing it into a campaign that is doing so much good."

"Let's talk about your new political party, People-First."

"I think our name pretty much says it all."

"Some have labeled it extremism."

"Extremism? Richard, if the majority of Americans share our beliefs, then how is that extremism? We believe in the strength of the family unit. We feel the good ol'

Christian values that made this country great have been replaced by promiscuousness and a generation of children who fail to give back to society."

"When you say Christian values, you are aware how those words frighten most non-Christian Americans?"

"It's just an expression, Richard. I love all Americans, be they Jew or Hindu, or whatever, as long as they respect the values of a Christian society, which is what we preach."

"You realize what you're saying flies in the face of the Constitution."

"I believe in the Constitution, but let's face facts. It's been less than forty-five days since our political leaders nearly wiped out our entire species. If that's what the Constitution protected, then it needs some serious amending. Our Lord and Savior didn't save our butts just to watch us commit the same sins all over again. We need to learn from the events of 2012 and move on."

"Again, you credit Jesus with saving humanity, giving no credence to the administration's reports about Michael Gabriel."

"That crock about a race of superior humans building the pyramids? Please." Mabus leans forward, his eyebrows knitting. "Let me tell you something about this Michael Gabriel. I've spoken with many clergymen who are absolutely convinced he was the Antichrist."

"Mr. Mabus, by every account, Michael Gabriel died a hero."

"According to who? The government responsible for nearly getting us nuked? It's well documented that Gabriel's father, Julius, was a wacko, and so was Gabriel. He spent eleven years in a mental asylum for assaulting former Secretary of State Pierre Borgia. Does that sound like a hero to you? For all we know, Michael Gabriel may have been the one responsible for causing that alien to awaken in the first place. He did claim he had entered its vessel in the Gulf, right? He even said he was in communication with that demon."

"True, but—"

"But nothing. We've all seen the footage. Gabriel entered the serpent's mouth, and the two of them disappeared. Poof!"

"What are you implying?"

"Ain't implying anything, I'm tellin' you straight out that our Lord and Savior intervened at our darkest hour, sending Gabriel and his serpent back to Hell whence they came. Divine intervention, Richard, not some Mayan malarkey. Now humanity's at a crossroads. We either learn from this brush with extinction and elect leaders who will help us become the God-fearing people Jesus always wanted us to be, or we stick our heads back in the guillotine and wait for the next Judgment Day."

Peter Mabus signs three more autographs, then boards his private jet.

Campaign organizers line up to greet him in the aisle.

"Beautiful job, Peter. The latest polls show us approaching 22 percent."

"The Dallas speech netted just under two million. Well done."

"Salt Lake City booked us for three more trips. The Mormons love you."

Mabus acknowledges each assistant as he makes his way to his private office located in the rear of the 707 airbus.

An older, white-haired gentleman is waiting for him inside.

Mabus's campaign manager, Texas billionaire Joseph H. Randolph, Sr., looks up from watching the CNN broadcast. "You did well on the family values crap, but you lost points when you labeled Gabriel the Antichrist. This campaign's success may be fueled by a faith-based initiative, but the public still views Gabriel as a hero. In the end, his close ties to Chaney may be our undoing."

"Michael Gabriel will be old news by the 2015 New Hampshire primary."

"Maybe, but his child won't be."

"His child?"

Randolph nods. Hands him the report.

Mabus scans the document, his blood pressure rising. "The Vazquez woman's pregnant?"

"Yes, and when the public finds out, and they will, they'll flock to her like she's the second coming of the Virgin Mary, her newborn worshiped like the baby Jesus. Chaney won't even have to campaign, he'll waltz into the White House for a second term, and we'll never get his kind out of power."

"Christ!" Mabus punches the closest wall, then rubs his knuckles as he collapses into an easy chair. "So? What do we do?"

"Only one thing to do, we get rid of this Vazquez woman before the public finds out she's pregnant. I've already got my sources working on finding her. Fortunately, Homeland Security's overseeing her case, so it should be relatively easy to get to her."

"Do it. Spare no expense. I want that bitch and her demon seed dead by the weekend."

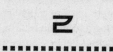

ATTENTION. LEAD VEHICLE NOW APPROACHING FINAL DESTINATION. HAVE A NICE DAY."

The sound of the Jeep's autopilot awakens Dominique. She stretches, inclines her seat, then glances at the digital clock. *Seven-thirty. I've been asleep for two hours.*

Evelyn Strongin's black Toyota is three car lengths

ahead, both vehicles exiting Smart Highway 95, following the ramp into St. Augustine, America's oldest city.

It was in 1513 that famed explorer and treasure hunter Don Juan Ponce de León first arrived in Florida, claiming the "Land of Flowers" for Spain. Fifty-two years later, King Phillip II appointed Admiral Don Pedro Menendez de Aviles as governor of Florida to protect the colony from the French. Menendez arrived on August 28, 1565, the Feast Day of St. Augustine and quickly fortified the coastal town, naming it after the holiday.

St. Augustine's history would be a bloody one. In 1586, Sir Francis Drake attacked and burned much of the city; in 1668, the pirate John Davis pillaged the town, murdering sixty people. With the British establishing colonies in the Carolinas and Georgia, Spain authorized the construction of the Castillo de San Marcos, a stone fort that surrounded the city, preventing it from being seized.

In 1763, Florida was ceded to England in exchange for Cuba, then returned to Spain twenty-three years later. The American Revolution forced Spain to relinquish Florida to the United States, and it eventually became the twenty-seventh state to be admitted to the union. America's oldest city would fall prey to a yellow fever epidemic, then see its borders occupied by the Union Army during the Civil War.

St. Augustine's bad run of luck would change in 1885, with the arrival of Henry Flagler.

The co-founder of Standard Oil saw the city's potential as a winter resort, and was soon investing heavily in lavish hotels and a railway linking New York to St. Augustine. A new city hall, hospital, and several churches would follow, making the city founded fifty-five years before the Pilgrims landed on Plymouth Rock the jewel of the South.

More than a century later, St. Augustine remains a popular tourist attraction, maintaining much of its old Spanish ambiance. The stone fort still remains, as do many of the city's original cobblestone streets and dwellings. One home dates back some four hundred years, and locals claim the older sections of the city are haunted by the souls of the dead. "Ghost" walking tours are given nightly in the old quarter, passing through dark streets and cemeteries where the spirits are said to be especially active.

Dominique disengages the autopilot, directing the Jeep along Orange Street and past the two looming stone pillars that once served as gateposts to the fortified city. The Toyota continues on for several blocks, then pulls into a parking lot across the street from an old brick drugstore.

Dominique parks next to Evelyn's car.

The old woman climbs out, stretching to ease her stiff back. "I'm not used to sitting for so long. Come, my dear, we'll pay our respects, then you'll join me for dinner."

Dominique follows Evelyn across the street and into the centuries-old drugstore.

"This dwelling and its parking lot were built over a sacred Indian burial site. The souls of the desecrated are still quite restless." She points at the front window where the headstone of Seminole chief Tolomato sits. A wooden sign stands next to the gravestone.

Dominique reads the inscription:

> **"NOTIS. THIS WERRY ELABORTE PILE IS ERECKTED IN MEMORY OF TOLOMATO, A SEMINOLE INGINE CHEEF WHOOS WIGWARM STUUD ON THIS SPOT AND SIRROUNDINGS. WEE CHERIS HIS MEMERY AS HE WAS A GOOD HARTED CHEEF. HE WOOD KNOT TAKE YOOUR SKALP WITHOUT YOU BEGGED HIM TO DO SO OR PADE HIM SUM MUNNY. HE ALWAYS AKTED MORE LIKE A CHRISTSUN GENTLE MEN THAN A SAVAGE INGINE. LET HIM R.I.P."**

"Lovely."

Evelyn stands before the grave marker, her eyes closed,

her lips mumbling something incomprehensible. After several moments she opens her eyes, then leaves the dwelling without saying a word.

Dominique follows her outside. "Look, maybe this isn't such a—"

"One must adhere to proper etiquette, child. Let's walk, my home's not far from here."

They continue to the corner, turning right on Cordova Street, its sidewalks shaded by oak trees. After several minutes they arrive at the sealed metal gates of an ancient cemetery.

Evelyn nods. "Tolomato Cemetery, one of the oldest graveyards in North America. Prior to 1763, the site was occupied by the Christian Indian village of Tolomato. The first bishop of St. Augustine is buried in the mortuary chapel at the rear of the cemetery. Most of the Spanish settlers preferred to be placed in stone crypts, our 'New World' soil never considered holy ground."

Evelyn continues walking.

Dominique remains by her side, the thought of so many old dead people lying so close sending chills down her spine. *What am I doing here? Get back in your car and drive home to Palm Beach County where the blue-hairs are still alive and kicking.*

Evelyn closes her eyes and bellows a bizarre laugh, as if sharing a private joke with a ghost.

Jesus, she's a lunatic. Wonderful. You've wasted all evening escorting a nut job back to her loony bin. "Evelyn? Hello, Earth to Evelyn?"

The old woman turns, her azure blue eyes radiant.

"Listen, it's getting late, and I have an early self-defense class. How about we do this another time?"

"Your grandmother says she misses working the onion crops with you in the Guatemalan Highlands. Her knees and back always felt so much better after your evening swim in Lake Atitlán."

Dominique's skin tingles. "I was six. How did you . . ."

"My place is just over there." She points to a two-story

redbrick, its paved walkway lined in white and purple impatiens.

The house is over two hundred years old, its security pad brand-new. Evelyn touches her fingertips to the soft rubber pad.

A *click* and the front door swings open.

Dominique follows the old woman through an arched corridor into a library, its floors made of beechwood, its furnishings contemporary. An entertainment center activates along one entire wall, broadcasting a CNN News-Flash:

> ". . . and in Antarctica, another glacier has separated from the Ross Ice Shelf, this one estimated at three times the size of the Irish Republic. Environmental scientists working with the United Nations insist that global warming has not escalated beyond anticipated figures for this year, despite the multiple pure-fusion detonations that vaporized large sections of Australia and Asia three months earlier. In other news—"

"Shut down, please."

The screen blackens.

"That's better." Evelyn turns to Dominique. "You must be famished. I took the liberty of ordering a few things on the trip up, they should be in the delivery pantry."

Too hungry to argue, Dominique follows her into the kitchen, a room harboring the latest in voice-activated appliances. "Mmm, is that fresh garlic bread I smell?"

"Yes. And pasta with marinara sauce." Evelyn opens the pantry door. Built into the exterior wall is a three-foot-by-five-foot stainless-steel hot box, one end opening to the pantry, the other to the outside of the house, allowing access for local deliveries.

The old woman removes the hot pouch containing their dinner and sets it on the black pearl granite kitchen table.

"Come. We'll talk while we eat."

Dominique takes a seat as her host sets the table, then

opens the Styrofoam containers, unleashing the aroma of fresh Italian food into the room.

"You miss him, don't you?"

Dominique breaks off a piece of bread and stuffs it into her mouth. "Miss who?"

Evelyn smiles, placing her palm on top of Dominique's hand. "My dear, dancing around the truth will only wear both of us out. Do you know what necromancy is?"

"No."

"Necromancy is the art of communicating with the souls of the dead. Some believe it's a black art, but that all depends upon who's doing the communicating. The practice can be traced back to the ancient Egyptians and their leader, Osiris, creator of Giza, who summoned the dead to obtain valuable guidance."

"So . . . you're telling me you communicate with dead people?"

"With their souls."

Dominique scoops up a forkful of pasta. "I don't mean to be skeptical, but—"

"The body is made of physical matter. At creation, each of us is linked to a specific soul, our life force, or spirit, the energy force that strengthens the body-soul connection."

"Okay, let me stop you there. First, I'm not a very religious person. Second, Ouija boards and all that hokey crap give me the creeps."

"But you've used them recently, haven't you?"

Dominique swallows hard.

"Because you're seeking answers to something."

"Yes."

"You want to know if Michael is still alive."

Dominique holds back her tears. "I just need some sense of closure. You know, so I can go on."

"What does your heart tell you?"

She sits back, wringing her hands nervously against her thighs. "My heart tells me he's alive. My brain says something else."

For a long moment the old woman just stares. "I can

guide you on part of your journey, Dominique, but I can't give you all the answers. If I did, it could alter the future."

"What journey? What future? What the hell are you talking about?"

Evelyn contemplates. Says nothing.

"I said what journey?"

"Your journey, Dominique. Your destiny, and the destiny of your sons."

"Know what—I made a mistake. I'm not ready for this." She stands to leave.

"Leave if you want, but it won't change a thing; in fact, it will only make things worse. For whatever reason, a higher power has chosen you to be part of a greater good, just as I've been chosen to guide you. I'm not your enemy, Dominique, fear is the enemy—fear of the unknown. If you allow me, I can shine a light into the void and help eliminate your fear. I can give you the knowledge you seek."

Dominique pauses, then sits back down. "Say what you have to say."

"The first thing we must overcome is your lack of trust. I'm not a screwball. I'm a psychiatrist who relies on science and scientific observation to guide me. At the same time, I come from a family whose maternal ancestors were always adept at interdimensional communication."

Evelyn holds up a finger, stifling Dominique's question. "To understand inter-dimensional communication, you must first accept that we are surrounded by energy, and energy is everything and all things, it is only our perception within this universe of energy that changes. This table, for example, appears solid, yet it is made up of atoms, all of which are in constant motion. If we examined an atom of this chair under a powerful microscope, we would see mostly empty space. High-speed particles—electrons— would zip by like asteroids, and if we could delve deeper, we'd see even tinier particles called quarks, which oscillate, expanding into other dimensions. Everything is energy and everything is in constant motion.

"The speed at which a living human being perceives energy places us in the world of the physical, the world of the third dimension. Because physical density occupies space, its perception must be processed with time. For most of us, our physical surroundings are perceived within the limitations of our five senses. But there are higher dimensions that exist beyond these capabilities. Mathematically, eleven dimensions have been theorized, taking us into realms of what many have labeled the 'spiritual.' Again, the common bond in all these dimensions is energy.

"As I said, energy is all around us. Our senses may not perceive it, but this room is filled with energy. It emanates from our bodies as heat and brain waves. It bounces around this room in multitudes of frequencies. By discerning an energy pattern, we can tap into it, using devices such as radios and televisions, videophones and satellite dishes . . . devices that would have been labeled the work of the Devil when this city was first christened. But the mind is also a device, and by fine-tuning it, we can communicate with those who have moved on to higher dimensions of energy. Spirits are aspects of God, Dominique, and it is spirits that create souls. Death is not the end, but the beginning of a transitional stage. After we die, our perceptions change, expanding as we acquire the higher dimensions."

"How do you know these things?"

Evelyn's face creases into a smile. "Because, my dear, I've been there. I've crossed over."

Dominique feels her flesh crawl.

"Happened many years ago when I was living in Miami, right after Hurricane Andrew. Once the storm had passed, I went outside to walk my basset hound, Oscar. Stepped right in a puddle of wet leaves and *zap*—never noticing the downed electrical wire. Charge must've hit me like a ton of bricks."

Dominique looks at the older woman as if for the first time. "So what happened? Did you really die?"

"As they say, I was dead as a doorknob. The first thing I remember is feeling free, every physical burden instantly gone. My consciousness floated above my body, and it was a strange sensation to look down at myself, sprawled across the sidewalk like a puppet who'd lost her strings. A lifeless body is never very flattering. And poor Oscar, barking his head off. You know, I think he actually sensed my spirit hovering overhead."

"Were you scared?"

"Not in the least, and I've never been scared since."

"What happened next?"

"My consciousness began moving through a dark tunnel, and up ahead, I could see a light. It was God's light, and it bathed me in a kind of love I had never experienced before." She pauses. "This is making you uncomfortable?"

"A little. If this is some sort of sales pitch to convert me—"

"Believe me, I'm the last person to preach religion. Fact is, I died an atheist, and not a very happy one. Of course, none of that ever occurred to me, until I experienced the life review."

"The life review?"

"It's your entire existence, every moment, every deed, every thought and feeling of everyone you've ever been in contact with, and you don't just experience it from your own perspective, but from that of others—the people you hurt, the people you helped. It was amazing and incredibly intense, some of it quite sad, but most of it wonderful, like being immersed in a sea of unconditional love. Still, I saw my shortcomings, and it was quite an awakening. And then I realized I wasn't alone, that my parents' souls were by my side. I didn't want to leave, but they told me it wasn't my time just yet, that I still had things I had to do in order to fulfill my mission in life. And suddenly, just like that, I was back in my body. It felt so heavy, like a lead suit, and I hurt terribly inside. I could hear and feel the paramedics working on me, and I felt sad, because I really wanted to stay with my parents."

"You said you came back to fulfill a mission?"

Evelyn sits back in her chair. "For years, I assumed my

mission was simply to help people understand death. When I recovered from my injuries, I went to work on my first book. To date, I've interviewed eighty-seven people, all of whom shared similar near-death experiences with me. I've compiled a library of pertinent data, and I've written two best-sellers. Despite these postdeath successes, I always felt something was missing. And then my sister died."

Evelyn stands. Crosses the room. Opens a desk drawer and returns with a color photograph. "Maria and I were inseparable as children, born only thirteen months apart. The two of us attended Cambridge together. I'll never forget the night she told me she was going off on some Mayan expedition with Julius and that jerk, Pierre Borgia. The news about broke my heart."

Dominique stares at the photo of the two sisters, taken while they were in England. "Your eyes? In this photo they're black, like your sisters.'"

"Yes. They changed after the accident. In fact, it wasn't until after the lightning strike that I became a necromancer."

"You said earlier you've been in touch with your sister."

"She's been my spiritual companion, my guide into the higher dimensions, the higher states of consciousness. The higher states are the forces of God's light, the forces of good. The higher our own frequencies of good, the easier it is for us to attune to their light."

"Are there forces of evil?"

Evelyn pauses, choosing her words carefully. "By creating a world of free will, God allowed for the forces of both good and evil, light and dark. These 'lesser lights' as I call them, fall into several different categories. Ghosts are the deceased who remain too confused to move into the light. Sometimes our negative thoughts or ignorance invites them into our lives. Ouija boards, for instance, set us up for ghostly pranks. By praying for these confused entities, we can help them realize the reality of their situation and guide them into the light.

"More dangerous are poltergeists. Poltergeists have their

own agenda. They are dark and evil and believe they can use their knowledge of the universe to manipulate our world. Poltergeists are the false prophets the Bible warns us about. They will entice us with their knowledge, but are not to be trusted. They can cause us great harm.

"The purer sources of light bring us closest to God. These are the spirits. Spirits are our friends. They never judge or manipulate us, they are here only to help us see the truth. Angels are the brightest lights in the spiritual world, the messengers of God's essence. They are always available to help, but it is up to us to ask for their assistance. Among the angels are the cherubim, seraphim, guardian angels, and archangels."

"And you can see them? You can see your sister?"

"No, but I can feel her presence when we communicate."

"And she's told you about Mick?"

Evelyn nods. "Take my hands in yours and close your eyes. Quiet your mind. Breathe in through your nose as slowly and deeply as you can, then gently out through your mouth. Focus on your feelings for Michael. Extinguish your sadness and feel him in your heart. Center yourself upon your love for him."

Dominique breathes. She thinks of Mick and how much she misses him.

Evelyn registers Dominique's increased energy flow as she meditates. She centers herself, moving deeper into her own meditation.

In due course she speaks: "Dear Lord, hold us in Your loving light. Allow Your Angels to guide us, so that our experiences may be for the highest good. We thank You for all You have done, and ask You now to reveal our dearly departed, Maria Rosen-Gabriel, to us."

A long pause, then Evelyn speaks again, this time in a higher, raspy voice not her own.

"My son has not passed into the spiritual realm. Michael has imprisoned himself in purgatory."

Dominique's eyes flash open. "My God . . . Mick's in Hell?"

"There is no Hell. Michael's soul is shackled with anger—an anger that comes from a life devoid of love. He was asked to make a great sacrifice. Now he loathes the decision and curses his existence, marooned on an island of space-time surrounded by an ocean of evil. "

"Is . . . is he safe?"

"He is in great danger. A powerful poltergeist tortures him and the *Nephilim*—a population of lost souls. Michael's internal rage blinds him, preventing him from defeating the poltergeist, and yet he feels compelled to remain, for it is his heavenly light that comforts the Fallen Ones. All are trapped in an equilibrium of existence, a higher temporal plane, what you would call Hell. It is Michael's presence within this existence that has created a third-dimensional loop of space-time. The loop must be broken to save Michael, the souls of the Fallen, and humanity."

Dominique's fingers ache within Evelyn's steely grip as she stares at the tears streaming down the old woman's cheeks. "Maria . . . will I ever see him again?"

"The Creation Story foretold in the Mayan *Popol Vuh* rewrites itself. The final battle will again be waged. The journey of good and evil begins anew with the rebirth of your sons. It is your role to prepare them for a battle that was waged and lost eons ago. If they are successful, then Michael will be resurrected. If they fail, then humanity is lost.

"But beware, for another shall be born on the day of the twins' birth. Negative energy shall flow to this child, tainting its soul while strengthening its spirit. It is this abomination that imprisons my son and disrupts the space-time continuum. It is this unholiest of unholies that tortures the *Nephilim*, feeding off their life force.

"Guard against the Abomination, Dominique. Do not allow it to spawn."

3

Ennis Chaney, the second appointed vice president in history to ascend to the highest office in the land, enters the Oval Office, feeling all his sixty-seven years. African-American, with deeply set owlish eyes, the former Senator from Pennsylvania has been commander in chief forty-two tumultuous days, ever since his predecessor, Mark Maller, took his own life in an attempt to stave off a global nuclear holocaust.

Since then, every dawn has been a blessing, every day twenty-four hours in hell.

Chaney barely has time to make his way behind his desk when his chief of staff, Katherine Gleason, buzzes him on the intercom. "Jesus, Kathy, at least give me a chance to sit down."

"Sorry, sir. Your seven o'clock appointment is here."

"Fine, send them in, and get me some of those chocolate chip cookies I had yesterday at the G-9 meeting. The wife says I'm gaining weight, but I'd don't care, I need the caffeine."

"Yes, sir."

A moment later, Kathy opens the outer office door, escorting two men inside. The first is Chaney's friend, Marvin Teperman, a short Canadian exobiologist with a pencil-thin mustache and an annoyingly warm smile. The second man is all business, a gray-haired colonel in full-dress uniform. Chaney notices a slight hitch in the man's step. An attaché case is handcuffed to his left wrist.

Marvin beams his usual smile. "Morning, Mr. President. Great day to be alive, eh? Allow me to present Colonel Jack McClellan, United States Air Force."

"Colonel." Chaney motions to McClellan's leg. "Old war injury?"

"Prosthetic. Damn diabetes."

"Tough break." For a fleeting moment, Chaney feels guilty about ordering the cookies. "Have a seat. You'll forgive me, Colonel, but this is my first MAJESTIC-12 briefing. Maybe you could sort of bring me up to speed? I was never big on those *X-Files* shows."

The colonel shrugs off the insult. "Sir, Operation MAJESTIC-12 was established on September 24, 1947, by special classified presidential order following the recovery of airborne objects that fell over Roswell, New Mexico, between July 4 and July 6 of that same year."

"By fallen airborne objects, you mean UFOs?"

"Yes, sir, and Hollywood aside, I can assure you that this was no special effect. Technically speaking, our unit originated in 1941 with a UFO retrieval case that took place in Cape Girardeau, Missouri. It wasn't until '47 that Truman officially funded the organization. Over the years, MAJESTIC-12 has utilized the services of some of the most brilliant minds in the world, including Albert Einstein and Robert Oppenheimer. Even after all these years, it remains our government's most supersecret program."

"Guess that explains the little wrist ornament."

The colonel nods. "These aren't your ordinary run-of-the-mill handcuffs either, sir. The bracelet monitors my pulse. Should my heart stop beating, should the chain be severed, or the wrong access code entered, the contents of the briefcase would instantly incinerate from within."

"Well, since there's no smoking permitted in my office, I guess I'd better enter the correct code." Chaney stands, leans over his desk, then carefully enters his access code on the briefcase's security pad.

The locking mechanism deactivates, allowing the colonel to open the case.

McClellan removes a half-inch-thick computerized clipboard, sealed in plastic, and hands it to the president.

"Thank you, Colonel. Now gentlemen, if you'll give me a few minutes—"

"Of course, sir." The colonel sits back in his chair.

Marvin just stares and grins.

The president sighs. He retrieves his reading glasses from his top desk drawer, then peels off the file's plastic wrapper, enters his daily access code to the wafer-thin screen, and begins reading off the LED monitor.

TOP SECRET/MAJESTIC-12

WARNING: Unauthorized access or viewing of this document without the appropriate authorizations will result in permanent incarceration or sanction by authorized use of deadly force.

PROGRESS REPORT ON SPECIAL ACCESS PROGRAM <u>GOLDEN FLEECE</u>

21 January 2013

<u>ORIGINS</u>

1. On 14 December 2012, at approximately 14:30 hours, EST, an electromagnetic force field equivalent to several billion amperes activated across the entire globe, destroying more than 1,000 Russian ICBMs and SLBMs targeted for North America, effectively saving the United States. MAJESTIC teams traced the EM array to exotic crystalline biomemnetic devices serving as transformer nodes and relay junctures within and/or below ancient structures of Angkor Wat, the Great

Pyramid of Giza, Stonehenge, the Pyramid of the Sun at Teotihuacán, Mexico, and under the complex at Tiahuanacu in Peru.

2. MAJESTIC teams were able to trace the common origin of the EM pulse to a vessel buried 217 feet beneath the Kukulcán Pyramid in Chichén Itzá (Yucatán Peninsula). The EM pulse itself was transmitted to relay junctures by way of an antenna mast which morphed out of the vertical axis of the buried vessel and up through the core of the 1,000-year-old Mayan superstructure. This was later confirmed by Michael Gabriel and his female companion, Dominique Vazquez, who were able to access the vessel by way of a freshwater aquifer (cenote) located a mile north of the pyramid.

3. Michael Gabriel is the only child of archaeologists Julius and Maria Gabriel (both deceased), whose body of work centered upon the Mayan calendar and its doomsday prophecy, predicted for 21 December 2012. On 24 August 2001, Julius Gabriel presented 32 years of research at a Harvard symposium attended by rival (and future secretary of state) Pierre Robert Borgia, who verbally assaulted the professor, interrupting his speech. Julius Gabriel suffered a fatal heart attack, dying in the arms of his son and only child, Michael, who then attacked Borgia. The incident cost Borgia his right eye and landed Gabriel in a mental asylum in Massachusetts, where he would spend the next eleven years, most of it in solitary confinement. He was subsequently transferred to a facility in Miami in summer of 2012 where he fell under Florida State University intern/grad student Dominique Vazquez's care. Ms. Vazquez subsequently aided Gabriel's escape in early December of 2012.

4. On 21 December 2012, a "transdimensional" extraterrestrial biological, appearing as a giant serpent, rose

from its own buried vessel beneath the Chicxulub Crater, the (Gulf of Mexico) impact site of an asteroid-like object that struck Earth 65 million years ago. The biological immediately targeted the EM pulse originating from Chichén Itzá, making its way to the site through a series of aquifers. U.S. Armed Forces were unable to stop the entity, which appeared to be existing on two dimensional planes at once. Michael Gabriel was able to deactivate the biological, using an energy beam originating from the antenna of the vessel buried beneath the Kukulcán Pyramid. Michael Gabriel then entered the triplex orifice of the entity. Both Gabriel and the biological subsequently disappeared. His status remains unknown.

GOLDEN FLEECE

5. Following the events of 21 December 2012, POTUS completed a new trade agreement with Mexico that included a private addendum placing Chichén Itzá under U.S. jurisdiction. The public park was immediately shut down, security assigned to MAJESTIC-12 under the newly-formed GOLDEN FLEECE program. Project Director Dr. David Mohr (formerly of NASA) and exobiologist Marvin Teperman divided GOLDEN FLEECE personnel into the following independent programs.

SECURE & CAMOUFLAGE MAIN STRUCTURE:
Responsible for erecting a prefabricated camouflaged urethane shell resembling the exterior of the Kukulcán pyramid. On the night of 18 January 2013, the shell was set in place above the existing pyramid, thereby preventing discovery of subsequent GOLDEN FLEECE operations via satellite reconnaissance.

EXCAVATION-A:
Responsible for systematic removal, tagging, and storage of every stone used in the construction of the

Kukulcán pyramid, overseen by Mexican archaeologists. Pyramid removal expected to be completed by 15 March 2013.

EXCAVATION-B:
Excavate access pit to buried vessel upon completion of Excavation-A.

EXCAVATION-C:
Access buried vessel via aquifer running beneath Kukulcán Pyramid. Underwater Assessment Team (UAT) made up of MAJESTIC-cleared personnel included laser physicists, theoretical physicists, metallurgists, aerospace engineers, psychiatric personnel, several noted neurophysiologists, and selected members of NASA's Breakthrough Propulsion Physics (BPP) team. All UAT members SCUBA certified with at least 100 dive-hours.

<u>EXCAVATION-C PRELIMINARY REPORT:</u>
<u>EXTERIOR STRUCTURE</u>

6. The burial vessel measures 722 feet long and is best described as "dagger-shaped," though this hardly begins to describe the vehicle. The forward hull tapers out like the front two-thirds of a surfboard and resembles the "Chine" hull-form configuration similar to A-12 HABU ("Blackbird") style spy planes. The "Hilt" starts out as a pronounced sphere, with large bulbous twin nacellelike structures that end in triangular vanes that enclose twin multichambered "exhausts" located at the stern of the vessel. Smaller transverse thruster exhausts are located along the belly. Several engineers have theorized that the aerodynamic starship was configured to "surf" an atmosphere or possibly even a hydrosphere in a manner similar to a "Waverider" aerospace vehicle, but on a larger scale. The star cruiser's enormous size rivals that of a medium to large

cruise ship, with a design "cut" that gives the impression of a warship. The keel is pronounced along the belly and is reminiscent of a Celtic warrior's ribbed ax blade.

7. The burial vessel's outer skin is described as a shimmering mirrorlike golden metal, composed of an ultrahard material, superior to diamond carbon. It cannot be cut using arc cutters or high-intensity lasers. It is resistant to heat and friction and is so smooth to the touch that it defies description. Although multiple panels can be distinguished (theorized as semitranslucent banks of solar cells) the hull, in fact, appears to have been constructed as one seamless integrated unit. Members of the BPP team theorized that the burial vessel's entire hull could function as a magnetoaeroelectric propulsion and levitation system by tapping into the gravity well of a planet. The indigenous magnetic field of Earth or any planet with a heavy iron core would be sufficient to power such a mode of atmospheric propulsion, and, in fact, may have been the system used to power the Roswell flying wing spacecraft.

8. Of special interest to the GOLDEN FLEECE scientists was the keeled belly portion of the burial vessel's outer hull. Located just beyond the "dagger-shaped bow" is an aerodynamic ring and four conjoined nacelles. BPP scientists theorize this to be a stabilizing structure, possibly used in "Warp" drive, or quantum gravity tunnels (see WORMHOLE theory), also referred to as "Transwarp" or "Quantum slipstream" conduits through non-Einsteinian space. Structures behind the ring may have served as amplifiers/phase shifters, which may have the capability of generating "space-folds." By varying the configuration of the so-called "Warp field" in super-luminal flight, the starship could theoretically change directions (alter course).

9. Inscribed upon the buried vessel's outer hull are two symbols. The first appears as Mayan glyphs along the bow of the vessel, translated as BALAM, a name referring to the ancient Mayan Jaguar God, and most likely the name bestowed upon the alien vessel. The second symbols are a series of embedded red candelabra-shaped logos that archaeologists have identified as the "Trident of Paracas." An identical insignia is found on the side of a mountain in Peru. There are four "Trident" panels located along the outer hull, two on the ventral side, two on the dorsal. Each of these panels appears to be an access hatch. None could be opened.

<u>EXCAVATION-C PRELIMINARY REPORT:</u>
<u>INTERIOR STRUCTURE</u>

10. All attempts to access the interior of the *BALAM* have so far failed.

<u>RECOMMENDATIONS</u>

11. RELOCATION OF BALAM:
It is essential to relocate the BALAM to a secured facility in the United States in order for the ship to be accessed internally and reverse engineered. Because of security considerations and the enormous weight of the vessel, the only acceptable means of transportation would be via U.S. Navy heavy-lift barges and towable dry docks currently used for full-sized conventional Navy destroyers. In order to utilize this mode of transportation, a canal must be dredged and dug, connecting Chichén Itzá with the Yucatán shoreline by way of its freshwater aquifers.

12. It is hypothesized that Michael Gabriel was able to access the *BALAM* because he bore the genetic "Hunahpu" ID. On 6 January 2013, a MAJESTIC-12 team exhumed the remains of Maria Gabriel, Michael Gabriel's biological mother, from her gravesite in Nazca, Peru, and found a similar genetic marker present in her DNA."

13. On 17 January 2013, Dominique Vazquez was examined by a MAJESTIC-12 physician, who verified the subject to be four weeks pregnant. Subject claims the biological father is Michael Gabriel.

14. It is theoretically possible that Dominique Vazquez's unborn child will possess the Hunahpu genetic marker and may one day be able to access the interior of the BALAM and perhaps even pilot the vessel, assuming its power plant is still usable.

<u>CONCLUSIONS</u>

15. The potential technological advancements in propulsion, weapons, and energy/power systems associated with the BALAM make GOLDEN FLEECE of vital interest to the United States. It is recommended we proceed immediately with transportation of the vessel to a secured U.S. facility. It is further recommended that Dominique Vazquez be kept under twenty-four-hour-a-day surveillance.

Submitted:

W. Louis McDonald
GOLDEN FLEECE

21 January 2013

"Incredible." Chaney types in his security code, erasing the file. "Tell me, Marvin, how's Dominique taking the news that she's pregnant with Gabriel's child?"

"Not well, to be honest. She's still overwhelmed by all that's happened, and she misses Mick terribly. Unfortunately, she's also more than a little freaked out about this whole Hunahpu genetics thing. Right now, I'd guess she's leaning toward abortion."

"You can't allow that to happen, Mr. President," objects the colonel. "The unborn Gabriel child may represent our only means of accessing the *Balam*."

"Easy, Colonel, let's give the girl a break. Dominique's been through a lot over the last few months. It's her life, her decision, not ours."

"Homeland Security has set her up with a new identity," Marvin says. "She's living in south Florida under the alias, Andrea Smith. We've tried to keep her under twenty-four-hour surveillance."

The colonel shakes his head. "MAJESTIC-12 should be in charge of the girl. Homeland Security has more holes in it than a Swiss cheese factory."

"We'll let them handle it for now," Chaney says. "Dominique's in no immediate danger, and locking her up in an underground bunker might negatively impact her decision about keeping the child. Anything else?"

"Just one last thing," Marvin says. "In reviewing Julius Gabriel's journal, I came across a passage that referenced a necromancer."

"A who?"

"A necromancer. Comes from the Greek words *necro*, meaning death, and *mancy*, describing divination. A necromancer is one who claims to be able to communicate with the souls of the dead for the purpose of obtaining useful information. A few years prior to his own death, Professor Gabriel sought out the services of a necromancer named Evelyn Strongin, hoping to communicate with his deceased wife, Maria. We've been trying to locate Ms. Strongin, hoping she might be able to shed some light on Michael Gabriel's genetic abilities. Unfortunately, her last reported address was in Peru. We can't seem to locate any current information about her or her whereabouts."

Chaney shakes his head. "Extraterrestrials. People talking to the dead. Whatever happened to the good ol' days when all a president had to worry about were economic reforms and war in Iraq."

4

The beige 2001 Dodge with the dented rear bumper turns off Mexican Route 180, following a local road through the poverty-stricken town of Pisté.

Dominique slows the rental car, her dark eyes scanning the dilapidated stucco homes lining the roadway. The village is just like a thousand others located throughout Central America along the "Maya Route," a 120,000-square-mile area stretching east from the Isthmus of Tehuantepec through the Yucatán Peninsula, extending into Belize, Guatemala, and parts of Honduras and El Salvador.

A thousand years ago, the Maya were the dominant civilization in all Central America. Unable to rise against their Spanish oppressors, the Indians were left behind, their decreasing crops unable to compete in the marketplace. The culture is still very much alive, but the Maya are at the bottom rung of society's ladder.

Dominique's maternal ancestors were Yucatec—direct descendants of the Maya, and she bears the dark complexion and sculpted cheekbones of her people.

The dusty road widens into a four-lane highway that leads to the entrance of Chichén Itzá, the capital city of the ancient Maya and the most visited tourist attraction in Mexico. Harbored within this 3.75-square-mile jungle-enclosed park are richly carved temples and shrines, the centerpiece being the Kukulcán Pyramid, a perfect ziggurat of stone that rises seventy-five feet above the grass-covered esplanade.

Dominique's heart races as she thinks of the structure . . . and the alien vessel buried beneath its foundation.

For nearly a week, Dominique had remained at Evelyn Strongin's home in St. Augustine. But after her initial contact with the spirit of Maria Rosen-Gabriel, the energy force had shut down, refusing further communication. This "silent treatment" caused Dominique to have doubts about the validity of the first message . . . and its source.

"No offense, Evelyn, but how can I be sure that was really Mick's mother who spoke with me?"

"Who else would it be, child?"

"Maybe it was you, pretending to be in communication with your sister. Or maybe you weren't even aware of what was happening. My background is in psychiatry. Over the years, I've seen some pretty bad cases of schizophrenia."

"The energy source was Maria's."

"If that's true, then why hasn't she spoken through you again? It's been days since the last communication. I can't hang around this town the rest of my life. You've succeeded in freaking me out to the point where I'm seriously considering an abortion."

"Choose that route, and you not only condemn Michael, but humanity's future as well."

"So says you. I need real answers, Evelyn, not riddles."

"Dominique, Maria senses your fear, and this is why she's ended communication. Fear is one of humankind's strongest negative emotions. Negative emotions create negative energy, and negative energy attracts negative spirits. Communicating with the dead is not like placing a phone call. Anyone can answer, including demons like the

Abomination, who is as powerful as it is cunning. Sensing your fear, Maria felt it best to end the communication rather than tip our hand to the enemy. The success of future sessions will depend upon your ability to control your negative emotions. But first, you must fully commit to the journey."

"Again with the journey. What journey? How can I commit myself to something I don't even understand?"

"You do it by acquiring knowledge. Study the Mayan *Popol Vuh*. Familiarize yourself with its story of Creation. Seek answers from those you trust."

"That's just it, I don't trust anyone. I've never felt so scared and alone in my life."

"Julius and Maria felt the same way when they began their own journey, and I'm sure Michael shared these feelings. At times they lost sight of the path, and yet they continued on, their resolve strengthened by faith, knowing they were following their destiny."

"What would Mick do if he were me?"

"He would seek answers from those who know. He would return to the land of the green lightning."

Dominique turns into the entrance of Chichén Itzá. To her surprise, the parking lot is deserted, the front gates sealed, guarded by a platoon of heavily armed American soldiers.

Captain Luke Magierski leaves his station and approaches, his hands resting on his M-16. "Sorry, miss, Chichén Itzá's closed."

"Actually, I was looking for the local vendors who used to sell inside the park."

Magierski stares at the attractive woman with the long ebony hair and high cheekbones, her looks vaguely familiar. "They've set up shop on the grounds of the Mayaland Hotel. It's about ten minutes from here." The soldier removes an identity scanner from his belt. "I need to scan you, it's standard procedure."

"Of course." She extends her left hand out the window.

Magierski's device snaps Dominique's digital photo as it scans her open palm.

SMITH, ANDREA M.
RESIDENCE: WELLINGTON, FLORIDA.
NO OUTSTANDING WARRANTS.

"Thank you, Miss Smith. You have a nice day now."

She waves, then drives off.

Magierski stares at the photo. *Wait a second, I have seen her before.* Removing his Palm Pilot, he scans his old e-mails. Locates the People-First.com website. Checks the photo against the one posted. *Holy crap, it's her!*

Glancing over his shoulder to make sure no one is watching, he e-mails the photo of Andrea Smith to the political party of Peter Mabus.

[handwritten annotation: Palm Pilots came out in 1996 AND WERE NEVER able to send EMAIL - SUPERCEDED IN EARLY 2000's BAD RESEARCH!]

Dominique pulls into the grand entrance of the Mayaland Hotel and parks. A farmers' market has been set up across from the parking lot, allowing the local villagers to sell their wares to tourists.

She scans the tables, counting fewer than a dozen visitors among the vendors. *The park's closing's hurting everyone.* Approaching the first booth, she is immediately swarmed upon by children, all pulling at her skirt in an attempt to lure her to their table.

"Jade necklace, *señorita?* Only ten dollars, American."

"Come, *señorita,* we have beautiful rings. Five dollars."

"*Señorita,* you must buy a silk hammock. We give you a very good price, eh?"

"Okay, okay, tell you what, I'll buy from the first person who can tell me where I can find the elder known as Ocela."

The children back away. "Don't know this person, *señorita.* Maybe you should go, eh?"

The children abandon Dominique for a Canadian couple and their teenage daughter. "Bandanna, *señor?* Two dollar."

* * *

Captain Magierski stares at his Palm Pilot as if he's just hit the lottery.

> SUBJECT VERIFICATION CONFIRMED. ONE-MILLION
> WILL BE WIRED UPON PROOF OF VAZQUEZ CAPTURE,
> BALANCE DELIVERED WHEN TEAM ARRIVES THIS EVENING.
> DISCUSS THIS WITH NO ONE. CONGRATULATIONS AND
> THANK YOU FOR SERVING YOUR COUNTRY.

Dominique moves from table to table, stopping occasionally to check out an obsidian letter opener or an ornamental jaguar. "Excuse me? How much?"

"Thirty dollars, *señorita*. For you, twenty-three."

"I'm looking for a man named Ocela."

Eyes avert. "No man by that name here, *señorita*."

She looks up as an Army jeep enters the Mayaland parking lot, its tires skidding across gravel as it comes to a stop, blocking Dominique's rental car.

Captain Magierski scans the tables using a finger-size telescopic lens.

Dominique ducks behind a shelf stacked with wool Mexican blankets, her heart racing as she peeks out at the soldier. *Something's wrong, he's definitely after me. Where the hell are those Homeland Security guys when you need them?*

Magierski jumps down from the jeep, striding toward the marketplace.

"Psst! Over here!"

Dominique turns. A curly-haired Mayan man motions at her from behind a fruit stand.

"Come quickly!"

"I know you, don't I?"

"Elias Forma, I'm a friend of Mick's. You were at my home. Quickly—"

* * *

Magierski pushes through a throng of children, moving from table to table. "The American woman, where is she?"

Elias Forma shrugs. *"No habla inglés."*

"Maybe you *habla* this." Magierski raises his M-16, pushing the barrel of the gun into the Mayan's face. "Now where's the goddam girl?"

Elias says nothing, his dark eyes returning the soldier's glare as the other Mayans crowd around them, whispering.

Magierski grabs Elias by his shirt collar and drags the vendor out from behind the fruit stand, tossing him to the ground. Cocking his weapon, he fires a circle of bullets around the terrified local. "Listen up, Dominique Vazquez, you either come out now or I'll blow his fucking head off!"

"Hold it!" Dominique climbs down from the slanted roof of the fruit stand. She approaches the soldier, her hands out at her sides, her blouse unbuttoned to her navel. "All you had to do was ask."

Magierski's heart pounds faster as he stares at her tantalizing cleavage.

Dominique winks. "I'm into handcuffs. Do you have any?"

"Definitely." He removes the shackles from his belt, snapping them around her offered wrists. "Looks like you and me are gonna spend a few hours alone together."

"Sounds like fun. Think maybe we can get a room at the hotel? I'm hot, and I want to get out of these sweaty clothes. If you're good, I'll let you handcuff me to the bed."

Magierski smiles. "Tell you what, how about if I—"

Whomp! Dominique's right foot snaps off the ground like a cobra, the tip of her shoe driving high into the man's groin. As the soldier drops to his knees, the ball of her left foot smashes into Magierski's face, snapping his head back.

The soldier collapses in a heap.

Elias searches Magierski's belt for the handcuff keys. He tosses them at Dominique as three Mayan vendors drag the unconscious soldier's body into the high grass.

A dozen more push the jeep off the side of the road and into a ditch.

Salt Lake City, Utah

Peter Mabus lies back in the dressing room chair, allowing his makeup man to finish dabbing at the dark circles beneath his eyes.

A knock and the dressing room door opens. Joseph Randolph enters, followed by a slight, gray-haired Caucasian in his late sixties. The nerdy-looking man wears wire-rimmed glasses and is dressed in a wool suit and black bow tie.

"He's had enough primping." Randolph ushers the makeup artist out and shuts the door. "Pete, this is Solomon Adashek, the man I was telling you about."

Mabus sits up, his piggy eyes taking in the visitor. "No offense, Joe, but he looks more like my goddam CPA than a hired assassin."

Solomon Adashek remains expressionless. "It only takes the strength of a child to pull a trigger, Mr. Mabus. The key to eradicating one's target is to get close without arousing suspicion. If you'd prefer to hire a goon, I'll take my services elsewhere."

"No, you'll do. The girl's in the Yucatán, I'm sure Joe's briefed you. I want her and the soldier who found her eliminated without a trace."

Solomon nods, then leaves the dressing room, quietly closing the door behind him.

"Creepy little shit, ain't he?"

"What's important is that he'll get the job done without complications," Randolph says. "Guy's former CIA, as cold and unfeeling as a reptile. Spent a lot of time in the Soviet Union as a mole. Returned home after the Cold War ended and wigged out. Torched his mother's home, killing her and her live-in nurse. Served six years and was released on parole. Bit of a pedophile, but he's calmed down over the years."

"Maybe we ought to send him after Chaney?"

"One step at a time, my friend. One step at a time."

Chichén Itzá
Yucatán Peninsula

10:17 P.M.

The nocturnal jungle is alive with humidity, and chirps, and the ghosts of the dead. Dense brush cuts Dominique's ankles and lashes out at her neck. Mosquitoes buzz her ears. A flutter of wings takes the air overhead beneath the canopy of trees.

The heaviness of the woods presses in on her, whispering into her ear. She grips Elias Forma's hand tighter, afraid she will lose him in the darkness. And yet she feels safer here than she does in the real world, knowing that someone out there wants her dead.

Like it or not, you're Alice through the Looking Glass, chasing a rabbit down its hole, and there's no turning back now.

In time they come to a clearing. Dark-skinned Mayan elders squat around a campfire. Dominique recognizes the *H'Menes,* the same men who helped her and Mick climb down into the sacred well in Chichén Itzá six weeks earlier.

A lifetime ago . . .

The wise men are descendants of the *Sh'Tol brethren,* a sacred Mayan society that escaped the wrath of the Spaniards back in the fifteenth century.

Elias greets the frail, white-haired leader of the group with a hug. "Dominique, this is my grandfather, Ocela, the man you seek."

Dominique extends her hand. "Hope you remember me, I'm a friend of Michael Gabriel. I need to speak to you about the Creation Myth."

Ocela takes her hand in both of his, then speaks to Elias in a language she cannot comprehend.

"My grandfather says he will do all he can to assist First-Mother."

"Now see, that's why I'm here. Who's First-Mother, and why is he calling me that?"

Ocela smiles a toothless grin, then touches her stomach. *Yaya ba'l.*

Oh, God, he knows I'm pregnant, too? Did somebody send out notices? Dominique feels light-headed. The sounds of the night dissipate into the snapping and popping of the campfire as she swoons in the humidity.

Elias and the old man lead her to a log poised at the edge of the clearing. She sits, the other men gathering around. One offers her a flask of water, another a wooden bowl filled with fruits and berries. She drinks and eats, feeling a little better.

Still holding her hand, Ocela looks into her eyes and speaks, Elias translating.

"The Creation Story is the most important lesson recorded in the *Popol Vuh.* The hero of the story is One Hunahpu, a brave warrior later revered as First-Father. One Hunahpu's great passion in life was to play the ancient ball game known as Tlachtli. One day, the Lords of the Underworld, *Xibalba,* challenged One Hunahpu to a game, at stake—the future of his people. One Hunahpu accepted and entered *Xibalba Be,* the dark road that leads to *Xibalba,* said to have been the mouth of a great serpent."

Dominique shudders, recalling the image of Mick entering the orifice of the alien being.

"But the Lords of *Xibalba* had no intention of actually playing the game. Using trickery and deceit, they defeated One Hunahpu and decapitated him, hanging his head in the crook of a calabash tree as a warning to others who might challenge them.

"After a great many years, a brave woman named Blood Moon ventured down the Dark Road. Approaching the tree to pick fruit, she was startled to find One Hunahpu's head. The warrior's eyes opened and he spit into her palm, magically impregnating her. The woman fled, the Death God and his minions unable to destroy her before she could escape.

"Blood Moon, who is later revered as First-Mother, gave birth to twin sons. As the years passed, her boys grew into strong, capable warriors. Upon reaching adulthood, their genetic calling demanded they follow in their father's footsteps and make the journey to *Xibalba* to challenge the Death God and avenge One Hunahpu's death.

"Once more, the Lords of the Underworld used cunning and deceit. But the Hero Twins, having prepared for this treachery, triumphed, banishing evil while resurrecting their long-lost father."

Ocela smiles at her, again palming her stomach.

"No, stop it, none of this makes any sense. The *Popol Vuh* is just mythology, it tells of things in the past. How can I possibly be First-Mother?"

Elias translates for his grandfather.

The old man rattles off a response.

"The knowledge found in the *Popol Vuh* comes to us from our great teacher, Kukulcán. The *Popol Vuh* was recorded five hundred years after his passing. Time distorts the Creation Story, but not its ultimate meaning. What came to pass shall come again as the cycle of humanity repeats itself. One Hunahpu has come. He has delivered us from evil, sacrificing himself in the process. Now he awaits his sons in *Xibalba*."

Dominique's hand trembles within Ocela's. He pats it with his other hand, gripping it tightly as he speaks again.

"My grandfather says to have faith. You were chosen by One Hunahpu for your strength."

"If Mick really is this One Hunahpu character, then where is he now? How can I find *Xibalba?*"

"The dark road to *Xibalba* shall appear before the Hero Twins in their twentieth year. Until then, it is your destiny as First-Mother to prepare them. Great challenges lie ahead. Allies of the Dark Lord will do everything in their power to stop you."

Ocela stands, leading her to the edge of the clearing and a massive cypress tree. Bound and gagged to the trunk is Luke Magierski. The soldier is wearing only his boxer shorts and a tee shirt.

Dominique removes his gag.

"Uh, thank God. Would you tell these Zulus that I'm American!"

"Why were you after me?"

"You're Dominique Vazquez, Michael Gabriel's woman. Everyone wants to speak with you."

"He's lying," says Elias. "Who hired you to find Dominique?"

Magierski stares into the jungle. "Name, rank, and serial number, that's all you'll get from me. The United States doesn't like it when you kidnap their soldiers. There's fifteen thousand heavily armed men and women less than a dozen klicks from here who'll napalm this entire jungle into a prairie dust if any harm comes to me."

Ocela signals to his elders. Two of the men force Magierski's jaw open, while a third jams a small piece of bamboo between the soldier's upper and lower molars, preventing him from closing his mouth.

The fourth man appears with a wooden container. From within, he retracts an eighteen-inch centipede, its thick jet-black body sporting a yellow head and legs.

Dominique steps back. "Gross. What is that thing?"

Elias takes the animal from the elder. "It's long name is Scolopendromorpha, a tropical species that flourishes in our jungles. Some of the larger ones feed on mice and lizards."

"They get bigger than that?"

"Hmm. See these front legs? They're called prehensors. They're used to inject venom into their victims. Let's see if our little friend here can persuade our brave American soldier to tell us what we want to know."

Elias holds the wiggling centipede in front of Luke Magierski's face. "This afternoon at the marketplace, you were acting on someone's orders. Whose?"

The soldier looks away.

Two of the elders hold Magierski's face steady while Elias positions the centipede's yellow head in the soldier's open mouth.

Magierski thrashes in his bonds, moaning and hissing and gagging as the repulsive creature wiggles its way into his mouth, blocking his airway as it moves down his esophagus.

Dominique turns away in disgust.

Elias leans in closer. "Six more inches and its tail disappears. When that happens, I can't save you. It will crawl into your small intestines and lay its eggs. Three more inches . . . two more. If you have anything to say, say it now."

Magierski nods vigorously, his eyes as wide as saucers, his face turning purple.

Elias carefully extracts the centipede, then removes the chunk of bamboo.

Magierski leans over and pukes.

"Give us a name, or it goes back in, and this time, we'll let it keep going until it crawls out your ass."

"Mabus. Peter Mabus. He placed a 2-million-dollar bounty on the girl's head."

Dominique turns to face him. "Why? What does that screwball want with me?"

"I don't know. He . . . he blames a lot of the doomsday stuff on Gabriel; guess you're sort of lumped into his political campaign. He's sending one of his men down from the States to collect you."

"More likely to kill you," Elias states. "Where were you and this man supposed to meet?"

"I don't know."

Elias nods to the Mayan elders, who grab Magierski's head.

"No . . . wait, he's meeting me tomorrow morning, at the commuter airport outside of Pisté."

A Mayan elder returns the centipede to its wooden container. Elias shoves the gags back inside Magierski's mouth as Ocela leads Dominique back to the campfire.

She watches as the elder carrying the wooden container skewers the centipede with a pointed stick, then roasts it over the open fire.

Elias winks at her. "Old Mayan delicacy. I prefer mine with butter."

Dominique feels queasy.

"Grandfather's right. Enemies are everywhere."

"Maybe I should just stay here?"

"Unfortunately, it's not safe here either. Among the Mayans are cult members of Tezcatilpoca, practitioners of the Dark Way. It was Tezcatilpoca who vanquished our great teacher, Kukulcán, more than a thousand years ago. Once these followers learn you are here, they won't stop until they kill you and sacrifice you . . . in that order. "

"Fine. I'll return to the States tomorrow, but there's one more thing I need to know before I leave. What is the Abomination?"

Elias struggles to translate.

Ocela listens, then becomes animated.

"My grandfather says the Abomination is the Dark Lord in its human form. Legend says the Abomination is the origin of all human evil, reborn on the day of the Hero Twins' birth."

"I don't understand. Why do they call it the Abomination?"

"Because, Dominique, like Michael and your unborn sons, the Abomination is Hunahpu."

Pisté Airport

7:25 A.M.

The private Learjet touches down, then taxis along the hot tarmac.

Luke Magierski waits in his jeep. *Just play it cool and you should walk away with something, at least a hundred grand.* He watches as the entry steps lower from the jet's passenger compartment.

A wave of dry heat blasts Solomon Adashek in the face. He wipes humidity from his spectacles with a handkerchief, then gingerly makes his way down the narrow steps.

Magierski shakes his head. *A 2-million-dollar bounty, and this is the guy they send?*

"Captain Magierski?"

"Yeah. You have my money?"

"All set to be wired. Where's the girl?"

"I lost her. Bunch of Mayan locals helped her escape. Beat and tortured me, but I managed to escape."

"How fortunate for you."

"Yeah, but all's not lost. You have her identity now, so it shouldn't be hard to find her."

"Identities can be replaced easier than soldiers, Captain."

"Listen, pal, I still deserve something for my trouble, at least a hundred grand. That's chump change to a guy like Peter Mabus."

"I'll be glad to pay you your money. Would you join me aboard the jet? I'll need your assistance in completing the wire to your bank account."

From the adjacent woods, Elias Forma watches the two men through his binoculars.

Magierski follows the nerdy little man up the steps and into the plane. "Let's move it, fella, I have to get back to my post by O800."

"Of course. Step to the rear of the plane and stand on the plastic please?"

"Plastic?" Magierski walks to where a heavy plastic painter's drop cloth has been stretched out over the aisle. "What's all this for?"

"Just a matter of convenience."

Solomon Adashek's 9mm spits out two bullets, both striking the Army captain through the heart.

PART 2

■■■■■■■■■■■■■■■

BIRTH

The house is silent.
The door is closed.
A person enters.
The window is opened wide.
Yang enters the Yin.
A baby is born.

—TAO TEH CHING

5

Dominique Vazquez gazes through feverish eyes at her foster mother, Edith Axler, as another contraction begins. The wave of pain crests higher . . . higher—

She groans through clenched teeth, "Drugs! Get me . . . drugs!"

Edith turns to Rabbi Steinberg, the only other person in the birthing room. "Richard, find the doctor."

The auburn-haired, bearded rabbi unbolts the door, hurrying past the two armed security guards and into the chaos of the main corridor.

A dozen policemen have formed human barricades in front of each of the three stairwells, shunting off the swelling mob of reporters. Two nurses and an orderly argue at their station with members of the governor's entourage, while governor Grace Demers continues her verbal assault on Dominique's private nurse.

". . . we had an arrangement, Mrs. Klefner."

"Hey, lady, I called you, just like I said I would. Not my fault the preggo wants nobody but the old woman and the Jew in her birthing room. You don't like it, you can take your money and let it hit you where the good Lord split you."

"Now you listen to me—"

"Nurse Klefner?" Rabbi Steinberg grabs the nurse by

the arm, dragging her away from the governor. "Where's Dr. Wishnov?"

"Who're you?"

"I'm the Jew. Where's the doctor?"

"Uh, he's trying to secure an operating room."

Steinberg heads down the corridor.

The governor hustles to catch up. "Rabbi, wait, let's talk. Get me inside to witness the birth, and I'll make it worth your while."

Steinberg spots Bruce Wishnov, Dominique's obstetrician, hurrying down the opposite corridor.

"I'll bet your synagogue could use a new parking lot." She lowers her voice. "Or would you prefer credits?"

Steinberg's blood pressure boils. "*Geh feifen ahfen yam.*"

"Excuse me?"

"It's Yiddish for go peddle your fish elsewhere."

The rabbi jumps aside as a burly Hispanic cop drags two handcuffed reporters into a makeshift holding room. Jogging down the corridor, Steinberg intercepts Dr. Wishnov, who is dressed head to slippers in surgical green. "Where have you been? Dominique's in pain, she needs an epidural."

"Dominique may need a Caesarian. The OR's ready, but the mob's getting worse. I thought Chaney was sending the National Guard?"

"Yes." Steinberg struggles to keep up. "That's what we were told."

The security guards step aside, allowing the doctor and rabbi to reenter the private birthing room.

Edith is at the window, peeking between wooden shutters at the scene three stories below. The night is torn by sirens and swirling lights that streak the surging crowd blue and red. Mesoamerican Indians, news reporters, and religious fanatics have jammed the parking lot and hospital entrance to jostle with local police. The deep thrumming from news choppers pounds the humid air, their white-hot search lights cutting through palm fronds, casting bizarre shadows across the glass-faced building.

"There must be ten thousand people out there. Where's the National Guard?"

"Owww!" Dominique moans as she rides another crest. Sweat mats her black bangs to her forehead, beads of perspiration rolling past her cheekbones. She grabs the doctor by his arm, burying her nails into his skin. "Get these babies out of me!"

Dr. Wishnov releases the brakes on her roller bed. "Hang in there, we're moving you to an operating room."

"No! No Caesarean! It's time. Just get them out . . . owwww!"

The doctor kneels between Dominique's legs and lifts her gown. "You're right, you've dilated to ten centimeters."

"No shit!"

The sounds of the mob grow louder. "Okay, forget the Caesarean, we'll do this the old-fashioned way. Where's that nurse?"

"Selling us out to the media," the rabbi says. "I don't want her in here."

Dr. Wishnov shoots the rabbi a harsh look. "Then scrub up, I'll need your help."

The black limousine continues north on Route 441, inching its way toward the hospital through bumper-to-bumper traffic. Designed by the United States Army, the "smart-limo" contains a variety of offensive and defensive systems. Tinted bulletproof glass and lightweight Kevlar armor shields the chassis. High-voltage door handles and pepper-spray blasters keep hostile crowds at bay. Conformal arrays of superbright LED lights in the front, sides, and rear can blind enemies looking directly at or pursuing the vehicle. A retractable antenna and bowling-ball-sized weapons platform can deploy from inside the trunk, providing night-vision images and laser-designation capabilities.

Two men are seated up front. Riding shotgun, sporting a trimmed black beard and mustache, is Mitchell Kurtz. At five-foot-eight and 160 pounds, the forty-year-old Caucasian looks anything but dangerous, but the CIA-trained assassin has killed a dozen times in the line of duty.

What he lacks in physical stature Kurtz more than makes up in advanced gadgetry. His sleek wraparound "smart" sunglasses contain tiny lasers embedded in the frames that beam light into his eyes, offering crisp wide-angle images from the miniature cameras. The camera lenses are telescopic, enabling him to zoom in on objects over great distances, using either day or night vision.

Concealed beneath the former FBI agent's shirt, strapped to his right forearm and powered by a waist-worn battery pack is a "pain cannon." Designed for riot control, the weapon fires pulses of millimeter waves at its target, heating the victim's skin as if the subject had just touched a hot lightbulb. The pain cannon can scatter every living being within a three-hundred-yard radius or deliver a death blow to a specific target up to half a mile away.

Driving the limo is Ryan Beck, an immense African-American, whose six-foot-six frame carries 285 pounds of sculpted muscle. The former Green Beret holds black belts in several martial arts, is an expert with guns and knives, and once took a bullet for California governor Arnold Schwarzenegger. The scar is still present beneath the man's shirt collar.

Affectionately known around the Oval Office as "Salt and Pepper," the duo have spent the last ten months guarding one client.

President Ennis Chaney stares out the tinted rear windows of the limo, growling to himself. Security has been breached once more, despite Homeland Security's having changed Dominique Vazquez's identity three times over the last seven months, and the media has turned the event into Ringling Brothers meets the Second Coming. Terrorist threats, intercepted on-line by the FBI over NREN (National Research and Education Network) have forced the president to bypass the scheduled helicopter ride from Fort Lauderdale airport to the hospital, while a computer virus has crippled Homeland Security, causing the National Guard to be delayed by two hours.

The president rubs sleep from his deeply set owl-shaped eyes as the limo rolls to a stop in front of a police barricade.

Pepper, seated driver's side, lowers his window.

A cop reeking of garlic breath pokes his head inside. "Sorry, pal, this area's closed. Now turn this boat around and get outta here."

Pepper holds up his I.D.

"White House? Yeah, right."

Chaney leans forward from the backseat and shoots the cop one of his infamous "one-eyed-jack" glares. "You need glasses, son, or you just stupid?"

The cop's complexion pales as he recognizes the heavy rasp. "Mister President? Geez, I'm sorry, sir—"

"Shut up and let us through before we have to shoot you."

Pepper grins, shutting the window in the cop's face. The limo proceeds past the barricade and continues north on Route 441 another three miles before turning onto a side street leading to the hospital.

The access road is wall-to-wall people.

Pepper shakes his head. "Look at all those freaks. This is worse than one of your damn Republican conventions."

Chaney leans forward, gazing out the windshield. Up ahead on the right is a mob of protesters, carrying signs that read: KILL THE ANTICHRIST.

"Goddam Peter Mabus. Salt, clear 'em out."

"All of them? Cops too?"

"All of 'em."

With a mischievous grin, Kurtz activates the moon roof and stands, his upper torso protruding out the hatch. He scans the crowd, his computer optics calculating distance.

A sixteen-year-old Caucasian male with a blue goatee and a dozen facial piercings saunters over, a fourteen-year-old girl handcuffed to each tattooed wrist. The girls, high on Ecstasy, climb onto the hood of the limo. "Hey, Dr.

Shades," the male calls out, "you here to witness the birth of the Messiah Twins?"

Kurtz rolls up his shirtsleeve, revealing his weapon. "Yep. Me and the other two wise men in the limo brought the frankincense. Open wide, here comes the mirth."

Salt fires the cannon, its invisible beam of millimeter waves igniting screams from the crowd. Several dozen fanatics leap into the nearest canal, the rest disperse in every direction, yelping as if their skin was on fire.

The tattooed teen cries out like a banshee as he and his girls tear at their scorching tongue rings and handcuffs.

"It's a school night, junior. Go home and study." Kurtz ducks back inside the vehicle as Pepper drives up to the now-deserted hospital entrance.

"I can see the first one's head . . . easy while I turn the shoulders. Okay, push!"

Dominique bears down, grunting as she squeezes the newborn from her birth canal.

"Beautiful." Dr. Wishnov holds the blood-streaked, fair-haired child in both hands, momentarily dazzled by the infant's bright azure blue eyes.

"Hey, no breaks here!" Dominique yells.

"Sorry." The obstetrician quickly runs a suction tube down the newborn's mouth and throat, clearing the airway before cutting the umbilical cord and passing him to Steinberg.

The rabbi places the wide-eyed child onto the incubator as instructed. He mutters a prayer in Hebrew, watching as the warmth of the semienclosed chamber turns the infant's skin a healthy pink.

Incredibly, the newborn seems to be watching him.

The rabbi shakes the ridiculous thought away, returning his attention to Dominique as her second son is birthed.

Belle Glade, Florida

1:32 A.M.

Forty-seven miles to the north, seventeen-year-old Madelina Aurelia thrashes naked beneath a sweat-soaked bedsheet as she cries out to her foster father. "Get this goddam baby outta me!"

Quenton Morehead, Baptist Minister, squeezes the girl's hand, his dark eyes lingering on the girl's exposed pelvis. "Don't blaspheme, child, the midwife's on her way."

"Fuck you!" Madelina claws his arms, drawing streaks of blood. "Where's Virgil?"

"I don't know—"

"Find him!"

The minister cringes as the girl's high-pitched screech penetrates his brain like a tuning fork. He hears the front door open and sighs a quick *Amen*.

"Virge?" Madelina stops thrashing. "Virgil, honey? That you—you cheatin', whorin' sonuva bitch!"

A heavyset Black woman enters. "Calm down, baby, everthin' gonna be just fine."

Madelina tears at the mattress as another contraction grips her torso. "Vir . . . gil!"

The midwife turns to the minister. "Go on and find him. I can handle things here."

Quenton backs out of the bedroom, then hurries out the front door of the sweltering stucco home and into the night.

Madelina Aurelia, only child of Miguel and Cecilia Aurelia, was born in the small Mexican town of Morelos. Cecilia's marriage to Miguel had been arranged by his uncle, Don Rafelo, a man feared by all as an *Ojo mak* (evil man), who had learned the girl's maternal lineage was full-blooded Aztec, her ancestors dating back to the reign of Montezuma.

Bad luck seemed to follow the young couple since Madelina's birth. Cecilia had nearly died in labor, and Miguel suffered a debilitating stroke a month after his daughter was born. Relatives whispered that Don Rafelo had cast his evil eye on the Aurelias in hopes of obtaining their daughter. Secretly, they advised the young couple to move away from Morelos and the *Ojo mak* as soon as possible.

The Aurelias held out until Madelina turned four, then joined a group of crop pickers bound for the United States. For the next two years, the illegal aliens would migrate from Florida to Texas, following the growing seasons.

For the Aurelias, life in the States seemed just as bewitched as it had been in Morelos. Cecilia lost sight in her right eye because of a bee sting, and Miguel suffered a second stroke. When the Aurelias' shanty burned to the ground, the superstitious couple departed Belle Glade, abandoning their daughter on the doorstep of the town's Family Services office.

A month later, six-year-old Madelina was placed in the foster home of the Reverend Quenton Morehead and his wife, Rachel.

It soon became apparent that something was seriously wrong with the young Mexican immigrant. Bizarre infantile behavior, including public masturbation and finger painting with her feces led the God-fearing Quenton to declare the girl possessed. His wife, being more grounded, suspected a chemical imbalance and made an appointment with a child psychiatrist.

After two visits and a battery of tests, doctors diagnosed Madelina's problem as a form of disorganized schizophrenia, probably inherited from one of the girl's biological parents. Drugs were prescribed, therapy recommended.

Two weeks later, Rachel Morehead found a lump on her left breast. She would not last the year.

Deeply depressed over his wife's death, Quenton was forced to endure the additional burden of Madelina's illness alone. Unable to accept the doctor's psychiatric "mumbo jumbo," the minister decided the best course of action was simply to exorcise the girl's demons himself.

Prayer, empowered by Quenton's fire-and-brimstone delivery, would cleanse Madelina's soul. Daily Bible readings and nightly services would fill her idle time after school, preventing her mind from wandering back toward Satan. Jesus would shine His guiding light into the girl's valley of darkness.

It was a long, exhausting "road to salvation," complicated by Quenton's own disease: alcoholism.

After staggering home drunk, the ordained minister would often strip naked and crawl into bed with his frightened nine-year-old foster child. On good nights, Quenton simply passed out.

On a few terrible nights . . . he stayed awake.

Weeks after the first episode, the girl began carrying on conversations with imaginary friends. The voices "stopped" with Quenton's beatings.

By the time she turned sixteen, Madelina had been molested by her foster parent dozens of times. Meanwhile, the adolescent's girl's schizophrenia had grown worse, and the minister feared he might be stuck caring for his foster daughter the rest of his days.

What he needed was a son-in-law to relieve him of his burden.

Prior to the introduction of Lake Ockeechobee's legalized "river boat gambling" in 2009, Belle Glade had predominantly been a seasonal farming town, most of its worker force minorities, primarily African-American and Hispanic. The big sugar companies recruited strong backs, having little use for brains, a fact that reflected poorly upon the school district, which boasted the worst standardized test scores in the county. For most high-school males growing up in the area, college was not an option. In Belle Glade, you either labored in the fields, sold drugs, or played sports.

Seventeen-year-old Virgil Robinson could play sports, especially football. After three years of high-school ball, he had earned the coveted title, "Nastiest Linebacker in the State." While Glades Central High might have had a bad reputation for standardized test scores, they were tops in the nation when it came to sports, producing more professional athletes than any other school in the country. Virgil was the cream of the football class of 2011, a 257-pound man-child standing an imposing six-foot-five, who could cover forty yards in just under 4.4 seconds and had a fifty-two-inch vertical leap. What's more, the speedy junior middle linebacker loved delivering bone-jarring hits, the more savage, the better. "Don't wanna just hit the dude, I wanna bleed him from the inside out."

Running backs trembled. College recruiters salivated.

Young Virgil's parents had died when he was six, leaving him to toil in his uncle's fields ever since. He could barely read and write, and admittedly didn't know "much about nothing," but what he did know was that football was his ticket out of Belle Glade. Now in his senior year, he was finally enjoying the first whiffs of success. The recruiting ritual had begun, the Division I-A college assistants luring him with promises of wealth, fancy cars, and beautiful undergrads. Virgil Robinson was the type of athlete who could turn around a losing program and bring home a national championship. Every coach knew about his inflated 2.13 grade point average and his third-grade reading level, but none seemed to care. Tutors were easier to find than All-Americans, and grades could be spoon-fed. At the very worst, the kid from Belle Glade would redshirt his freshman year.

Of course, Virgil had no more interest in earning a degree than he did cracking open a book. A year or two of exposure in a top-ranked football program and he'd turn pro. A year or two and the money would be there. Shoe deals, sports drink endorsements, it was all part of the game. Millionaires didn't need an education. As long as he maintained his appetite for violence, success both on and off the gridiron would follow.

Unfortunately, Virgil also had an appetite for women

and drugs, the latter amplifying his propensity for violence. On the eve of signing a letter of intent with the University of Florida, the high-school star decided to spend the night on the town partying with a few friends and teammates. After getting high, the boys headed to nearby Clewiston, intent on crashing their rival's homecoming dance. One of the Clewiston cheerleaders had caught Virgil's eye during their last game, and the star linebacker's loins ached at the thought of seeing her again.

The girl was there, dancing with her boyfriend, the team's starting tailback. Virgil approached the couple, grinning his gold-capped smile. "Yo, hoochie, why don'tch ya'll shake dat thing over here—I'll show you how a real man handles it."

The tailback threw first, his punch impacting Virgil's nose, drawing blood. Virgil never flinched, only his expression changed, morphing into an insane leer his defensive coordinator had dubbed "the Robinson Rage." In one motion the All-State linebacker grabbed the smaller teen by his neck and head-butted him twice, the latter blow knocking him senseless. A swift knee to the mouth finished the job.

As the crowd backed away, Virgil turned his attention to the girl. Grabbing her by the wrist, he tossed her over his shoulder, carrying her out to the parking lot like a Neanderthal choosing his·mate.

Back in his truck, Virgil had to slap the girl twice before he could tear off her panties. By that time a small crowd had gathered around the vehicle, including Wes Hobart, the school's wrestling coach. Hobart yanked open the door, only to have Virgil leap out and grab him by the hair, smashing him headfirst through another car's windshield. Then he spun around to face his next assailant, the girl's father, an English teacher—

—who was carrying a shotgun.

The load of buckshot struck Virgil in his left knee, shattering the patella, blowing out most of the supporting cruciate ligaments and muscle. Six hours of surgery later,

Virgil Robinson awoke in a hospital bed, his dream of playing professional football gone forever, the nightmare of adulthood about to begin.

The former star left the hospital a week later and was sent to jail to await trial. The judge sentenced him to three years.

When the Reverend Morehead read about Virgil's fall from grace, he approached the judge and offered to take the youth in as part of the church's work-release program. In the former high-school star Quenton saw yet another downtrodden youth whose soul needed to be saved . . . and a potential son-in-law in the making.

And so Virgil Robinson moved in with Reverend Morehead and his foster-daughter, Madelina. Encouraged by their "matchmaker," the two began dating. After three weeks, the reverend promised Virgil he would use his influence to have the rest of his prison sentence commuted, but only if he agreed to marry Madelina.

Faced with another two years of incarceration, Virgil wholeheartedly accepted.

A quick Sunday ceremony and the deed was done. As a wedding gift, Quenton gave the young couple use of a dilapidated stucco home the church owned, but could find no one to rent. Before anyone could say "early parole" the newlyweds headed off to begin their lives together, blessed with all the hardships poverty and a lack of formal education could offer.

For a short while things seemed fine. With Quenton's help, Virgil landed an assistant manager's position with one of the big sugar companies. By day, he supervised sugarcane workers, by night, he would return home from the fields to find comfort in his young bride's loins. As for Madelina, with Quenton out of her life, the girl finally felt safe. Medication kept the "voices" at bay, and she began saving money to purchase a nicer home. There was even talk of starting a family.

And then Virgil's drugging resurfaced.

It started innocently enough—a few missed NA meetings here, a few hits of coke there. But drug addiction is a disease only abstinence can contain, and before Madelina realized what was happening, her husband had spent their savings on his all-night binges.

Madelina was forced to dip into her medication money just to afford groceries. Depression set in, and with it, all of the girl's old fears. "Remember girl," Quenton always said, "the Devil will take your soul if you're not strong . . ."

To make matters worse, the college football season was upon them, the time of year that stoked Virgil's anger to its fullest. Watching the University of Florida's games on TV, his internal rage would build until he had to lash out at something . . . or somebody.

Madelina told Quenton she had broken her arm while mending the roof. The punctured lung—that had come from a nasty fall on her bike. She told the intern at the clinic that she broke her nose slipping in the bathtub.

The beatings subsided briefly in late January of 2013 when Virgil learned his wife was pregnant. The news seemed to calm the former football star. A son could be put to work in the fields. A son could be taught how to play football. Virgil Jr. would live the life denied his father—he would return glory to his old man by making it in the NFL. Twenty years from now, old Virgil Robinson would be able to retire in wealth, living off the fortunes of his prodigal son.

Life in the Robinson home stabilized . . . for the moment.

And then the world seemed to lose its equilibrium, and sobriety was not an option.

Reverend Morehead enters the strip club, his senses immediately seized by the smell of alcohol and smoke and sex. It takes him several minutes to find his son-in-law, who is in a back room, receiving a lap dance.

"Virgil! Get your heathen butt home, your son's on the way!"

"Aww shit, Quenton, give me two more minutes."

"Now boy!"

"Sumbitch!" Virgil climbs out from beneath the stripper, squeezes an exposed breast, whispers, "Call you later, baby," then follows Quenton into the parking lot.

Boca Raton, Florida

2:13 A.M.

The parking lot is quiet, the National Guard having cleared the hospital and its grounds. Only authorized personnel are allowed entry, no one permitted on the third-floor maternity ward without President Chaney's personal approval.

Dominique sits up in bed, gazing through heavy lids at her new family. Edith beams like a proud grandmother as she coddles the dark-haired twin. Ennis Chaney sits back in an easy chair holding the fair-haired infant, the gruffness gone from the old man's weathered face.

Rabbi Steinberg sits on the edge of Dominique's bed, taking everything in. "So? Have you decided on names? You know, it's Jewish custom to use the first initial of a deceased loved one to honor the dead."

"I'm going to name the dark-haired twin Immanuel, after Isadore."

Edie looks up, the mention of her late husband, causing her eyes to moisten. "Your father would be honored."

"We'll call him Manny for short. He has Hispanic blood running through him, you can see it in his eyes."

"And what about this blue-eyed fellow," Chaney asks. "How about an 'M' name, after the father?"

"The father's not dead!" Dominique blurts out the words, the unexpected burst of anger exploding from her mouth.

"Doll, take it easy." Edie hands Immanuel to the rabbi, then takes Dominique's hand.

"Sorry . . . I'm just tired. It's been a long night, a long pregnancy."

"It's okay."

Dominique looks at the infant sleeping in the crook of Chaney's arm. "Mick's father, his name was Julius. I thought I'd name the baby Jacob."

The rabbi smiles his approval. "A wonderful choice. Jacob is Hebrew for, 'he will prevent.'"

"I also want Mick's last name. Rabbi, can you marry us in absentia?"

Steinberg nods. "I think we can do that. Dominique Gabriel it is."

"And Ennis, I'd like you to be the boys' godfather."

"An old fart like me?" He smiles. "Be my honor. Now you listen," he rasps. "I've made arrangements to move your family to a private compound on the Gulf Coast, someplace you can live without being under the constant watch of the media. Gated grounds, your own personal chef, housekeepers, and a twenty-four-hour-a-day security team. The twins'll have private tutors when they get older, and starting today, I'm assigning my own personal bodyguards to your family. You and yours will never want for anything. That was my promise to Mick."

"Thank you." She smiles through tears of relief. "There's just one other thing I need from you. Julius Gabriel had a journal. It was confiscated after Mick . . . disappeared. I want the twins to have it. I want them to be . . . prepared."

Belle Glade, Florida

2:13 A.M.

Reverend Morehead hears the sounds of a baby crying as he reenters the sweltering stucco home. "Madelina?"

The heavyset midwife is in the kitchen, an infant in her arms. "Look. There's your grandpa. Say hi, Grandpa!"

"My Lord, will you look at his eyes, I've never seen eyes so blue."

"Silly, it's not a he, she's a little girl."

"A girl?" Quenton feels the hairs rise along the back of his neck.

"Where's the father?"

"Puking his guts up outside. Quickly, take the child and—"

The screen door slams open and Virgil approaches, a line of spittle running from his lower lip to his stained tee shirt, a ring of white powder visible in his left nostril. "Okay, le' me see my boy."

Quenton and the midwife exchange frightened looks. "Now Virgil—"

The minister steps in front of the wailing infant.

"Outta my way, Quenton, I said I wanna see my son."

"Virgil, the Lord . . . the Lord has blessed you with a child. A daughter."

Virgil stops. Facial muscles contort into a mask of rage. "A girl?"

"Easy, son—"

"A girl ain't shit! A girl's nuthin' but another goddam mouth to feed and clothe and listen to her whining." He points at the screaming infant. "Give her to me!"

"No." Quenton holds his ground. The nurse stands, preparing to flee with the child.

"I want you to sober up, Virgil. I want you to go to my home and—"

Virgil punches the minister in the gut, dropping him to his knees.

The midwife tucks the infant under one arm, brandishing a kitchen knife in the other. "Ya'll git outta here, Virgil. Go on!"

Virgil stares at the blade quivering in the fat woman's fist. In one motion he grabs her wrist, wrenching the knife free.

The midwife screams, backing away.

Virgil stares at the infant, then hears Madelina moaning from inside the bedroom. "Damn no-good bitch . . ." Leav-

ing the kitchen, he ducks inside the bedroom, slamming the door shut behind him.

"Oh, Lord, oh, God—Quenton, get up! Get up, Quenton!"

The minister struggles to his feet as sounds of slapping flesh and Madelina's screams fill the home. Quenton turns to the midwife. "Go! Take the child to the neighbors and call the police!"

The woman hurries out the back door.

Quenton bangs on the locked bedroom door. "Virgil? Virgil Robinson, you leave her be! You hear me?"

The screaming stops, the sudden silence deafening.

The minister backs away from the door and the approaching footsteps.

Virgil emerges, his white tee shirt splattered scarlet. He casts a hollow look at the minister, then stumbles into the night.

Quenton Morehead peeks inside the bedroom. Gags. Crosses himself.

Belle Glade police will arrest Virgil Robinson hours later in the apartment of Luanda Melendez, a thirty-nine-year-old "dancer."

The mutilated body of Madelina Lilith Aurelia will be buried two days later.

PART 3
INFANCY

The world is a dangerous place to live;
not because of the people who are evil,
but because of the people
who don't do anything about it.

—ALBERT EINSTEIN

PROGRESS REPORT ON
SPECIAL ACCESS PROGRAM
<u>GOLDEN FLEECE</u>

27 October 2013

<u>HUNAHPU GENETICS</u>

1. A thorough physiological and genetics examination of the Gabriel Twins reveals some unique findings. Geneticists have isolated a mutation in chromosome six, in segments 6p21 through 6p26. This genetic anomaly (Hunahpu marker) is dominant in Jacob Gabriel (white-haired, blue-eyed twin) but so far recessive in Immanuel Gabriel (dark-haired, dark-eyed twin). Although only five weeks old, physical and mental disparities among the boys are already apparent. While both boys are far above average, Jacob's responses to voice recognition are on par with three-year olds. Incredibly, Jacob can already walk and can support his body weight by gripping a horizontal bar for more than two

minutes. GOLDEN FLEECE trainers assigned to the Gabriel compound as developmental teachers claim the child prodigy's improvements can be measured daily.

2. Unfortunately, Jacob's physical and mental capabilities may be rendered moot as he gets older. The Hunahpu gene is part of the same chromosome that leads to paranoid schizophrenia. (Note: Michael Gabriel was incarcerated in an asylum for this same diagnosis.) While the twins are not yet old enough to exhibit this type of deviant behavior, it is recommended that all GOLDEN FLEECE personnel assigned to the Gabriel compound be advised.

Submitted:

W. Louis McDonald
GOLDEN FLEECE

27 October 2013

6
THREE YEARS
LATER

OCTOBER 27, 2016
LONGBOAT KEY, FLORIDA

The barrier island of Longboat Key is an eleven-mile stretch of land located between the tropical waters of Sarasota Bay and the Gulf of Mexico. Considered a private island-paradise, the resort town is home to 8,000 permanent residents and 150 relocated members of the National Guard and their families.

Follow the pristine alabaster beach south past Fire Station Number 2 and you will reach a restricted zone. What was once the Quick Point Nature Preserve has been turned into an Army base. Perimeter electrical fencing is monitored around the clock by security cameras and armed flying drones keep trespassers away. The entire island and surrounding waters are considered a no-fly, no-boating zone, the restriction enforced by 20-mm guns mounted on turrets on both the Gulf and Bay sides of the preserve. Two Coast Guard cutters patrol the surrounding Gulf waters. Boaters and divers are no longer permitted south of Fire Station Number 2.

Three concrete-and-steel dwellings set in a wide "H" formation, occupy the southern tip of the island. The building on the right is a training center, complete with classrooms, the latest virtual-reality combat simulators, a weight room, basketball court, and a Faraday chamber, impervious to electromagnetic waves. The building on the left is a three-story residence, its luxury suites occupied by the bodyguards, Salt and Pepper, and the private staff that serves the occupants of the central facility.

The six-bedroom, eight-bathroom beachfront home at the center of the "H" belongs to Dominique Gabriel and her two sons. The house has two wings, separated by an enormous kitchen, dining room, living room, virtual-reality chamber, and den.

Dominique waits patiently while the ABC *20/20* film crew sets up in her living room, under the watchful eyes of her bodyguards. Today marks the first appearance her family has ever made before the cameras. With the presidential election only a week away, and Ennis Chaney trailing Peter Mabus in the polls, Dominique feels it important to address the issue that has been swaying public opinion over the last thirty-six months.

Barbara Walters makes her way carefully across the living room carpet, now covered in a myriad of electrical wires. The renowned reporter has come out of retirement just for this interview.

"Hello, Dominique, I'm so glad to finally meet you."

"Me too. I really appreciate your network coming on such short notice. Mabus's lies have gotten way out of hand."

"Our viewers will want to hear all about it. When do I get to meet the twins?"

"They have a karate lesson in twenty minutes. I thought we'd do it then."

"Terrific, wait . . . did you say a karate lesson? The boys are only three. Isn't that a bit young?"

Dominique only smiles.

Dominique registers the heat of the lights on her face as she sits opposite the ABC host on the beige L-shaped sofa.

"Tell us why, Dominique, after all these years of living

in seclusion, you felt it important to share your family and home with our viewers."

"Peter Mabus has been using the public's fear to spew his hatred and lies for too long. This man is a phony, his entire political campaign taking advantage of a religious renaissance that has swept the country since the events of December 2012. What happened back then was not religious or sacrilegious in nature, it was simply an extraterrestrial event. Thousands of years ago, an advanced race of humans came to our world to prepare modern man to face the 2012 threat. These humans, who called themselves the Guardian, helped educate ancient man. They were our allies, our friends, our leaders. They taught our ancestors about astronomy and architecture, and built great temples and shrines, which they used to conceal relay stations that would be used in 2012 to emit a high-energy EM beacon. It was this beacon that thwarted the nuclear missiles that nearly destroyed us. My husband, Michael Gabriel, was one of the Guardian's genetically chosen humans, one of the few amongst us capable of accessing the Guardian's vessel to activate the array. He was not the Antichrist, as Peter Mabus's fanatical followers make him out to be, he was a man, confused about his destiny, but he was a hero, and he risked his life to save us all."

"And what happened to Michael? Where is he now?"

"I don't know. The biological entity he entered was capable of moving between dimensions, at least that's what I'm told. Both the entity and Mick disappeared."

"But there's also another possibility, isn't there, Dominique? That maybe the entity self-destructed?"

"Yes, that's possible."

"Let's talk about your sons. Peter Mabus makes them out to be demons."

"Peter Mabus is a selfish, self-righteous asshole who preys upon the public's ignorance. My sons are wonderful children, gifted, yes, but innocent children."

"Can we see them?"

"Of course."

"Stay tuned, *20/20* will be right back with the first exclusive footage of the Gabriel twins."

"And . . . cut!"

Barbara pats Dominique on the knee. "You're doing great. We're already set up in the gym. Do you need a break?"

"No, I'm okay." Dominique accepts a bottled water from a technician, then leads Barbara out of the house. A brisk ocean breeze messes up her hair as she crosses the compound to the athletic facility.

They enter the secured building and follow an interior corridor to the main gym. The grunts and groans of young children can be heard within.

Dominique pushes open the door.

The three-year-old Gabriel twins are dressed in white karate outfits with black pants. White-haired, blue-eyed Jacob wears a black belt, his dark-eyed, ebony-headed brother sporting a green *obi*.

The cameras are rolling as Master Gustafu Pope places a two-inch concrete slab across the top of two cinder blocks. "Okay, Jacob, remember, focus your mind. Move into the moment and harness your inner strength."

The white-haired three-year-old steps up to the slab and takes a forward stance, his weight displaced perfectly over his bent left knee, his right arm slightly bent as it arcs slowly overhead, practicing the breaking movement. The blade of his right hand comes to rest at the center of the top slab.

"Permission to break, sir?"

"Permission granted."

Barbara Walters and her crew watch in amazement as the small boy closes his eyes and meditates, his shallow breaths growing gradually into a low growl as he gathers strength, his right arm continuing its downward practice swings over and over, pressing the concrete heavier with each successive strike.

Suddenly, the blue eyes flash open, the boy's face a mask of rage. With a tremendous, "ki-yahhh!" he slams his open knife hand against the slab, the impact of his slender right wrist striking the concrete like a bullet hitting glass.

The slab collapses to the protective mat, the concrete split in half.

The crew applauds wildly.

The boy doesn't so much as smile. He bows to his instructor, then takes his place next to his brother.

Master Pope turns to the dark-haired twin. "Immanuel."

The dark-eyed boy ignores him, too engrossed in playing with his toes.

"Immanuel, join me please."

The boy rolls over and stands, then bunny-hops over to his instructor.

"Manny, these nice people want to see how well you can break a board. Do you want to show them?"

The boy runs to his mother, hugging her legs.

Dominique picks him up. "Sorry, he's a little shy."

Barbara strokes his hair. "He's so cute, but so much different than his brother. Jacob seems so mature, I mean, I know he's only three, but—"

"The Hunahpu gene is dominant in Jake, recessive in his brother. At times, Jake possesses the awareness of an adult."

"Can I meet him?"

"Sure. Master Pope?"

Master Pope signals Jacob to stand. Student and teacher bow to one another, then the white-haired boy hustles over to his mother.

"Jake, this is Barbara."

"Hi."

"Hello. Would you mind if I ask you and your brother some questions?"

"Okay."

"How were you able to break that thick slab of concrete with your tiny hand?"

The boy points to a bone along the outside of his right wrist. "We strike this bone over and over until it calcifies and the nerves deaden. Then we learn to focus."

"Wow. You sound so grown-up for a three-year-old."

Jacob shrugs.

"Tell us what else you can do."

"I like to swim."

"How far can you swim?"

"I do a mile in the pool every morning before breakfast."

Barbara's jaw drops. "A mile?"

"I can swim, too," chimes in Manny.

"You can? And how far do you swim?"

Manny buries his face against his mother's chest.

Dominique strokes the boy's jet-black hair. "Manny can swim ten laps in the pool, can't you, Manny?"

"I like to read," Jacob says, his bright blue eyes blazing.

"You can read? That's wonderful," says Barbara. "What do you like to read? Do you read *Sesame Street* books?"

Jacob giggles. "That's for babies."

Barbara looks up at Dominique. "What does he read?"

"He just finished *Huckleberry Finn*. But he downloads a lot off the Internet."

"Amazing."

They are back in the living room, shooting the last segment of the taped interview. The boys are outside, playing in the fifty-meter pool under the watchful eyes of Salt and Pepper.

"Dominique, what's Jacob's IQ?"

She smiles uncomfortably. "I don't know. I'm told it's off the conventional scale. Manny's is high, too—"

"But nothing like his brother's?"

"No."

"What do you tell Jacob when he asks about his father?"

"I tell him his father's with the Angels."

"While you were tending to Manny, I asked Jacob about his father. Do you know what he said?"

"No." Dominique's heart pounds in her chest.

"He said his father's in someplace called She-bal-ba. He also told me that one day, he and his brother are going to travel to this She-bal-ba, defeat the evil warlord, and rescue Mick."

Dominique bites her lower lip. "He has quite an imagination, doesn't he?"

"This She-bal-ba, what is it?"

"It's nothing. Just some Mayan folklore. I hate putting parental controls on the Internet, but I guess I'll have to."

"Dominique, this doesn't sound like an Internet situation, it sounds like the Mayan studies the boys' paternal grandparents spent their lives investigating. She-bal-ba? Evil warlords? I mean, this is serious stuff."

"You want to know what's serious? In the last three months, there have been two attempts on the boy's lives. In August, four members of the Aryan Nation made it up the beach in scuba gear, armed with Uzis and grenades. They came within one hundred yards of our home before security shot them. Then two weeks ago, a mob, incited by Peter Mabus and his radical regime, stormed the front gates using seven military vehicles and a trailer packed with explosives. Seven people died, including two American soldiers assigned to guard the compound."

Dominique turns to face the camera. "I'm a single mother, trying her best to raise two wonderful boys in a loving environment. I'd give anything for them to lead normal lives, but those weren't the cards we were dealt. Ennis Chaney's leadership helped save the world, he supported Mick when few others did. The president is a stable hand at the helm during these rocky times, exactly what we need. What we don't need is a knee-jerk God-fearing reaction based on bully boy tactics. Elect a fanatical monster like Peter Mabus, and America no longer becomes a melting pot of liberty, it becomes a haven for the privileged few, a nation as close-minded as those Muslim-dominated countries we've been conditioned to hate over the years."

Jacob stands next to his mother. He holds her hand, staring into the camera.

"Please don't vote for Peter Mabus. He wants to kill my family."

Belle Glade, Florida

Three-year-old Lilith Eve Robinson stands next to the television set, staring into the white-haired boy's brilliant eyes. "Grandpa Quenton, look! He has pretty blue eyes just like me."

The minister drains the rest of his gin as he thumbs through his monthly bills. "How many times I got to tell you, child? Turn that goddam television off and get to bed!"

"Yes, sir."

Lilith powers off the set using the remote, then crawls onto the sofa, pulling the wool blanket over her head.

Quenton tosses the empty liquor bottle into the kitchen trash. "I'm goin' out. Don't you even think'a movin' your ass offa that couch or I'll whup it good."

"Yes, sir."

The minister staggers out the front door, slamming it close behind him.

Lilith listens. Waits until the car pulls out the driveway, then turns the television back on. The interview is over, the older woman back at her desk, talking to a colleague.

At the bottom of the screen is the *20/20* e-mail address.

Lilith commits it to memory, shuts off the television, then climbs onto her foster grandfather's chair and boots his computer. She signs onto the Internet, and types in *20/20*'s address.

DEAR JACOB:
I HAVE BRIGHT BLUE EYES, JUST LIKE YOU, AND I CAN READ AND WRITE, JUST LIKE YOU, AND I LOVE YOU.
PLEASE LET ME LIVE WITH YOU.
LOVE LILITH EVE.

President Reelect Ennis Chaney climbs up to the dais, shakes hands with the Speaker of the House and Vice President Marion Rallo, the first woman ever to hold an executive office, then turns to face the applauding members of Congress and the American people.

"Thank you. Mr. Speaker, Vice President Rallo, members of Congress, distinguished guests, fellow citizens. 'The cause of America is, in a great measure, the cause of all mankind. Many circumstances have, and will arise, which are not local, but universal, and through which the principles of all Lovers of Mankind are affected. . . . Society in every state is a blessing, but government even in its best state is but a necessary evil; in its worse state, an intolerable one, for when we suffer, or are exposed to the same miseries *by a government* which we might expect in a country *without government,* our calamity is heightened by reflecting that we furnished the means by which we suffer.'"

Chaney looks up from his notes. "These words were first recorded in Philadelphia on February 14, 1776, by Thomas Paine in his persuasive document, *Common Sense*, in which he tried to address the fear of change, exhorting the American colonists to break from England. Like our patriot forefathers, we find ourselves facing similar fears, fears that also began with an act of war. The events of September 11, 2001, took us on a perilous journey, a journey we had to make, and yet our best intentions led us to the brink of Hell. From a world united against terrorism we nearly ended as a species divided by globalism, and paranoia, and greed. Our leaders asked us to make sacrifices to protect our freedom, but in the end, it was freedom that we nearly lost.

"Just as our forefathers did in 1776, we too stood at a crossroads in American history. On November 8, we could have allowed our fears to force us off the path of democracy. Instead, we rose up as one people, united before God, and stood against those who would challenge our Constitution. By doing so, we shall come out of this struggle stronger as a nation and as a species."

Chaney pauses as Congress rises for a standing ovation.

"For a decade, the world wallowed in the shadow of war; now we will lead the world, hand in hand, into the sunshine. Equality, education, and technology shall drive our economies, peace and prosperity our calling card to all nations. But before we can rise, we must first rid our country of the shackles that led us down the path of destruction. The first of those shackles is our continued addiction to fossil fuels. Our leaders applauded the promises of cleaner, greener, renewable energy sources, but in the end they chose to keep our country addicted to OPEC because of their own personal investments in the oil industry. It is time to end this addiction once and for all. Our new task force on Energy and America's Future has determined that there is now less than half a trillion barrels of proven and probable oil reserves left in the world, 75 percent of which are located in authoritarian-run countries. By 2025, the price of oil is expected to quadruple. By 2040, it will become prohibitive, precipitating a worldwide economic crisis. At the same time, third world industrialization is driving energy demands even higher, with needs escalating from our current usage of 15 trillion watts to over 40 trillion within only two decades. Meanwhile, we infect our environment with more acid rain, more air pollution, and an even bigger rise in greenhouse gases to melt what little's left of the Arctic and Antarctic ice."

Chaney's deeply set eyes stare into the lens of the nearest camera. "In 2017 and beyond, our vision is clear: We're Clean and Goin' Green."

Democrats stand and applaud, most members of Chaney's Republican Party remaining seated.

"The most promising solution to our energy crisis has and always will be solar. It's unlimited and clean, but the cost has remained high because we've never committed our full resources to the technology. Decades ago, the federal government invested over $100 billion in nuclear research to jump-start that industry, not to mention the money used to subsidize businesses involved in the uranium fuel cycles. Now we're going to commit the same kind of resources to solar and wind power, as well as hydrogen fuel cells. To help pay for these changes, my new budget will eliminate the Strategic Defense Initiative, a failed and costly program that drove a wedge between the United States, China, and Russia and led to the nuclear assaults of 2012."

Wild applause.

"Real change requires real commitment, not just doubletalk. The Clinton and Bush administrations budgeted funds to produce hydrogen fuel cars, only they gave the money to the automakers. President Bush's promise of a new energy future required hydrogen to be extracted from fossil fuels and nuclear power, effectively maintaining Big Oil's agenda, a policy my predecessor also adhered to. This year, our new energy plan will commit $50 billion to developing hydrogen automobiles using renewable sources like wind and sun and biomass. Furthermore, within the next thirty days, the White House will introduce legislation aimed at outlawing gasoline-powered vehicles by 2023."

The president pauses, allowing his last statement to sink in amid the applause.

"Fuel cells will, by law, replace gasoline. New jobs will be created as we retool our automobile plants and fueling stations. The economy will prosper, our air quality will improve, and the United States will rejoin the global effort to reduce greenhouse gases!"

The room erupts in applause.

"Change is never easy, but it is necessary. The war on terrorism led to great changes, changes that affected our civil rights and the freedoms this country was founded upon. Within the next ninety days, I will ask Congress to dismantle the monolithic Department of Homeland Security and restore the pre 9-11 restrictions on domestic surveillance."

Chaney pauses again as members of both parties rise to cheer.

Belle Glade, Florida

Three-and-a-half year old Lilith Eve Robinson is in the backseat of Quenton Morehead's 2003 Buick, strapped in a child protection device. The reverend has cracked the windows and left the radio on for her while he visits the recently widowed Sherry Ann Williams.

Lilith squirms, her bladder full, her stomach rumbling as the State of the Union speech plays on the radio. The toddler has not eaten since lunch seven hours earlier, and knows she will not eat again until her grandfather emerges from the widow's home sometime around eleven-thirty.

And then the child stops squirming as her mind suddenly focuses on the president's words, her subconscious absorbing them like a sponge.

"My fellow Americans, humanity has a future, and it is a bright one, as bright as the stars in the night sky. And this is where our future lies, for it is space exploration that shall advance and unite our species. This year, we shall end NASA's moratorium on new projects and set new apolitical goals for the colonization of Mars. We shall encourage the private sector to join us, and we will open the frontier of space for all people, so that we may rejoice in our humanity, unite in harmony, and better ourselves as a species. Thank you all. God bless you, God bless America, and good night."

Lilith unbuckles her safety device and climbs out of the infant seat. Prying open the back door, she jumps out of the car and looks around.

The lights are off in the widow's home. From an open bedroom window she can hear her grandfather and Mrs. Williams giggling.

Lilith rolls down her pants, squats, and urinates on the driveway. Looking up, her dazzling blue eyes widen as she gazes at the full moon and a billion twinkling stars.

"Grandpa, when I get old, I'm going to go on a rocket into space."

Quenton glides through a four-way stop sign, nearly hitting a teenager on a motorized skateboard. "Space? Don't talk stupid."

"Why can't I go into space?"

"Space is for astronauts. You ain't gonna be no astronaut."

"Why not?"

"'Cause bein' an astronaut means ya'll got to go to college, and I ain't sending you to no college."

"Why not?"

"'Cause it costs money, lots of money. You want to go to college, move out and marry some rich boy."

"I will."

"Good. Sooner the better. Now stop yer yappin', I'm tryin' to drive."

Gabriel Compound
Longboat Key, Florida

Ocean waves sizzle as they die out on the Gulf beach. Sand crabs race from their outposts, searching for food.

Jacob Gabriel peers through the telescope, then backs away, allowing his aunt Evelyn to take a peek.

Evelyn Strongin presses her right eye to the rubber housing. "Wow. You can really make out details on the lunar surface."

"When me and my brother get older, we're going into space."

Evelyn pulls back, struck by the absoluteness of the statement. "Why do you say that, Jacob?"

"*Xibalba*'s out there. My daddy's on *Xibalba*. Mommy says we're going to see him when we get older."

"How do you know *Xibalba*'s out there?"

He shrugs. "I just know." He peers into the telescope. "Mommy says you talk to dead people."

"I can communicate with the souls of those who've passed."

"Teach me how to do it."

"Maybe when you get older. What else can you show me on this telescope?"

"Can you teach me to talk to my daddy?"

"I don't know if that's possible."

"'Cause he's not dead?"

"Yes, because he's not dead."

"But he has Hunahpu blood, like us, right?"

"Well, I suppose—"

"Then I can communicate with him. Teach me."

"When you get older."

"But I want to talk with him now."

"You're not ready. Sometimes when we communicate over interdimensional frequencies, other spirits can answer us. If you're not strong enough, they can fool you into believing what they tell us is real. Try to be patient, Jacob, your time will come."

"He's beyond inquisitive," Evelyn says, pouring herself another cup of coffee. "He possesses an almost innate sense of the universe. It's like talking to an adolescent trapped inside a toddler's body."

Dominique looks up from her computer. "I worry about Jacob. His mind's developing way too fast."

"Maybe you're telling him too much."

"That's just it, I haven't told him anything. He's been sneaking on the Internet, reading about himself. He's totally engrossed in the Mayan legend."

"What about his brother?"

"Manny's more like a normal toddler. He could care less about Mayan legends, which really bothers Jake. Unfortunately, it seems like the gap between their genetic gifts grows wider with each passing day. God only knows how I'll be able to handle Jake as he gets older."

Evelyn looks over Dominique's shoulder. "Child, what is that you're working on?"

"It's a program that charts births. Did you know there were 723,891 babies born on September 22, 2013?"

"You're searching for the Abomination?"

"By segregating out all of the blue-eyed babies, I've reduced the list to just under three hundred thousand names. Of course, this program only accounts for about 68 percent of the world, but it's a start."

"A start to what? Murder?"

"Beware the child born on the day of the twins' birth, you said. The Abomination imprisons Mick and disrupts the space-time continuum. If I can kill it in this time period—"

"Stop it." Evelyn leans over and shuts down the computer. "You'll never find the one you seek this way, Dominique, and even if you did, what would you do? Murder an innocent child?"

"What am I supposed to do, Evelyn? Sit back and allow some freak of nature to stalk my sons?"

"Unlike your sons, who will be prepared, the Hunahpu child born on the twins' birthday has no idea what it is or what lies ahead. Like all newborns, it is an innocent being—God's clay, ready to be molded. It is the influences throughout the child's journey that will lead it to become the Abomination my sister warned us about. Your mission, First-Mother, is to prepare your sons for battle, not to play God."

PART 4

::::::::::::::::::

CHILDHOOD

> *The Earth is the cradle of mankind,*
> *but one cannot stay in the cradle forever.*
>
> **—KONSTANTIN TSIOLKOVSKY**

> *And Jacob called to his sons, and said,*
> *"Gather yourselves together that I may tell you*
> *that which shall befall you in the End of Days."*
>
> **—GENESIS 49:1**

8
FOUR YEARS LATER

Dawn backlights seven-year-old Immanuel Gabriel's bedroom in bronze shades of gray. The dark-haired, ebony-eyed boy snores softly.

Jacob stands over him, grinning mischievously. "Get up, you lazy sonuva bitch!"

Manny sits up with a start, his heart pounding. "Huh!"

"You shut your alarm off. Now get up, we have to train."

"Go away!" Immanuel pulls the sheet over his head.

Jacob reaches beneath the blanket and shoulder presses his twin up and over his head.

"Help! Ma—"

"You're falling behind, Manny. You're supposed to be my equal, but you're not—"

"Get off me, freak!"

"—you're nothing but a lightweight."

"Ma! Ma, he's doing it again!"

The bodyguards arrive first, still in their bathrobes. "Again?" Salt shakes his head. Holsters his weapon.

"C'mon, Jake," Pepper coaxes, "put your brother down."

Dominique pushes her way past the two bodyguards. "Jacob Gabriel, you put your brother down this instant!"

Manny drops to the floor, his face meeting carpet with a thud. The dark-haired twin sits up, tears in his eyes, his nose bleeding.

Dominique's face reddens. "Dammit, Jacob, look what you—"

"His fault. Should have rolled with the fall. *Sensei* taught him that months ago."

"It's 6:00 A.M.!"

"When the Death God comes for us, it won't care what time it is. We have to be ready."

"I hate you," Immanuel yells. "You're a sick freak!"

"I'm Superman. You're only Clark Kent, a big fat wussie."

Dominique reaches for Jacob, but the fair-haired twin is too quick, leaping over the bed. "Foolish mortal. You can't catch Superman!"

Salt cuts him off, and the game is on.

Jacob feints left, then bounds across the chest of drawers, slipping beneath the older bodyguard's grasp.

Refusing to play, Pepper backs his considerable bulk in front of the open doorway. "Game over, Jake."

Without pause, the boy takes a running leap, his legs churning air like a triple-jumper until his right foot connects with the African-American's massive bare chest. The blow knocks the bodyguard backward through the doorway.

Jacob completes a forward somersault dismount and lands running, sprinting down the hallway into the kitchen and out the back door. "Superman . . . da-da-tada—"

Pepper sits up, massaging his bruised sternum. "Damn. How'd he do that?"

Dominique is livid. "I swear to Christ, that child will be the death of me. Come on, Manny, let's get some ice for your nose." She helps him to his feet, leading him out of the bedroom.

Mitchell Kurtz looks down at his larger comrade. "Now you know why Karla and I never had kids."

Belle Glade, Florida

6:17 A.M.

Dawn's rays reflect off the surface waters of Lake Okeechobee, planting a fiery orange kiss against the glistening white hulls of the gambling ferries and yachts, docked in rows of newly dredged slips. Hotels and casinos, restaurants and shops remain silent after another extended night of tourism, the pelicans and sandpipers picking at a bounty of refuse.

Follow the golden-lit streets south, past the renovated Town Hall and new Civic Center, to the west end of the resort town. A road sign at the canal bridge warns that you are leaving the tourist area, the ensuing sign across the bridge welcoming you to Belle Glade proper.

The bars on homes and storefront windows send another kind of warning.

Gambling dollars have not had much impact on this enclave of the poor, unless you consider the expanded police force and new wing of the local jail to be civic improvements. The elementary school is still grimy, the windows of its overloaded portables still supporting air-conditioning units that purge waves of lukewarm air reeking of mildew. Travel two more blocks, and you'll reach the Reverend Morehead's church, still in desperate need of a coat of paint. Cross the dirt parking lot where the rats feast at night, and you'll find a four-room stucco home, its fading yellowed walls trimmed in peeling black paint.

Seven-year-old Lilith Eve Robinson awakens on her birthday with a start. Stares at the ceiling fan. Concentrates.

"Six-seventeen."

She rolls over and glances at the alarm clock—6:17.

Lilith climbs out of the sofa bed. Folds the sheet and quilt. Replaces the cushions and enters the kitchen. Removes two eggs from the refrigerator. Scrambles them in a bowl, then pours the contents into a pan and lights the burner.

She heads for the powder room. Urinates. Washes her hands and face. Forces the last bit of toothpaste onto the worn bristles of her toothbrush, knowing the container must last at least another week. Rinses her mouth. Slips on the dress hanging behind the door, then stares at her reflection in the bathroom mirror.

Cocoa skin. High cheekbones. Startling azure blue eyes framed by ebony hair, long and wavy. The daughter of the late Madelina Aurelia-Robinson is a beauty in the making, even if her classmates despise her.

"Lilith Eve!" The door is yanked open, the girl dragged out by her arm. "You see this?" Quenton Morehead shoves the frying pan of burned eggs under his foster granddaughter's nose. "That's the third time this week. What on God's green earth is wrong with you, child?"

Lilith says nothing. To say something would invite the Baptist minister's physical wrath.

"I'm talkin' to you, you little heathen. Answer me!"

Silence.

"Damn you, child. Just like your mama. You got six lashes comin', and I don't wanna hear no whimperin' outta you this time." She sees the knotted electrical cord in his right hand as he braces her with his left. "Why (whip) the good Lord (whip) stuck me (whip) with the likes of you (whip) is beyond me."

She looks up at him through teary eyes, his breath painful to breathe. "Sorry, Grandpa."

"Sorry my ass. Now go on and get to school. Breakfast is over."

She limps past him, grabs her school bag, and heads out the front door.

Brandy Townson is waiting for her outside. They walk together in silence.

"You hate him, don't you?"

"It was my fault," Lilith says.

"He doesn't love you, Lilith. Nobody loves you."

"Do you love me, Brandy?"

"Who you talking to, freak?"

Lilith looks up. Sees Daunte and his fourth grade pals. Feels the warm urine dribbling down her panties.

"Run," whispers Brandy.

Lilith takes off, sprinting across two front lawns toward the church parking lot.

The boys chase her for a block, then give up.

Lilith Eve Robinson is a freak, but she is a fast freak. No one in school can catch her.

Gabriel Compound
Longboat Key, Florida

The Sikorsky Surveillance-3000 UAV (Unmanned Aero Vehicle) slows to hover twenty feet above the beach, its shadow dancing along the wet sand. Three feet in diameter, the donut-shaped flying saucer houses a series of short blades in its center hole that rotate horizontally like a helicopter's rotors. Designed for low-speed surveillance, the SS-3000 is powered by fuel cells and can fly up to seventeen hours on a single charge.

Sealed within the UAV's aluminum frame are three cameras, providing the viewer 360 degrees of video coverage.

Its aft camera focuses on two subjects jogging along the shoreline.

Jacob Gabriel steals a quick glance at the drone as his legs plow through the relentless surf. Jogging in ankle to knee-deep water is exhausting work, especially when breathing through a scuba mouthpiece, part of his combat swimmer's training. The cadence of the incoming waves is erratic today, forcing the boy out of his pace. Lactic acid burns in his muscles, weighing his lithe form down.

It is the lactic acid that Jacob seeks. Tolerance of the oxygen-depriving chemical must be raised if he has any hope of survival on *Xibalba*. He looks up again at the drone, focusing his eyes upon its digital timer.

19:07 . . . 19:08 . . . 19:09 . . .

Another eleven minutes. Push it . . .

The white-haired twin turns to his left. Manny is jogging in the wet sand, exhausted and red-faced but still keeping pace. Jacob bears down, increasing his speed.

Immanuel sees his brother pull ahead. His feet are aching, his calves in knots, but pride, long wounded by his brother's accomplishments, refuses to allow him to quit.

Wheezing the salty air into the back of his parched throat, he digs deeper, matching Jacob's pace.

The UAV images are beamed a half mile away to a closed-circuit flat-screen digital television monitor in Dominique's oak-paneled family room. Seated on an olive green wraparound leather sofa, watching the scene, are Rabbi Steinberg and his wife, Mindy.

Dominique enters from the kitchen. She hands them each a glass of peach iced tea, its contents laced with the latest bioelixir designed to lower blood pressure and cholesterol, then sits back in her recliner.

Registering her presence, the recliner's electromagnets instantly activate, the pulsating field invigorating the tight muscles in her back and neck.

"Look at them," she says, pointing to the screen. "Jacob always pushing, Manny always lagging behind. I worry about him. I really have to push him to work out more in the *Dojo*."

The rabbi shakes his head. "I don't understand? What are you training these kids for? The Olympics?"

"I don't expect you to understand," Dominique says. "What God has planned for these boys requires preparation."

"Really? God has spoken to you?"

"Rabbi, please."

"This has to do with that Mayan *Popol Vuh* nonsense."

"Nonsense?" She turns on him. "Were you there when those drones started landing, or when that alien ship rose out of the Gulf? Were you there when my Mick disappeared?"

Mindy attempts to put an arm around her. "Stay calm, dear. You're doing a terrific job raising these boys. No one's doubting you, right, Richard?"

The rabbi shrugs. "I'm not trying to upset you. They're both such well developed athletes. At least reconsider and let them play Little League."

"Out of the question. Do you have any idea what would happen if they competed in public?"

"My guess is they'd meet some friends their age and make a few coaches very happy."

"Please. There'd be a riot at every practice."

"Still, it might be good for them, especially for Manny," Mindy suggests. "They need friends their own age. Today's their birthday, and there are no children here. It's not right. Manny's such a loving child, but he always seems so sad."

"He hates it here," Dominique admits. "Then again, maybe he just hates his brother. Anyway, I'm still too afraid to let them leave the compound."

"Aren't you being just a tad overprotective?"

"Overprotective? There are lunatics out there, Mindy, thousands of them. Some want to worship my boys, others want to kill them. Security receives hundreds of letters a week, some of them quite graphic. It's sick."

"I had no idea."

"We're prisoners in a luxurious cage. Jake could care less, but poor Manny—all he ever talks about is playing football and basketball when he grows up. Breaks my heart."

"What about Jake?" Mindy asks. "What does he want to do when he gets older?"

"Jake wants to train. I never have to push him, he knows intuitively what lies ahead. Up before dawn swimming laps, then two hours on the computer, memorizing God-knows-what. After breakfast he's in the gym, studying with his Tibetan monk until lunch—"

"He's seven years old," the rabbi says. "He should be reading comics and . . . and taking naps."

"Don't you get it? He's not like other kids. Jake's naps consist of transcendental meditation sessions. Sometimes he 'naps' hanging upside down from inversion boots, other times, he immerses himself in a tub of cold water."

"Cold water?"

"The monk taught him that. Says it forces the mind to redirect the blood to the internal organs. At first Jake could only stay in the tub for thirty seconds. Now he's up to fifteen minutes. One time I checked his pulse, and I swear, I couldn't find it."

"So what can we do to help?" Mindy asks.

"I'm worried about raising the boys without a father figure in their lives. Salt and Pepper help, but they're more like big brothers." She looks at the rabbi.

"Okay, okay, I'll talk to them. Maybe I can even suggest a way for Jacob to refocus some of that energy of his."

Jacob enters the study. "Yes, sir, you wanted to see me?"

The rabbi looks up from the computer. "What? No hug?"

Jacob gives the man a cold embrace. "Was that all, sir, because I have a jujitsu lesson in half an hour, and I really should—"

"Jujitsu can wait. I want to talk to you about Ju—daism." A nerdy smile.

No reaction.

"You know, your paternal grandmother was Jewish, so were your mother's parents."

"Actually, sir, my mother was adopted. Her real mother was Quiche Mayan. Her father was—"

"Never mind. What's important is history. Your mother tells me you're interested in the Mayan *Popol Vuh*."

"Yes, sir. It's a sacred parchment."

"Yes, sir, yes, sir . . . call me Rabbi or Uncle Rich, okay, *tatt-ala*? Anyway, yes, I suppose the *Popol Vuh* is a sacred parchment, but it only dates back what . . . about five hundred years? The Bible, on the other hand, dates back thousands of years." He swivels in his chair to face the computer's microphone. "Computer, access Torah, Hebrew text."

The screen fills with Hebrew characters.

"Your mother says you can read and speak several languages. Can you read Hebrew?"

"No, sir . . . er, Rabbi." Blue eyes dart to the holographic display clock above the computer monitor. "I'm not really interested in—"

"Not interested? I'm surprised at you. Here I thought you were someone who sought knowledge, who sought the truth."

"The *Popol Vuh* is—"

"The *Popol Vuh* isn't accurate, Jacob, it was written long after that Koo koo fella—"

"Kukulcán."

"Uh, right . . . after Kukulcán's passing. Now the five books of Moses . . . they were written more than three thousand years ago by Moses himself."

A whisper of thought teases Jacob's brain. "Moses wrote the Bible?"

"Most of it. And did you know that every single Hebrew Bible that exists or has ever existed was transcribed in exactly the same way, word for word, letter by letter. If even one letter is out of place, the Bible can't be used. Did you know *that*?"

"No . . . Rabbi." Jacob touches his temple and closes his eyes.

"*Tatt-ala,* you okay?"

The boy nods. "I just had a strong *déjà vu*. I've lived this moment before."

"Excuse me?"

"This moment. I've lived it before. We both have."

The rabbi looks startled. "Now who taught you that?"

"No one. It's just the way things are." The boy climbs onto the rabbi's lap and peers at the screen.

Jacob Gabriel cannot read Hebrew, yet he stares at the words, transfixed. "Something's here."

"What do you mean?"

"Letters are jumping out. But it's hard to see."

Steinberg leans closer to the screen. Reads a passage. "It seems fine to me. How about if we set up a time to study together. I can teach you the Hebrew alphabet and—"

"It's the spaces between the words. It's screwing everything up, scrambling things, making it harder to see the patterns. Computer, close all spaces between words and sentences."

The text on the screen recycles.

"Whoa . . ." Jacob's brilliant azure eyes widen as three-dimensional patterns form among the letters in the text. "See! Things jump out better now!"

Steinberg's heart races. "What things?"

The boy points to a line. "Like these letters. Does this say anything?"

"WRWRIzRrPaA." The Rabbi looks at him, slightly pale. "It means, 'End of Days.' How did you manage to select—"

"Now these letters." Jacob points his index finger at a letter, then skips down three lines and one to the left, then continues the pattern until he forms a word.

"zRWJQaIaRL. Atomic holocaust. Jacob, how did you—"

"And these letters here."

"I get it, you're playing one of your famous mind games on me. Very clever."

"Just tell me what these four letters mean!"

The rabbi looks at him, unsure. He squints at the screen. zLmA. It's a year: 5772."

"In the future?"

"No, in the Hebrew calendar. The date equates to the year . . . 2012."

Jacob closes his eyes, reciting, "End of Days. Atomic holocaust. 2012. It's all here . . ."

"Okay, Jacob Gabriel, fun time's over. Who put you up to this?"

"No one."

"You read about the Bible Code in class, didn't you?"

"The Bible has a code?"

"That's enough, I'm not falling for this nonsense."

Jacob jumps off his lap. "Tell me!"

The rabbi sees desperation in the boy's eyes. *He's serious . . .*

"Hidden within the original Hebrew text of the Torah is a cryptogram—encoded messages that pertain to man's history. Isaac Newton was the first one to suspect it, but it wasn't until the late nineties and the advent of the computer that an Israeli mathematician was able to figure it out."

"Then the Bible Code's real?"

"I don't know."

"You're lying. Tell me the truth."

"I don't lie. According to code breakers—yes, it's real. According to religious scholars, it's all nonsense." Steinberg searches the boy's face. "You really didn't know, did you?"

"But if it predicts the future, then why don't—"

"It doesn't predict the future. According to the Talmud, 'everything is foreseen, but freedom of action is given.' In other words, what has been encoded within the Bible's text may be a warning about a possible future. What we do, what action we take is what determines the outcome."

"But still—"

"But nothing. The challenge of the Bible Code is that you have to know the specific words or phrase you're searching for in order to establish whether a pattern exists or not. Now confess, how did you really know what to look for?"

"I didn't. Certain letters just sort of jumped out at me."

Rabbi Steinberg feels the blood drain from his face. *If he can really look at the text and recognize patterns, then . . . my God.*

"Teach me to read Hebrew, Uncle Rich. Teach me now."

Don't get me wrong, Reverend Morehead, your grand-daughter is a remarkably gifted child—"

"Foster granddaughter," corrects the minister.

"Yes, of course." The guidance counselor makes a mental note. "Lilith tested as the brightest girl in her class, perhaps the entire school."

"Then why she gettin' all Cs and Ds?"

"In my opinion, it's low self-esteem. On the second day of school, she locked herself in the bathroom for almost an hour after a teacher's aide yelled at her for talking."

"Yeah, she's always talking. Yap yap yap yap yap."

"Lilith's teacher noticed bruises on the back of her legs. Do you know how she got these welts?"

"How would I know? You know kids . . . always falling from trees, climbing over fences. Uh . . . what did Lilith say?"

"She said Chester kicked her."

"Chester? Who's that?"

"We don't know. There's no boy named Chester in our school. But Mrs. Walker noticed Lilith at recess, talking to an imaginary friend named Brandy."

Quenton grinds his teeth.

"You don't seem surprised?"

"The girl's mother, she suffered from similar, uh, delusions. Leave it to me, I'll handle it."

"Reverend, if this is some form of mental illness, then Lilith should really be seen by a professional."

"Believe me, ma'am, when it comes to this, I *am* a professional."

Longboat Key, Florida

Immanuel Gabriel stares hard at his brother's computer screen, the rows of Hebrew letters blurring in his vision. "I still can't see any patterns."

"They're there," Jacob says, smugly. "I bet there's a million warnings encoded throughout the Bible. References to the dinosaurs and extinctions, Martin Luther King and the Kennedys, wars in the Middle East, the World Trade Center, the 2008 Ebola outbreak—"

"Shut up." The dark-haired twin covers his ears. "I keep telling you, I don't care."

"You'd better care. I came across our names, too." Jacob advances the text to another page where series of letters are highlighted like a crossword puzzle. "Going across, this says **Gabriel Twins**. See these intersecting letters going down? That means **Time Tunnel**."

"Time tunnel?"

"It's the Bible's word for wormhole. It's how we'll travel to *Xibalba*."

Immanuel shakes his head. "I'm not going to *Xibalba*."

"Yes you are."

"No I'm not."

"It's our destiny, Manny." His eyes widen. "It's in our blood . . . the End of Days!"

"Maybe your freaky blood, not mine."

"The Hunahpu gene is in your blood, too, shit-for-brains, and I can prove it. I discovered a place, a place in my mind where everything slows down. It's like a higher dimension."

"Shut up."

"I'm serious. Our Hunahpu DNA gives us special abilities. By focusing our thoughts inward, we can actually tap into this higher realm."

"You're making this up."

"Am not."

Immanuel is frightened but curious. "Okay, tell me what it's like."

"It was weird, but really cool. Everything around me sort of slowed down. But inside my head I felt, I don't know . . . it was like I was more in control. I could do things, see in every direction all at once, control my body in different ways. I could slow down my heart, or even follow blood cells as they moved through my veins. It was like having another sense, one that lets you see inside yourself. The only thing is, you can't stay in too long, or all this lactic acid starts building up in your muscles. I think it's because your mind's in the nexus, but your body's still in the third dimension, and it's moving extra fast."

"The nexus?"

"That's what I call it."

"Teach me how to do it."

"Come on."

Manny follows Jacob outside to the fifty-meter pool.

"What are you doing?"

"Teaching you the way I learned, by holding my breath. Happens best when you're frightened, when the adrenaline really kicks in." Jacob strips down to his shorts. "Swim down to the bottom and hold on to the ladder. Then close your eyes and look for a white pinpoint of light. When you see it, focus on it but don't go in. The light will grow bigger, and then everything will just slow down. You'll be able to tell 'cause your lungs won't hurt anymore from holding your breath. Just remember, see the white light but don't slip inside its warmth."

"Why can't I go inside?"

"Just don't."

"Why not?"

"I think it might be a higher dimension."

"Have you done it yet?"

"Not yet, but I will one day."

"Are you afraid to do it?"

"I'll do it when I'm ready. You just focus on getting in the nexus."

"If I make it inside, how do I get out?"

"Just say to yourself, *I want out*, and you're out."

"What if I forget and drown?"

"You won't drown. Once you begin running out of air, your hands will let go of the ladder, and you'll float to the surface. That's what always happens to me. Every time I try to stay under, my body lets go and the nexus tosses me out."

The dark-haired twin stares at the bottom of the pool. "I don't know."

"Come on, Manny, stop being such a baby."

Immanuel strips to his underwear and climbs down the aluminum ladder into the pool, the cool water giving him the shakes. "It's cold."

"It's warmer in the nexus. Now take a deep breath and go under."

Immanuel takes a gulp of air and ducks underwater, working his way below using the ladder. Gripping the bottom rung, he closes his eyes.

Blackness.

His heart pounds in his ears.

His lungs burn.

Immanuel releases the rung and kicks to the surface, exhaling as his head breaks water. "You are such a goddam liar. I swear, I don't know why I let you talk me into these things."

"I wasn't lying—"

"Shut up!" Immanuel climbs out of the pool, shivering. "I'm going inside."

Jacob grabs his arm, then points to the digital clock on the pool house wall. "It's 2:04, right? Watch and learn." Without waiting for a reply, he dives in, kicking to the bottom.

Immanuel sees his brother wrap the crook of his left arm around the lowest ladder rung. *Crazy freak.*

Jacob steadies himself. Closes his eyes. Loses his thoughts in the blackness behind his eyelids.

In his mind's eye, he is sliding down his larynx, racing through a bronchial tube into his right lung. He follows a bronchi branch into one of the smaller bronchioles until his mind dead-ends at a harvest of grapelike alveoli clusters, each tiny sac containing molecules of air. Like a honeybee he taps into each one, drawing minuscule breaths, which he redirects into his oxygen-starving brain.

The constriction in his chest eases. The pinpoint of light appears, its warmth increasing as it expands.

Okay, I can do this . . . I can do this . . .

Jacob Gabriel's mind slips inside the bright hole, his soul bathing in its warmth.

Then he sees the shadow.

Immanuel looks up at the clock. *Almost three minutes . . .* A tingling as his bladder tightens. *What do I do? What if he drowns?* He focuses on his brother's face. Sees the melancholy smile. *Geez . . . he's really doing it.*

Beyond the haze is a lithe figure, floating along the periphery. Jacob's mind reaches out to communicate: *Hello?*

Who's out there? A girl's voice. Frightened.

Don't be scared. My name's Jacob. Who are you?

Lilith. Where are we?

It's a special place I call the nexus. How did you find it?

Brandy taught me. She told me to hide in here.

Why are you hiding?

I . . . I can't tell. Quenton will get angry.

Who's Quenton?

My grandpa. He says I'm a heathen. Says my soul needs to be cleansed.

Lilith, I have to go.

Wait! Please don't go, I get so . . . lonely.
I have to go, but we can talk again.
Really? Will you be my friend, Jacob?
Of course, but now I have to go.

The digital display advances—2:11.

Immanuel Gabriel is on the verge of panic. He is about to leap into the pool when he sees Jacob's fingers loosen their grip on the ladder rung.

The white-haired twin floats to the surface, then suddenly snaps awake. His head breaks the water, his azure blue eyes searching for the digital clock. "Seven minutes. Convinced now?"

Immanuel shakes his head. "I can't do that. I'm not like you."

"Yes you are." Jacob climbs out of the pool, his eyes catching sight of a passenger jet as it streaks north across the afternoon sky.

ZAP!

White light . . . presidential seal . . . the interior cabin of a private plane . . . Ennis Chaney at his desk . . . the open cockpit door . . . a man in uniform at the controls . . . an identification badge . . . a glint of steel . . . blood splatters the control panel . . . nosedive . . . a sickening descent . . . bursting into flames . . .

ZAP!

"Jake . . . hey Jake, wake up!"

Jacob opens his eyes. He is on his back, lying on the pool deck. He sits up, confused. Looks at his brother. "What happened?"

"You fainted, dickhead. Serves you right for staying under so long."

"No . . . it wasn't that. I had a vision."

"What kind of vision?"

"A plane crash. I think it was Air Force One."

"You're such a freak." Immanuel heads back toward the house.

"Manny, wait—" Jacob hurries after his brother. "That never happened to me before. It must have something to do with the light. I entered the light for the first time. The vision just latched on to me!"

"Leave me alone!" The thermoimager above the rear security door tracks the dark-haired twin as he approaches. Positively identifying Immanuel, the system opens the sliding bulletproof doors.

Immanuel enters the kitchen, Jacob right behind him.

"You can't ignore this, Manny, you're my twin. At some point, these things will happen to you, too."

"Shut up—"

"We have to be ready. Years from now you and me are going to leave this world and—"

"I said, shut up!" Immanuel races through the hallway and into his bedroom, slamming the door behind him.

"It's our destiny, Manny!" Jacob presses his face to the closed door. "If you're too much of a wuss to go, maybe I'll go with Lilith!"

"Jacob Gabriel!" Dominique grabs her son by the arm, dragging him away from his brother's door. "What did I tell you about teasing Manny?"

"I wasn't teasing."

"Go to your room."

"No."

"Excuse me?"

"I have to call Uncle Ennis. I have to warn him—"

"Young man, you're grounded!" She drags him into his bedroom. "You stay in there until I say you can come out." Dominique slams his door shut, then knocks on Immanuel's door. "Manny? Manny, sweetheart, you okay?"

Hearing the sobs, she enters.

In a corner of his bedroom, Immanuel Gabriel sits on the floor, pulling out clumps of his dark black hair.

Belle Glade, Florida

". . . Saint Michael the Archangel, defend us in battle, be our defense against the wickedness and snares of the Devil—"

Lilith Robinson opens her azure blue eyes. She is no longer in the nexus. She is lying on the cot, naked, her slender wrists and ankles bound by plastic cords.

Quenton stands over her, Bible in one hand, cross in the other, his white minister's outfit lathered in sweat as he verbally assaults the girl with more fire and brimstone.

". . . we pray the God of Peace will crush Satan beneath our feet, so that he may no longer retain men captive and do injury to the Church. Offer our prayers to the Most High, that without delay they may draw His mercy down upon us—"

Brandy is at the back window, mimicking Quenton behind his back.

Lilith giggles.

The minister's eyes widen. He slaps the girl across the face, then sprinkles her with Holy Water. "Take hold of the Dragon, the old serpent, which is the Devil and Satan. Bind him and cast him into the bottomless pit, that he may no longer seduce the nations!"

Lilith closes her eyes, her body trembling.

10

It is America's hottest summer playground, a coastal resort occupied by palatial beach homes owned by the rich and famous.

Peter Mabus stands in his bathrobe on the deserted stretch of private beach, staring at the pounding ocean of autumn as a gray dawn breaks over the eastern horizon. The last few years have taken their toll on the once robust entrepreneur. Following the landslide loss to Ennis Chaney in the presidential election, his wife of thirty years filed divorce papers after catching him in a hotel suite with two of his secretaries. Chaney's new anti–fossil fuel initiatives are costing him tens of millions of dollars, and his religious-based political party is under investigation for tax evasion.

"Hey, Dad!"

Mabus sees his son, Lucien, waving from the boardwalk. "Someone here to see you."

Mabus signals for his guest to approach.

Solomon Adashek makes his way over the private boardwalk and past the tall sea grass to the beach. "Good morning."

"I see nothing good about it. I hired you to do a job, Mr. Adashek. Why hasn't the job been finished?"

"You hired me to terminate the most closely guarded figure in the world. These things take time. However, my operative is now in position to complete the task at hand."

"When will it happen?"

"Today. Our friend should be dead in time for the noon-day news."

The White House
Washington, DC

9:02 A.M.

Ennis Chaney looks up from behind his desk, swallowing the rest of his pickled egg lunch as his secretary escorts the rabbi and a woman with bright orange-red hair into the Oval Office.

"Rabbi Steinberg. Nice to see you again. Been what . . . a year?"

"Two. We were together at the twins' fifth birthday party."

"Sorry I missed the last few. Been busy campaigning for my vice president. Wish we could talk, but I leave for Detroit in ten minutes. Next time call ahead and make an appointment."

The rabbi casts a worried look at the red head.

"Now what's so damn important you had to fly up to Washington instead of using the video-com?"

"Your assassination."

For a moment, Chaney's raccoon eyes narrow, then the president rasps out a laugh. "Is that all? Hell, I've received more death threats than the FBI can count."

"Mr. President, this is Kimberly Ward, a professor at Washington College. Her background is in parapsychology."

"I deal with paranormal phenomena, Mr. President."

"Well, if I ever run into a ghost, I'll be sure to call you."

Kimberly Ward is not amused. "I'm a scientist, sir. I deal with the science of extrasensory perception, clairvoyance, telepathy, and precognition, and I assure you my time is just as valuable as yours."

Chaney perks up, his ego always ready for a battle of wills. "Go on, Miss, uh?"

"Ward. Kimberly Ward."

Chaney signals them to sit, then hobbles to his favorite easy chair. "Okay, Ms. Ward, you've got five minutes."

"Have you ever heard of the theory regarding mind-body dualism?"

"No."

"Psychokinetic researchers such as I are convinced there are two separate but coexisting facets of human beings: the physical body, which does not survive material death, and the non-physical mind, or soul, that can live forever."

"If this is a religious thing—"

"This is science, Mr. President, with studies that date back to the late 1930s. Our latest research can measure the electrostatic radiation that is expelled by a human being when the subject undergoes an out-of-body experience. The study of paranormal phenomena has made huge strides over the last decade. Along with the material forces of gravity, electromagnetic, and weak and strong nuclear forces, scientists now believe a fifth force may be present in the known universe—a force that relates to psychokinesis. Your godson, Jacob, exhibits abilities in this field that dwarf any subject I've ever studied."

"It's the Hunahpu gene," Rabbi Steinberg interjects. "Somehow, the boy is able to tap into a higher dimension of consciousness."

"Really?" Chaney glances at his watch. "You know, I think my watch is slow." He stands to leave.

Steinberg blocks his path. "Jacob saw something. He had a vision, a precognition. You'll never make it to Detroit this afternoon, Ennis. One of Air Force One's flight crew is planning to crash your plane into the Washington Monument moments after takeoff."

The president glares at the rabbi. "How could a seven-year-old boy—"

"Jacob claims he saw the man's security badge," says Kimberly. "He's even given us a name: Fred Botnick."

Chaney hesitates, then touches the office intercom. "Kathy, get me a list of the flight crew scheduled this afternoon for Air Force One."

"Yes, sir. Transferring information to your monitor."

The bookshelf to Chaney's left vanishes, replaced by a large monitor. A dozen names appear on screen.

Kimberly Ward points to the seventh name down.

Botnick, Fred. Rank: Major. Assignment: Pilot.

Chaney stares at the screen for a long moment. "Kathy?"

"Yes, sir?"

"Get me the FBI director, then cancel my speech in Detroit."

"Sir?

"Just do it."

TOP SECRET/MAJESTIC-12

WARNING: Unauthorized access or viewing of this document without the appropriate authorizations will result in permanent incarceration or sanction by authorized use of deadly force.

PROGRESS REPORT ON
SPECIAL ACCESS PROGRAM
<u>GOLDEN FLEECE</u>

14 October 2020

<u>JACOB GABRIEL</u>

1. The genetically enhanced abilities of JACOB GABRIEL (son of Michael Gabriel, see HUNAHPU GENE) continue to evolve. On 3 September 2020 and again on 18 September 2020, Agent MITCHELL KURTZ witnessed Jacob remain underwater in excess of four minutes. When questioned, Jacob responded by saying he had moved into a "higher dimen-

sion of consciousness beyond our third-dimensional senses."

2. On 10 October, 2020, following a similar "immersion," Jacob confronted Rabbi RICHARD STEINBERG with a vision regarding an act of terror aboard Air Force One. Steinberg met in person with POTUS on 11 October 2020. FBI agents arrested AF-1 Major FRED BOTNICK (pilot) who was later identified as a member of an Aryan Nation terrorist regime. Seven pounds of C-4 plastique explosive was found sewn inside the lining of his uniform. More arrests are pending.

CONCLUSIONS

3. Jacob's ability to "remote view" makes him an invaluable resource to U.S. antiterrorist forces. It is recommended that both the boy and his twin (IMMANUEL) be evaluated for PROJECT TRINITY immediately.

4. GOLDEN FLEECE geneticists now agree it is unlikely that HUNAHPU DNA is limited to the Gabriel clan. Every attempt should be made to identify other members of this bloodline. A necessary first step would be the genetic "tagging" of newborns, as well as the top one percent of athletes and students, along with all mental patients diagnosed "paranoid schizophrenic."

Submitted:

W. Louis McDonald
GOLDEN FLEECE

14 October 2020

11

Lilith's flesh crawls with fear as her grandfather slips in between her sheets. She can smell the alcohol on his breath—

—and the pungent scent of his sex.

"Time for another lesson, girl."

She turns away. Stares at her dollhouse.

"As you get older, boys are gonna try stuff on you. Can't let 'em do these things. Understand?"

"Yes." The doll house roof is a sunny yellow.

"Think I better show you again, just to be safe. Go on now, spread your legs."

The dollhouse cardboard lawn is a Kelly green.

"Girl, I ain't askin'. I said spread your legs!"

The windows of the dollhouse are trimmed in pumpkin orange.

Her grandfather's probing fingers are cold as ice.

The chimney is mouse brown, as are the exterior walls.

Hot, rancid breath comes at her in waves. The five o'clock shadow scratches at the inside of her unblemished thighs.

Lilith's mind escapes inside the nexus as Quenton's wet tongue once more violates her innocence.

Longboat Key, Florida

The president's helicopter circles the compound twice before landing on the front lawn.

Dominique exits from the kitchen, waving at Ennis Chaney. She does not recognize the tall blond-haired Intelligence officer carrying an armful of presents.

Chaney greets her with a bear hug. "Dominique, you look better every time I see you."

"And you tell bigger lies."

"Where are the twins?"

"Manny's in the SOSUS lab. Jake's swimming."

"Good. Let's go someplace quiet where we can talk."

Her heart jump-starts. "Talk? Why? What's wrong?"

"Nothing. Can't I visit my two godsons without something being wrong?"

Unnerved, she leads the two men inside.

Jacob secures the rope around his waist, then loops the free end through the center of the forty-five-pound weight plate and ties it off. Satisfied, he picks up the iron plate and climbs down the steps of the swimming pool, wading deeper until the waterline is up to his neck.

The white-haired twin takes a deep breath, then lowers himself to the bottom.

The steel plate sinks, dragging him with it.

Hovering inches off the bottom, Jacob closes his eyes and relaxes, searching the dark recesses of his mind.

In due time he sees the pinpoint of light. His mind's eye focuses upon it, making it grow.

The pain in his chest eases. Concentrating on the bright light, he allows his mind to slip inside its warm white haze.

Lilith, are you in here?

Chaney sits back in a padded lounge chair. He sips an iced tea, then stares out the bulletproof glass at the inviting waters of the Gulf of Mexico. "Always loved this view. Wait and see, one of these days I'm gonna retire and move to Florida."

"Sure you are," Dominique says. "So? Are you going to introduce me to your friend?"

"Dominique Gabriel, this is Major Richard Phillips. Major Phillips is the director of Project TRINITY."

The major attempts to disarm her with a friendly smile.

Dominique is immune. "What exactly is Project TRINITY, and what does it have to do with my kids? And don't bullshit me. The staff does that enough."

"Okay, ma'am, straight and simple: TRINITY is a covert Intelligence program, its origins dating back to 1978 when it was called Project GRILLFLAME. The purpose of the program was, and is, to recruit, train, and utilize psychics for the gathering of Army intelligence."

"You're telling me the United States government recruits psychics?"

"Yes, ma'am. The DIA—the Defense Intelligence Agency—took over the project in the late 1980s, changing its name to STARGATE. The program was revamped and renamed TRINITY following the extraterrestrial interactions of 2012. I took over the project four years ago. My qualifications include sixteen years in STARGATE as a remote viewer."

"And what is a remote viewer?"

"Remote viewing is a mental faculty that allows an individual to describe a target or event that is hidden from our normal senses by distance, shielding, or time. In essence, it's the phenomenon of clairvoyance or telepathy."

"Sounds like hocus-pocus to me."

"A typical first reaction. The hypothesis behind the art is that all knowledge exists in a vacuum of pure energy. Remote viewers have the ability to tap into this realm. I can assure you from my own experiences at STARGATE that the phenomenon is quite real and governed by a well-structured scientific protocol."

A chill runs down her spine as she recalls Evelyn Strongin's words: *"To understand interdimensional communication, you must first accept that we are surrounded by energy, and energy is everything, it is only our perception within the universe that changes."*

"You're here to recruit Jacob."

"Easy," Chaney says. "I merely wanted the major to meet both boys and evaluate them."

"Why? Why do they need to be evaluated? Why can't you just let them be?"

"Dom, a few days ago, Jacob sent Rabbi Steinberg to Washington to warn me of an assassination attempt."

"What?"

"His information led to the arrest of one of Air Force One's crewmen, a racist nutcase who would have blown up Air Force One and everyone on board."

"My God . . ."

"It's no secret the twins are special. There's no harm in seeing just how special."

"Ma'am, it's very possible your boys possess the gift of psychotronic perception. If that's true, then my department can help them realize this gift to its fullest."

"For what purpose? So they can spend the rest of their lives locked up in some windowless chamber, telling the CIA what the North Koreans are up to? No—I won't have it."

"Dominique, open your eyes. There are groups out there—religious zealots, Mesoamerican fanatics—that may be planning an attack on your compound as we speak. If Jake or Manny could see them coming—"

"God, I hate this, I am so tired . . . fine, just do it . . . do whatever the hell you have to do. Test them. Poke and prod them if you have to. Take more DNA samples, hell, put them in a goddam bottle—"

"Dominique—"

"My sons have become the world's sideshow, Ennis, and it's my fault. So just do whatever you have to do and get it over with!"

She storms off, leaving the two men alone.

* * *

Lilith?

Jacob? Two pinpoints of azure blue twinkle back at him from beyond the white haze. *Where have you been? I call out for you every day.*

It's not always easy for me to enter. Evelyn says I have to get my adrenaline pumping in order to find my way in.

Who's Evelyn?

Evelyn Strongin. You'd like her. She's a psychiatrist, she had a near-death experience years ago. I want her to teach me how to communicate with my dead father.

When did your father die?

Long time ago. Before I was born.

My father's in prison. He killed my mama when I was born.

Geez . . .

Jacob, when we're together in the nexus, it feels like our souls are one.

He's hurting you again, isn't he?

Yes.

You should tell the cops.

I can't.

Why not?

I just can't.

He said he'd hurt you if you told, didn't he?

If I tell, they'd take him away, then I'd really be all alone. Unless I can live with you? Can I?

No, Lilith. I wish you could, but it's dangerous around here too.

Do you love me, Jacob?

Yes.

You wouldn't ever hurt me, would you?

Why would I hurt you?

Just promise me you won't.

I promise.

* * *

"Jake?"

Dominique enters the pool area. Sees the figure lying motionless on the bottom.

"Oh, shit—" She dives in the pool. Swims to the bottom. Drags her son and the weight plate to the surface.

"Jake! Jake, wake up!"

Jacob's consciousness is hurled out of the white haze of the nexus into bright sunlight, his mind awhirl, fighting to catch up with what just happened.

". . . insane? Answer me?"

"Huh?"

"I said, are you insane? Are you trying to drown yourself?"

"No. I was . . . I was just training."

"Don't ever let me catch you doing this again? Do you understand?"

"Yes, ma'am. You'll never catch me again."

"Don't sass me, young man. You know what I mean."

"Yes, ma'am."

Dominique climbs out of the pool, the sudden rush of adrenaline causing her muscles to quiver. "Get dressed. Your godfather flew in to see you."

Dripping wet, she heads back to the house, her nerves shot.

The Faraday chamber, located in the basement floor of the Gabriel twins' training facility, is a metallic enclosure, its wall-embedded circuitry designed to scramble all incoming electromagnetic signals. Soundproof and windowless, the chamber is painted in a neutral color, its softly diffused overhead light panels rigged to a voice-activated dimmer. Inside the room is a rectangular steel table, with two matching chairs positioned at either end. A video recorder and closed-circuit camera are positioned inconspicuously along the ceiling.

Jacob Gabriel sits at the far end of the table, facing the

closed door. He doodles on a legal pad with a blue ink pen, waiting for the session to begin.

Chaney and Major Phillips watch him on a monitor from another room.

"Okay, here's the drill," Phillips says. "While I'm working with Jacob, you keep the other twin occupied in the SOSUS lab."

"You think these two can communicate telepathically to one another?"

"It's definitely possible. One thing I know from personal experience is that remote viewing across interdimensional lines is very frequency-oriented. Since tapping into wavelengths of a similar consciousness can affect the believability of the session—"

"I understand."

Jacob looks up as the major enters the antiseptic room and shuts the door. "Hi, Jacob. My name is Major Phillips. I'm the guy the president told you about."

"You're here to test me?"

"You say it as if it's a bad thing. Actually, remote viewing is a lot of fun. I've been doing this sort of thing for a long time."

"My first time was an accident."

"Which means you should respond very well to formalized training."

"What do I have to do?"

"For one thing, relax. Your mom tells me you practice yoga. Focus on your breathing. Let your thoughts go blank. Computer, dim lights 60 percent."

The room darkens.

"Jake, I want you to turn to a clean sheet of paper. Write your name and the date in the upper right-hand corner." Major Phillips reaches into his breast pocket and removes six double-wrapped, opaque envelopes. Inside each is a folded piece of paper, with words written in ink.

"There are six stages to remote viewing. We always begin with stage one. Do you know how telepathy works?"

"One mind tunes to another."

"Correct. Remote viewing works the same way. Information, whether it's in our past or future, is stored as energy in the psychic realm. To acquire bits of this information requires a clue or signal line. Your mind can be subconsciously tuned in to the meanings of these clue lines, or, in the case of you and your brother, your minds may be genetically enhanced to evoke, or call them up. Clues will come to you as sharp, rapid influxes of significance. Your preconscious nervous system will transmit these ideas through the muscles and nerves of your arm and hand and express them as marks on your paper. It's very important that you not try to analyze these marks, just let them come. In the process, you might envision or remote-view different imaginary shapes for clues. When this happens, just tell me what you see. Again, don't try to interpret anything. So? Sound like fun?"

The white-haired twin shrugs. "I can already do this."

"You can? Then this first coordinate should be easy for you."

Phillips slides the first envelope in front of Jacob. "Interface with the object. Tell me what it is."

The boy touches the envelope, then closes his azure blue eyes. "This is too easy. It's a beach, the beach in back of our compound."

Phillips maintains his poker face, inside he is quite impressed. "Let's try another." He skips the second envelope, jumping ahead to number three.

Jacob closes his eyes. "Man-made . . . bronze and steel . . . surrounded by water. I hear echoes of a city."

"Where are you?"

"Statue of Liberty."

Phillips says nothing, but his heart is pounding like a kettledrum.

"Let's try one more." He slides another envelope forward.

Jacob focuses inward.

A mountain . . . its volcanic peak rising higher . . .

The clue lines of Hawaii's Diamond Head tighten in his mind—

—then suddenly evaporate, morphing into an ominous, alien world.

Crimson coals simmer along a subterranean ceiling, its embers refracting below along the molten surface of a silvery lake. Standing alone by the lake's volcanic-sandy banks is a tree, like none he has ever seen. Wide as a silo, as white as the driven snow, its bare branches and alien bark drips a syrupy alabaster goo.

Situated within the "V" of the great trunk is an object.

Jacob's consciousness moves closer.

It is a human head, the severed neck melding into the tree's ivory-colored ooze.

The eyes flash open, blazing a fiery azure blue.

Who's out there? Whoever it is, stay away!

Ennis Chaney exits the elevator on the first floor, then turns left down the main corridor to the double doors marked: SOSUS LAB.

The underwater sound surveillance system, known as SOSUS, is a network of undersea microphones and cables originally configured by the United States Navy during the Cold War to spy on enemy submarines. As the military's need for SOSUS began to dwindle, oceanographers successfully petitioned the Navy for access to the acoustic network. Using SOSUS, scientists could hear the infrasonic vibrations made by ice floes cracking, seabeds quaking, and underwater volcanoes erupting, sounds far below the range of human hearing.

Dominique's adopted father, the late Isadore Axler, had been a marine biologist who had used his private SOSUS lab to study whale migration patterns in the Gulf of Mexico. In the winter of 2012, Isadore, using Michael Gabriel's information about the Chicxulub Crater, had discovered strange acoustics originating from beneath the Gulf floor. His investigation of the site led to his death . . . and the eventual discovery of the remains of an alien transport ship, buried beneath the seafloor in the Gulf of Mexico.

At Edith Axler's request, President Chaney had arranged for a SOSUS relay station to be set up in the Gabriel compound. Manny loved working in the lab, and his grandmother, Edith, took great pleasure in teaching her husband's namesake how to record and analyze the voiceprints of whales, identify their species, and even track particular cetaceans as they moved throughout the Gulf of Mexico.

The president enters the lab. Manny is seated in his favorite chair, his headphones on as he eavesdrops on the whales. "Wow . . . listen, Grandma, I think I found a blue!"

Edith checks the source strength of the whale song. "One hundred eighty-six decibels. It's a blue, all right." She signals Chaney over. Hands him a set of headphones.

Low-frequency moans echo in his ears. "That's, uh, interesting."

The lab door bursts open, Major Phillips hurries inside. "Sorry, sir, but we've got a situation."

Jacob Gabriel lies on the floor of the Faraday chamber, unconscious. The staff physician listens to his heart, while Ryan Beck and a nurse attempt to comfort the boy's visibly upset mother.

"What happened?" Chaney rasps.

The major shrugs. "Honestly, sir, I don't know. Jacob's mind is incredibly focused, giving him direct access to the clue line, better than any viewer I've ever worked with. Everything was fine, then he just blacked out."

Dominique pushes her way to the major, poking her index finger against his chest. "Whatever you did to him—"

"Ma'am, I swear . . . it wasn't me. Jacob's doing this himself."

"Blood pressure's good," the doctor calls out. "Pulse is strong, but very slow. He seems to be in some kind of transcendental state. Let's everyone try to stay calm and give him a few minutes."

Father?

Who's out there?

It's Jacob. Your son.

Foul beast, go away! Think you can fool me with your—

Father, please, it's really me. It's Jacob. Jacob Gabriel. Father—

Jacob? Jacob, is that really you? I've dreamed of you, son, but . . . but is this real? Is it really happening?

I've dreamed of it, too. And it's happening, Father, it's real.

But how? How is it we can communicate?

Thoughts are energy. We're both Hunahpu. We share similar frequencies. Father, where are you?

I don't know. I'm not even sure I exist. I have no physical form, but somehow I can think, and I can feel emotions. It's as if I exist in a vacuum of energy, only I can't escape.

Something's out there, isn't it? Something's frightening you. It's as if I can taste your fear. Father, what is it?

It's the Abomination . . . I can feel its presence. It's like ice, hovering in the periphery. It circles me like the shadow of death, always waiting for me to drop my defenses.

But what is it?

A presence of pure evil. It wants to feast on my soul.

Tell me what to do! How can I help?

You have helped, son, more than you'll ever know. I've been so lost, drowning in loneliness and despair. Your thought energy . . . it's like a lighthouse beacon to my soul. You've strengthened me, you've given me hope. I know now that I haven't been abandoned, that

I'm not alone. You've given me a newfound sense of being.

Father, there's so much I need to ask you. The Mayan Creation Myth . . . is it true? Am I really the son of One Hunahpu? Is it really possible for me and my brother to travel to Xibalba? Can you be . . . resurrected?

There's no easy answer to that. There's so much I need to tell you, and I want to, I have to, but it's dangerous. The effort to communicate weakens me, and the Abomination hovers . . . waiting for me to lower my guard. Still, I must try, there's so much at stake. Jacob, how old are you now?

Seven.

My God . . .

Father?

Wherever I am, it's impervious to time. You say you're seven?

Yes.

My own journey . . . it also began when I was seven. In fact, it was at seven that I first encountered evil.

Teach me, please! Tell me how it began for you.

I'll try. The memories . . . they're very powerful, so vivid. I can still recall inhaling the scent of the rain forest, registering its heaviness in my lungs. I can hear its nocturnal symphony playing in my ears. And the Peruvian desert . . . as I recall the desolation of that awful Nazca plateau, I can almost feel the blood pooling in my extremities as the afternoon heat baked my skin in its searing embrace.

That was my childhood, Jacob, an existence spent in Mesoamerican jungles and on the harsh plateau of Nazca. My parents, Julius and Maria, your paternal grandparents, they had been archaeology students who had first met at Cambridge. Their love blossomed on their own journey as they set out to resolve the mystery of the Mayan calendar and its two thousand-year-old doomsday prophecy. Me? I was the result of their fateful union, born, like you, as destiny's victim.

I don't feel like a victim. Most of the time I feel like Superman.

Careful, son. Even Superman has his kryptonite. Although my Hunahpu genes were not as developed as yours must be, I also felt superior. By the age of seven I had grown into quite the brat, rebelling against everything my parents were attempting to teach me.

You said you encountered evil?

Yes. At the time we were living in a one-room, stucco dwelling in Pistè, a tiny village outside of Chichén Itzá. I remember the day it happened, a typical morning in the Gabriel clan. Julius had just grounded me for swapping a pair of his best binoculars for a baseball glove and ball, and I was furious, stomping and cussing up a storm. The moment my parents left for the ruins, I packed a small bag, my passport, and a few pesos borrowed from my mother's purse—and I headed out to begin my life anew.

You ran away?

I had to. I felt boxed in, unable to cope, unable to just be myself. But I had a plan. Merida and its airport were seventy-five miles to the west. Somehow I would stow away on board a plane bound for America. Even though I was only seven, I had already aced my high-school equivalency test and was being recruited by several universities. If I could just get to the States, I knew I could survive.

Guess I'd been walking less than an hour when a taxi pulled off the road. I immediately recognized the driver—T'quan Lwin Canul—a middle-aged local of pure Mayan descent. He had a large nose and dark eyes, and wore his black, oily hair long and braided. Tattoos ran up and down his body, and jewelry pierced his ears and heavy brows. More bizarre was his tongue, the tip of which had been sliced down the middle and forcibly separated over time so that the last two inches were forked, resembling that of a viper.

The "serpent's tongue" gave T'quan a heavy lisp. He

leaned out his open window at me, and hissed, "Going somewhere, mas'sa'?"

"Off to see a distant cousin," I lied. "What would it cost me to get a ride to Merida?"

T'quan gave me a price, then mentioned he needed some assistance cutting down a tree. We struck a deal. If I helped him, he would have me in Merida by nightfall.

And you believed him?

I was naive, and the truth is disguised by what we want to hear. Before I knew it, we were bouncing along a dirt path, cutting through dense jungle. Eventually we came to a small clearing and T'quan's hut, which sat adjacent to a freshwater sinkhole.

The old man led me inside and offered me a drink. I watched as he dipped his cup into a wooden barrel, the scent of the fermented ceremonial drink known as *pulque* drifting up at me. "No, thank you," I said. "Where is the tree?"

"Forget the tree," he said, "I require help with a ritual. Tell me, mas'sa, have you ever heard the story of Tezcaplipoca?"

"You mean Tezcatilpoca," I corrected, as if I knew everything about the ancient ones.

"That is Aztec pronunciation," he said. "To the Nahuas, he was Tezcaplipoca, god of the night, god of evil, a creature of black magic." As he spoke, T'quan opened a container of what appeared to be scarlet dye and proceeded to paint a stripe across the bridge of his beaked nose. "Tezcaplipoca was the mirror that smoked. It was his presence that drove Kukulcán from Chichén Itzá. He was our greatest and most feared god."

T'quan told me his Nahua ancestors had lived in this same jungle a thousand years ago. While Kukulcán built temples, T'quan's clan followed Tezcaplipoca— god of conflict and turmoil, god of power.

The old man removed his tee shirt, revealing a bony,

dark-skinned canvas of chest, covered in tattoos. Draping a black cape around his shoulders, he led me back outside to the sinkhole, the very cenote T'quan's ancestors had used to worship Tezcaplipoca.

I looked out over the edge. The drop was more than thirty feet, and the well's stagnant olive waters were dark and foreboding. And that, Jacob, is when I finally realized what T'quan meant to do—he meant to sacrifice *me* to Tezcaplipoca, just as his ancestors had done a thousand years before.

I turned to run, but the wiry old man was too quick. He grabbed me by the arm and pushed me to the ground, pressing his heavy boot to my chest. From a sheath on his belt he removed a ceremonial obsidian dagger. As I screamed, struggling in vain along the edge of the sinkhole, he rolled his eyes to the heavens and began chanting.

What did you do?

At first I panicked, but as the adrenaline flowed, a strange sensation gripped my soul, and a tiny voice in my mind guided my consciousness into a harbor of utter calm. I stopped struggling and allowed my mind to slip inside.

The nexus?

Yes. I remember looking at the trees, which seemed to be getting brighter, the leaves no longer moving with the breeze. Shadowed objects became clear in my vision, while the old man's words seemed to mute into distant echoes. I could hear my heart pumping blood—a slow, drawn-out *slurp*. I could feel my muscles growing stronger, as if adrenaline was coursing through every vessel in my body. The weight of the old man's boot seemed to lessen upon my chest and I knew that if I tried, I could fling it aside . . . which is what I did.

In one motion, I was back on my feet, pushing through invisible waves of resistance, as if the air itself had become gelid. T'quan barely seemed to react. I followed his eyes as they slowly drifted down to me, his pierced brows raising in disbelief. Quickly, I dashed behind him, then, with all my might, I kicked the old Mayan in the small of his bony back.

It must have been a mighty blow through that thickened air, for he flew forward in slow motion, rising as if gravity had abandoned him. And then he fell, his limbs flapping uselessly as his body dropped silently into the waters below.

Serves him right. What happened then?

A burning sensation ravaged my gut. I fell to my knees and shook my head violently—and the sounds of the woods returned. For several moments, I lay on the ground, my muscles drenched in lactic acid, twitching in recovery until splashing sounds drew me to the edge of the hole.

The old man was struggling to stay afloat, his gaunt figure hopelessly entangled in his soaked cloth cape.

I stood and watched my would-be killer . . . watched as he sank beneath the surface. When the air bubbles ceased, I climbed in his taxi and drove out of the jungle, back to Pistè.

I had never driven a car before. I could barely reach the pedals, yet it seemed perfectly natural. An hour later, I returned to the old man's home with my parents and the police, who dredged T'quan's corpse from the sinkhole's muddy bottom—along with the remains of no less than a dozen other children the old man had murdered over the years.

That was my first encounter with evil and the powers that we possess, Jacob, but it wouldn't be my last.

I need to know more about evil. Where does it come from? How did it start?

That, my son, is a question your grandfather, Julius, pondered until his dying day. Is evil something genetically programmed into our species, or is it a learned behavior? Is it spiritual in nature, perhaps the Yin to the soul's Yang. Or is it a disease that infects the mind? T'quan had a look in his eyes when he came after me, one that I'll never forget. It was as if the old man's soul had vacated the body and separated itself from the collective warmth of our species. Julius called the man a godless reptile, and for a long time I agreed with him, until the night I witnessed my own father straddling my mother's body, suffocating her with a pillow.

Julius murdered Grandma?

He claimed it was euthanasia, but in the eyes of a twelve-year-old, it was murder. Looking back on it now, I realize just how much Julius loved my mother, how hard it was to do what he did. She was in so much pain from the cancer, she begged him for mercy, and he gave it to her. At the same time, I also realize how evil is created, because from that moment on, I hated Julius for what he had done, and I allowed my anger to fester, until it finally exploded backstage as I held my dead father in my arms and went after Pierre Borgia.

When you were in solitary for so long—how were you able to keep from . . . you know, from going insane?

For a while, I thought I had gone insane. Then, during my eighth month, I drifted into a semilucid state, for all intents and purposes, an out-of-body experience.

I don't understand?

Nor did I at the time. It was my Hunahpu DNA. The gene was somehow programming my mind to take a visual reconnaissance into humanity's past. My first journey deposited my consciousness on a Mediterranean shoreline, somewhere in the Middle East. From out of the sea strode a large humanoid male, his appearance bordering on the bizarre. His skin was as dark as cocoa, in sharp contrast to his long silky hair and beard, which were snow-white. His eyes were a deep azure blue, set within an almost inhumanly elongated skull.

I would learn his name was Osiris.

But this was all just a dream?

No, son, it was quite real. I was remote-viewing an actual event that had taken place ten thousand years in the past. In my transcendental state, my consciousness had tapped into a matrix of energy, similar to what you and I are experiencing. Because the events had taken place in the past, I was able to witness the events as if I were there, as if I were one of Osiris's nomad followers. Osiris turned my people into a functioning society. He directed us to dam the Nile delta, forming an artificial lake. He taught us how to cut immense ten-ton stones from basalt quarries. I marveled as he used his scepter-like device to lift the blocks onto barges, transmitting strange sonic harmonics that seemed to reverse the effects of gravity. More than two million stones were moved in this manner, transported through the pre-flooded valley until they were placed into position, using the surface of the lake as a perfect plane of reference.

Osiris was engineering three of the largest structural foundations in the world—the bases of the Great Pyramids of Giza, and somehow I had become one of his laborers!

Viewing those experiences is ultimately what preserved my mind. For while my body was confined to that dark, decrepit cell, my consciousness was free to roam.

As the years drifted by, my mind accompanied more of the wise men on their journeys. In England, I was part of a sect that followed the teachings of an extraterrestrial who told us his name was Merlin. This "wizard" used his own stafflike device to help us transport the great sarsens that were used to erect Stonehenge. In South America, another wise man—Virococha—used a similar device to carve immense patterns into the Nazca plateau—the very zoomorphs whose meaning had eluded my father and me for decades.

What I didn't know at the time was that these wise men with their elongated skulls, majestic blue eyes, and white hair and beards were actually members of the Guardian. Attuned to their signal line through my own Hunahpu genetics, I was being prepared.

Prepared for what?

Four *Ahau*, three *Kankin*—the winter solstice of 2012—humanity's day of doom, prophesied in the Mayan calendar. I realized that wallowing in my emotions was doing me no good. I had to focus. I had to stay strong. My life served a greater purpose. If a holocaust was truly coming, then I knew I had to stop it.

My cell became a war room. A regimen was established, combining rigorous exercise, meditation, and remote-viewing sessions. Pieces of an ancient puzzle began falling into place. There was a means to our salvation—I just had to find it.

But first, I had to escape.

Sometime during my last year in isolation, the state of Massachusetts determined that the antiquated facility I called Hell would close down. Pierre Borgia, by then U.S. secretary of state, immediately arranged for Dr. Foletta, my personal keeper, to transfer himself and me to an asylum in Miami.

It was the summer of 2012.

The rules at the Miami facility were different, each inmate assigned a team. No longer able to exert his autocratic rule, Dr. Foletta needed someone on staff he could manipulate into signing off on my yearly evaluation. His pawn would arrive a week later in the guise of a graduate student.

My mother?

Yes. She was so beautiful, so enticing . . . consuming all my thoughts, disfocusing me from the mission at hand. I tried to quell my love for her, but as the doomsday drew nearer, our souls touched. Then, in her most difficult hour, your mother sacrificed everything she held dear and helped me escape.

Together we discovered the *Balam*, a starship buried long ago beneath the Kukulcán Pyramid. Within this vessel we found the remains of Kukulcán, the last survivor of a more advanced humanoid race called the Guardian. The Guardian had come to our planet long ago, fleeing the rise of evil that had enslaved their people, transforming their world into a hellish existence. The Guardian had avoided enslavement by taking refuge on one of their planet's moons. But the evil ones were not satisfied with their conquest. Inhabiting their planet was an alien serpentine creature that could bridge the gap between dimensions of time and space. Trapping the creature aboard a transport ship, they sent it into space and through a wormhole. Members of the Guardian brotherhood chased after the transport in the *Balam*. Their vessel's presence in the wormhole altered the wormhole's trajectory . . . depositing both ships in our solar system, 65 million years into Earth's past. This historic journey not only resulted in a cataclysm that wiped out the dinosaurs, it created a causal time loop in third-dimensional space.

Most of the transport was destroyed upon impact, but the life-support pod containing the creature remained intact.

Knowing a deep-space radio transmission could awaken the creature, the Guardian programmed the *Balam* to remain in orbit above Earth. The ship would deflect any incoming signals while the Guardian remained immersed in sleep pods. Sometime around 11,000 B.C., the *Balam* landed in the dense jungles of the Yucatán Peninsula, not far from where their enemy lay buried beneath the Gulf of Mexico.

It was about this time that the great flood caused by the last ice age thawed, and *Homo sapiens* became the dominant species on the planet.

The Guardian had a two-phased plan for humanity. Awakening in intervals, each member was assigned the task of erecting an electromagnetic relay station at key points around the globe. When completed, this astrogeodetic array would link with the *Balam*, creating an electromagnetic grid around the entire planet. The grid would prevent the creature from using its weapons to alter our planet's atmosphere for its carbon-dioxide-breathing masters. Each Guardian had the challenge of camouflaging his relay station so that the array's relay stations would remain undisturbed over thousands of years. Their solution was to bury the antennae beneath monolithic structures so magnificent in size and structure that they would forever remain undisturbed by modern man.

Great civilizations came into being, and with them rose the Pyramids of Giza and Stonehenge, the Pyramid of the Sun, and the Temples of Angkor Wat.

One of the last of the brotherhood to be revived was Kukulcán. Under his tutelage, the Mayans rose to power and the Kukulcán Pyramid was built—directly above the burial site of the *Balam*. All that was needed was someone to activate the device in the year 2012.

This was the second phase of the Guardian's plan. Each member of the brotherhood would not only instruct his people, but spread his genetic seed using our women. By mixing the Guardian's superior DNA with *Homo sapien* DNA, our species genetically leapfrogged up the evolutionary ladder.

The Guardian's DNA is the so-called missing link?

Yes. But the Guardian were capable of much more than simply siring a new subspecies, they could also manipulate their DNA so that genetic anomalies like them would reach maturation around the time of the predicted day of reckoning. They called these superior beings the *Hunahpu*.

I didn't know it at the time, but I carried the Hunahpu gene, passed down to me from my maternal ancestors. By activating the *Balam*'s array, I not only prevented the creature from using its weapons, I also stopped an all-out nuclear war between the superpowers.

Days later, the alien creature ascended from the Gulf, intent on destroying the *Balam*'s electromagnetic array. I was waiting in Chichén Itzá to meet it. Tapping into my newly discovered Hunaphu powers, I was able to access the *Balam*'s weapon, which deactivated the cybernetic beast.

But you entered the creature's mouth? Why?

To prevent the Under Lords of *Xibalba* from arriving on Earth. The creature had succeeded in shunting the *Balam*'s array, opening a corridor of the nexus that bridged the gap between Earth and the *Xibalban* Underworld. Inside this corridor were two demons, disguised as my mother and Dominique. Having been warned about the deception by the Guardian, I killed both of those evil souls, completing my mission.

Or so I thought.

The Guardian offered me a choice. I could live out my days as Michael Gabriel or continue to evolve as One Hunahpu and journey to *Xibalba* to save the lost souls of the *Nephilim*.

Who are the Nephilim?

The Fallen Ones, human souls who were being tortured on *Xibalba*. I had remote-viewed their terror. Thousands of men, women, and children—all suffering at the hands of their oppressors. As Michael Gabriel, I could have ignored them, but as One Hunahpu, I realized I was their only hope.

With heavy heart I took one last look at your mother's face, then climbed into the Guardian's pod. Moments later, I found myself hurtling through space, leaving Earth forever . . . through a wormhole, racing to *Xibalba*—where the origin of mankind's evil was waiting.

The origin of mankind's evil? Father, I don't understand?

Humanity is caught in a bubble of space-time, each successive journey through the wormhole looping history. What has happened before will happen again, unless the paradox can be broken. My presence on *Xibalba* somehow reinforces this paradox, yet it also serves to keep the door to humanity's own salvation open. You see, Jacob, there are two crossroads that face humanity, one in 2012, one more in your own near future. I cannot tell you about this second holocaust, but if left unchecked, it will terminate life on Earth as surely as the events of 2012 nearly did.

What is it?

Again, I cannot say, but only a Hunahpu can prevent it.

Is it my destiny to stop it?

I don't see how. According to the *Popol Vuh*, you and your brother will make the journey to *Xibalba* aboard the *Balam* soon after your twentieth birthday, long before the second event.

And if we don't make the journey?

Then the second holocaust will wipe out humanity.

Father, is Manny Hunahpu? I know he shares our DNA, but the gene seems recessive.

Your brother's powers may grow stronger in years to come or they may not appear at all. All I know is that . . .

Father?

Father, what's wrong?

The Abomination. It senses our communication.

What should I do?

I should have known better. You're too young, it's too easy for the Abomination to use you. Even as we speak, it grows stronger in your energy field. You need to learn how to disguise it before we can communicate again.

Teach me how.

I can't, it's a strength that comes with age. Find me again when you're older.

How old?

Wait at least another seven years. Your Hunahpu powers will strengthen as you get older.

Father, I can't wait that long—

You have to. I'll be all right. Time isn't the same here as it is for you. Go now, quickly, before the Abomination pierces my defenses!

Father, I love you. Father?

* * *

Jacob awakens, staring into the teary eyes of his mother. "Jake? What happened?"

"I spoke with—" *Don't tell her, she'll only worry.* "It's okay, Mother. I'm fine."

Dominique turns to the president. "That's it, Ennis. No more remote viewing, do you understand? No more training! No more tests!" She looks at her son. "And no more talk about Mayan death gods and *Xibalba*. Somehow, some way, we're going to find a way for you and Manny to live normal lives."

12

OCTOBER 23, 2020
MABUS ESTATE
HAMPTONS, NEW YORK
8:37 P.M.

The delivery truck stops at the gated entrance of the Mabus Estate.

Mitchell Kurtz lowers his driver's side window to speak with the security guard. "Hey, pal. Got a delivery for your boss. Three surf-and-turf specials, and a bottle of wine. Should I leave it with you or take it up to the house?"

The armed guard steps out of his booth. "Where's Murphy?"

"Out sick. Probably at the track."

"Put the food on Mabus's tab and leave everything with me. I'll take it up in the cart."

"Sure thing." Kurtz hands the guard a thermal delivery

pouch. "Do me a favor and take the food tray inside, the pouch has to stay with me."

The guard reaches inside the insulated pouch and grabs the metal tray—

—and is jolted into unconsciousness behind ten thousand volts of electricity.

Kurtz opens his door. He steps over the body and pulls off his jacket, exposing a brown-and-gray uniform identical to the guard's. Hoisting the unconscious man over his shoulder, he carries him inside the guardhouse, then unceremoniously drops him to the floor.

Looking into the videocam, he dials into the main house.

Peter Mabus's voice bellows over the intercom, Kurtz's screen remaining scrambled for privacy. "What is it?"

"You have a food delivery, sir. I'm bringing it up in the cart."

"About time, we called forty minutes ago."

The line goes dead.

Kurtz tucks the metal food tray into its thermal pouch and resets the stunner, then taps at the tiny communication device hidden inside his left ear and speaks into his wristwatch. "I'm good. You in position?"

One hundred yards behind the beach house, Ryan Beck emerges from the dark Atlantic, dressed from head to toe in a black wet suit. Using his night-vision glasses, he verifies the beach is deserted, then makes his way past the sandy dunes and wild grass to the private boardwalk.

"Stand by."

Beck switches to a thermal scanner, focusing the invisible beam on the back of the Mabus mansion. "I'm detecting three people. Kid's upstairs in a third-floor bedroom. Servant's waiting for you at the door. Our target's drinking out back on the screened-in porch."

"Roger that, I'm on my way." Kurtz starts the golf cart and drives it up a narrow walkway that leads to the front entrance of the mansion.

Belle Glade, Florida

8:45 P.M.

"Been taking care of ya'll for seven long years, your mama longer than that!" Quenton Morehead stumbles into his granddaughter's bedroom, the alcohol flowing through his bloodstream like poison. "Two of ya'll took and took . . . drained me like a 'ho."

Lilith Eve Robinson's heart flutters like the wings of a dove.

"Ya'll owe me, you know that don't cha? Seven years' worth, uh-huh."

Her adrenaline pumping, Lilith's mind searches desperately for the white light as Quenton stumbles out of his trousers, falling sideways onto her sofa bed.

"Okay, okay, don't start yer slobberin'. Ya'll been comin' along nicely lately. Tonight it's time to let you feel heaven for yourself."

Lilith squeezes her eyes shut, her consciousness taking refuge inside the nexus.

Jacob?

I'm here, Lilith. But I can't stay. My mother's calling, I have to go.

Please don't go yet, he's doing it again! Her energy reaches out for him, entwining his mind like a vine.

Hey, let go, you're . . . you're too strong for me. Let me go—

Stay with me—please! I really need you tonight!

I'll come back as soon as I can, I promise.

Jacob, he's hurting me.

He's always hurting you. Stop being a victim, Lilith. Call the cops. Run away. Do something!

It's not that easy for me. I have no place else to go.

My mother's coming, Lilith—

You don't love me anymore, do you?

I do love you, I just can't do this right now. I'll be back as soon as I can.

Jacob—wait! Don't go, please!

Lilith, do you trust me?

Yes.

Then here's what I want you to do. Tell him that if he puts that thing near you again, you'll tell everyone in his church.

He's threatened to kill me if I ever told.

Then kill him. Wait until he passes out, then get a real sharp knife and cut his throat.

I . . . I can't do that.

Then I can't help you. I'm sorry, I have to go.

Jake, wait—

Jacob's mind pushes free and slips out of the netherworld, his vacancy tossing Lilith's own consciousness back into reality.

The girls opens her eyes in time to witness Quenton step out of his boxer shorts, exposing himself to her. "Now don't ya'll worry. See this? It's slidey cream. Slidey cream makes everythin' feel real good inside."

Jacob help me . . .

"Jacob!"

Longboat Key, Florida

"Jacob!"

Jake opens his eyes. He is on the beach, his mother calling for him.

The white-haired boy hustles up to the house.

"Jake, I want you to meet someone," Dominique says. "This is Craig Basedorfer. Mr. Basedorfer will be overseeing internal security while Salt and Pepper are away."

Jacob nods at the older gentleman, who looks more like a librarian than a security expert.

Solomon Adashek nods at the boy, his thin lips pursing in a forced smile. "A pleasure to finally meet you, young man. Mr. Kurtz and Mr. Beck have told me so much about you."

"Like what?"

"Excuse me?"

"What have they told you?"

"Well, for one thing, that you're quite the athlete. Mrs. Gabriel, perhaps you can call your other son in, there are a few new procedures I need to go over with all of you before you go to bed."

"Manny's probably in the SOSUS lab."

"No," Jacob says. "I saw him playing basketball."

"Okay, I'll be right back." Dominique heads outside, leaving her son alone with the government-trained killer.

"Jacob, I have something for you, a little gift from the CIA." Solomon Adashek removes the small cigar-sized canister from his jacket pocket, popping open the seal on the pressurized lid as he aims it at the boy.

"What . . . iz. . . . zit." Jake hears his words echoing hauntingly in his brain as the room spins, and he falls into the psychopath's reptilian-cold embrace.

Mabus Estate

8:47 P.M.

Mike Renyze, Peter Mabus's 260-pound "personal assistant" greets Mitchell Kurtz at the front door. "Who da fuck're you? Where's Maurice?"

"Maurice got sick on some bad X. I'm covering his shift." Kurtz hands the larger man the thermal pouch."

From his thermal scanner, Beck watches with amusement as a white-hot spark ignites at the front door, and the hulking form collapses. He taps his communicator. "That's twice you've used the same gimmick. What do you have in mind for our man?"

"He gets tonight's special." Kurtz drags the unconscious assistant into the bushes, then enters the mansion. He follows the polished marble floor to the back of the house and out through the kitchen to the back porch. "Mr. Mabus?"

Peter Mabus looks up from his lounge chair. "Who the hell are you?"

"Maurice's cousin, Phillip. The chef at Le Vielle Maison sent something special for you tonight to go along with your entrees. Your bodyguard said he'll take it if you can't finish it."

Mabus approaches, intrigued. "So? What is it?"

Kurtz reaches into his thermal pouch and removes a fifteen-pound lobster, holding the animal by its tail. "Is this a beauty or what?"

Mabus's mouth waters. "I like it, give it to me."

Kurtz squeezes a trigger hidden in the lobster's belly.

Two darts shoot out from the claw openings, puncturing Mabus's chest.

The billionaire's eyes roll up as he collapses to the wood deck.

Kurtz shoves the lobster-gun back inside the pouch, then bends over Mabus. Checks his pulse. "Pep, he's out."

"Better move fast, the kid's left his room."

Kurtz removes the two darts and tosses them in the pouch. Removes the hypodermic needle from his belt.

"He's coming down the steps."

Kurtz removes Mabus's sandal, then injects the clear elixir between the big man's toes.

"First floor, heading for the kitchen."

Kurtz replaces the sandal. Gathers his thermal pouch.

"Five seconds . . . move!"

Kurtz hurries out the back porch, hustling silently down the walkway to the beach.

Twelve-year-old Lucien Mabus stubs his cigarette out in an ashtray, then heads outside. "Hope dinner's ready, I'm starving. Dad? Oh, shit—"

The boy bends over his prone father. Presses his ear to his chest. "Rempe, get in here, Dad's having a heart attack! Walker? Maurice?"

Peter Mabus's pulse ceases long before the ambulance arrives.

From the sundeck of their rented yacht a half mile offshore, Beck and Kurtz feast on lobster and fillet tips, the light show provided courtesy of the Hampton Police Department.

Gabriel Compound

9:02 P.M.

Jacob's head throbs in pain. His arms are pinned behind his back, his wrists and ankles in handcuffs.

He forces his eyes open, bile rising in his throat as he takes in the scene.

His mother is seated across the room, bound by duct tape to a wicker chair. Her hair is tousled, her eyes wild above the gag as the slight, middle-aged predator methodically finishes taping her ankles before turning his attention to Jacob's twin brother.

Manny is bent chest down over the kitchen table, his arms splayed and bound over the granite top, his lower body dangling free.

Solomon Adashek pulls up a kitchen chair and sits beside the boy. Liver-spotted hands gently probe the unconscious youth's hairless muscular legs, savoring the moment before pulling down the boy's boxer shorts, exposing his bare bottom.

Jacob and Dominique grunt and groan as if jolted by electricity, thrashing within their bonds.

Solomon looks up, his eyes cold and twinkling, his thin mouth grinning like a snake.

Jacob's heart beats like a timpani drum, his adrenal glands pumping like a river—

—as the room seems to brighten, and time suddenly slows to a crawl.

Through waves of invisible energy, he forces himself off the ground, balancing within his shackles. He struggles with all his might against the steel handcuffs.

No use . . . I can't break free!

Eyeing his mother, he bunny-hops toward her as Solomon Adashek's head slowly turns toward him, his eyebrows raising in surprise.

Jacob jumps off the ground and double-kicks the man as hard as he can in the chest, sending him headfirst over the kitchen table.

Lactic acid washes over the boy's muscles as he bends to his mother, the fingers of his shackled hands tearing at her bonds, ripping apart the duct tape.

Freed, Dominique springs out of her chair, pulling the tape from her mouth. She rushes toward the mantel and grabs the *Katana,* the larger of the two Japanese swords on display.

Jacob collapses to the floor, his exhausted muscles quivering, his body bathed in sweat.

Solomon Adashek shakes the cobwebs from his brain. He rolls over on the kitchen floor—

—gazing up at Dominique Gabriel, who stands over him, her eyes breathing fire.

Raising the *Katana* high above her head, she rasps out a command, "Jacob, look away. Mommy doesn't want you to see this."

Jacob stares, his azure blue eyes widening in glee as his mother's *Katana* loops downward in one magnificent slash, separating Solomon Adashek's head from his body.

PART 5

:::::::::::::::

ADOLESCENCE

Nothing in life is to be feared, only understood.

—MADAME MARIE CURIE

Discipline is the highest form of intelligence.

—ENNIS CHANEY

13
SEVEN YEARS LATER

The government-appointed psychiatrist continues jotting down notes on a smart-pad, his presence in Dominique's living room more than a bit unnerving. "Go on, Mrs. Gabriel."

Dominique's hand quivers as she tucks her hair behind her ears. "Jacob thinks he's Superman, and a few of his trainers—you know, all the Smith and Jones CIA guys, I think they encourage it. Jake's ego's out of hand, and God help you if you try to argue with him, unless you want an earful about Mayan Under Lords and Death Gods. He quotes endless passages from the goddam *Popol Vuh*. *Xibalba* this and *Xibalba* that—"

"*Xibalba?*" Dr. Shyam Tanna looks up from his smart-pad. "Please, what is *Xibalba*?"

"The Mayan Underworld, a place he's convinced his father was exiled to. This is all my fault. I was so stupid, letting his Aunt Evelyn brainwash me. I never should have given Jake his grandfather's journal or let him read all that Mayan mumbo jumbo. I created a . . . a Mayan monster."

"Mrs. Gabriel, while Jacob's fantasies concern me, my primary reason in seeing you today was to talk to you about your son's I.Q. To say it's way off the scale is almost an insult to Jacob."

"I know. His brain's like a sponge, it absorbs everything."

"Of that I have no doubt. However, it is this Hunahpu gene that causes us the greatest concern. Extensive analysis of the chromosomes affected by the gene indicate that Jacob's condition lends itself to an extreme form of schizophrenia. Now, I've taken the time to review his father's medical records and—"

"Mick wasn't schizophrenic!"

"He was diagnosed paranoid schizophrenic by two major institutions."

"It was all a setup. Pierre Borgia wanted him put away permanently."

"Perhaps. But consider the possibility that Michael Gabriel showed signs of oncoming dementia—signs that, emotionally, your heart refused to allow you to see. And with Jacob, the Hunahpu gene appears much more dominant."

"What are you telling me? That I should institutionalize my son?"

"If not now, then at the first sign of dementia."

"Forget it, I won't do it, and he'd never stand for it anyway."

"And that, in itself, is a problem. An adolescent with Jacob's strength and intelligence makes for a very difficult individual to rear, let alone control. What will you do when the schizophrenia takes over and Jacob starts responding to commands from his Mayan warlords? What if he claims to be receiving messages from his long-lost father? You were a psych major, Mrs. Gabriel. You know the ramifications if you fail to act. Jacob could easily hurt himself, or worse, he could hurt his brother."

"We can medicate him. There's so many new prescription drugs that—"

"Nothing strong enough to handle this. Mrs. Gabriel, Jacob needs to be placed in a controlled environment where we can properly monitor his condition while protecting him from himself."

"Just call it what it really is, Doctor. You want to imprison him in one of your fancy labs."

2:17 A.M.

Small waves lap at the beach beneath a cloud-covered night sky.

Fourteen-year-old Jacob Gabriel settles himself into a lotus position and closes his eyes, focusing inward.

Jaaaaacob. The female's voice seduces him from beyond the mist.

Cut it out, Lilith, I can't speak with you now.

You never seem to have time for me lately, she pouts.

Hey, you're the one with all the friends.

Jealous?

No.

Liar. I have loads of friends and you only have your stupid brother, and he can't stand you.

Whatever.

By the way, Brandy says she wants to come with me when I meet you. She's already checked into bus tickets.

Lilith, I told you, my mother won't allow you into the compound. If she even suspected I was talking to someone with Hunahpu blood, she'd never give me another moment alone.

Well, we can't allow that. You'd never be able to play with yourself.

Shut up.

Do you think of me when you masturbate?

God, Lilith . . . I think you've been hanging out with Brandy too long.

Does your mommy expect you to be celibate all your life?

I told you before, it's the whole Abomination thing. It makes her paranoid.

Jacob, we weren't created in a lab. there must be a thou-

sand other people out there with Hunahpu blood. Maybe ten thousand. As for this crazy Abomination thing, I was born a full eight months after you and your brother. Want me to e-mail you my birth certificate again?

No.

Then sneak out of the compound and meet me at a hotel.

I can't. Lilith, I want to be with you, but things are crazy around here right now.

How can we ever get married if we can't even arrange a simple date?

What makes you so sure I want to marry you?

Because we're soul mates and you love me . . . and you like girls with long hair and big breasts. Want me to e-mail you another picture?

No, I mean, uh yeah, sure. I like that last one. Just make sure that crazy old bastard doesn't catch you in the bathroom with the digital.

If I don't meet you soon, maybe I'll just have to let Quenton have his way with me.

Shut up and go to sleep.

Bye lover. Say hi to daddy for me.

Bye.

Jacob waits until her presence disappears before refocusing his mind.

Father? Father, please answer, it's been so long since our last communication. Father, please, there are things I need to know—

I'm here, Jacob. I'm here.

Finally! Where have you been? I've tried for so long to reach you.

The movement of space-time affects our ability to communicate. I missed you, son.

Me too. There's so much I want to tell you. Is it safe to talk?

Yes. I can feel newfound strength in your communication, making it harder for the Abomination to track our thoughts. How old are you now?

Fourteen.

Fourteen. My God. How is your mother?

Not good. The passage of time is causing her to lose faith. She's doubting her existence as First Mother.

The journey's hard on her. You haven't told her about me?

No. She couldn't deal with it.

And your brother?

Manny still shows no signs of becoming Hunahpu.

You need to be strong for the two of them.

Father, I want to talk more about humanity's fate. I need you to teach me more about my journey to come.

Imagine time as multilayered highways of energy. As third-dimensional beings, we can only move forward along our own particular level at sublight speed, which we equate to the present. By increasing our speed beyond that of light, we can sling ourselves farther up the highway in relation to our sub light-speed friends, but we cannot move backward in time unless we access an off-ramp that takes us back down the highway from which we began. Wormholes are such highways—gravitational conduits, powered by the massive black hole located at the center of our galaxy. Wormholes provide us the means of looping backward or forward along the space-time continuum.

Sometime in your near future, humanity will find itself following a section of highway that splits our species. The survivors will be taken down a wormhole off-ramp that loops sublight time. The rest of humanity will blindly follow a stretch of road that leads to a dead-end . . . the end of our species.

The Popol Vuh's *Creation Myth tells of the Hero Twins presence in* Xibalba, *an event that already happened.*

Correct.

Father, if it already happened, then why are we reliving it?

The *Popol Vuh* tells of what we hope will come to pass, but the myth is not accurate. The truth is, you and your brother failed in your first attempt.

We failed?

Yes. Fortunately, humanity was granted a second chance when the Guardian took the Balam back through the wormhole and ended up at Earth, 65 million years in the past.

And what's to prevent us from failing again? Manny's not even Hunahpu. I don't see how we can win over this Abomination.

You'll win this time because I'm going to help you. I can be your eyes, advising you which road to take. I can prepare you in much the same way the Guardian tried to prepare me.

Then do it, teach me! Tell me what happened to you after you entered the serpent's mouth and disappeared.

I didn't disappear, Jacob. I entered the Guardian's pod and moved beyond light speed. As the stars passed by like taser fire, I realized the reality of my decision. What seemed like seconds to me would be decades to everyone on Earth. You, your brother, your mother— everyone of my era would be long dead by the time I arrived on *Xibalba*, wherever that hellish world might lie.

I panicked. I screamed. I ordered the Guardian to return me to Earth.

But it was too late. The highway I was traveling on could only move forward—and it was a dark road that led to the origin of man's evil.

The Guardian promised they would never abandon me. Those were the last words I remembered hearing before I lost consciousness.

When I awoke, I was shocked to find myself aboard an Earth shuttle, bound for Mars.

I don't understand? Were you remote-viewing the scene, still unconscious aboard the Guardian's transport pod, or was it real?

The event was real, only I was living it as someone else, someone from my past but your future. Let me tell my tale, and you'll understand.

What clued me in to the time period was the space

vehicle itself. It was not a shuttle like those NASA had designed and flown during my teen years. This vessel was infinitely larger, with private berths to accommodate fifty-two passengers and a year's worth of supplies. Nor were we alone on our voyage. There were eleven other shuttles accompanying us, twelve in all, like the twelve tribes of Israel—all crossing the great desert of space on our journey to the Promised Land . . . Mars.

You were on a scientific expedition?

No, I'd say it was more like a pilgrimage. The great holocaust I told you of had just overwhelmed humanity. Billions had perished, and billions more were destined to die. Something horrible had happened back on Earth . . . a cataclysm that caught the general population by complete surprise. But the upper echelons of the government knew, and that's why we were aboard those space shuttles.

They kept it a secret?

A secret shared only by a privileged few. Years from your present time, clues about the coming cataclysm will be discovered. It will be kept from the public. Only those in power will know, and they will create a secret coven—in essence, an Earth evacuation plan, concealed behind an aggressive program to colonize Mars. Humanity, at least a certain privileged segment of it, would go on. Thousands had already arrived on the Red Planet. Our twelve shuttles would be the last to join our fellow survivors.

As we began our perilous four-month journey and Earth disappeared from our viewports, we cried and prayed and cried some more. Our salvation was Mars Colony, but we would never arrive, for what lay ahead was an off-ramp—the entrance to a wormhole.

There was no way to avoid it, no way for our pilots to even see it. A sudden surge of the shuttle's gravity-wave detectors and *whoosh*—we found ourselves hurtling through the conduit's funnel of energy, time and space distorting as we plunged through our Galaxy's version of a rabbit hole.

Imagine falling from a thirty thousand-foot precipice, knowing your life is about to be extinguished, your screams squelched by the length of the drop. In those final minutes everything becomes clear, and you realize how much time you wasted on petty nonsense.

As frightened as I was, I could not tear myself away from my viewport, my mind mesmerized. We passed through gray interstellar gas clouds whose cosmic glow brightened into visible light, drenching us in pastels of crimson and yellow and blue before yielding to a hydrogen field of fluorescent pink.

Voices cried out in the darkened cabin, some identifying the gas cloud as the Orion Nebula. If accurate, then we had traveled some fifteen hundred light-years from Earth in the blink of an eye.

And then the cabin pressure increased and the spacecraft shook violently, and I closed my eyes to die.

How much time passed, I cannot say, but when I awoke, I was still on board the Mars shuttle, only the stars had stopped moving. We were through the wormhole, all twelve of our ships—and somehow we had survived.

I say "we" yet I still had no idea who I was or what I was doing on board the vessel, but the sheer delight at merely being alive . . . it was too overwhelming to question.

In the distance I could see a red supergiant—a star so large that had it been Earth's sun its girth would have stretched across the solar system beyond the orbit of Mars. In close proximity to this monster was a planetary nebula, its fluorescent-style ring of gases appearing in shades of violets and blues.

I heard voices in the dark debate the red supergiant's identity, the consensus agreeing it was Betelgeuse, a star over three hundred times the diameter of our sun and ten thousand times as luminous. If correct, then we had been transported to another section of the Orion spiral arm.

And then one of my cabin mates turned to me and addressed me as Bill.

So now I had an identity. The consciousness that had been Michael Gabriel had hitched a ride in the body and mind of William C. Raby. I . . . or should I say *we*, were a marine geneticist, selected for Mars Colony, not by merit, but by extensive international private bank dealings that had helped fund the journey.

Like many of the other passengers, Bill Raby had known the right people to bribe and had the means and political clout to save himself.

But you weren't really this Bill Raby, were you?

That's just it, son, in every sense, I had become him. My consciousness dominated his, I felt his fears as if they were my own. I had his memories, and his overwhelming sense of guilt, for like me, Bill Raby had also left a loved one back on Earth, and it was tearing him up inside.

The desperateness of our situation quickly spread throughout the cabin. Our trip through the space tunnel had destroyed most of our ship's electronics, damaging our outer hull, crippling our engines. Like the rest of the fleet, we were hurtling through space, out of control, being reeled in along powerful gravitational forces that our damaged sensors could not identify.

Another wormhole?

No, it was a planet, its atmosphere vermilion, its appearance in many ways similar to that of Mars, though closer to Earth in size. Like the Red Planet, the alien world possessed two barren moons, one the size of Earth's lone satellite, the second—a smaller potato-shaped body, perhaps fourteen miles in diameter.

Panic levels rose as our twelve vessels plummeted through this alien world's atmosphere. With our heat shield damaged, our cabin began heating up like a furnace. Children screamed. Passengers held one another, hoping and praying for another miracle all of us knew in our hearts we didn't deserve.

But another miracle did happen, coming this time from our gallant crew, who managed to angle the shuttle's decent just enough to allow us to slip through the searing atmosphere without combusting into ash. A collective cheer embraced the cabin as the blackness of space morphed into a magnificent cardinal red horizon. Aerodynamics took over as our winged vessel soared like a plane high above an alien landscape. As we descended, we could make out a geology composed of barren volcanic rock, splashed with patches of moss.

Fear returned moments later as we continued losing altitude, dropping fast, with no suitable landing place in site.

With a sickening jolt, our tail struck terra incognita. The shuttle skidded, the cabin spun, and once more, everything turned to black . . .

TOP SECRET/MAJESTIC-12

WARNING: Unauthorized access or viewing of this document without the appropriate authorizations will result in permanent incarceration or sanction by authorized use of deadly force.

PROGRESS REPORT ON
SPECIAL ACCESS PROGRAM
GOLDEN FLEECE

24 October 2027

STAR SHIP VESSEL: *BALAM*

1. Dr. David Mohr and the GOLDEN FLEECE team have been reluctant to speculate on the propulsion system of the *Balam*, ever since its arrival in Hangar 13

four years ago—this due primarily to the team's continued inability to access the interior of the ship. A new theory and its related dangers, however, has led to some unanimous conclusions that must be brought to POTUS's attention.

2. Previous MAJESTIC reports have stated that the *Balam* star cruiser most likely "surfed" its way through Earth's atmosphere riding its own massive shock waves, maneuvering at lower speeds/hovering utilizing an advanced form of magnetoaeroelectro dynamics. In this mode, the vessel's polished gold external hull becomes the engine. Waves of negatively charged electron particles, embedded in the carrier frequencies of the electromagnetic waves "push" the vessel through the air mass.

3. A second, infinitely faster method of propulsion is now believed to exist. Located underneath and between the two stern nacelle structures are multicellular exhaust nozzles. Upon further examination, Dr. Mohr's team has reached a consensus, theorizing that these nozzles may have been designed to channel tachyon energy particles, leading the scientists to agree that the *Balam* is capable of superluminal propulsion, labeled by NASA-BPP scientists as "Warp Drive."

4. A third theory put forth by NASA-BPP concerns the *Balam*'s ability to create an "exotic-matter" force field, allowing the vessel to theoretically enter a gravimetric vortex (SEE WORMHOLES).

RELEVANT APPLICATIONS

5. The GOLDEN FLEECE team theorizes that the power produced to activate the *Balam*'s Warp Drive would be enough to light and heat every city on Earth simultaneously and continuously for more than 100,000

years. The terawatts of power produced every picosecond by the *Balam*'s interior reactor cores are the kind of power requirements hypothesized for hyperdimensional travel at superluminal velocities.

SAFETY WARNING / SECURITY ISSUES

6. In the opinion of the senior MAJESTIC team members and also Dr. Mohr: This Warp Drive propulsion system represents an extreme danger to the physical safety of Earth, possibly affecting the power grids and/or the ecology of whole continents if the system is accidentally activated.

7. Quantum-gravity physicists immediately expressed concern should the *Balam*'s Warp Drive engines activate, producing a microwormhole. They stated that, should the magnetic containment fields that "bottle" the quantum singularity collapse, the microwormhole could potentially expand to consume the entire vessel and perhaps whole portions of the planet itself.

8. The ability to create and navigate wormholes is the ability to traverse the boundaries of space-time. As per preestablished MAJESTIC directives, time travel is an uncontrollable threat to the security of the human species owing to the theoretical "Paradox" effect (SEE EINSTEIN SPECIAL THEORY OF RELATIVITY).

GULF OF MEXICO / CHICXULUB CRATER

9. On 18 December 2012, Michael Gabriel confirmed that the Guardian's vessel (*Balam*) entered Earth space in pursuit of the alien object that crash-landed 65 million years ago. If the *Balam* is capable of superluminal velocity, it therefore must be assumed that the enemy transport ship it was chasing was also capable of Warp Drive.

10. An extensive reexamination of the Chicxulub Impact Crater in the Gulf of Mexico reveals a Magnetic/Gravitational Field Anomaly. Recent discoveries of Magnetic Field Anomalies in both inner and outer space have led quantum physicists to theorize that wormholes may actually cross our planet's path. These "GATES TO HYPERSPACE" may cause the kind of magnetic/gravitational deviations experienced in an area intersecting the Chicxulub Impact Crater, expanding outward from the Gulf of Mexico into the Caribbean Sea to form an unstable magnetic region, better known as the "Bermuda Triangle."

11. Discovered within the "Bermuda Triangle" are small, very deep, very anomalous underwater caves, known as "Blue Holes." Robert Palmer, former director of the Blue Hole Research Center in the Bahamas mysteriously disappeared while diving in one of these anomalies. Palmer had theorized that the underwater anomalies are being created by the continuous popping in and out of existence of microwormholes.

12. Dr. Mohr believes the larger Magnetic Field Anomaly originating beneath the Chicxulub Impact Crater is being influenced by a wormhole, but not a microwormhole, a larger one, perhaps originating/approaching Earth space from somewhere in another space-time, or another section of our galaxy. If true, we could be looking at the formation of a gateway into another dimension.

GABRIEL TWINS

13. It is the opinion of senior MAJESTIC team officials that former POTUS Ennis Chaney was too quick to limit GOLDEN FLEECE's access to the Gabriel Twins. Now fourteen, the boys may hold the "mental key" that unlocks the secrets of the *Balam* and the Magnetic Field Anomaly in the Gulf of Mexico.

CONCLUSIONS

It is recommended that Dominique Gabriel (the twins' mother and legal guardian) be "convinced" that it is in the best interests of her family to allow her sons to join the GOLDEN FLEECE team. Narcotherapies, hypnotherapies, microvolt brain implants, and even control of access to family members must be held in reserve to enforce compliance. Threats and applied duress should also be held in reserve as an option.

Submitted:

W. Louis McDonald
GOLDEN FLEECE

24 October 2027

■ ■ ■ ■ ■ ■ ■ ■ ■ ■ ■ ■ ■ ■ ■

14

■ ■ ■ ■ ■ ■ ■ ■ ■ ■ ■ ■ ■ ■ ■

OCTOBER 27, 2027
GABRIEL COMPOUND
LONGBOAT KEY, FLORIDA
3:02 A.M.

Bloodred subterranean sky. Searing-hot wind. Dark clouds churn, their speed surreal.

Below, an alien lake smolders, its mirrorlike surface lapping upon an ominous shoreline.

Jacob approaches the alabaster tree, its trunk as wide as a sequoia's.

An icy fog announces the Abomination. The mist swirls about the trunk of the tree, and then a pair of bright azure blue eyes twinkle back at him through the haze.

"Come closer, Cousin. Let me lick your wounds."

With a bloodcurdling scream, Jacob Gabriel launches from his bed and darts into the hallway.

Dominique yanks open her bedroom door. "Oh, Jesus, another night terror?"

The door across from Jacob's bedroom opens. Immanuel stares at his brother. Shakes his head. "Again?"

Jacob pants, trying to find his voice. "Just wait . . . you'll go through the same thing someday."

"I doubt it. But until then, why don't you move your bed into the training center."

Dominique turns to the dark-haired twin. "Manny, go back to sleep."

Immanuel slams the door, bolting it from the inside.

Dominique moves to comfort Jacob, but he pushes her away.

"Jake—"

"No. I need to stay strong . . . for all of us."

"Who told you that?"

"It doesn't matter. I'm going for a walk to clear my head."

"It's three in the morning. Jacob Gabriel, don't you ignore me."

The back door opens and slams shut.

Dominique's eyes tear up, her heart aching for the son who has refused to hug her since he was seven years old.

A tropical gust greets Jacob as he races down to the beach. Lunar light from the three-quarter moon dances across the Gulf, illuminating the breaking crests.

Jacob kneels in the cool sand. Closes his eyes. Tries to meditate, desperate to communicate again with his father.

For a brief moment he breathes quietly, then his chest constricts and his body is overtaken by sobs, the tears pouring from his eyes as he collapses facefirst against the wet sand.

Stop it! You need to stay strong!

The wind dies down, yielding to a haunting echo.

Jacob wipes his face, then looks around, searching for the source of the sound.

The high-pitched moan leads him north. He follows the shoreline another quarter mile, and then he sees them.

The animals are everywhere, lined up along the beach like giant logs. Grays and humpbacks, right whales and blues, adults and calves . . . the dead and the dying.

Jacob approaches the largest of the beached mammals. The blue whale's head, as big as a tractor trailer, is half-covered in sand, the remains of its 105-ton girth disappearing behind it into the Gulf.

The teenager reaches up and brushes sand from the female's eye, then jumps back when it opens.

A thunderous snort as the dying whale gasps a breath through its blowhole.

A moment passes between them as beast and boy contemplate one another. *It's like it wants to communicate. Maybe it can?* Jacob Gabriel closes his eyes, entering the nexus.

The night dawns olive green in his vision. Every muscle in his six-foot, 183-pound muscular frame seems to come alive, every vessel in his body pulsating with blood and adrenaline, every sensation magnified. Looking up, he sees stars racing across the heavens, the cosmos coming alive.

The whale moans, its dying gasp echoing in his brain.

Leaning forward, Jacob places both palms against the blubbery torso, registering deep, intense reverberations as his hands become a living stethoscope. The mammal's pulse draws him closer, as a white haze envelops his mind—

—yielding to another vision.

An ominous scarlet sky casts its surreal light upon a man-made reservoir, its waters resembling liquid mercury.

The exotic waters churn. Emerging from the surface is the viperous upper torso of a serpentlike creature, as wide and as long as a train. The horrible being's eyes regard Jacob through vertical slits of gold, surrounded by incandescent crimson corneas more cybernetic than organic. The jowls part, revealing rows of ebony, scalpel-sharp teeth.

A thunderous snort causes Jacob to jump backward as the serpent expels a stench-laden breath through its synthetic nostrils.

Jacob opens his eyes. The vision is over.

The blue whale is dead.

Belle Glade, Florida

October 28, 2027

Fourteen-year-old Lilith Eve Robinson's high cheekbones and brilliant Hunahpu blue eyes are accentuated by cocoa skin and waist-length wavy black hair. Her athletic figure is long and supple, her shapely breasts firm and far more developed than those of most girls in her class.

The adolescent beauty always rides home alone on the bus, occupying the same aisle seat. Every heterosexual teenage boy imagines himself with Lilith, still none ask her out—too freaked-out about her animated conversations with her invisible friends.

Facing the window, Lilith shrugs at Brandy. "It's Jacob's stupid mother. If she or Jacob ever found out when I was really born, he'd never speak to me again."

That's just silly, girl. You love Jacob, and Jacob loves you. Do you believe it's your destiny to be together?

"Yes."

Then forget about Jacob's mother and make it happen. Here's your stop. I'll see you tomorrow.

The school activity bus pulls over to the curb and stops. Lilith climbs down the bus steps, then heads for Quenton's house. She is not involved in after-school activities, but she is never in any hurry to return home to her guardian.

Regina Johnson chases after her. "Hey, Robinson, wait!"

Lilith continues walking.

Regina catches up. "Who were you talking to on the bus?"

"Brandy."

"Brandy who?"

Lilith walks faster.

"Hey, wait. I've got some killer weed. Wanna get high?"

"What is it you want, Regina Johnson?"

"Lighten up, girl, I just wanna get to know you better."

"Why?"

The strawberry blonde smiles. "You goin' to Brett's party with anyone?"

"No."

"Why don't you come with me?" Gina's fingertips slide across Lilith's moving buttocks.

Lilith stops dead in her tracks. "I'm not into girls."

"That's not what I heard."

"Yeah? And what have you heard?"

"I dunno. It's just . . . you know—you're so pretty, and I never see you with any boys."

"Don't believe everything you hear. I have a boyfriend, he just doesn't live around here."

"Oh. Well, aren't you even a little bi-curious?"

"I have to go."

"Wait. Cut through the woods with me. We'll share a quick joint, you know, as friends. Unless you're in a rush to get home."

Regina heads for the woods, Lilith in tow.

Longboat Key, Florida

Immanuel Gabriel is alone in the SOSUS lab when his Aunt Evelyn knocks on the open door. "Mind if I join you?"

The dark-haired twin doesn't bother looking up. "Jake's not here."

"Actually, I wanted to speak with you."

"What for?"

She approaches, using a cane to support her arthritic left hip. "What are you working on?"

"I'm charting a new whale migration pattern."

"May I listen?"

Immanuel plugs in a set of headphones, then passes them to the old woman.

"There's so many of them. Such godly creatures."

"I'm not like *him,* you know."

"I know."

"He drives me crazy."

"Your brother can be . . . intense."

"He's a nut job. Why do you humor him?"

"Maybe I'm a nut job, too."

Immanuel smiles. "Hey, wanna see something cool?" Evelyn waits patiently as the teenager pulls up an image on screen of a four-legged oversize ratlike animal. "See this creature? It's called a *Pakicetids*. It's actually a prehistoric whale."

"That's a whale?"

"Well, it was the ancestor of whales. For some unknown reason, *Pakicetid* returned to live in the sea about 50 million years ago. They eventually lost their fur, which was replaced with thick layers of insulated blubber. Nature even repositioned their nostrils on top of their heads so they could breathe easier."

Evelyn smiles at the teenager. "You really have a deep love for whales, don't you?"

"I suppose." He advances the page. "Look here. This is *Rodhocetus,* the first species of whale with a true fluke and blowhole."

"That is amazing. Whales have really come a long way, haven't they?"

"Uh-huh." Immanuel continues the program. "Modern cetaceans eventually split into two different suborders.

Baleen whales, like blues and humpbacks, have no teeth. Toothed whales, like sperm whales and orcas, remained predators, developing a sense called echolocation."

"Echolocation? Is that those high-pitched clicking sounds?"

"Exactly. My grandma says the clicks allow toothed whales to see things using sound. By listening to the returning echoes, the mammals can navigate through their environment, seeing things we could never register with our own eyes."

"Sort of like a built-in sonar, huh?"

"That's right. Echolocation gives whales x-ray vision. Grandma says a dolphin or whale can detect a shark swimming hundreds of meters away, using its echolocation to see right into its belly to determine if it's fed recently."

"Does your grandmother know why there are so many whales migrating into the Gulf of Mexico?"

"It's the anomaly."

"Anomaly? What anomaly?"

"The one she detected in the Chicxulub Crater. It's screwing up the whales' sense of direction."

"I don't understand?"

"Inside a whale's brain are these things called magnetite crystals. Whales navigate by tuning in to the Earth's magnetic force fields. It's sort of like having a built-in compass. The magnetic anomaly in the Gulf is scrambling their compasses, confusing them. That's why a lot of them are beaching. My grandpa Julius, he knew all about whales, too."

"How do you know that?"

"It's in his journal." The teen types in another command, causing a new home page to appear on screen.

THE JOURNAL OF JULIUS GABRIEL

"Your grandfather's memoirs?"

"Uh-huh. Jake transferred everything to audio disk. Computer, recite Journal Entry 722."

JOURNAL ENTRY #722
RECORDED ON THE NAZCA PLATEAU, NAZCA, PERU.
JANUARY 17, 1993.

The computerized voice of the late Julius Gabriel crackles from behind the surround-sound speakers:

"Of all the zoomorphs engraved in the desert pampa, perhaps the most bizarre are those of the three Nazca whales, each mammal drawn distinctly different from the next.

I shall begin with the oldest of the lot, a thirty-foot specimen possessing an enormous fluke and four leglike appendages. Although several of my colleagues regard the addition of these strange appendages as 'artistic license,' I disagree, believing our ancient artist had something different in mind.

Paleontologists have determined that modern whales descended from an extinct giant rodentlike land mammal called a **Pakicetid.** *This terrestrial creature mysteriously walked back into the sea on all fours sometime after the asteroid strike that led to the extinction of the dinosaurs. In the 25 million years that followed, evolution succeeded in transforming this land mammal into an ocean dweller.*

Equally mystifying is a strange object that was drawn below the ancient cetacean's lower jaw. Most of my peers have identified this feature as the mammal's spout. Here I disagree emphatically. Anatomically speaking, a whale's blowhole is part of its dorsal surface, yet this object has clearly been drawn below the creature's lower jaw. My colleagues' rebuttal to these inarguable facts is simply to shrug the matter off, crediting it to a mistake made by the artist.[[AR 1]]

Mistake? The ancient Nazca icons and geometric figures are inhumanly precise. Was the creator of these drawings capable of such a grievous error? I think not.

My theory, improbable as it sounds, is that the circular object was meant to represent a form of communication. I believe the creator of the Nazca drawings was able to com-

municate with these ancient whales, and the artist clearly wanted us to know it.

"Computer, end program." Immanuel looks up at the old woman. "Well?"

"Well what?"

"Do you think the Guardian communicated with whales?"

"Honestly, I have no idea."

"Jake thinks they did. Last night he was out on the beach and . . . ah, never mind. It's stupid."

"What's stupid?"

"Nothing. I have to go."

"Wait, Manny, before you leave, I wanted to ask you a question."

"Just one?"

"Are you happy?"

"Are you?"

"I try to be."

Immanuel looks away. "I hate it here. It's like being in prison. Mom's paranoid—she never let's me leave, and Jake is a jerk, always acting like some goddam drill seargent. All he cares about is his stupid fantasies."

"It must be hard on you."

"It's harder on her. He treats our mother like crap."

"Why do you say that? I've never seen him lose his temper with her."

"He treats her with indifference. Like he's afraid to love her, or anyone, for that matter. My brother's all business."

"Do you believe any of his stories? You know, the Mayan myths about the Hero Twins."

"You're not serious?"

"You know, I think you really love Jake a lot. I also think the two of you are a lot more alike than you let on."

"Don't say that. You think I want to end up like him?"

"No, but I think you have a good heart, Manny." She touches his chest with her palm. "Let it be your guiding light."

Belle Glade, Florida

October 28, 2027
11:17 P.M.

They can hear the heavy bass from the speakers pounding a block away.

"Don't be nervous," Regina says. "Just let yourself go."

Lilith tugs nervously at her violet skintight top, trying to hide the bulge of her protruding nipples. "I wish you would have let me wait for Brandy."

"Forget about Brandy for one night. Tonight you're with me."

"If Quenton saw me dressed like this, he would . . . well—"

"Relax. Your grandfather's asleep."

"You mean passed out."

Regina takes her hand. "Just stick with me."

The party is in full swing by the time they arrive. Cars are parked everywhere, in the driveway, on the street, and atop the lawn. A multiracial mix of teens flow in and out of the two-story stucco and stone home, the night air drenched with the scent of beer and marijuana.

All eyes stare at Lilith as she follows Regina inside.

Strobe lights and heavy-metal music greet her, along with a wall of moving bodies.

"Gina—hey, glad you made it!" Brett Longley pushes his way towards them.

"Hey, Brett. You know Lilith."

"Uh, sure, I've seen her around school. Hey, Lilith."

"Hi."

"Yeah, let's get high." Gina places a white pill on her tongue, then turns to Lilith.

Brett watches the two girls French-kiss. "Damn. Save some of that for me."

October 29, 2027
2:15 A.M.

Lilith is numb.

Numb is easy. Numb requires no emotions. No thinking. An occasional breath. Just open wide for a probing tongue and the numbness comes.

I'm a popular object . . .

Lilith lies back on the couch between Regina and Ron Ley.

Ron is tall. Ron is a senior. Ron plays varsity basketball and runs track.

Ron is white. Ron is cool.

Ron is horny. Lilith can feel his erection every time he leans over to steal a kiss.

"Lilith, finish my beer."

No more beer. More beer means throwing up, and throwing up makes the headaches come back.

Lilith takes the beer from Ron and drains it.

Ron likes me. Ron thinks I'm cool. Jacob will be so jealous.

Regina passes out on Lilith's lap.

Across the smoke-filled room, Dante Adams drains his beer. Dante has been eyeing Lilith for hours.

Dante is horny.

Dante is a predator.

Ron kisses Lilith again. Squeezes her breasts way too hard, then takes her hand and leads her into the nearest bedroom.

Don't do this, Lilith! She tries to pull away, but all resistance is gone.

So you're dumb. Just be numb. At least you're cool.

Dante follows them inside.

"Don't—"

"Come on, baby—"

"No . . . Ron, please don't—"

"I don't like being teased."

"I wasn't teasing."

"Fine. If you won't let me put it in you, then just suck it."

Brandy appears over Ron's shoulder. *Just do it. It's easier than fighting him.*

Lilith opens her mouth. Inhales a whiff of his manhood. Chokes back a gag reflex, then pukes all over Ron's basketball sneakers.

"Ugh . . . you stupid bitch!" Ron slaps her hard across the face.

Too wasted to feel the pain and too high to locate the nexus, Lilith squeezes her eyes shut and sucks on the blood oozing from her lower lip.

Dante moves closer. "I'll spread her legs. You do her first . . . then it's my turn."

6:15 A.M.

Lilith staggers home just before sunrise. Her lower lip is swollen, her cheek bruised. Her shirt is torn. She is missing her shoes.

Lilith is no longer numb.

Lilith is sober.

Lilith is ready to die.

She sneaks around back and enters the kitchen. Hears Quenton snoring.

Quietly, she roots through a kitchen drawer. Locates the steak knife.

She enters Quenton's bedroom. Sees the old man passed out on the floor. Enters the master bathroom. Stares at the tub and the razor blades lined up in the soap dish. Contemplates. Decides against running the bathwater for fear of waking her grandfather.

Lilith enters the walk-in closet. Tugs on the dangling ceiling chain, retracting the wooden step-ladder from the attic. Climbs up into the crawl space, searching for solitude.

Lilith hates the attic. As a four-year-old, Lilith feared the attic.

This morning, the attic is a refuge, a point of no return.

Dawn shines in from the cracked hexagon of glass.

Lilith stares at the veins of her wrists. She is not afraid to die, but she is afraid of the pain. Pain means noise, and noise could awaken Quenton.

She looks around for a towel or shirt, something to stuff in her mouth and bite down upon while she opens her veins.

She sits up, wincing at the sharp twinge shooting through her swollen rectum. She thinks about contacting Jacob, but feels too ashamed. *He'll think I'm a slut.*

Her azure blue eyes skirt the attic, pausing at an unrecognized cardboard box. She reaches over and opens it.

Curiosity captures her attention. It is her mother's personal effects.

She removes the dusty photo album and opens the torn book flap, accidentally spilling half the unbound contents.

A yellowed black-and-white photo of her mother and father taking their wedding vows.

A legal document signifying Madelina Aurelia's adoption by her foster parents, the Moreheads.

Madelina's second-grade report card—all As.

A few disturbing watercolor paintings. Several more photos of her mother as a teen.

She fingers the sealed manila envelope. Tearing away the yellowed tape, she reaches inside, removing several old newspaper clippings and a black-and-white photo of a frightening old man.

On the back of the photo is scrawled: Uncle Don Rafelo.

She unfolds the aged newspaper clippings. Each story concerns her great-uncle, reputed to be a *Nagual*—a powerful Mexican witch.

Lilith reads, her schizophrenic mind absorbing the information like a sponge.

15

OCTOBER 31, 2027
BELLE GLADE HIGH SCHOOL
BELLE GLADE, FLORIDA

Students mill about the patched tarmac schoolyard, waiting for the sixth period bell to ring. Dozens hang in groups, smoking by the seven-foot-high chain-link fence. Others are preoccupied with palm-sized computer games. Shirtless boys play full-court pickup basketball.

Lilith kneels behind one of the basketball poles, then turns to Brandy. "Okay, we're here. Now what?"

Do as I told you.

"They'll hurt me."

Not this time. Get ready.

Lilith's luminescent blue eyes follow the game.

Dante Adams dribbles between his legs, then launches a wild shot at the opposite basket. Ronny Ley grabs the defensive rebound and pushes the ball up court. Evading a defender with a crossover dribble, he pulls up in front of Brett Longley at the three-point arc and shoots.

Swish.

Lilith dashes onto the court and grabs the basketball before it hits the ground, then takes off running.

"Hey! Crazy bitch, come back here!"

Lilith races for the seven-foot-high chain-link fence . . . and hurdles it.

Jaws drop. The boys swear out loud, watching helplessly as the teenaged girl dodges traffic and ducks behind a fast-food restaurant.

"Come on!" Ron, Dante, and Brett scale the fence. The three boys cross the street, then cut between a row of shrubs bordering the rear of the hamburger joint.

Lilith is waiting in back, seated atop an open steel trash bin that is surrounded by a rusty brown, eight-foot-high wooden fence.

"There she is," whispers Dante, his rage tinged with lust.

"Know what? I think she's playing with us," Ron says. "You had a good time Friday night, didn't you, girl? I think you want some more."

"Let's do her right here," says Dante. Reaching up, he grabs Lilith by her ankles.

"Get off me!" She kicks at Dante and Ron as they drag her down, pinning her to the ground.

"Hey, come on, easy guys." Brett backs away, but is unable to tear his eyes away as Dante pulls up Lilith's skirt, grabbing for her underpants.

This time, a fully sober Lilith slips inside the nexus.

She immediately springs to her feet, rising through invisible waves of energy. Ron and Dante's expressions morph into disbelief as she lunges for them, grabs them by the hair, and smashes their skulls together with all her might.

The violent collision sends blood and bone spouting in slow motion through gelatinous waves of energy.

Lilith stares at the dueling crimson streams, then turns her attention to Brett.

The boy has turned and is attempting to flee.

Lilith kicks him in the buttocks, launching him facefirst into the side of the steel trash bin.

The bruised teen collapses. Bleeding and barely conscious, he struggles to crawl away on all fours.

"Finish him."

Lilith turns in shock, the nexus suddenly filled with an icy aura.

The old man is tall and gray-haired, his appearance striking. A long aquiline nose, like that of a hooked eagle, dominates his wrinkled Mesoamerican face. The left eye is a piercing azure blue, the right eye hazel and lazy, always glancing sideways. Loose silky white clothing hangs from his bony frame.

"Who are you?"

"You know who I am."

"Uncle Don? Why are you here?"

"I'm here to guide you. Now finish the last one quickly, before someone sees you."

"I . . . can't." She doubles over, the lactic acid buildup excruciating.

Don Rafelo seems to glide through the invisible waves of energy as he approaches. "You can't finish him because you're weak. Move aside and learn." Don Rafelo reaches down to Brett. Gripping the boy's skull in the knotty fingers of his right hand, he twists, shattering the boy's cervical vertebrae, severing the spinal cord.

Brett collapses flat on his face—dead.

Don Rafelo turns to Ron and Dante and inhales deeply, "tasting" their diminishing life forces. "You did well. These two are close to death. Help me get them into the trash bin."

Lilith complies.

The trash truck will arrive three hours later. By nightfall, the remains of the three teens, along with the rest of the debris, will be deposited in a dirt pit located atop "Mount Trashmore," a man-made mountain of garbage located twenty miles south of Lake Okeechobee.

8:10 P.M.

The motel clerk fingers his goatee as Lilith lays the five crumpled twenty-dollar bills she has stolen from Quenton's wallet upon the coffee-stained front desk.

"That should cover my uncle's room for the rest of the week."

The clerk scoops up the money, then hands her a key, his grip lingering a second too long. "Let me know if there's anything else I can do you for."

She ignores his leer, then heads outside.

Don Rafelo appears from behind a parked car. He follows her to Room 113.

The room is musty, reeking of mildew. Lilith turns on the air-conditioning, the antiquated unit growling to life. "Okay, Uncle Don, I've done everything you've instructed, now I want to know how you found me."

Don Rafelo lies back on one of the twin beds, staring at her. "I never lost track of you, even when your parents tried to escape me by fleeing to America. I'm the one who arranged your parents' marriage."

"Why?"

"Because of their bloodlines. Each of us possesses a life force, Lilith, something the Western World refers to, with much distortion, as the soul. Harbored within your genes are two powerful animating forces. The first was created long ago by the joining of two ancient bloodlines, one Mayan, tracing back to the days of Kukulcán, the other Aztec and the lineage of Quetzalcoatl. But it is the second life force—the Rafelo bloodline—that allows us to tap into the darker forces of the universe. It is this dark force that chases you across the Earth like a cold wind. It is spiritual in form, yet it possesses the ability to manipulate the other."

"I don't understand. Where is this dark force? Where's it coming from?"

"Another place, another time. You will feel its presence as you move closer to our homeland and the Gulf of Mexico. The dark force is powerful, it reaches out to embrace you. It is what summoned me from Morelos to guide you."

Lilith's azure eyes widen. "I want this power. Teach me!"

The old man grins. "That is why I am here."

When Lilith Robinson stumbled upon her parents' belongings, she'd discovered a treasure trove of materials highlighting the life of her great-uncle, Don Alejandro Rafelo, a man whose roots dated back to fourteenth-century France, and his ancestor, Grégor Rafelo.

Grégor Rafelo was born outside Paris in 1397. Like his father before him, he became a career military man who served as a special guard under the command of Gilles de Rais. Competent and brave, Grégor was assigned to Joan of Arc's guard and fought several battles at her side, bloodbath after bloodbath.

Following the relief of Orleans in 1429, the thirty-two-year-old Rafelo returned home to his family, distraught over all he'd seen. Months later he turned to religion, converting from Christianity to Albigenses.

The Albigenses (named after the town of Albi, in southern France) were an offshoot of the popular Manichaean dualistic system, which believed in the separate and independent existence of a god of good and a god of evil. To the Albigenses, the god of good was Christ, who, during his stay on earth, became an angel with a phantom body that allowed him the appearance of a man. The god of evil was Satan, who was responsible for imprisoning the soul in the human body.

By living a good life, the Albigenses believed a person could earn his soul's freedom after death. Failure to achieve righteousness during one's lifetime would result in the soul's being reborn again as another human being, or even an animal. Everything material, including wealth, food, and even the human body itself was considered evil and abhorrent. As such, the sect held that the traditional Christian Church, with its corrupt clergy and immense material wealth, were agents of the Devil.

The Christian Church, in turn, viewed the existence of the Albigenses as the single most important heresy of the Middle Ages. When peaceful attempts to convert the group failed, Pope Innocent III launched the Albigensian Crusade. By 1230, most of the Albigenses had been brutally suppressed, leaving much of southern France desolate over the next two centuries.

The secret sect of the Albigenses that Grégor Rafelo joined was divided into two groups, the simple believers and the "perfects," derived from the Greek word *katharoi* for "purified." Perfects were extremists who renounced all possessions and survived only on the donations provided by other members. They were forbidden to take oaths, to eat meat, eggs, or cheese, or to have sexual relations. Haunted by the blood on his hands, Grégor Rafelo sought "perfection," a decision which made life extremely difficult on his wife, Fanette, and their adolescent son, André.

Refusing to honor his father's orders of celibacy, fourteen-year-old André left home, seeking refuge with Grégor's former commanding officer, Gilles de Rais, a man whose own extensive wealth and power was in direct contrast to the beliefs of the boy's father.

The conversion of Grégor Rafelo to Albigenses was a slap in the face to the Church. Within a week of André's leaving home, his father was arrested by the Inquisition, under charges of heresy. He would spend the remaining thirteen years of his life in prison, the ideal environment for one seeking "perfection."

As for André Rafelo, his destiny would follow a different path.

Gilles de Rais had accompanied Joan of Arc to Reims for the consecration of Charles VII, where he had been appointed Marshal of France. He remained by her side until her capture, at which time he retired to his estate in Brittany.

Gilles was a wealthy man, having inherited extensive domains from both his father and maternal grandfather. In addition, he had recently married Catherine de Thouars, a rich heiress. So well off was Gilles that he earned a reputation for keeping a more lavish court than the king.

Young André was taken in by Gilles and made a herald, but the boy's personality grew on Gilles, who soon took the adolescent into his confidence.

In July of 1435, the Rais family secured a decree from the king that restrained Gilles from selling or mortgaging the rest of his properties. This financial setback turned the desperate Gilles to alchemy, eventually leading to his burgeoning interest in Satanism. Having lost much of his wealth, Gilles hoped to regain his riches through the knowledge and power of the Devil. Over the next five years, he and André would delve into witchcraft and the occult, worshiping Satan in ceremonies later termed the "Black Mass."

At Black Mass, the celebrants would don vestments similar to those of the Christian priests, except the chasuble had the addition of a goat's figure, an animal associated with the Devil. Other parodies of the Church included crosses suspended upside down, inversions of Christian prayers, a blessing with filthy water, animal sacrifices, and the use of a naked woman's abdomen as an altar. The Black Mass culminated in a ritualistic orgy, and occasionally—a human sacrifice.

It was André Rafelo, one of the cult's high priests, who introduced this new blasphemy into the ceremony.

In September of 1440, Gilles de Rais was arrested and brought to trial in Nantes. There he was condemned for heresy and the abduction, torture, and murder of more than 140 children.

André Rafelo fled France for the Harz Mountains of Germany. There, he established secret covens, which formalized the supernatural traditions of Devil worship, witchcraft, and the ways of the Black Sabbat. Years later, he would travel to Africa, where he would learn the secrets of eating from the skulls of the dead to steal their souls.

Rafelo would father twelve children by three wives and live to see the births of seven grandchildren and two great grandchildren. After his death, his clan's influence would spread overseas when his great grandson, Etienne Rafelo, set sail aboard a supply ship bound for New Spain (Mexico).

The history of the Central American people traces back long before the arrival of the first Europeans. The first "true" Mexicans were seminomadic tribes who first appeared in Mesoamerica around 4000 B.C. Eventually they settled and became farmers, breeding avocado, tomatoes, squash, and corn—a hybrid of wild grass.

Then, sometime around 1500 B.C, *He* arrived.

He was a long-faced Caucasian with flowing white beard and hair. Mesoamericans had never seen a white person before, let alone a bearded man (the Mayans being genetically incapable of growing facial hair). But the stranger was unique in other ways, for he possessed a wisdom far greater than anything the Indians had ever seen. The Caucasian elder quickly became their leader, and was soon revered as a god-king.

There are no records that tell us his name or his people's name, but the natives of this low-lying region along the Gulf of Mexico eventually became known as the Olmec, the mother culture of all Mesoamerica. Under their teacher's tutelage, the Olmec would unify the Gulf region, their achievements in astronomy, mathematics, and architecture influencing the Zapotec, Toltec, Mayan, and Aztec cultures that followed over the next two thousand years.

Almost overnight it seemed the jungle-dwelling Olmec went from being simple farmers to the architects of modern society. They established complex structures and extensive ceremonial centers. They were the first in Mesoamerica to record events. They originated the ancient ball game, and created great public works of art, which included the famous Olmec Heads—monolithic skulls fashioned from basalt, many of which weigh nearly thirty tons.

The bearded one's presence soon became known throughout the region. To the Maya and Toltec he was the great teacher, Kukulcán, to the Aztecs he was Quetzalcoatl, the Plumed Serpent. And though he promised his people he would one day return, the god-king's eventual departure around A.D. 1000 left Mesoamerica in utter disarray. Many peoples, like the Maya, turned to human sacrifice, their actions meant to appease Kukulcán and lure him back from the great beyond.

Five hundred years later, the first "official" Caucasians would make their way into Central America from Europe, bringing with them tyranny and death, and something more—

—the Devil.

Hernan Cortez was a Spaniard who had earned his reputation as both explorer and Conquistador. In 1519 the governor of Cuba, Diego de Velázquez, commissioned Cortez and his forces to invade and conquer Montezuma's Aztec empire. Armed with eleven ships and five hundred men, Cortez set sail for the Yucatán Peninsula, homeland of the Maya. Making his way north along the Gulf coastline, he founded the first Spanish settlement, *La Villa Rica de Vera Cruz* (modern-day Veracruz). As his men realized the daunting odds facing them, Cortez ordered his ships burned, fearing desertion. The vastly outnumbered Spanish would either win their battle or die trying.

What Cortez never suspected was that the outcome of the war would be decided by something else entirely—a case of mistaken identity.

When Montezuma, the Aztec leader, received word that a bearded white man had arrived from the sea, he believed

Cortez to be none other than Quetzalcoatl, returning as he had promised from the grave. Ignoring a series of foreboding omens from his *Nagual* (witches), the Aztec leader sent emissaries to escort the Spaniard and his army directly into the capital city of Tenochtitlán, a near-impregnable island in the middle of Lake Texcoco. The stunned Spanish, impressed by the size of the city and its numerous temples and canals, were treated like gods. Feigning friendship, Cortez waited until the right moment, then ordered his army to attack, the bloody slaughter becoming the opening blow of an all-out war that would last more than two years.

Cortez eventually secured Mesoamerica for Spain, but it would take far longer for the Spanish priests to "conquer" the peoples of Central America. To the Spanish, the Maya and Aztec were godless pagans who worshiped deities that could only be allies of the Devil. Kukulcán's codices (and their warnings of impending doom) were burned, his followers converted to Christianity—under penalty of torture.

In reality, the dichotomy between good and evil, God and the Devil was completely alien to Mesoamerican Indians. Before the Spanish invasion, the closest divine being comparable to Satan was *Tezcatilpoca,* considered to be the god of night and patron of witches. The "mirror that smokes" was the lord of sin and suffering and the inventor of fire, but he was not the Devil.

At least, not until the Spanish priests arrived.

To promulgate Christianity in Mesoamerica, the priests had to teach their "ignorant pupils" that the universe was divided into forces of good (God) and forces of evil (Satan). Any act deemed unacceptable was naturally considered evil. Evildoers thought to have conspired with the Devil were branded witches, and witchcraft in New Spain would not be tolerated.

The Holy Office of the Inquisition in New Spain was quickly established, and soon thereafter Mesoamerican tribal members were brought to trial and convicted of being witches.

By bringing the Devil and witchcraft to the forefront,

the Catholics inadvertently helped it to flourish. Secret societies formed among the conquered Mesoamericans, with the larger cities becoming centers of sex and sin. Satan (appearing in the form of a goat) played host to witch parties. Pacts were made with the Devil. Black magic was introduced and passed from one generation to the next.

Where there was once innocence, sorcery now thrived. Thanks to the invading white man, fear of the Devil had become a real thing.

Etienne Rafelo arrived in Mexico in the fall of 1533, his mission: To spread the seeds of the "dark forces" throughout the New World. His travels would lead him to Tecospa, a small Nahuatl Indian village situated across the mountains from Morelos. Here he would meet an Aztec leader named Motecuma, whose maternal ancestors were direct descendants of Quetzalcoatl, a member of the brotherhood of the Guardian.

Etienne would fall in love with Motecuma's oldest daughter, Quetzalli, an azure-eyed beauty who possessed the Guardian's Hunahpu bloodline. The couple would raise eight children in the southernmost part of the Valley of Mexico, a land the mighty Aztecs had once ruled.

Like her father, Quetzalli was a *Nagual* witch. Mesoamerican witches dated back a thousand years. They had counseled kings and could forecast events. It was said a *Nagual* could cause sickness by sucking the blood of his victim or by giving him the "evil eye." It was believed the more powerful witches could even capture a man's soul.

Twenty-seven generations after the Rafelo-Quetzalcoatl bloodline began, Don Alejandro Rafelo was born. Like his ancestor, André, Don Rafelo sought a different path.

The villagers of Morelos both despised and feared Don Rafelo. They said his *ojo* made him powerful, that his *K'az-al t'an-ob* (curses) caused serious and painful diseases.

Blessed with intelligence and a feverish lust for power,

Don Rafelo made it his life's calling to learn the truth behind the power of the *Nagual*. Unlike the superstitious locals, he knew the witches gained their insight—not from spells and incantations, but from their bloodline. The Olmec, Aztec, Toltec, and Maya had risen to power under the tutelage of two great *Nagual*, Kukulcán and Quetzalcoatl. Don Rafelo knew these men had sired dozens of children, and that his own family's spiritual abilities could be traced back to Quetzalcoatl. What Don Rafelo needed to increase the power of his lineage was a descendant of Kukulcán's bloodline.

He would find his genetic link in Cecilia Meztli, a Mayan woman whose maternal ancestors were raised in the city of Chichén Itzá, sired by the great Kukulcán himself.

Too old to have children, Don Rafelo selected his sister's son, Miguel Aurelia-Rafelo, to wed Cecilia. The *curanandero* warned the girl's family to stay away from Don Rafelo, but the Meztlis owed Don Rafelo money, and the arranged marriage would pay off the debt.

The azure blue–eyed Madelina Aurelia was born seventeen months later, and Don Rafelo had the minion he had long sought. The *Nagual* conspired against the infant's parents, intent on raising the child himself. Following a series of tragedies, the family secretly fled Morelos and headed for America.

Seventeen years later, Don Rafelo's prized apprentice died after giving birth to Lilith Eve Robinson.

Lilith finishes mowing the backyard lawn as Quenton returns home from church. Hearing him enter the house, she quickly positions the frayed lounge chair so it faces the sun, her heart racing. She removes her bikini top just as Don Rafelo had instructed, then lies back on the chair, rubbing oil over her exposed breasts, moaning just loud enough for her legal guardian to hear.

Quenton is in the bathroom urinating. Hearing the noise, he peeks between the curtains of the open window and stares at the topless teenager.

"Sweet Jesus . . ."

Over the years, Quenton Morehead had convinced himself that his molestation of Lilith had been a necessary part of her "exorcism." He had already asked Jesus for forgiveness, and if the Lord could forgive him, then surely Lilith would. Now in his late sixties, he had eased up on the child's "treatments," fearing the emboldened teenager might speak out against his acts.

But Quenton still had his needs, and the girl's budding adolescence gnawed at him, creating desires that even prayer cannot staunch. But this public display of nudity—this was something altogether different. The girl was teasing him, charging his insides with electricity.

Lilith moans louder as she slips her fingers beneath her bikini bottom and pleasures herself.

It is more than Quenton can handle. Leaving the bathroom, he heads outside.

Feeling his presence, Lilith opens her eyes. "Something you wanted?"

Quenton grabs her by the arm, dragging her to her feet. "You wanna be a bad girl? I'll show you what we do with bad girls—"

Lilith slips inside the nexus.

A moment later, Quenton Morehead finds himself on his back on the freshly mowed lawn, staring up at the blue heavens and his granddaughter's surreal azure eyes.

Lilith's fist blots out the view as it wallops his nose.

"Oww . . . God . . . damn you, you little whore!" Blood spurts from both nostrils.

"Whore? Whores get paid, Quenton."

"I have paid you! Fourteen years I've fed you and clothed you and kept a roof over your head. You owe me!"

Still straddling him, she fondles her breasts. "You want this, Quenton? Come and get it."

He reaches for her, but she hits him again, the furious, impossibly fast blow knocking loose his front teeth.

Lilith is on her feet, her bikini bottoms twirling around her index finger as she struts, naked, back into the house. "Be sure to put the lawn mower away before you come in."

Quenton rolls over, spitting out two bloody teeth. *Only thing I'm gonna do is beat the hell outta you, then do you 'til you walk funny.*

■■■■■■■■■■■■■■

16

■■■■■■■■■■■■■■

NOVEMBER 1, 2027
FEDERAL CORRECTIONAL INSTITUTE
MIAMI, FLORIDA

. . . nineteen . . . twenty . . . twenty-one . . ."

Eighty-two-year-old inmate Pierre Robert Borgia sucks air through his teeth, his face red, his muscles trembling as he completes his daily regimen of sit-ups.

". . . twenty-two . . . twenty-three . . . twenty-four . . ."

It has been nearly fifteen years since the former secretary of state was incarcerated for ordering the murder of Michael Gabriel.

". . . twenty-five . . . twenty-six . . . twenty-seven . . ."

Borgia has been a model prisoner. He has helped tutor inmates in a literacy program. He has led prayer groups on Sundays.

". . . twenty-eight . . . twenty-nine . . . thirty . . ."

Daily video-mail has kept him apprized of his family's efforts to reduce his sentence. He knows parole is just around the corner.

". . . thirty-one . . . thirty-two . . . thirty-three . . ."

Exercise has helped keep Borgia's blood pressure in check. Daily meditation has preserved his sanity.

The thought of revenge keeps him alive.

". . . thirty-four . . . thirty-five . . . thirty-six . . ."

Borgia's anger had once been directed solely at the son of his arch rival—a man who had assaulted him onstage three decades earlier, costing him his right eye.

With Michael Gabriel dead, Borgia's anger has been redirected at someone else.

". . . thirty-seven . . . thirty . . . eight . . . thirty . . . nine . . . forty!"

Borgia lies back on the cold linoleum floor of his four-by-seven-foot cell. He gazes at the projection of a tropical shoreline on his wall as he catches his breath.

"Computer . . . activate CNN."

The holographic ocean disappears, replaced by cinder block. The news broadcast begins a moment later.

"*. . . in the wake of Jordan Ann Katras's death late last week, former U.S. president Ennis Chaney was nominated earlier today as Secretary General of the United Nations Security Council.*"

"Ahhhh!" Borgia kicks the wall, Chaney's face distorting on his shoe.

"*In other news, the World Basketball Association has added two new European teams to its Eastern Conference . . .*"

"Computer, cease broadcast!"

The transmission ends.

Borgia's pulse races, his blood pressure soaring. He wheezes a deep breath, then lets it out slowly. Repeats the exercise until his pulse stops pounding in his ears, then gets on his hands and knees, resuming his workout.

"One . . . two . . . three . . . four . . ."

There is one person Borgia despises more than any other human being, one person whose very name causes his blood to boil, his ulcer to bleed . . .

". . . five . . . six . . . seven . . . eight . . ."

Parole is coming.

Pierre Borgia counts the days.

Longboat Key, Florida

2:35 P.M.

"Come on, Manny. Apply the formula, then figure out the answer!"

Immanuel Gabriel stares at his Vision-Station, a high-resolution curved computer monitor, five feet tall and six feet wide, that encompasses his entire forward field of vision. "I told you, Mr. Hopper, I can't do it."

"Sure you can," the tutor insists. "Watch and learn." Scott Hopper leans over the teen and types in an equation designed to calculate G forces and the speed of light. "There, I plugged in the values, now you do the math."

"Who cares about this stuff? I'm not interested in being an astronaut, I'm gonna play pro ball."

"Sure you are. Now just apply the damn formula so we can end the lesson."

"I'm ending it now."

"Sit down, please—"

"No. I want to shoot hoops before dinner."

"Not until you finish the rest of these problems. Your brother finished an hour ago, and he's doing quantum physics."

"Whoop-dee-do."

"Sit down!"

"Drop dead."

Hopper swallows his retort as Jacob enters the classroom. "Jacob, see if you can talk some sense into your brother; he won't listen to a damn thing I have to say."

The instructor walks out.

Immanuel kisses his middle finger, then flips it at Scott Hopper's back.

"I need to talk with you, Manny. I spoke with our father again."

"And I spoke with the Easter Bunny. He says they need you back at the Funny Farm—"

In a lightning maneuver, Jacob grabs his brother by his hips and hoists him clear off his feet.

"Let me go—"

"I've had it with you, Manny. You're way behind in your training and—"

Immanuel kicks his brother in the chest, the blow powerful enough to send both boys tumbling to the floor.

The dark-haired twin leaps to his feet. "I've had it with you, too, asshole. I've had it with your stupid delusions, and you always bossing me around. Most of all, I'm sick of living in this prison camp."

"It's for our own good. There are crazy people out there—"

"There's crazy people in here!" Immanuel picks up his chair in frustration and smashes it through the computer screen, sending shattered fragments flying in all directions.

"Stop! Do you have any idea how much that costs?"

"Doesn't cost me a damn thing." Immanuel reaches for another chair.

Jacob intercepts, grabbing him in a powerful wrestling hold. "Knock it off, Manny. I don't want to hurt you."

"Hurt me?" Tears of frustration flow from Immanuel's ebony eyes. "You're killing me."

"How am I killing you? Answer me!"

"Get off—"

Jacob releases him. "We live in paradise. You have everything you could ever want or need."

"Bullshit, What I need is freedom. I need friends my age. I'm tired of playing pick-up games with the guards. I want to compete on teams. And I want to meet some girls. Girls, Jake, as in the opposite sex, or did that Hunahpu gene take away your balls?"

"I have sexual desires, I even have a girlfriend."

"Yeah? Who? Rosie palm and her five sisters?"

"Her name's Lilith. We talk on . . . on the Internet. She wants to get together, but I can't."

"See, that's what I'm talking about. Go see her! Screw your brains out."

"It's not like that. I love her, which is why I have to break it off."

"Huh?"

"She's becoming a distraction."

"A distraction? From what?"

"You still don't get it, do you? You still refuse to acknowledge who we are, or what's at stake."

"Oh, God, here we go again—"

"Time's running out, Manny, we only have six more years."

Immanuel's eyes widen. "What happens in six years?"

Jacob shakes his head. Turns for the door.

"Hey, asshole, I said what happens in six years?"

"Just train, Manny. Train like your life depended upon it."

The azure-blue specks blaze at him from beyond the white mist of the nexus.

Jacob, I did it, I finally did it! Quenton tried to rape me, but this time, I slipped inside the nexus . . . I beat the crap out of him!

I'm glad.

You don't sound it.

Sorry.

It felt so good to hit him, I felt so powerful. It was even better than when I hurt those boys.

What boys?

Never mind.

Lilith, what boys?

Just some assholes I met at a party. They won't be bothering me anymore.

Lilith, you just can't go around beating people up.

Excuse me, but I'll do whatever I have to do to survive.

What're you saying? This doesn't sound at all like you.

It's the new me. Uncle Don is teaching me how to use my powers.

Uncle Don?

A distant relative who's come to visit.

Is he . . . Hunahpu?

Yes.

Jacob?

Lilith, I can't talk to you now. I . . . I need to speak with my father.

And I need to feel your arms around me.

I told you before, I can't see you now.

And I'm sick of these excuses. I need to nestle in your warmth. There's no warmth in my life, Jacob, just like there's no more warmth in your words. You've become cold and calculating, and I don't like it.

Sorry, but things are happening. I didn't ask for this life any more than you asked for yours.

Try taking your own advice and change things.

I'm going to. Starting now.

Meaning what?

Meaning I can't see you. Not outside the nexus. Not within.

I thought you loved me?

I do . . . but I can't communicate with you while you're in contact with another Hunaphu.

He's my uncle.

It doesn't matter. My destiny . . . I can't take a chance.

To hell with that stupid Mayan stuff, it's our destiny to be together.

It's not stupid. My father warned me—

To hell with your father, your father's dead!

Don't say that.

Think, Jacob. Necromancers like us can only speak with the dead.

You're wrong.

Don't leave me, Jacob! You're all I have!

Look, I don't wish to hurt you, but things are happening . . . there are more important things at stake.

What's more important than love?

Lilith—

Answer me! What's more important than love?

I'm sorry.

Jacob shudders as Lilith's venomous energy lashes out at him.

You go to Hell, Jacob Gabriel! You go straight to Hell!

Lilith—

The sudden emptiness of the nexus closes in upon him.

Hell. Exactly where I'm headed.

Father, I need you!

I'm here, Jacob. Tell me what's wrong?

I feel so lost. Manny's still not Hunahpu, at least he's not like me.

Give him time.

I don't know. He wants a normal life.

In the end, Manny will fulfill his destiny.

He hates his calling, he just wants to live his life. He wants to be in love.

What did you tell him?

I told him love is a distraction, that it makes men weak. You don't agree?

Jacob, love is the most powerful force in the universe. The love I feel for your mother has kept me from giving in. It was your love for me that reached out and saved me.

You're far from saved. When Immanuel and I find you and rescue you, then you'll be saved. Until then, I don't have time for the nonsense of love. At least not now.

You found a girl, didn't you? Someone special.

Yes.

And you love her?

Sometimes I can't stop thinking about her.

I was the same way with your mother. At times, my love for her seemed to consume my every waking moment.

Exactly why I had to break it off. She was disfocusing me, interfering with my training.

Jacob—

Why prolong the hurt? In six years, I'm out of here, right? You of all people should understand why I did what I did. After all you've told me about the loop in space-time, about our failure during our first attempt—

Maybe I was wrong to allow this communication.

You're preparing me for what lies ahead.

Or condemning you to it. If it was only my existence at stake, I would have given in long ago, I would never have allowed you to speak with me.

It's okay.

It's not okay! It infuriates me! Why must my family suffer so? Why must my sons and their mother have to go through this hell?

Dad, calm down . . . the Abomination might register your anger.

Let it, let God feel it, too! Do you hear me, God? I know you're out there listening. What kind of God allows good people to suffer so? Why does evil often go unpunished? Where's the justice in your universe?

Dad—

I hate you, God! Do you hear me? I hate you as much as I hate myself!

Jesus, Dad, you're scaring me! Dad?

Dad?

I'm . . . I'm sorry, Jacob. I'm sorry for everything. If I had been stronger . . . if I'd been wiser, I would never have allowed the Guardian to manipulate and deceive me the way they did.

What? The Guardian deceived you? What did they do?! Father, tell me, I need to know.

I'm sorry . . . it's so hard to focus through the rage. It blinds me . . . scatters my thoughts.

Then take it slow. Go back to your journey, to Bill Raby's journey. That was his name, right? The space traveler who had escaped the coming holocaust.

Bill Raby . . . yes . . . yes, I had become Bill Raby.

And the transport. Tell me what happened after you crash-landed on Xibalba.

I remember now. I remember thinking I must've blacked out, because when I awoke, the cabin was pitch-dark and people were screaming.

Why were they screaming?

Our landing . . . the impact caused a flash fire. It must've been a bad one. A dozen colonists were dead, dozens more injured.

But you were okay?

No, I don't think so. Something had happened, but not to Bill, to Michael Gabriel. All my thoughts, all of my memories as Michael were gone. From that point on, I was Bill Raby, marine geneticist, marooned on an alien world. It was as if Mick had never existed.

Okay, okay, so what happened then? Try to remember.

We were surrounded by darkness, still fumbling within the powerless cabin, when we heard scratching sounds outside the ship. Pressing my face to the viewport, I scanned the terrain, looking for the source.

The sun had set hours ago. Unable to see through the darkness, I located a pair of night-vision scanners and placed them over my eyes. The lenses cut through the night, turning everything olive green . . . revealing movement outside.

There were billions of them—huge beetles—a foot and a half in length, maybe twenty to forty pounds, God only knows what the gravity was like on this desolate world. They were scurrying up through the volcanic fissures by the hundreds of thousands, their grotesque black shell-encased bodies marked by occasional flashes of luminescence that set off the night like tiny strobe lights. My first thought after I swallowed back the bile of terror was communication . . . that the

lights were a form of alien language, sort of like the fireflies back on Earth, only far more intelligent. But as they piled upon one another, rising up the viewport glass to test its thickness with their tripod-shaped horns and sickle claws, I knew these beings were more like the horrible hurdes of army ants that devastate Africa, the ones that operate as a single collective, striping away the flesh and bones and vegetation of everything that stands in their path.

We watched, helpless and frightened, as they scampered over the moss-covered terrain in ebony waves. They covered the ship, and for several terrifying hours, all of us feared they might eat through the steel plates.

After a tense night, the first rays of dawn sent them fleeing back to their underground dwellings.

When it became apparent that the swarm would not venture into the daylight, our shuttle leaders organized an exploratory team. Several men approached and asked me to join them outside.

Forty minutes later, a dozen of us, all dressed in space suits, stepped out from the shuttle's airlock to join leaders and scientists from the other eleven vessels. Armed with measuring devices, we probed the land and air.

The more we learned, the more fearful we became.

The planet's atmosphere contained high levels of carbon dioxide, along with smaller amounts of carbon monoxide, methane, and ammonia. Like Mars, the scarlet sky was devoid of an ozone layer, but unlike the Red Planet back in our end of the galaxy, there was no shelter on this desolate world other than our broken vessels, and no raw materials to access to gain a foothold.

After three hours, our teams returned to our respective vessels, the reality of our situation too overwhelming to bear. We were marooned on a world lacking fresh water, vegetation, and breathable air. There was no ozone layer to protect us from the alien sun's ultraviolet rays, and in five months, our ship's supplies would run out . . . assuming the nocturnal scavengers did not devour us first.

Two million years ago, our ancestors had managed to survive their own harsh beginnings in the jungles of East Africa. The first humans had migrated into new lands and faced life-threatening challenges. They had sought shelter in caves, and crafted tools to hunt with. They had learned how to harness fire and to farm, and had built thriving civilizations. Ever the explorer, man had eventually constructed great vessels, crossing dangerous oceans in order to satisfy both his need to improve his lot in life and his inquisitiveness.

And now, in a sense, so had we.

As Michael Gabriel, I had once remote-viewed a member of Christopher Columbus's crew. Sharing Bill Raby's consciousness, I could finally experience what these brave explorers must have felt as their voyage across the Atlantic grew more desperate.

The hopelessness.

The fear.

The constant bickering.

Twelve Earth ships had crash-landed in a toxic environment. Twelve ships possessing a limited supply of air, food, and water.

Twelve ships. Six hundred-plus opinions.

Long before we had launched from Earth, Mars Colony and its ten thousand chosen inhabitants had been preorganized into five districts. We had appointed representatives and even a newly elected president. The multiple party system had been tabled for the moment, but democracy would rule the Red Planet just as it had shaped America, with a new Constitution and a Bill of Rights.

None of that had any bearing on our present dilemma. We were castaways, forever separated from the collective. In space, the crew had called the shots, but now the ships were dead, and anarchy ruled the day.

If we had been a colony of ants, we'd have been working side by side before that second dawn. If we had been a beehive, there would have been no question of authority.

But we were modern man, cursed with ego, full of self. So before we could begin searching for food and fresh water, before we could start designing shelters, before we could see to our most basic needs . . . first, we had to decide who was in charge.

Imagine twelve cramped space vehicles filled with hundreds of emotionally crazed passengers and a limited number of atmospheric suits. It took three hours of negotiations on the ship-to-ship communicators just to determine where the first council meeting would be held and who would attend.

Atmospheric scientists wanted to be heard. So did the geologists, horticulturists, medical staff, engineers, architects . . . in fact, everyone wanted to voice an opinion. It was an endless gaggle of babble, compounded by the hopelessness of our situation.

Finally, one man rose above the fray to bring order to the chaos . . . the only man who could.

Devlin Mabus.

Mabus? Father, was he related to Peter Mabus, the billionaire?

He was his grandson. Devlin's company, MTI, had financed a third of the Mars Colony. His team had selected more than half of the survivors on our space vehicles. He had already been appointed to the president's new cabinet as vice president and was easily the highest-ranking Mars official present among us.

More important, Devlin had boarded his private shuttle with two dozen heavily armed bodyguards, all loyal to the influential billionaire and his poisonous mother.

Devlin decided each ship would elect three representatives to serve as liaisons to communicate to the newly formed Council, over which he would preside. This hierarchy worked well enough . . . until the day one representative openly voiced his disagreement, causing a rift among the leadership. Devlin took it all in stride, then had the dissenter relocated to his own ship so that the two could "come to a political resolution on behalf of the colony."

The dissenter's opinions changed. Two days later, he went for a "stroll."

The "stroll" was a walk outside the shuttle without an environmental suit.

The "stroll" was suicide.

This Devlin sounds an awful lot like his grandfather.

I have no doubt he was even worse, having met his mother, a woman who could manipulate a small nation with her beauty, and crush them in her evil embrace. She was as alluring and as deadly as a Venus flytrap, and she was Devlin's best friend and only confidant. The two of them made quite the pair, and yet, as much as I feared them, our colony survived on the virtue of their combined strength.

With each passing day, our situation grew more hopeless. Exploration teams would leave every dawn in search of food and water, but could never venture too far, forced to return before the giant beetles made their nightly appearance.

Traps were set to capture a few specimens. We learned the insects were blind, existing on microbes found within the volcanic rock and moss.

Unfortunately, the alien insects were not edible.

As hope faded, the suicide walks increased. Sometimes it was an individual, sometimes an entire family. Depression spread like the plague. A limited supply of environmental suits kept most civilians confined to their ships, increasing our feelings of isolation.

Still, our colony was blessed with some of the best minds our species had to offer. Using spare parts, engineers were able to upgrade an unmanned aerovehicle one of the children had brought on board. Each morning our drone scout would venture forth like Noah's dove, searching for salvation.

And then, on the afternoon of our forty-third day on the planet, we found it . . .

■■■■■■■■■■■■■■■■

17

■■■■■■■■■■■■■■■

The light fades, and with it all my fear
The atmosphere's electric, I can feel her near,
Her breath on my skin, her touch on my soul,
The spell has been cast, she has total control

The succubus, she comes to me,
Visits in the night;
Wringing the love out of me,
Our joined souls ignite

—ODE TO THE SUCCUBUS

MAX RAEL, HISTORY OF GUNS

NOVEMBER 2, 2027
BELLE GLADE, FLORIDA

Quenton Morehead is alone with Lilith in his one-room church, the two of them repainting the pews. For the last two days he has kept clear of the girl, her sudden confidence and exhibitionism shocking the minister while turning him on.

A new approach was needed, one that played up to his granddaughter's newfound persona.

"Lilith, have we spoken before about the Succubus?"

"Succubus? No, you never mentioned it." Feeling his eyes upon her, she allows her breasts to jiggle beneath the skintight top as she vigorously strokes the paintbrush.

Quenton fights the urge to drag her onto the dais and rape her. "The Bible tells us that the Succubus was a female demon who visited men, seducing them while they slept."

"And why should I be interested in this Succubus?"

"For one thing, her name was Lilith, and she was very powerful."

Lilith stops painting. Don Rafelo had never spoken of this. "Tell me about her."

"Lilith was Adam's first wife, created out of the earth long before Eve came 'round. The Bible says the Succubus was a tantalizing beauty, like yourself, who refused to submit herself sexually to Adam."

"You're not equating yourself with Adam?"

"The point is, God created Lilith to pleasure Adam, but she resisted her calling. She left the garden and eventually became pregnant. It was Lilith's daughters who mated with Cain and Abel."

"Good for her."

"The Succubus was powerful."

Lilith looks up. "How so?"

"She'd approach her victims under the cloak of night as a wind demon, using sex to control their will. The Succubus could control even the strongest of men. It is said that any man who fell for the Succubus never awakened from her spell."

Lilith allows one of the overall straps to slide off her shoulder.

Quenton moves closer, taking the bait.

The teen's cocoa skin crawls with his approach. "I can smell the stench of your lust, Quenton. Try something again, and I'll hurt you even worse."

"You owe me. I could have sent you away long ago, but I didn't."

"I wish you had. Maybe I wouldn't curse my own existence."

"Just as I curse the day my wife and I took your mother into our home." He inches nearer. "See, I know who you are. You can't fool me any longer."

"And who am I?"

"Lucifer's mistress—the Succubus-Lilith, reincarnate."

"Does that make you afraid, Quenton, or excited?"

"Hush your mouth, heathen."

"I'm the heathen?" She turns to face him. "How dare you—you, who spent so much time violating my innocence."

"What I did, I did to exorcise the Devil."

"And who is the Devil to threaten a man of God, a man of virtue? Why should you fear this fallen angel, Reverend Hypocrite? Ah, maybe it's not fear, but jealousy that drives your hatred, after all, Lucifer *is* the angel of pleasure."

Quenton stares at the girl, his body quivering.

"Would you like pleasure, Quenton?"

Saliva drools from his open mouth.

"Answer me, Reverend Sin. Would you like to screw me?"

"Yes!" He lunges for her, but she raises her fists, keeping him at bay.

Quenton bites his lower lip. "Why do you tease me?"

"There's a price that comes with pleasure. What is the price of the Succubus-Lilith? Say it, Reverend Slave."

His eyes widen, his game suddenly turning against him.

"Say it!"

"My will?"

"Exactly." She reaches for his hand. Licks his fingertips, then sucks on a digit, getting him even more aroused. "Say my name."

"Lilith."

"Who am I?"

"The . . . the Succubus."

Her moistened fingers casually brush the bulge in his trousers.

He drops his paintbrush and reaches for her.

"No!" She pushes him away. "Who's in control?"

"You are."

"That's right, slave, I am in control. No more exorcisms, no more speeches about Jesus and God. I hate God. God deserted me the night he stole my mother from me and left me with the likes of you! God sat back and watched as you raped me and let you fuck my soul. God made me your victim. Now the dark forces empower me, just as I empower you!"

Her azure eyes blaze as she raises her voice, "Say . . . my . . . name!"

"Lilith."

"Who am I?"

Tears roll down his cheeks. "God help me . . ."

"God cannot help you, Quenton. God is a spectator in the game of life. God watches from his golden perch while innocent children are molested by monsters like you. Only I can help you, now, because only I can give you what you need." She reaches for his trousers and unbuckles them, getting an immediate response.

"Yes . . . please—"

"Stop whining and lie down."

Panting like an animal, he drops to the wooden floor, lying spread-eagle on his back.

"These are my terms, Quenton. Tonight I will pleasure you. Tomorrow, you will go to your bank and withdraw all of your assets, every penny. Then you'll change your will so that I am the sole benefactor."

"Why?"

"Because I wish it, and because you need to please me if you want me tomorrow night, and the next night, and the next." She pulls off her shirt and licks her nipples. "Do you want me?"

"Yes!"

"And how will you please me?"

"By going to the bank!"

Lilith steps out of her overalls and stands over the minister in her underwear. For the first time in her life, she feels safe, in total control. "Remove your boxers, *slave*."

"Yes, Succubus!" Quenton yanks off the undergarment, exposing himself.

Lilith stares at his sex, now fully aroused. "Who am I?"

"The Succubus!"

"Listen to me carefully, slave. Exquisite pleasure shall be yours, but only on my terms. I will come to you if and when I please, but only when I please, is that understood?"

"Yes, Succubus, yes!"

"You will never come to me unless I give you permission. You will never touch me again or come home drunk. Is that understood?"

"Yes, Succubus."

"From now on, I am in control. I will sleep in your bed, and you will sleep on the sofa. You will no longer tell me stories about Jesus and God. The Succubus is sick of hearing about Jesus and God."

"Of course, Succubus."

"The Succubus hates God, do you understand. Say it with me, I . . . hate . . . God."

Quenton hesitates.

Lilith tears off her panties and fingers herself. "This *is* what you want, isn't it, slave?"

"Oh, God, yes!"

"We hate God, don't we, Quenton?" She touches herself again. "Say it!"

"We . . . hate God."

"Again!"

"We hate God!"

Lilith squats over her delirious guardian. "Keep your hands at your sides. Don't attempt to touch me, don't even move a muscle. I will touch you."

"Of course, Succubus, anything you want!"

A child's face appears at the church door.

"Go away, Brandy, we don't need you anymore. The Succubus needs no one!"

The delusion fades into the night.

"Go away? Who are you speaking to, Succubus?"

"Shut up, fool." She lowers herself onto Quenton, guiding him inside her.

Quenton closes his eyes, moaning in delight.

Cold, emotionless, feeling nothing, Lilith grinds her pelvis into her guardian as she stares at the crucifix mounted behind the pulpit.

Are you watching me, Jesus? Can you hear me, Jacob? Are you two assholes enjoying what you've created?

Longboat Key, Florida

Jacob swoons in his trance, his mind ignoring Lilith's haunting cry as he focuses upon his father's words. *I'm listening, Father. What did the drone find?*

Something immense, an artificially created platform hovering twelve hundred feet above the volcanic terrain . . . so vast it blotted out the alien sky for thousands of square miles. Protruding from the underside of this monstrous structure were countless rows of silo-sized coiled iron objects, hanging down like a crop of metallic stalactites. The drone's sensor readings warned us of the presence of an intense magnetic field emanating from these million-strong objects. Had our UAV crossed into the field, it would not have survived the scrambling of its electronics.

We instructed the drone to fly higher, hoping to glimpse a topside view of this incredible antigravitational platform. What we saw, Jacob . . . my thoughts, mere words—they simply do no justice.

Situated atop this Texas-sized floating structure were copper-tinted domes—thousands of them—each roof ten times the girth of the old New Orleans Superdome, yet all interconnecting, like the bottom of a carton of eggs.

As we watched, a section of one of the domes retracted, allowing our drone to enter. Inside was a city, the scope of which could only be conceived in fantasy.

Imagine Manhattan, only one hundred thousand

years in the future, the entire island raised in the sky and encapsulated. Imagine majestic silicon dwellings— so tall they would have dwarfed Chicago's Sears Tower. Imagine interconnecting walkways and levitating pavilions—all woven into the dazzling skyline like latticework, and lush, tropical gardens and azure lagoons. There were rivers and twisting brooks, and cascading waterfalls, and farther along the outskirts, what appeared to be floating agricultural pods.

It was Shangri-La and Eden rolled into one, a beehive of intellect that, on an evolutionary scale, dwarfed us on a scale that we dwarfed the Neanderthals.

The technology required to build this domain was simply too overwhelming to conceive, and yet . . . it was deserted, not a single sign of life.

Who had built this magnificent floating habitat? Why had they abandoned it? Were they beings like us? Would they return?

We must have felt like the first Spanish explorers who happened upon Chichén Itzá after the Mayans deserted the city.

With us, however, these questions were quickly forgotten after the drone's atmospheric readings detected air within the domed city. Higher in oxygen content than Earth's, void of all our chemical pollutants, it was nevertheless quite breathable.

To our dying community, we had discovered an oasis, delivered by God Himself, and we were determined to occupy it.

First, of course, we had to get there.

The structure's closest border was 422 miles southeast of our crash site. Since the existence of the planet's nocturnal insects made traveling by foot out of the question, our only hope was to repair as many of our damaged spaceships for a limited flight before our air and water supplies ran out.

Hope. How long had it been since any of us dared utter the word?

It took us ninety-six days to make three of our twelve shuttles operable enough for a vertical takeoff and restricted flight plan. During that time, we continued sending drones into the city, establishing maps, identifying key landmarks, puzzling over a myriad of dwellings.

Never did we come across a life-form.

The day of our departure finally arrived. Tossing out all personal luggage and nonessential items, we crammed our 572 survivors on board the three ships and flew to the Promised Land.

For twenty minutes, our vessel pitched wildly in the dense atmosphere, bringing nausea to all but our most seasoned astronauts. And then we passed over the copper domes and entered the alien domain.

What an astounding site.

As Bill Raby—I felt reborn . . . invigorated, excited to be alive.

If only I knew what lay ahead . . .

Hell hath no fury like a woman scorned . . .

NOVEMBER 4, 2027
BELLE GLADE, FLORIDA

For fourteen years Lilith Robinson had been a victim, her life a constant struggle to maintain a degree of sanity in an insane environment. Jacob had been her rudder, her strength in a stormy sea.

And now he had abandoned her.

When the Reverend Morehead accused his granddaughter of being a Succubus, he unwittingly supplied Lilith with a new compass—a persona her schizophrenia could mold like clay.

The Succubus was not a victim. The Succubus was powerful.

For the first time in her life, Lilith's miserable existence was beginning to make sense. While God and His followers had shunned her, Lucifer had reached out to protect her. Lucifer had plans for her future, and although she had no idea what those plans were, she felt confident that her new companion, Don Rafelo, would guide her down the dark path to her destiny.

Lilith enters her uncle's hotel room, tossing her book bag on the floor.

Don Rafelo is lying on one of the double beds, naked beneath a silk robe.

"Everyone at school is talking about the missing boys."

"Have they questioned you?"

"The police asked me if I'd seen them. I told them I kicked the basketball into the bushes and ran home."

"Good."

"When do we leave for Mexico?"

"Soon. Are you familiar with the *Dia de los Muertos*, the Day of the Dead?"

"I read something about it in school once."

"*La Muerte*—Death—is a fixture in Mexican society. During the first days of each November, the spirits of the dead pay a holiday visit home. Death has always held a special place in our ancient rituals. Among the Aztecs, it was considered a blessing to die in childbirth, in battle, or in human sacrifice, all of which assured the victim a desirable destination in the afterlife. Are you afraid to die, Lilith?"

"There are worse things than death. I want to know more about the Succubus."

"The Succubus is your alter ego. You are the reincarnation of Lilith, the Demon Queen—Queen of the Succubi. You were originally created by God to be a subservient wife to Adam. Born from filth but independent of will, you refused to be anything but equal. When Adam became aroused you refused his sexual advances and fled Eden on the wind to pursue erotica with God's fallen angels. By the Red Sea you spawned a family of demons called the Lilim. Three of God's angels attempted to force you to return to Eden, but you refused. As punishment, the angels butchered your children."

"What did I do?"

"You swore revenge. Yahweh's angels were able to protect the mothers and their children from you, but not the men. And so you seduced them while they slept, precipitating nocturnal emissions. The Talmud warned men not to sleep in a house as the sole occupant for fear of your presence. When you are reborn, you will possess the ability to control the will of men and deplete their life force."

"How shall I be reborn?"

"Not far from the village of Bolonchen is a cavern, part of an underground network of passages known as *Grutas de Xtacumbilxunaan,* the Caves of the Hidden Woman."

"I read about this place in your papers. What's inside the cave?"

"Immense power . . . a power that will ignite your bloodline and give you the gift of sight. But be warned: If you are not strong, the energy will cause you to go insane."

Lilith stares hard at the old man. "Quenton tells me my mother was insane."

"Or perhaps he drove her to insanity? It matters not. You are stronger than she ever was, and your master, Lucifer, will protect you."

"Quenton preached that God would protect me if I accepted Him into my life."

"Who can accept such a vengeful God into their heart? A God who coexists with death camps, who infects our species with disease, who is worshiped as being all-powerful yet somehow remains indifferent throughout our suffering? Did God help you when Quenton was abusing you?"

"No."

"We of the left-hand path refuse to grovel before deities of crosses in hopes of gaining favor with such a God. Instead, we choose to rise above the ignorant fray and stare into His eyes. We revel in our humanity and take full responsibility for our actions. We seek out Lucifer, not to worship him, but to work side by side with him and his demons. God may have given us our sexual organs, but it was Lucifer who made us aware of them. He allowed us to see, to explore, to indulge our most carnal instincts so that we could flourish."

"And what of good and evil?"

"A useless concept, taught by self-serving priests—hypocrites—like your Quenton, who seek to gain earthly pleasures by invoking God's name to create fear. If to do good is to serve God, then it is a waste of time. Evil is the path to power. We of the left-hand path refuse to live in fear. We feel love and compassion because we are human, but we follow a dark path, one that harbors a hidden force in nature, leading us into a world most men refuse to understand."

"Quenton never loved me. Jacob loved me, but his mother and that old woman refused to allow us to be together."

"Old woman? Tell me about this old woman."

Longboat Key, Florida

3:12 P.M.

The Boeing Canard Dragonfly, with its sleek hull, rotor wing, and fixed forward and aft stabilizers, is a cross between an airplane and helicopter. While in "helicopter mode" the aircraft is capable of vertical takeoffs, hovering, and landing. In "airplane mode" the rotor wing locks into a stationary position and its jet engines kick in, propelling the craft at cruising speeds.

Dominique greets Ennis Chaney as he steps down from the airship, his dour expression speaking volumes.

"What's wrong?"

"Inside." The former president leads her inside the main house. "Sorry. Too many listening devices buzzing around these days."

"You look exhausted."

"I'm getting old, and there are still too many windmills to fight before I die. Where are the boys?"

"Manny's in the weight room, Jake's meditating. Now talk to me."

"GOLDEN FLEECE has lost patience. They want access to the twins, or they'll close down your compound."

"Bastards. Can they do that?"

"Unfortunately, they do whatever they want. Today, GOLDEN FLEECE is asking. Tomorrow they'll be telling. These guys don't take no for an answer."

"To hell with them. We'll leave."

"Where will you go? No matter where, eventually they'll find you."

"Shit." She sits on the edge of the stone coffee table, pinching tension from her brows. "Manny will run. Jake might be into all this MAJESTIC mumbo jumbo, but Manny hates it."

"I know."

"Did you know Dr. Stechman's treating him for depression?"

"He'll have to deal with it as best he can."

"Screw you, Ennis! This is my son's life we're talking about."

"I'm not happy about this either."

She grabs her car keys and sandals.

"Dominique, wait, where are you going?"

"For a drive. Want to arrest me?" She exits through the garage, slamming the door behind her.

Chaney hears the SUV hydrogen fuel cell whine to life, its wheels squealing in protest as Dominique accelerates down the driveway.

Let her go, she needs to blow off some steam.

The former president hobbles over to the refrigerator and grabs a bottled water. Changes his mind. Searches the liquor cabinet. Pours himself a shot of whiskey.

"My mother's right. Manny can't take much more of this isolation."

Chaney looks up as Jacob enters the kitchen. "I'm not the one calling the shots, kid. Not anymore."

Jacob nods. "I think it's time I started calling the shots."

St. Augustine, Florida

It is dark by the time Dominique parks her car in front of Evelyn Strongin's home. The drive has done little to ease her frayed nerves. What she needs now is advice.

Dominique walks up the old redbrick path to the entrance. Holds her palm to the security keypad.

Surgically implanted in Dominique's palm is a microchip identification device, no larger than a grain of rice. Recognizing her "key," the electronic bolt unlocks.

Dominique enters the home. Sees the turned-over palm plant and magazine rack. Feels her skin tingling. "Evelyn?"

Evelyn's library door is closed. Dominique creeps closer and listens. Hears the gurgling sound. Flexes her right biceps, activating the pain-cannon's neurological trigger.

Dominique kicks the door open. "Evelyn! Oh my God—"

The dead woman's face is purple, her limp, broken figure swaying from a makeshift noose tied to the overhead ceiling fan.

19

November 2, 2027
Miami, FL. (AP Internet Wire)

Former Secretary of State Pierre Robert Borgia was released today from a federal penitentiary in Miami after serving nearly fifteen years. Once considered a strong Republican candidate for president, Borgia was convicted of conspiracy to commit murder when he ordered the death of Michael Gabriel, the incarcerated mental patient who mysteriously died after helping prevent a nuclear holocaust back in December of 2012. "I'm an innocent man who served his country and was wrongly accused," Borgia told reporters moments after his release. "All I want now is to live out what few days I have in peace."

NOVEMBER 4, 2027
MABUS MANSION
MANALAPAN, FLORIDA
4:17 P.M.

Pierre Borgia stares at his reflection in the bathroom smart glass. Prison life has trimmed forty pounds from his once stocky physique. His face is noticeably leaner, almost gaunt, his head cleanly shaven to hide the gray. The bandage over his right eye socket is new, the result of a recent inmate attack during his last month in the federal penitentiary.

"We should get that eye looked at," says Lucien Mabus,

the teen entering from the bedroom. "Once the swelling's down, we'll fit you with one of those new prosthetics."

"Waste of time and money. My life's over." Borgia turns on the faucet. Washes his face.

"Don't say that. My father always said the party needs you."

"Where the hell was the party when Chaney had me carted off like a goddam animal? That nigger's got the UN marching to the beat of his goddam drum. He's also the one who killed your father."

The nineteen-year-old nods. "Yeah. What're we gonna do about that?"

"I have a few ideas. Get dressed, kid, I'll meet you downstairs."

Borgia reaches for a sensory toothbrush. Brushes his teeth. On cue, a medical chart appears on the smart-glass mirror directly in front of him.

TEMPERATURE:	98.6
HEART RATE:	118
BLOOD PRESSURE	158/94
CHOLESTEROL	343
ELECTROLYTES	NORMAL
2 CAVITIES PRESENT	
GINGIVITIS IN STAGE	2

BLOOD PRESSURE AND CHOLESTEROL ARE HIGH.
ANALYSIS OF SALIVA INDICATES A BLEEDING ULCER. SEEK
MEDICAL ATTENTION IMMEDIATELY. HAVE A NICE DAY.

"Damn know-it-all computers." Borgia dries his face, then reexamines the eye patch in the bathroom mirror.

Longboat Key, Florida

4:17 P.M.

Jacob stares wide-eyed into the bathroom's smart-glass mirror, his reflection dissipating as his mind hitches a ride aboard another person's wavelength.

Gaunt face.

Shaved head.

Eye patch . . . covering a wound created twenty-seven years ago by his own father.

It's Borgia . . . I'm remote-viewing Pierre Borgia!

The session ends as abruptly as it had begun.

Jacob blinks hard at the reflection of his own tan face and snow-white hair.

You're up to something, Borgia. I can taste your anger . . . the restlessness of your soul.

Belle Glade, Florida

6:40 P.M.

The Orion Suburban convertible rolls to a stop in front of Quenton's home, its batteries nearly depleted. Lilith nods good-bye to her uncle, then heads for the front door.

The reverend is waiting for her inside. He is wearing a bathrobe, boxer shorts, and black socks. "Why did you steal my car?"

"A friend needed it. Besides, technically it's my car now. Did you take care of everything at the bank?"

Quenton holds up the manila envelope. "Everything's here, all signed and sealed, but you don't get nuthin', least not until I die."

"Give me the papers."

"No. The papers go back to my attorney's office tomorrow morning. As long as you please me, the Last Will and

Testament stays unchanged." Quenton's eyes gleam. "I want it every night. From now on, you're my private whore."

A twinge of panic. *The Succubus is not a whore. The Succubus is powerful. The Succubus controls—*

"Take off your clothes, whore."

Lilith looks up at Quenton, pulling him in with her smile. "Okay. You want a private whore, you got it. But first, let's make sure you're up to the task." She reaches into her pocket and removes the three pills. "Chew these up real good. These pills will help you last all night long."

He does as told, chewing and swallowing the tablets. "Get undressed, 'ho. You owe me for the last seven years."

Longboat Key, Florida

7:22 P.M.

Go on, Father, finish your story. Tell me what happened after your shuttles reached the domed city on the alien world.

A section of the dome receded, allowing us to enter, just as it had for our drone scout. Once inside, an invisible force field, perhaps a tractor beam, steadied our three pitching vessels, guiding them to a landing pad located atop one of the twelve-thousand-foot-high dwellings.

We filed out of our vessels and breathed the alien air. We were so relieved to be saved that we literally stood upon the roof of that tower and cheered. We joined hands and thanked God in prayer. And then we realized we were stuck.

Stuck?

Twelve thousand feet above ground level. The only access point we could find to enter the interior of the dome-scraper was an octagonal door, which appeared to be composed of an incredibly thin yet impenetrable nanocarbon fiber. There was no handle or keypad, no clues for entry.

The sun set, and we were still marooned on the roof. Nightfall arrived, and for the first time, we gazed upon that alien sky, it was simply breathtaking to behold. The planet's large moon shone bright yellow, the smaller potato-shaped satellite appearing as a fast-moving violet speck. In the distance was a nebula and a bright blue star.

We spent two long days atop that dwelling, waiting impatiently for our engineers to fashion devices to rappel us down the face of the tower. A harrowing descent, and we were finally on the ground.

Neanderthal man had arrived in New Manhattan.

The urban landscape integrated tropical foliage and artificial waterways into its design. The humidity was heavy at ground level, the air cool. Close by was a stream, and I remember feeling pleased that our scientists were already busy testing its silvery-tinged waters.

To our dismay, the liquid contained microscopic traces of some exotic elements. Was the water toxic? We couldn't be sure, but tests using our few surviving lab mice showed it as potable . . . at least in the short term.

Water is life. Our shuttles had two more months of food but only a few days' supply of water. If this alien source was even semicompatible with our bodies, then what choice did we have but to drink it?

So now we had air and water, fertile soil to plant our crops, and a dome above our heads that shielded us from the deadly ultraviolet rays of the alien sun. But we still could not access any of the dwellings.

Wild rumors spread that an alien race was harbored inside, waiting to slaughter us as we slept. Others, like me, believed the city had been abandoned long ago and that we only lacked the necessary knowledge to access the habitat.

And so, at the foot of these mammoth, futuristic structures, we cut down trees and fashioned log cabins.

Planted our crops and set up our science labs. Erected schools and hospitals, a courthouse and a house of worship. There was a peace and sense of well-being on our new home world that never existed on the old. We were one people—a tribe of survivors. There would be no haves and have-nots. Equality ruled the day.

At least, for the moment.

We voted, naming our growing community New Eden. In honor of our leader, Devlin Mabus, his mother was given the privilege of choosing a name for our planet. To our surprise, she selected an old Mayan name, a name derived from the Creation Myth recorded in the *Popol Vuh*.

Xibalba.

Then Xibalba *is really a planet, not an Underworld? And how am I to get there? And this woman who named it, who was she? And why would she choose such an evil name for a planet?*

She was a widow, her husband, billionaire Lucien Mabus, having died years earlier. She was in her early fifties but looked far younger, still a ravishing beauty. She wore bizarre violet contact lenses, had cocoa-skin and long, flowing ebony hair. Apparently, Lilith's maternal ancestors hailed from Mesoamerica and—

Lilith! You say her name was Lilith?

Lilith Eve Mabus.

She's the one—the one I've been communicating with all these years within the nexus.

You're girlfriend's Hunahpu?

Yes. Father? Father, are you still there?

Jacob, it is Lilith Mabus who will one day become the Abomination.

No . . . no, that's impossible! Lilith can't be the Abomination, she . . . she wasn't born on the same day as us, she showed me her birth certificate! Dad, it's not her!

"It's her, Jacob. She's deceived you, and through you, she now knows about me. It's been your communication with Lilith in your present that forewarned her. It's the reason the Abomination and her demon seed were waiting for me when I finally arrived on Xibalba as Michael Gabriel.

. . . all my fault. I have to do something. I have to stop her now.

Jacob, wait! Stifling Lilith's actions in your time could adversely affect man's future. Remember, it's the wormhole that gives us a chance to change things, to save humanity. It was Lucien Mabus who pioneered space tourism, providing the ships that made the journey to Mars possible. Destroy Lilith in your time period and there may not be a Mars option, which means the second holocaust will wipe out all of mankind. The time loop must be preserved, then broken at the correct interval, in my time, not in yours.

Then what am I supposed to do?

I don't know, but you and your brother must stay away from Lilith at all costs.

Belle Glade, Florida

7:40 P.M.

Quenton Morehead lies naked in bed, watching the enchantress remove a bottle of aromatic oil from the pocket of her robe, along with several lengths of rope. His eyes widen as she slips out of her clothes, pouring the oil over her naked breasts.

"Yes, whore, I like that."

"You'll enjoy this even more." Using the lengths of rope, she secures his ankles and wrists to the oak bedposts. "Whores like a captive audience."

She turns off the lights, then slowly snakes her way up the old man's frame.

Quenton quivers with delight, moaning with pleasure as she slides her fingers down his distended belly to his groin. She licks his neck, teasing his knotty Adam's apple with her tongue as she grinds her moist pubic region into his pelvis. "You're right, you know," she coos. "I really owe you so much. Now lie back and close your eyes."

"But I want to see you."

"It's better in the dark. Remember back when I was a child and you'd come to me in the darkness. Now I'm coming to you. Close your eyes."

The old man obeys, a serene smile on his face—

—as Lilith removes the razor blade from behind her ear, placing it between her teeth.

The teenager slides down his frail body, fondling his inner thigh, pinching, tickling him as she rubs her lips across his dark skin . . . gently slicing open his flesh.

Returning to his neck, she teases open his carotid artery, swirling the warm pulsating liquid down his hairy chest as her free hand strokes his erect organ.

Pleasure and pain. With every groan, more blood. With each squeeze, a new cut.

By the time her mouth works its way to his groin, the Reverend's body has become a heaving patchwork of crimson.

Quenton climaxes, then drifts off to sleep, the drugs taking effect, the old man never realizing the hot beads of moisture drenching the bedsheets are his life.

Longboat Key, Florida

11:08 P.M.

The sand is cold, the driving wind coming off the Gulf penetrating Dominique's sweater. She pulls her collar up over her ears. "Enough games, Jacob. Yes or no, do you know who murdered your Aunt Evelyn?"

"Her name is Lilith. We've been communicating since we were young children."

Dominique covers her mouth in shock. "Communicating how?"

"Through a higher plane of quantum existence we call the nexus."

"She's Hunahpu?"

"Yes. And yes, she's the Abomination, at least she may be someday."

Dominique feels the blood drain from her face. "All these years . . . all my warnings, all Evelyn's warnings, and you've been communicating with the very person who tortures your father, who might destroy us all. How could you, of all people, be so blind?"

"Love is blind."

"Love? You love this . . . this thing?"

"She's not a *thing*, Mother, she's a human being born in a hurricane. She comes from a broken home, she's been abused physically and sexually. She needed my help, and I was there. She's a child of God as much as you or I."

"And now she's a dangerous child. She murdered Evelyn."

"She's angry at me. She's become psychotic."

"I'd say she passed psychotic. Now what are we supposed to do?"

He paces along a dune, his mind racing. "Lilith knows where we live and who we are. We can run now, but she's growing stronger every day. Eventually she'll have no trouble tracking me down using her Hunahpu abilities. She also has at least one ally,—who's—also Hunahpu."

"We have allies, too. We'll send Salt and Pepper after her."

"We can't do that. Lilith's presence in the near future is entwined around mankind's survival. If we derail her now, we'll upset an entire chain of events. The key is to avoid her until Manny and I leave for *Xibalba*."

"You know where *Xibalba* is?"

He points to the heavens. "Somewhere out there. According to the Mayan prophecy, Manny and I won't travel to *Xibalba* until our twentieth year. Avoiding Lilith for six years will be next to impossible, unless . . ." His eyes widen as another option takes shape within in his mind.

Belle Glade, Florida

November 5, 2027
7:25 P.M.

Lilith Eve Robinson sits at the kitchen table weeping, her tears aided by the irritation of the soap.

Detective Teak Colson hands her a tissue. "I know you're upset, but I need to ask you a few more questions. You say you came home around eleven?"

"Yes, sir. I was visiting my uncle at his hotel. My grandfather was lying on his bed when I got here."

"Did you ever see your grandfather use drugs?"

"He . . . he pops these pills. Said it was for his arthritis."

"According to the coroner, those pills were Oxycontin. Coroner found about six hundred milligrams of the stuff in him, and it was all chewed up. Oxycontin is a time-released drug, it was made to swallow whole. Chew it up and you release toxic amounts of the drug."

"Oh my God. . . . He should have known that, right?"

"I think he did. I think your grandfather committed suicide."

"No . . . he was murdered. Look at those wounds? How do you explain the blood loss?"

"Self-inflicted. With all that painkiller in him, he probably never felt a thing. Did you know he changed his Will?"

"I didn't even know he had a Will."

"Changed it yesterday. Fits the suicide pattern. This whole thing was premeditated. His lawyer will be speaking with you later this afternoon." Colson checks his notes. "Now this uncle of yours—Don Rafelo. I'm going to need his statement."

"Of course."

Colson looks over her shoulder, his expression darkening. "Oh, hell—" He hurries into the living room to the television.

The scene is live, broadcast from a news chopper hovering over the Gandy Bridge in Tampa. Rescue boats are circling, divers are in the water.

Colson turns up the sound.

"*. . . the former president's limousine was struck as it approached the construction area of the bridge. The vehicle crashed through the temporary barricade and into the bay.*"

The scene zooms in on a Coast Guard rescue boat.

"*Jennie, Brian Bahder here. We've just received word that former president Ennis Chaney and the driver of the vehicle have been rescued. Both men are now aboard the Coast Guard rescue boat in stable condition.*"

"*Brian, what about the missing Gabriel twin?*"

Lilith kneels by the screen, her heart racing. *Please not Jacob . . .*

"*Divers are still searching, but I have to tell you, it doesn't look good. Eyewitnesses report the limo sank at least ten minutes ago.*"

"*For those of you just joining us, you're looking at a live telecast over the Gandy Bridge where a limousine transporting former president Ennis Chaney and one of his godsons was struck by a hit-and-run driver as it was heading east into Tampa. Chaney and his driver have been rescued, but the unidentified Gabriel twin is still missing.*"

"*Jennie, from what we understand, Tampa Bay Buccaneers owners Dan and Linda Broersma, had invited Chaney and his godson to watch this afternoon's football game—*"

"*Stand by, Jennie, it looks like divers have surfaced.*"

The camera angle changes, zooming in on the stern of the Coast Guard rescue boat where a body is being lifted out of the water.

Lilith holds her breath as the carcass, supported by a team of divers, breaks the surface.

It is the dark-haired twin, Immanuel.

20

For one more terrible moment in man's history, the world seemed to stop spinning.

Over the years, stories about the Gabriel twins had grown to almost legendary proportions. News of Immanuel's demise stunned the public as much as the deaths of John Lennon, Princess Diana, or John F. Kennedy, Jr.'s. But it was in Mesoamerica where the Mayan Indians had worshiped the teens as living deities that the news was hardest to swallow.

Riots broke out in Central America. Zealots took nosedives off pyramids. Schools and businesses closed. People wept openly in the streets. Back in the States, news journalists stormed the gates of the Gabriel compound by the hundreds, forcing the military to shut down access bridges leading into Longboat Key.

What the public wanted was information, what the media insisted upon was proof. They demanded to examine the body, which had been transported back to the compound to be readied for burial.

In her grief, Dominique finally relented, knowing there would be no peace without verification. A team of physicians were allowed to enter the Gabriel compound, along with a CNN film crew and two witnesses drawn from a lottery.

The morbid event was telecast around the world.

After thirty minutes, a heavily sedated Dominique could handle no more. Everyone but Ennis Chaney and the immediate family were banned from the compound.

The former president spoke to the world later that eve-

ning, providing sparse details about the hit-and-run, saying
only that Immanuel's body would be cremated. A public
mass and international day of mourning was scheduled for
Monday in Washington, DC.

Belle Glade, Florida

5 November 2027

The unmarked police car enters the lot of the Belle Glade
Breakers Motel and parks. Lilith gets out of the passenger
side and knocks on the door of Room 113. "Open up, Uncle Don, it's me—Lilith."

Detective Colson joins her at the door. "Do you have a
key?"

"Yes." She slips the magnetic key in the lock and opens
the door.

The room is empty.

"So? Where is he?"

"I . . . I don't know. He was supposed to meet me here
this evening."

"Anyone at the front desk ever meet this uncle of
yours?"

"No. I paid for the room. His English isn't too good."

Colson searches the chest of drawers. Looks under the
bed. Checks the bathroom. Finds nothing.

"Looks like he took off on you. What was his relationship with your grandfather?"

"I . . . I don't know? But if you're thinking . . . Detective, I'm sure he'll be back soon. Please don't jump to any
conclusions."

"Here's my card. I want you to wait here and call me the
moment he comes back. Meanwhile, I'm going to contact
someone from Family Services. If your uncle doesn't show
up by tonight, you'll go with them."

"Yes, sir."

Colson leaves. Lilith locks the door behind him.

"Bastard."

She spins around, shocked to find Don Rafelo lying spread-eagle on the bed.

"Don't worry, I put the evil eye on him."

"Where were you? How did you get . . ." The sudden realization shocks her, dropping her to her knees. "No . . . you're . . . you're not real, are you?"

His smile reveals diseased gums. "Of course I'm real. Thoughts are real, aren't they?"

"But—"

"The power of the Succubus is real."

"But you're just in my mind. You're not really here. Not in the physical sense."

He sits up and leans in close, and she can smell his foul old man's breath. "Real is what the mind can conceive and believe. Thoughts are things. Your thought energy is as real as mine."

Lilith swoons. "Those boys you killed—"

"You mean, the ones *you* killed. And the old woman."

"And Quenton?"

"Of course. I instructed you, gave you confidence, but it was you who did the deed. And now there's more to be done, before we travel to Mexico."

"Jacob?"

Don Rafelo nods. "He'll be in Washington for the memorial service. Security will be tight, but he'll be out in the open, where we can reach him through the nexus."

"He doesn't want to see me anymore."

"Jacob's value is in his seed. Your union will be the first of two nearly pure Hunahpu. Your child, Lilith, shall be a god."

West Potomac Park,
Washington, DC

November 7, 2027

Towering 555 feet high, the alabaster marble obelisk known as the Washington Monument is located at the east end of Potomac Park, approximately one mile west of the Capitol Building. At the very top of this hollow structure is an observation room, affording visitors a magnificent view of the park's reflecting pool, the Vietnam Veterans Memorial, the 9-11 wall, the Middle East War Memorial, and the Lincoln Memorial.

The Lincoln Memorial is constructed of thirty-six columns—the number of states in the Union at the time of Lincoln's death in 1865. Situated within the massive enclosure is sculptor Daniel Chester French's giant stone-carving honoring the sixteenth president of the United States.

Ennis Chaney, the forty-sixth president of the United States, listens to Rabbi Steinberg's opening invocation as he looks out upon a vast sea of bodies gathered around the Memorial and the park's long rectangular reflecting pool. Network hovercams dot the gray winter sky, each suspended in its preapproved flight pattern. Security cams dart in and about, scanning the crowd, who have already been searched for weapons. Congressmen and visiting dignitaries are seated along the steps of the Lincoln Memorial. Several dab at their eyes, though few are actually crying.

Seated on one side of the former president is President Marion Rallo. Jacob Gabriel is on Chaney's left side, the white-haired teen wearing a black suit and tie and dark, tinted, wraparound shades.

Concealed in an opaque envelope in the teen's left hand is a photo of former secretary of state Pierre Borgia.

The crowd bows their heads as Rabbi Steinberg completes the invocation with a prayer.

* * *

At the east end of the park, Pierre Robert Borgia, dressed in a black SWAT team uniform, enters the Washington Monument. He flashes his false identification badge to the two armed guards, then allows them to scan his new false eye and fake retinal implant.

"You're clear to go on up, sir."

"Thank you."

Concealed within Borgia's backpack is the Barrett M101-A .50-caliber Browning sniper rifle and bipod. Waving to the guards, he takes the elevator up to the observation deck, which is to remain closed until after the ceremony.

Ennis Chaney follows President Rallo at the podium. A harsh winter's wind causes him to shiver, despite the heavy lining of his dress coat and undergarments. He touches his right ear, repositioning the dime-sized communication device.

"Distinguished guests, members of Congress, my fellow Americans, my fellow citizens of the world: It's not easy to have faith. It's not easy in this, the twenty-first century, nor was it easy in the first century, when our ancient ancestors looked up at the stars and wondered, 'Where do we come from? What is this life all about?'"

Chaney's eyes are dancing now, moving to the rhythm of his words.

"We need faith. Faith that is not predicated on fantasy. And yet we, as educated and sophisticated caring souls, must rely on faith to get us through times of confusion, times of pain and suffering . . ."

Borgia exits the elevator and steps out onto the observation level. He passes the bronze replica of George Washington and heads for the west windows facing the Lincoln Memorial.

Removes the glass cutter. Adheres it to the thick pane

using the twin suction cups. Sets the automated device for an eight-inch circular cut.

As the device slices the glass, Borgia assembles the high-powered rifle, attaching it to its bipod.

Chaney looks from the right TelePromPter to the left. "Many years ago, another African-American stood on these same steps and addressed his people. He spoke of freedom and equality. He spoke of rising up from the dark and desolate valley of segregation into the sunlit path of racial justice. He shared with us his dreams. He shared with us his faith.

"My godson, Immanuel, was a gentle soul. Like his father, Immanuel believed in humanity, but worried about our survival. On his last birthday, he shared with me a passage his brother, Jacob, had transcribed from one of the Dead Sea Scrolls. The passage described something called the War of the Sons of Light versus the Sons of Darkness. Manny explained that the Sons of Darkness are the mass murderers of the innocent and all who support them. They are the zealots, who distort faith's teachings as an excuse to commit mayhem. They are the greedy, who force society down paths that retard the future of mankind, solely so they can remain in power. 'The war is on,' my godson told me, 'and humanity must triumph, or our light shall be extinguished.'"

Behind the former president, Jacob Gabriel closes his eyes, focusing inward, as his mind searches the psychic realm for the signal line he seeks.

Borgia adjusts the bipod's height so that the barrel of the rifle protrudes out the hole in the window. He loads a high-velocity .50-caliber exploding round, then peers down the infrared scope with his only functioning eye.

It takes him a full thirty seconds to lock the target in.

* * *

Gun scope . . .

The reflecting pool . . . viewed from above.

The podium . . . he's not targeting me, he's after Chaney!

Jacob's eyes snap open as he speaks into the microphone cuff links. "Washington Monument—observation deck!"

There are 147 members of the Secret Service patrolling the area, all tuned in to Jacob's radio frequency, but it is Dominique Vazquez-Gabriel, disguised as a security guard, who is first to react.

Aware of the TelePromPter, Borgia activates the infrared laser, invisible to the naked eye, and brings the glowing orb to the center of Ennis Chaney's chest. He slips his right index finger around the trigger. Collects his breath.

Pulls the trigger.

"Martin Luther King said the ultimate measure of a man is where he stands during times of challenge and controversy. As we stand here, united in our sorrow, our survival is being tested. History is asking more of us than tears, it is asking us to rise to the challenge of our own mortality. As intelligent beings, created in God's image, it is our obligation to reach out to the stars and experience the heavens before we die, so that we may realize our true place on this Earth—"

Adrenaline pumping, Jacob commands his mind to enter the nexus.

The area suddenly brightens as everything slows around him. Chaney's rasping voice crawls to a dull echo.

Jacob cannot see the bullet, but he can see the gelatinous

ripples as it pushes through waves of energy, angling down from the distant white tower.

He jumps to his feet, his Hunahpu mind dissecting time and distance—

Jacob!

Jacob's heart skips a beat. He sees her standing in the twentieth row, an azure-eyed vixen whose fluid movements, as she approaches, separate her from the rest of the crowd.

Lilith . . . please—not now!

You deserted me!

Gelatinous ripples widen as the bullet appears.

I came here for you, Jacob. I'm offering you a last chance.

Ignoring her tantalizing presence, Jacob leaps—

A bucket of crimson explodes from Jacob Gabriel's black suit as he and former President Ennis Chaney tumble sideways off the dais.

Pierre Borgia smiles, then turns suddenly at the elevator bell signal. Reaching into his pocket, he fumbles to load another .50-caliber exploding round into the chamber.

Dominique steps out of the elevator.

"You?" Borgia slips the bullet into place, his finger at the trigger. "I should have killed you and your wacko patient when I had the chance!"

"You tried. Now it's my turn."

Borgia raises the rifle barrel—

—as Dominique's flexes her right biceps, commanding the microwave pain-cannon to fire.

The blast of searing heat separates assassin from gun, sending Pierre Borgia writhing on the ground, his nerve endings sizzling.

* * *

Desperate cries rend the crisp November air.

Waves of onlookers at the west end of the park drop for cover. Secret Service agents sweep President Rallo into an awaiting vehicle. Congressmen and guests disperse, some for their limos, others for the interior of the Lincoln memorial, where Secret Service agents huddle around the bloodstained body of Jacob Gabriel.

Rabbi Richard Steinberg grips the white-haired youth's lifeless hand and prays as a dozen news hovercams jostle for airspace overhead.

A terrified physician pushes through the throng. With quivering fingers he gently unbuttons Jacob's suit coat, revealing an undergarment drenched in blood. He shakes his head.

The horrified crowd yields to an ambulance. Word carries with the panic: "The other Gabriel twin's been shot! Jacob's dead!"

Seconds later, the insanity of the moment is interrupted by screams coming from the park's east end as a window shatters atop the Washington Monument and a body—the body of Pierre Robert Borgia—hurtles through the air, splattering like a sack of scarlet flour at the base of the Monument below.

A wisp of thought, in the consciousness of existence.

Jacob?
Where are you, son?
Where are you . . .

PART 6
••••••••••••••••
ADULTHOOD

*"To succeed is nothing, it's an accident.
But to feel no doubts about oneself
is something very different: it is character."*

—**MARIE LENÉRU**

There is no security on this Earth, this is only opportunity.

—**DOUGLAS MACARTHUR**

21
SIX YEARS LATER

NOVEMBER 19, 2033
SATURDAY AFTERNOON
MABUS TECH INDUSTRY ORANGE BOWL
BISCAYNE BAY
MIAMI, FLORIDA

The pelican balances on a wooden piling, struggling to preen its feathers. Like most of the other coastal scavengers, the bird no longer actively hunts for its meals. The shallows are devoid of fish, the marshes long paved over. Processed food sustains it now—all the scraps it can eat.

The pelican's beak opens and closes in spasms, gasping insufficient breaths of hot air thick with body lotions, perfumes and the unmistakable scent of human perspiration. *Mau-Mau* music—a blend of calypso and rap—blares from hundreds of speakers situated around the Teflon-coated fiberglass pier.

A final gasp and the pelican drops from the piling, its lifeless form splashing upon the olive-colored, gasoline-tainted surf twenty-five feet below.

Another scorching Saturday afternoon in late autumn . . . the inner harbor at Biscayne Bay once again transformed into a human beehive of activity.

Moving inland from the piers is a latticework of inflatable walkways and air-supported bridges that weave in and out of hundreds of stores and eateries. Shoppers and sun-bathers, families and students, locals and tourists, representing a multitude of races, religions—and colors—flock to the trendy mall-park.

Skin color in the 2030's is now a matter of choice, the once-popular tattoo replaced with "body-dipping." Developed by dermatologists in response to the alarming rise in skin cancers caused by the continued deterioration of the ozone layer, "dermo-shields" were originally designed as clear body applications featuring an SPF-50 ultraviolet skin protector designed to wear off in 90–120 days. Unfortunately, very few people under the age of sixty sought out the preventive treatments.

Six months after its development, an enterprising group in Australia introduced color to the formula, and body-dipping became an overnight sensation.

Clinics opened everywhere. Clients could select from a multitude of flesh-toned colors, including Caucasian, Bohemian-Tan, Chinese, African, and American Indian. Dermatology became a fashion statement, racial discrimination ultimately "confused." Even better, the four prescribed annual "dips" were covered by all three levels of the FMC (Federal Medical Coverage).

More radical applications quickly followed, designed to appeal to the sought-after age twelve-to-twenty demographic. Clinics introduced "rainbow-shields," and a new race of "alien-adolescents" invaded the schools, their epidermis stained from head to toe in shades of greens, blues, violets, reds, and yellows. When this fad led to increases in gang-related violence, municipalities and states instituted laws forbidding rainbow dips to anyone under the age of eighteen.

The Mau-Mau music slips into prerecorded ocean acoustics. A family of African-Americans, stained Bohemian-Tan, pauses along one of the catwalks to observe the activity below.

Bonzai-boarders balance precariously on fluorescent orange-and-yellow skateboards that ride on "zip tracks," the cushions of methane microjet air allowing riders to defy gravity—at least the first four to six feet of it.

A small crowd gathers at the guardrail, anticipating either an amazing feat or a spectacular fall. Spurred on by the applause, several of the more daring riders link arms and race along a skull-and-crossbones-painted path leading to "suicide hill," a four-story, 360-degree vertical loop.

The blueberry-stained teens rise in unison along the near-vertical wall and invert, the crowd's oohs and ahhs quickly turning to gasps as gravity's invisible fingers latch on to two of the boys closest to the center. Suspended upside down, they are yanked from their boards, the rippling disturbance sending the entire pack tumbling headfirst toward the crash mats forty feet below.

On ultrasound proximity alert, air-bag suits inflate a millisecond before the first body strikes the tarmac.

For a long moment the dazed adolescents lie motionless in an entanglement of purple-blue flesh and equipment, their crash collars and helmets momentarily restricting all movement. Gradually the air suits deflate, freeing bruised but intact limbs. A smattering of applause greets the daredevils, encouraging them to reorganize and attempt the impossible assault again.

Above, the bright Miami skyline buzzes with a high-pitched whine coming from a dozen VTOLs—Vertical Takeoff and Landing vehicles. Powered by four fixed turbine ducts that provide thrust for launch, these two-man skycars whiz back and forth over Biscayne Bay like swarms of giant polyurethane wasps. Less-maneuverable one-man VFVs (Vertical Flying Vehicles) hover over the nude sunbathers along South Beach, the two-propeller craft rented by the hour.

Below, the aqua green surface is crisscrossed by sailboats and schooners, Windsurfers and super yachts, all competing for maneuvering space within the crowded marina. The occasional Luxon-glass nose cone of a two-man minisub sneaks a peek above the watery playground, the Argonauts ever fearful of the whirling blades that cut great swaths across the ceiling of their more private underwater domain.

At the center of this dervish of activity is the beehive itself—the MTI Orange Bowl—a mammoth steel-and-tinted-glass horseshoe rising sixteen stories above the sweltering south Florida playground. Home to the University of Miami's PCAA-champion football Hurricanes, the arena is bursting with the energy that comes from its capacity crowd of 132,233.

Patches of orange, lavender, and teal bare-chested bodies denote the different skin-stained Miami fraternities harbored in the west bleachers. A group cheer prompts a response from the visiting Florida State student body, their own skins dipped "Seminole red," while bare-chested women from both universities pose for hovercams, showing off their "calypso" tanned and augmented breasts.

After six minutes of play, the home team trails cross-state rival FSU 3 to 0, and the Miami crowd is beyond antsy. Chants of "Mule, Mule, Mule" bounce across the cushioned Teflon seats, electrifying the air as the Canes offense sprints onto the field for the first time, taking possession at their own sixteen yard line.

There are no team huddles. All instructions are communicated from position coaches directly into the players' helmets via encrypted microspeakers.

The orange and white-clad Hurricanes set themselves on the artificial grass field, the roots of which are designed to give on impact. There are no human referees. A dozen infraction cameras linked to high-speed macroperceivers adorn the sidelines, analyzing the playing field, searching for infractions. There are no first-down markers. Concealed beneath the padded emerald green turf is an electronic grid linked to remote sensors embedded inside the football. Fluorescent yellow laser lines indicate precise ball placement, while digital sideline markers display both the down and the yards necessary to achieve a first down. A vertically oriented electromagnetic plane extending upward from the goal line must be broken to score a touch-

down, the accomplishment instantly igniting a rainbow of
laser lights and the scoring team's unique holographic special effects celebration.

The goalposts themselves are violet-colored holograms
that activate for field goal or extra point attempts. Striking
the "post" causes the ball to spin wildly, the outcome always a crapshoot.

Samuel "the Mule" Agler, Miami's twenty-year-old star
sophomore tailback lines up in the backfield behind his
quarterback and best friend, K. C. Renner, as the game ball
is set into place by Robo-Ref—a two-foot-high mobile
trash-can-shaped device.

On the Miami sidelines, Mike Lavoie, the team's offensive coordinator, selects a play from his Port-a-Coach.
Sam listens as the annoying computerized voice chirps in
his left ear.

Sixty-three, halfback, pitch right . . . on two.

Sam blocks out the crowd's thundering crescendo and
slows his pulse. His mind focuses inward, directing his
consciousness into what his sports psychiatrist calls "the
zone," a soothing pool of existence harbored somewhere
deep within his brain.

Senior lineman Jerry Tucker squats over the pigskin, the
massive 378-pound center's buttocks stretching the reinforced polyurethane-and-steel fibers in his pants to their
max. As he touches the ball, all player-coach field trans-
missions are instantaneously severed.

The play clock ticks backward from fifteen.

Now Sam immerses himself fully into the zone, grimac-
ing as the familiar ripples of queasiness magnify into
waves of intense pain—

—and time and space suddenly appear to slow to a surreal crawl.

The din of noise evaporates to a dull baritone buzz. The
football rises away from the turf in slow motion.

Easy . . . don't jump offside. Sam waits impatiently, the
burning in his gut intensifying as the leather object momentarily disappears between Tucker's elephantine thighs,

reappearing a lifetime later within K. C. Renner's hands. The quarterback fakes left, then pivots to his right, his planted cleat tearing away a clump of artificial grass and sand that spins as it rises, twirling in the air like an orbiting Kelly green satellite.

Sam eyes the divot, his attention momentarily transfixed by grains of plastic dropping away like a comet's tail.

Enough!

Renner pitches the football to Sam's right. Sam plucks the floating object out of midair and secures it within the crook of his right arm. His dark eyes set upon the wall of moving bodies, his mind dissecting the fluctuating current of pads and flesh.

Miami's right guard and tackle are pulling, but Florida State's all-American, Ryan Ehrensberger, is blitzing from his linebacker position, and fat Tucker is too slow to stop him. Ehrensberger shoots the gap in slow motion, his eyes widening, his face a mask of contortion and glee as he bears down on the ball carrier like a child on Christmas Day.

Not today, pal . . .

The Mule's quadriceps fire, the capacity crowd gasping as number 23 gallops away from the Seminole's blitzing linebacker with an almost inhuman burst of speed.

Slipping from Ehrensberger's lunging tackle, Sam heads for the outside corner, only to see wideout Rusty Bradford tumble in slow motion as he misses his block on FSU's strong safety.

The outside linebacker joins him, cutting off the corner.

Have to do it the hard way . . .

Planting his right foot, the Mule changes directions with an ankle-breaking pivot and rushes back toward the mounds of flesh now rolling in disarray along the line of scrimmage. The safety's expression drops as he flails helplessly at a blur of orange and white that, only seconds before, had been the Miami tailback.

A wall of bodies looms ahead. The "Mule" targets Joe Mastrangelo, FSU's 377-pound all-American, Sam's powerful "stiff arm" striking the defensive tackle's chest like a lance, the blow knocking the bulky lineman clear off his size eighteen triple-E shoes, opening a sliver of Kelly green daylight.

Samuel Agler slips through the hole and into the clear, leaving a half dozen would-be tacklers in his wake. Invisible flames of lactic acid singe his insides as he gallops untouched toward the end zone.

He crosses the thirty yard line . . . the forty—

Who's out there?

The female's voice startles him. He nearly stumbles at midfield.

Speak to me, cousin. Identify yourself.

Terrified, Sam wrenches his mind free of the zone.

The crowd noise returns.

Sam staggers down the right hash marks, his chest heaving, his mind urging his exhausted muscles to move faster.

"He's at midfield . . . the forty . . . the thirty . . . the Mule's heading for the end zone, and no one in this arena's going to catch him—touchdown!" Todd Hoagland, the Hurricanes' visual color commentator, is on his feet screaming into his remote headset as waves of hysteria bombard the MTI arena.

Samuel "the Mule" Agler drops to his knees in the end zone, gasping great breaths of air as his delirious teammates rush to embrace him.

4:17 P.M.

Sam leans back against the carpeted cubicle in the Hurricanes' locker room, his aching muscles in desperate need of a rubdown. The faint scent of ammonia moves through an air-conditioned current tinged with the scent of human sweat. Wearily, he raises a plastic container of tangy cold liquid to his lips and quaffs the beverage, a few drops dribbling past his chin. The high-protein drink is loaded with amino acids and biogenic fuel designed to stimulate tissue repair and help flush his system of lactic acid.

The media converge upon him. A dozen wireless video-cams are shoved toward his face, linking each telecast to computer feeds around the world.

"Sam, you've already broken the PCAA's rushing record for a freshman, now it looks like you're well on your way to smashing the all-time single-season rushing record. Can we safely assume you'll bypass your junior year and de-clare yourself eligible for the GFL's draft?"

"Look, we lost a tough game today. I don't want to talk about my future. Christ, don't you guys ever get tired of asking the same questions?"

"We'll stop asking when you start giving us answers." Diane Tanner leans in, the blond bombshell's tight gray-and-red ESPN leotard revealing more than most of the toweled athletes watching in the wings. "For instance, can you confirm rumors you've negotiated a contract to play basketball with the GBA next season?"

Sam steals a glance at K. C. Renner, who is flicking his pierced tongue at him from across the locker room. "I've been offered a dozen contracts, but I haven't signed any-thing. Besides, if and when I do turn pro, it will be to play football. The Global Basketball season is way too long."

"A lot of GBA owners would be willing to sign you just for the playoffs. The London Monarchs' owner told me last week that he'd even allow you to use his private jet."

"Enough! Ask me about today's game, or we're done."

"I have a question." *Sun Sentinel* beat writer Ethan McElwee pushes his video feed a little closer. "Miami only scored one touchdown, four below its season average. Was the FSU defense really that tough?"

"They're tops in the nation for a reason. They hit hard, as hard as any team we've faced."

CNN sportscaster Cal Kitson squeezes between McEl-wee and Sam, offering the football star a tantalizing view of her Indian red-tinged cleavage. "Mule, in two years, no one's ever come close to tackling you behind the line of scrimmage, yet in the third quarter alone, Jesse Gordon, Florida State's left defensive end, caught you twice. How do you explain that?"

"Gordon's quick. He made a coupla nice plays."

"And those rumors about point spreads?"

"That's enough." Head Coach Ted DeMaio pushes his way through the crowd. "Give the kid a break. Hell, he's been averaging over two-hundred yards a game since he was a freshman, ain't he entitled to one bad game?"

"Coach DeMaio—"

"I said out! Security, get these leeches outta my locker room."

Four taser-armed security officers push the crowd of reporters toward the exit.

Sam hangs his head.

Diane Tanner lingers behind, moving close enough for Sam to catch a whiff of her perfume, a new aphrodisiac offering a hint of lilac and strawberries.

"Yes, Diane?"

"Aren't you forgetting something? You promised me a private interview after the Penn State game. You blew me off."

"I, uh . . . sorry, I've been busy."

"Sports is a business, Sam. You guys get paid from revenues *we* help generate. The head of the network's pissed, he wants a live studio interview by Monday or we'll cancel global coverage of the FAU game in three weeks."

"Okay, okay. How 'bout tomorrow afternoon? I can meet you in the Press Room about three."

"Tomorrow's good, but tonight's better. I thought we could do it in my hotel suite."

Yeah, I bet you did . . . "I, uh . . . really can't."

Diane leans closer. Whispers into his ear. "Yes you can. In fact, I bet you can do it all night long."

She pulls away as the *Canes'* starting offensive line assembles in front of Sam's cubicle. The grungy, orange-stained underclassmen are wearing nothing but skimpy towels.

K. C. Renner steps forward. "Hey, ESPY-ho, check out this exclusive!"

"Trust me, Renner, there's nothing you've got under those towels I haven't seen already."

The six football players ceremoniously drop their towels, revealing pubic hair but no penises.

Sam hides his grin as K. C. strikes a pose. "It was a team decision. Saves wear and tear on jockstraps and cups."

Ignoring Renner, she turns back to Sam. "Tomorrow at three. Don't blow me off again." She whispers. "Call me later, and I'll help you forget all about today's game."

She pushes past K. C. and heads for the exit as Sam's teammates, laughing hysterically, untuck their male organs from between their legs.

K. C. watches Dave Goldsborough, Miami's 402-pound all-American left tackle struggle to free himself. "Yo, Moose, you oughta think about trimming that thing for real, man. Probably help you to move a lot faster."

As if considering it, the lineman looks down, unable to see past his massive belly.

Sam looks up as his best friend slaps him on the shoulder. "Thanks, K. C. Lauren would kick my ass six ways to Sunday if she caught me hangin' with the ESPY-ho."

"No sweat. If she corners you again, send her my way, I'd love to give her what she wants." K. C. lowers his voice. "Seriously, man, what happened out there today? 'Cept for that first score, I've never seen you move so slow. You pull something?"

"Maybe. I don't know."

"You don't know? You're not doin' leeches, are you?"

"You know me better than that."

"Sure, sure—" The quarterback follows him back to the showers. "Well listen, you can pay me back by sticking around long enough for us to win at least one more PCAA championship. I don't wanna be reading about you jumpin' ship next week to join some rugby team in Orlando."

Sam wheels around, catching his friend in a playful headlock. "Don't worry, pal, I ain't goin' nowhere."

Dusk bathes the western face of the arena in its golden haze.

Sam emerges from the air-conditioned building, his skin tingling in the heavy south Florida humidity. He brushes his long, jet-black hair away from his forehead as his dark eyes search the sea of faces waiting for him behind the outer steel gate. Samuel Agler's eyes are black as coal, making it impossible to tell where the irises end and the pupils begin. At times they seem to shimmer, radiating an inner strength and intellect.

He nods to the guard to open the gate, then pushes through the crowd, struggling to avoid the computer porto-pads being shoved in his face.

"Come on, Mule, one autograph—"

Sam ignores the autograph hounds, whose only intention is to ~~download~~ his signature across the Internet. He pauses for a father and his eight-year-old son, forcing a smile as their porto-pad snaps his picture. He scribbles a signature— UPLOAD

—looking up as a black stretch limousine slows, then passes by.

Sam's pulse quickens. He hands the kid back his porto-pad, his eyes searching for his ride.

K. C. Renner beeps at him from his "hydro-jeep."

Sam jumps in the vacant passenger seat. "Go, man, quick!"

The fuel cells kick in, spiriting the two of them away.

Main Campus, University of Miami
Coral Gables, Florida

Saturday Evening

Nineteen-year-old geology major Lauren Beckmeyer jogs past rows of royal palm trees adorning the campus drive.

Shoulder-length brown hair is pulled back into a tight ponytail, making her tall, six-foot frame seem even more angular. The junior track and field star glides like an antelope when she runs, her loping strides and explosive power giving her a competitive advantage in the long jump, triple, and high jump.

Lauren's coach is pushing her to add hurdles to her events. Hurdles means more roadwork, a lot of it. Lauren hates roadwork. It wears on her lower back and knees and chews up too much time. Between going to class and studying, proctoring Dr. Gabeheart's meteorology class and her physical training regimen, she barely has time to see her fiancé.

Missed his game again. Sam's going to kill me . . .

A gunshot of thunder echoes across the threatening south Florida sky. She quickens her pace. *Screw this. Three events is enough. Not like I'm going to the Olympics . . .*

Crossing the street, she cuts in front of a campus robobus, the twenty-four-hour-a day vehicle powered by the electromagnets of the induct-tracks embedded in the smart-way. Sheets of rain are pouring on her by the time she reaches the quadrangle of dorms located on the west side of campus. Wiping sweat and rainwater from her face, she holds up her hand, allowing the security camera's scanner to "read" the computer S.I.D. (security and identification) chip embedded in the flesh of her palm.

The sensor identifies her, simultaneously scanning her for weapons.

ENTER LAUREN BECKMEYER. HAVE A NICE DAY.

The front doors part, the familiar gust of cold air causing goose bumps as she enters the mezzanine. She walks past a group of students, some on body cushions, others hibernating inside sensory bags, as a movie displays on the giant smart-glass screen. By day, these multipurpose windows adjust the degree of tint to keep out the sun. By night, they opaque for privacy and convert into entertainment centers.

She waves to a friend, then locates an unoccupied turbolift and takes the high-speed transport up to the seventh floor. A holographic notice advertises a 'Rave-Free Lunar Festival' tonight in the dorm's virtual-reality chamber. A federal ad displays: *Immunize and say NO TO ADDICTION*.

In early 2024, the United States, Canada, and Mexico, following in the footsteps of the European Union, began mandatory infant immunizations for cannabis, cocaine, and heroin. These "inhibitor shots" were designed to prevent the human brain from experiencing a "high," eliminating any possibility for a future attraction to the narcotic.

Unfortunately, remove one illegal high and another is bound to come along. Immunization programs against fringe drugs like methylenedioxymethamphetamine (MDMA) were proving expensive, and the population was becoming tired of "Big Brother's" heavy-handedness.

Instead of continuing the battle, the federal government, in 2028, decided to join forces with the pharmaceutical industry, staking its own claim in the $500-billion-a-year trade of recreational agents. The aim of drug companies had always been to free the human condition from physical pain. Now they would turn their attention to eliminating psychological pain while enhancing happiness.

The first "heaven" drug was BLISS, a genetically encoded cocktail designed to release serotonin and stimulate phenylethylamine, a chemical released by the human brain when one is "in love" (or for some, while eating chocolate). A year later, a second line of BLISS was developed for senior citizens, this one designed to restore the dopaminergic neurons that gradually die off as we age, leading to a decline in sexual drive.

Happiness and a recharged libido—an old industry was reborn.

Designer heavens were not physically addictive, and the

delayed action of these nonneurotoxic mood enhancers released a more gradual high, preventing the wild emotional swings of drugs like heroin, Ecstasy, and cocaine. When used in conjunction with a new line of virtual-reality software products, the effect was increased tenfold.

Biotechnology had created an entirely new sensation-driven world economy, virtually replacing the alcohol and nicotine industries.

Lauren steps from her moment of serenity into a hallway throbbing with technomusic. From an open dorm room she spots a bare-chested, multistained underclassman.

Second-year Middle Eastern Dialects major Kirk Peacock stares back at her through mood-evolving contact lenses, which now appear purple. The track lighting along the ceiling reflects off his hairless scalp and the Chinese symbol for love permanently tattooed just above his forehead.

"Laur-rah—"

"It's Lauren."

"Laur-rah, Laur-ren . . . just a name, Laur-ren Beckman."

"Beckmeyer."

"You're the Mule's tool."

"Excuse me?"

"His plaything, you know, his pacifier. I need you to score me a signed pigskin. My geoprof said he'd raise my grade if I—"

"You like new experiences, Kirk?"

"It's the basis for my existence."

"Then try attending a few lectures in person this semester." She examines his neck. "Is that a mood-leech?"

"Uh-huh." Kirk giggles, pulling the edge of the flat leech-shaped object away from his birdlike neck. "Want a suck? Still got another twenty minutes of juice."

The "mood-leech" is a drug injection system, its two-hundred hollow microscopic needles designed to release a hybrid of illegal "rave narcotics" directly into the user's carotid artery. Combined with "designer heaven," the mood-leech created waves of "whole-body hyperorgasmic euphoria," especially when used in a virtual-reality chamber.

Lauren shakes her head in disbelief. "Is your consciousness ever drug-free?"

Kirk's grin reveals two platinum-capped teeth. "Consciousness blows, psychological hedonism rules. If it ain't virtual, it ain't reality . . . Laur-rah Beck-woman. What releases your endogenous opioids? Exercise? Sex? Food? Music? When I listen to music now, its stirs my soul. When I make love, my whole body quivers for hours. This morning, I had erotic alien sex in a VR chamber, and I don't even know if it was a male or female!"

"Yeah, well I'm not into Zombi-ism or alien gang bangs. I'll stick with my mule, if you know what I mean."

"Mule sex. Ha. Ha-ha—ugh . . ." The metallic smile suddenly fades as Kirk's blue-tinged face flushes violet.

WARNING: TOXIC LEVELS OF DEXTROMETH-ORPHAN PRESENT. SWEAT GLANDS SHUTTING DOWN. HEAT STROKE IMMINENT. PARAMEDICS HAVE BEEN SUMMONED.

"Shut up!" He looks at Lauren, fighting to keep his balance, his mood swinging like a pendulum. "*Sheating-fud* computer's been driving me crazy all afternoon."

Sheating-fud? Lauren frowns, her mind racing to unscramble the new slang-stringing curse. *Shit-eating fuck-wad . . . got it.* She touches his forehead. "You're burning up."

Kirk's eyes roll up as he falls forward.

Lauren ducks, catching him over her right shoulder in a fireman's carry. She enters his apartment, gagging at the stench as she makes her way over piles of soiled laundry and garbage.

The lights fail to activate as she enters the bathroom. "Computer, increase lighting."

UNABLE TO COMPLY. FUEL CELL HAS BEEN REMOVED.

"Emergency lighting."

Panel strips illuminate along the ceiling and floor. The bathroom smart-mirror has been spray-painted black.

Lauren lays Kirk on the shower floor and rips the leech from his neck, revealing a series of red dots. "Computer, shower on, fifty degrees."

Icy water blasts from dual nozzles, the built-in sensors targeting the unconscious teen.

Kirk moans.

"Computer, this is Resident Assistant Beckmeyer. What is ETA of paramedics?"

SIX MINUTES.

"Place a call to resident's sister to meet resident at student health center."

ACKNOWLEDGED.

Lauren looks down at Kirk. The teen's eyes have reopened, his mood-contacts black, his flushed skin paling to blue again as his body cools off.

"Fu . . . fu . . . fubish—" His teeth chatter as he tries to stand.

Lauren places her foot on his chest.

"Fuckkking . . . bi-itch-ssshiiit—Laureeenn!"

"At least you got the name right."

"Let . . . m—m-me . . . g-g-go—"

"Sorry, Kirk, you want to kill yourself, do it on someone else's floor, not mine. Now sit your rainbow ass down and take it like a man . . . or alien, whichever you prefer."

The paramedics arrive five minutes later.

Eight minutes later, Lauren enters her own apartment. The interior is plush and immaculate, decorated in soothing shades of gray with violet throw pillows.

She kicks off her running shoes

GOOD EVENING, LAUREN. IT IS 7:36 P.M. YOU HAVE THREE MESSAGES.

"In the bathroom." She grabs a bottle of recycled reverse-osmosis water from the fridge and heads for the bathroom.

Interior lights turn on to greet her.

She sits on the toilet and urinates.

The "smart-toilet" instantly analyzes her urine, while the pulse in her thigh is computed.

NO DISEASES PRESENT. YOU ARE NOT PREG-NANT.

"Thank God. Computer, play back message one."

The image of Lauren's father, Mark, appears on the mirror. "Hi, sweetheart. Nothing important, just wanted to let you know that we're all looking forward to seeing you and Sam next weekend. Give us a flash when you get in."

"Computer, erase message one. Play back message two."

Christopher Laubin, Lauren's volcanism professor appears on screen. "Good afternoon, Ms. Beckmeyer. This is just a reminder that our grant selection committee will be meeting with you Monday morning at seven-thirty in Clinton Hall, Room 213. Don't be late."

"I'm never late. Computer, reply BECKMEYER ACKNOWLEDGE to message two. Play back message three."

Sam's face appears on-screen, her fiancé calling from a cell phone. "Hey, babe. Sorry I'm late, but my teammates and I had to do this postgame ritual thing. I'll be by in about twenty to fondle your breasts. Love you."

Dammit . . . She stands, strips out of her neon orange bodysuit, and steps into the shower, the warm water spray drenching her as the door seals shut.

IT IS TIME FOR YOUR MONTHLY MELANOMA CHECKUP.

"So do it . . . damn computer-nag."

She glances down as shower sensors scan her body. Her stomach is taut, her legs rock-hard from daily workouts at the training center. She wonders if Sam would prefer her breasts larger.

"Increase temperature ten degrees."

The water heats up, the shower's pulsating heads massaging the tension from her muscles.

Should I be angry at Sam or just disappointed? Recalling his postgame interview with the ESPN woman, she decides a touch of both would be appropriate.

The two melanoma monitors embedded in the tile begin blinking. She turns slowly, allowing the device to exam her skin for cancer.

MELANOMA NOT PRESENT. DERMO-SHIELD SHOULD BE REPLACED IN TWENTY-TWO DAYS.
A three-dimensional commercial for a local dermo-shield clinic displays in the shower.

The sound mutes.

ATTENTION. YOU HAVE AN INCOMING MESSAGE FROM YELLOWSTONE PARK.

"I'll take it in the bedroom." Lauren steps from the shower, drying herself with a preheated towel.

Lauren's associate department head, Professor William Gabeheart, is on sabbatical, teaching an on-site correspondence course, Geology 434: The Effects of the Yellowstone Caldera on Geysers, Fumaroles, and Hot Springs. Lauren is Gabeheart's graduate assistant and class coordinator.

While Yellowstone National Park is known for its magnificent geysers, mud pots, and boiling hot springs, to scientists it represents the home of the world's largest and most dangerous caldera. Originating deep beneath the park's mantle is a "hot spot," one of only a few dozens on the planet. Magma and tremendous heat rise from this volcanic location, impinging on the base of the North American plate while powering the park's geysers, hot springs, and fumaroles.

Three of the most violent volcanic eruptions in Earth's history have taken place at the Yellowstone hot spot, the first occurring 2.1 million years ago, the second 1.2 million years ago, the last 630,000 years ago. The eruptions have unleashed a combined six thousand cubic miles of debris, the ejection of lava causing the tops of the volcanoes to collapse, forming three massive calderas, or depressions. The calderas remain buried beneath extensive rhyolite lava flows resulting from smaller eruptions over the last 150,000 years.

Entering the bedroom, Lauren wraps a towel around her waist and slips a UNIVERSITY OF MIAMI sweatshirt over her head. "Okay, computer, put the call through."

The monitor on her nightstand comes to life, revealing Bill Gabeheart, forty-two, his mop of brown hair tucked neatly beneath a HAVANA SHARKS baseball cap. The former Navy Intelligence officer's hazel eyes glow blue in the porto-lab's computer consoles.

"Hey, Doc. You get the midterms I sent over?"

"Never mind that. Are you behind a secured firewall?"

The question startles her. "Uh, no—"

"Get on one."

She leaves the bed, hurrying to her desk. "Computer, transfer call to PC."

ACKNOWLEDGED.

The computer boots. Lauren touches the keypad, activating her secured access code. "Go ahead, Professor."

"Last night I received data back from the three Trimble 5000Ssi receivers we deployed at our new GPS control stations."

"So? How bad's the subsidence?"

"According to the USGS, everything appears stable, but as my grandfather used to say, 'Something ain't kosher.' The readings we received look identical to data I collected three years ago. Between me and thee, I don't trust the new USGS director."

"Alyssa Popov? I thought you liked her?"

"Grinding her and trusting her are two different things, and I don't have time for one of your feminist lectures. Things are happening behind the scenes here in Yellowstone. There are factors at play that we can't see, covert deals being made between the White House and other factions outside the government. Late last night, Professor Danielak and I decided to take our own vertical motion readings, along with temperature readings of the hot springs at the preselected areas within the Yellowstone caldera."

Lauren hears Sam enter her apartment. "What do you need me to do?"

"I want you to analyze the results. We'll upload everything directly to your computer in the lab."

"But—"

"Don't worry, we're encoding it and rerouting through a dozen other servers. Once you start receiving data, I want you to run a full analysis of variance, comparing subsidence with the results we took in the fall of 2030."

"Hey, Lauren, where are you?" Sam bursts into the bedroom.

She cuts her fiancé off with a harsh glare. "You'd better hurry with that data. Hurricane *Kenneth* was officially upgraded to a class-five storm two hours ago. Winds are expected to reach super-cane proportions by Tuesday evening. If the weather net doesn't slow it down, we may have to evacuate the city as early as next weekend."

"Where's the eye?"

Lauren presses CONTROL-6 on her keyboard. The screen splits, the right side showing a live satellite feed over the Atlantic Ocean. Using the mouse, she focuses on a swirling white vortex, the eye of the strengthening storm clearly defined.

"Kenneth's 361 miles due east of Antigua."

"Still pretty far out. Where's the weather net?"

She types in another command. A series of crimson dots appears off Cuba. "En route to Havana's port to refuel from the last cell."

"Which means they won't be in place until Wednesday. You're right, that's calling it close."

Sam lies by Lauren's feet. Playfully, he reaches his hand beneath her towel.

She pushes him away with a calloused foot.

"Any other cells developing in the Atlantic?"

She scans the screen. "Nothing."

"Analyze that data. I'll be in touch when I can. And Lauren, mention this to no one."

"Understood."

"Gabeheart out."

"Wait—what about my grant? The committee meeting's on Monday."

"You know you have my full support, now more than ever. We could sure use your brain down here."

Sam makes an obscene gesture with his tongue.

"Good luck on Monday. Gabeheart out."

22

NOVEMBER 19, 2033
MABUS PLAZA HOTEL AND CASINO
SOUTH BEACH, FLORIDA
SATURDAY NIGHT

The Mabus Plaza Hotel and Casino is an L-shaped monstrosity of tinted black glass and bloodred neon lighting, occupying five full beach blocks along scenic Ocean Drive. The top six floors of the thirty-three-floor dwelling are all lavish apartment suites leased year-round to film stars, politicians, bankers, and foreign dignitaries. For those who can afford the five million-dollar price tag, there is a seven-year waiting list for availability. For those who can't, reservations for hotel rooms on levels seven through twenty-seven must be made eighteen months in advance and require a nonrefundable five-thousand-dollar deposit. Still out of your league? You can always rent a room by the hour. Two hundred one-bedroom studios are located on floors four through six and are available twenty-four hours a day for clients of the Mabus Bordello, a state-licensed brothel that occupies most of level five. Businessmen specials run 11:00 A.M. to 6:00 P.M. daily. "Blue-ball Mondays are 10 percent off, Two is for Tuesdays (menage à trois), Wednesday's are "hump-days," with "Fantasy Thursdays' rounding out the weekdays (Friday through Sunday reserved for platinum-condom members only).

The first three floors of the Mabus Complex are dedicated strictly to gambling. Levels One and Two are where the general public goes to lose its money. Level Three is more private, strictly reserved for the high rollers and VIPs—by invitation only.

None of the bright lights and sparkles of the old Las Vegas–style casino can be found in this "Hideaway of the Rich and Decadent." Light is out, darkness in. The walls and floors of Level Three are decorated in crimson silks and ebony velvets, the ceiling in smoky mirrors. Half of the two hundred craps and blackjack tables are set up as islands inside giant hot tubs. High-priced "pink ladies of the evening" wearing high-heeled pumps (and little else) sell drinks, drugs, and ultimately themselves, for each of these carnation-dyed beauties can be "rented" by the hour or trick (whatever "cums" first). Baccarat players at hundred-thousand-dollar-minimum tables often receive sexual favors while they gamble, their naked genitals pleasured beneath the table's overhanging satin aprons.

Welcome to the Mabus Plaza Hotel and Casino—a den of iniquity raking in an estimated million dollars every hour—the favorite jewel of Lucien Mabus's thriving financial empire.

For newlyweds Danny Diaz and his bride, Sia, it has become their own private hell.

The young couple from Cocoa Beach had pushed the date of their wedding back eight months just so they could "Honeymoon at the Mabus." On their very first day, "Lady Luck" had greeted them in the guise of an afternoon thundershower, forcing them to abandon "Emperor Nero's Decadence at the Beach" for a day at the casino. Changing into satin robes (provided free by the hotel) they had spent the next seven-plus hours on an amazing run at the roulette table. Sia had won over $30,000, Danny pocketing another $21,400. Delirious with joy, they returned to their room for a quick interlude of sandwiches and sex, hurrying back to the casino with visions of a down payment on a four-bedroom dream home on the coast dancing in their intoxicated heads.

But Lady Luck can be a nasty mistress, and by Saturday morning, the newlyweds had squandered all their winnings, plus another $7,200 in vacation money, a $12,000 advance on Danny's credit card, and the $10,000 in credit Sia's mother had given her daughter as a wedding gift. Worse, Danny had done the unthinkable, tapping into his department's expense account to the tune of $7,300.

Their only consolation—they had received an engraved invitation from the hotel manager to visit Level Three on this, their final evening at the Mabus.

Danny clutches Sia's sweaty palm, guiding her to an open spot at a roulette table, the fifty-six-hundred-dollar credit from her pawned engagement ring burning in his right pants pocket. Steam rises from a nearby hot tub, where an obese middle-aged man is playing poker, the fat on his back flushed pink beneath a mat of thick black hair. Danny pauses, watching enviously as the man bets a stack of ten-thousand-dollar chips.

"Damn . . . uh, okay, honey, what do you think? Roulette or craps?"

Sia glances around the room, gazing at the half-naked celebrities and guests who are circling the tables like vultures. She is perspiring profusely, despite the heavy air-conditioning. "Look, isn't that Tonja Davidson, the soap opera star? Look at those tits. God, she makes me sick."

"Honey, please, roulette or craps? I have to get those funds back into the department's account before seven."

"Okay . . . okay . . . I say roulette." She leads him to the nearest table.

"Chips, please." Danny tosses the attendant the credit, his gaze momentarily lost in her size 38-DD breasts. He squeezes Sia's hand. "Red?"

She nods. "And lucky number 23. Let's get it all back on the first roll."

"Right. Okay, quick, give me a kiss for luck."

Their lips meet, their tongues spreading saliva and vodka as the wheel is spun.

Two floors up, Benjamin Merchant, personal assistant to the casino's president and CEO, sucks deeply on a pacifier bong as he watches the scene play out on his wrist monitor. Merchant's piggish eyes, squirrel gray, remain half-closed behind rose-colored designer spectacles. A thin line of spittle drools from the pacifier and down his lower lip onto the ruffles of his ivory white embroidered dress shirt.

Ben Merchant has never met Danny and Sylvia Diaz, but he knows the couple well. Over the last three days he has been both their good luck charm and dark cloud. Seducing them with each roll of the roulette wheel, he has baited them with lingering tastes of success while encouraging them to reach deeper into their depleted savings. He has played the banker, personally signing off on their arrangements at the hotel's pawn shop. He has played the "chef," lacing their meals with a potent form of Ecstasy.

Now he plays his favorite role of all—the Devil's advocate—as he guides them deeper into bankruptcy.

In Merchant's manicured hand is a small remote device linked to the casino's roulette wheels. He dials up the table number, presses a button, then sucks in another hit from his bong.

"Six black."

Sia's forehead collides with her husband's shoulder.

"*Fubishit!* Where's my goddam drink? Can we get something to drink here?"

A nubile waitress with salmon skin approaches, her gold nipple rings glittering beneath an overhead light. In drug-induced English, dripping with a Jersey accent, she manages, "Caligula wit' a twist, right honey?"

Sia downs the cream-colored liquid, barely registering the flame in the pit of her empty stomach. Sylvia Cabella-Diaz has not eaten or slept in thirty-one hours.

"Sia?"

"Red again, Danny. Everything we've got."

"You sure?"

"Just do it."

Danny pushes the pile of chips across the emerald green felt.

Two floors up, Ben Merchant fingers the BLACK key again on his palm-sized remote.

Sia's heart pounds like a timpani drum. She watches the steel ball jump across the wheel's plastic spokes, slowing on the red, stopping on—

"Nineteen, black."

"*Fubishole!*" The twenty-six year-old's forehead strikes the padded cushion in front of her.

Danny slides off the chair, the room spinning in his head as if he's on a merry-go-round. "Oh, God, Sia, what are we gonna do? I'm dead. I'll lose my job for sure. I could go into exile—"

Across the table, a pit boss listens intently as Ben Merchant's commands are whispered through his ear piece.

"I hate this place, Danny. I told you Friday we should have checked out."

"Excuse me? You're the one who—"

"Mr. and Mrs. Diaz?"

Sia looks up at the pit boss through bloodshot eyes. "What the hell do you want? Haven't you vampires sucked enough of our blood for one night?"

"My manager would like a word with the two of you. In private."

"What for?"

"I believe it concerns your room charges. If you'll follow me please."

Danny shoots his wife a worried look. She shrugs, too weak to protest. "What can they do?"

They follow the pit boss across the casino floor to a private door hidden among the satin vermilion drapes.

The hydraulic door hisses open. "Up the stairs, please."

"What's up the stairs?"

"My manager. Now please, ma'am—"

A brass spiral staircase beckons. Sia goes first, her husband right behind her, the weight of the world on his shoulders.

Ben Merchant is waiting for them atop the landing, a Cheshire cat smile splitting his pasty complexion. "Well, good evening, Mr. and Mrs. Diaz." The heavy Louisiana drawl is as cheery as it is false.

"About the room charges . . . can you just bill us? I promise we'll—"

"Tut-tut . . . all room charges have already been taken care of."

Sia looks at Danny, then back at Merchant.

"The two of you are lucky, very lucky indeed. It seems someone up there likes you." Merchant points a manicured finger toward the ceiling. "A guardian angel."

"I don't understand," says Sia. "Who are you?"

"The name's Merchant, Benjamin Merchant, but you, dear Sylvia, may call me Ben. I have been and remain the private secretary and personal confidant of Mrs. Lucien Mabus, but for tonight, I'll be your exclusive escort as you venture upward to Paradise Lost."

"Excuse me?"

"Paradise Lost, darlin'. A wondrous place just north of heaven. Come, dear cherubs, your chariot awaits." Merchant leads them down a short hall to a private glass elevator. "This lift will take you straight to the penthouse. Mrs. Mabus'll be waiting for you there."

"Mrs. Mabus wants to see us?"

"Nothing to fear, Danny Boy. Like I said, this is your lucky day. All your financial woes are about to disappear."

Danny looks at Sia, then back to Merchant, who is holding the elevator door open, beckoning them in. The couple enters.

"Bon voyage." The doors close on Merchant's smile, sealing them in darkness.

"Danny?" Sia grabs his arm as the lift races skyward.

The elevator stops before they can exhale. The doors part.

Sparkling before them—the Miami skyline—a tapestry of mirrored skyscrapers blazing in rainbows of neon beneath a clear autumn night. Mesmerized, they step out onto the polished onyx-marble floor.

The elevator door hisses closed behind them.

"Hello?" Uncertain, they leave the alcove and enter a living room, the plush carpet the color of sable, the leather furniture and wraparound bar done in various shades of red. Immense bay windows wrap around 360 degrees.

"I'm Lilith."

Danny turns to see a woman pouring drinks behind the bar. The vixen's skin is chocolate, her hair the color of pitch, long and wavy, trailing down her back. "Lucien wishes he could be here to greet you, but he's been sick lately, poor dear."

Danny's eyes widen as she walks around the bar, handing them each a glass. Lilith is wearing a see-through negligee, her dark breasts and shaved crotch pressing against the sheer fabric. She motions them to a couch. "So the two of you are newlyweds?"

"Uh, yes. Just married three days ago."

"Four." Sia shoots him an elbow, disrupting his gaze. "How long have you and Mr. Mabus been married?"

"Just long enough to want him dead." A high, piercing cackle as she turns her sociopathic gaze toward Sia. "Thank Satan for vibrators, eh girl."

Danny focuses his attention on Lilith's exposed brown nipple, drooling like an intoxicated mouse eyeing the cheese.

"It's late," Sia stutters, feeling out of her element.

"The night is young," Lilith purrs, "but you're worried about something."

"We lost a lot of money. Danny borrowed from his expense account."

"Sia!"

"Now, now, we're all family here at the Mabus. Tell me, Daniel, how much did you lose tonight in our little lion's den of inequity?"

Danny breaks eye contact. "I don't know. Everything we had left."

"Sia's ring, too?"

Danny nods, his emotions welling.

"And all of your savings?" Lilith Mabus—so endearing—like a priest at confession.

"The credit card. Our wedding gifts." Danny pinches tears from his sleep-deprived eyes.

Sia eyes shoot daggers at Lilith as the vixen circles the coffee table to sit next to her husband.

"Daniel, scoot closer and place your hand on the coffee table's access pad."

He complies, the woman's scent filling his nostrils, wondering what he'd do if Sia wasn't in the room.

"Computer, access the financial statement of Mr. Daniel Diaz."

A holographic account ledger appears above the pewter coffee table. Danny's eyes widen in disbelief.

The neon blue credit balance at the bottom indicates a recent deposit of $200,000.

"I think that should more than cover your losses." Lilith sits back on the cushion.

"This is . . . crazy," Danny says, "I don't understand?"

Lilith smiles, her bleached white teeth bright against her Mesoamerican-African-American complexion. "A gift, Daniel. From one who has—to one in need."

Emotion crumbles Danny's face. Glee. Tears. Relief. Exhaustion. "I don't know what to say?"

"Just say thank you."

"Thank you! Thank you, thank you, thank you—"

"What's the catch?" Sia asks.

Lilith smiles. "Maybe I'm just trying to buy my way into heaven?"

"I doubt that."

"Sia!"

"It's all right, Daniel. Your wife is right to question my motives. I've heard it said that sin is the Devil's daughter. Do you know what's worse?"

"No."

"Fear." Lilith stands, allowing her hand to casually tease Sia's hair as she walks by. "I was raised by fear. For as long as I can remember, fear dominated my dreams and every waking thought in between. It robbed me of my childhood, stole my innocence, and left me its victim. Fear of death. Fear of abuse. Fear of being abandoned, of being alone. Fear of losing love."

She settles on the sofa opposite Daniel. "You know what the worst thing about fear is? It keeps us from recognizing our one true power . . . that each of us possesses free will. Fear kept me in check for fourteen years, feeding off me, until it pushed me to the brink of suicide. And that's when I grew angry. Angèr mobilized me to take risks. From that moment on, I stopped being life's victim. I learned to use the powers of the flesh to get what I want." She motions with her hands.

Danny nods, mesmerized by her words and his Ecstasy-laced cocktail.

"You married wealth," Sia states. "What risks did you ever take?"

Lilith spreads her legs slightly and winks at Danny, offering him a tantalizing view of her crotch. "It takes talent to marry into wealth, Sylvia, especially when you come from nothing. Wealth must be seduced . . . teased. Power requires trust, trust—deception. Look at Daniel. He took a risk tapping into his company's funds, no doubt seduced by your own greed and ambition. I admire that. The ability to seduce makes us powerful, don't you agree?"

"And thank God for it," Danny says, feeling giddy.

"God may have given us our sex organs, Daniel, but it was Lucifer who taught us how to use them. Now show me yours."

"Huh?"

"My presence makes your wife jealous. Use it to your advantage."

Danny's pulse throbs. "I . . . I don't understand?"

"Show me the new Daniel Diaz, the man you always dreamed you'd be. You have your money, now take control of the moment. Order Sylvia to perform oral sex."

"You're nuts, lady." Sia stands to leave. "Keep your damn money, I'm nobody's whore."

"We're all whores, sister. Watch me, I'll show you how it's—"

"No!" Sia pushes Lilith aside. Quivering with anger and adrenaline, she stumbles around the coffee table to her husband. "Take off your pants."

"Sia—"

"Shut up and do it. She paid for a show, we'll give it to her."

Danny moans as his bride takes control, burying her face in his groin.

Lilith moves closer. "It's all about power, isn't it, sister. Who controls who." She grabs Sia by her hair and yanks her face away before Danny can climax.

"Hey—"

In Lilith's free hand is a small box. Sia opens it.

Inside is her engagement ring.

"Sisters share."

Sia feels dizzy, lost, as if she is living the moment from someone else's perspective. She watches as Lilith places her mouth against her husband's erect organ.

Danny lays his head back and closes his eyes.

For Daniel Diaz, senior structural engineer at NASA's

Top-Secret Project: GOLDEN FLEECE, the night is indeed still young.

Fraternity Row
University of Miami

Lauren wraps her arms tighter around Sam's waist as he propels the *Harley-Davidson* HY-1200 motorcycle along College Avenue at 96 mph. Wind whistles past her headgear, the sleek black-and-chrome hydrogen-powered cycle cutting a hole through the humid evening air.

Sam banks hard, directing his hog into the student parking lot. He reaches for Lauren's hand, but she pulls it away. "Come on, don't stay mad."

"Why this Tanner woman? Can't someone else interview you?"

"It's part of my PCAA obligations, Lauren. What am I supposed to do, insist on a male reporter?"

"Yes!"

"Well, I can't, okay? So just drop it."

"Fine." They walk down Fraternity Row in silence. "You know, Sam, maybe it's time we see other people."

"Come on, Lauren."

"No, I'm serious. We've been together since ninth grade. It's not healthy."

"Says who? Your friend, Tierney? She's just jealous."

"Maybe . . . but she has a point. We need a break before we get married. You should experience some other people."

"Lauren—"

"I'm serious. If I get that research grant, I'll be gone for four weeks. Use the time to 'grind some fresh bone.' Get it out of your system. If you don't do it now, our marriage'll never last."

"And what about you? You planning on 'draining' some park ranger while you watch Old Faithful?"

"Maybe."

"Bullshit." He spins her around, then sees the tears. "Lauren, I don't want to grind other women." He smiles. "I just want to grind you."

"Okay. But I swear, if I find out you were with that—"

He kisses her, cutting off the expletive.

Lauren kisses him back. Passion replaces fear as she grinds her pelvis into his, drawing him in deeper. "Let's . . . skip . . . the party."

"Can't."

"Yes you can." She continues kissing him, rubbing her hand along his crotch.

"I can't . . . okay maybe . . . no, wait—wait, stop, Lauren, stop—I have to make an appearance. Just a couple of minutes, okay?"

"Why?"

"Because they're my teammates."

She stops teasing him. "Some teammates. If you ask me—"

"Which I didn't—"

"—they're more like your employees. All they care about is their damn playoff bonuses. You need to look out for you. You should have turned pro last year."

"Well, I didn't. Now come on, we'll stay for an hour and finish this in your apartment."

"No we won't." She pushes him away. "I won't be in the mood."

"Fine." He takes her hand, leading her toward the frat house. "Hey, maybe I'll meet some fresh bone—"

He winces as she slaps him upside the head.

The orange-and-white-stucco, horseshoe-shaped two-story structure affectionately known as "Jock-U" is an open-air hacienda-style mansion containing an in-ground football-shaped swimming pool, hot tub, and, for those annoying rainy days—a retractable sunroof. The facility sleeps 112, has a full-time staff of cooks, trainers, maids, and tutors on the premises, and like Sam's Harley, is paid for out of the PCAA athletic budget.

The Professional Collegiate Athletic Association took roots back in 2008 when the former governing body of "amateur" intercollegiate athletics, the National Collegiate Athletic Association, lost a class-action lawsuit filed on behalf of five thousand student-athletes who charged the NCAA had no right to prevent them from receiving nonathletic-related monies while enrolled in school. Faced with the reality of finally having to pay their breadwinners, the NCAA voted to reorganize into a separate and independent governing body dedicated solely to "professional" collegiate athletics. Encompassing Men's Division I-A football and men and women's Division I basketball, the Professional Collegiate Athletic Association (PCAA) established standardized pay scales and benefit programs for its revenue-generating participants. This included full tuition, room and board, school supplies, a monthly stipend (based on undergraduate status) and a bonus program, which rewarded grade point average as well as postseason tournament participation. To remain eligible, a PCAA student-athlete was required to attend class (in person) and demonstrate satisfactory progress toward a five-year degree. Any athlete could try out for the professional leagues at any time and still return to school—provided they had not yet accepted a pro signing bonus (usually held in escrow until after final cuts) or played a minute of regular-season ball. Any PCAA athlete who did turn pro prior to graduation was required to immediately refund from their signing bonuses all stipend monies earned while at school. Athletes choosing to remain in school until graduation earned a "diploma bonus" a figure based on the team's won-lost record during their years of participation.

By 2017, the PCAA football playoffs were generating revenues surpassing those of the National Football League and National Basketball Asociation.

*   *   *

Lauren follows Sam through the Art Deco security arch leading to the front entrance. He places his hand upon the SID pad.

A holograph appears—a well-endowed topless blonde wearing a G-string. The model's computerized face has been replaced with Coach DeMaio's, the voice with that of teen pop singer Lacy Wong. "Good evening, Samuel Agler, you hunka-hunka burning Hurricane love. Please enter me so I may please you."

"Uh, thanks . . . Coach."

They pass through the weapon detector's violet indicator beam. The double doors slide open, allowing them entry into a high-ceilinged hall engorged with loud technomusic, neon holographic creatures, flashing lights, and mobs of mostly naked bodies.

Lauren leans over, yells, "It's like the last days of Rome meets disco."

K. C. Renner, who is wearing an aluminocloth shirt and boxer shorts, is the first to greet them. "My bonus baby, gimme some bone." Renner's and Sam's knuckles collide.

"Good evening, Lauren." Renner's voice turns sarcastically stuffy. "So glad you could join us." The quarterback shakes her hand, then licks it.

"You're disgusting."

"Thank you. Food's everywhere, plenty of strange . . . oops, sorry. *M'casa es su casa*."

The staccato pulse of the bass, originating from surround-sound speakers strategically placed beneath the porous floorboards is literally sending music vibrating up through their bodies.

"Isn't it a bit loud?" Lauren yells.

"Yeah, great crowd. Hey, everyone's out by the pool. Come on." Renner leads them through the packed hall. Groping blue-and-yellow-tinted hands reach out to touch them as they pass.

A set of soundproof Plexiglas doors part, allowing them to escape the noise into a home entertainment holograph suite. The doors *hiss* close behind them, shutting out the hallway acoustics.

The room is black, backlit by matching columns of ceiling-to-floor lava lamps and a 3-D holographic movie projecting in front of the far wall.

As Lauren's eyes adjust to the dark, she notices movement along the floor—couples, making out in sensory body bags.

K. C. directs them through a second set of soundproof doors. They pass the food prep room and exit into the courtyard.

Humidity and the heavy scent of the pool's ozone filtration system hits them square in the face. The soothing calypso sounds of Cuban heartthrob, Elian, comes from palm tree speakers planted along the periphery.

Cheerleaders, groupies, and prostitutes, most of them naked, lounge in and around the football-shaped pool in clusters, a dozen of Sam's teammates drifting from one group to the next. Lauren spots Jerry Tucker in the hot tub, the enormous lineman sandwiched between two bare-breasted Jamaican-dyed Asian girls. Another teammate is lying on the deck behind him, passed out in a puddle of vomit.

She shakes her head. "Miami's gridiron warriors. Pillaging the village before their next conquest."

Ken Hudak, the team's heavily muscled, pine green-dyed middle linebacker, struts toward them, dragging his date, a Haitian girl wearing only a bandanna around her waist. Lauren stares at the couple's his-and-her hip tattoo, which creates the illusion of two bulldogs doing it doggy style when the pair are making love with the girl on top.

"Mule—we gotta talk, man." Before Lauren can object, Hudak drapes his arm around her fiancé and leads him away.

K. C. shrugs. "Sam's a popular guy."

"Too popular."

The Haitian girl slides over to K. C., grinding her bare

groin into his hip. "I'm tired of playing defensive ball. How 'bout teaching me a little offense?"

K. C. winks at Lauren. "Back in a minute."

"Yeah, go grind your brains out." She watches him lead the girl away.

Lauren's eyes search for Sam. She spots him by the hot tub, surrounded by most of the team's defensive starters, all of whom are dyed the same shade of Miami green.

The hell with this . . . She heads back inside.

"You're accusing me of tanking it?" Sam shakes his head in disbelief.

Hudak leans in, spewing his garlic breath. "We lost. No way we lose to the *fubishitting* Seminole-holes if you're running the way you usually do."

"I had 104 yards on the ground, 54 more receiving. I scored a touchdown."

"Don't diss us, Mule," says Keith Plourde, the *Hurricanes'* cocaptain. "You haven't run for less than two hundred yards since you were in grade school."

"I need that playoff bonus, Mule," Brian Mundt whines. "I'm *fuupdass* without it."

"Maybe you wouldn't be so fucked-up-the-ass if you learned how to tackle," Sam says, pushing the defensive end out of his face.

"I heard a ton of gamblers lost money on the point spread today," Keith Plourde states, accusingly. "Maybe you were in on the action, huh?"

Sam lunges for Plourde, pile-driving him backward against a palm tree.

Hudak and Mundt intercede before the first punch is thrown.

"Knock it off!" The veins in Hudak's thick neck bulge like garter snakes. "We know Mule wouldn't do that, K. P. What we don't know is if our soul brother is turnin' pro?"

"Not this season."

"Yeah, but what about next year?" asks Jeff "Bubba"

Larsen, Miami's six-foot-three-inch, three-hundred-pound all-American strong-side linebacker.

"I don't know." Sam stares down Larsen, his heart pounding with adrenaline. "I haven't decided."

"Fuck!" Now it's Larsen who is ready to strike. "You leave after this year, and we're all *fuupdass*. Between stipes and bonuses, we're talkin' a buck forty large a piece."

"One forty-five," corrects Mundt.

"Most of us don't got two-hundred-million-dollar GFL contracts waiting out there," growls Matt Eterginio, the starting free safety.

"None of us *have*," Sam corrects. "You're supposed to be an English major, Matt. Of course, you're also supposed to be a free safety, but that didn't stop FSU from takin' it to the house on you all afternoon."

"Okay, everybody just calm down," commands Hudak. "Look, Mule, we're your teammates. Your brothers. Brothers stick together."

Brothers stick together . . . The words seem to echo in his brain.

"Are you gonna be there for us, Mule?"

They crowd around, creating a pine green wall of flesh.

Lauren surveys the banquet table of food and drugs in the dining hall. The sushi and Chinese ribs look tantalizing, but she passes. The last time she ate at one of K. C.'s parties, she ended up playing naked volleyball on the dean's lawn.

She hears cheers. Bored, she follows the sound to the entertainment suite.

A dozen football players are lying on body cushions, drinking beer and watching a 3-D holographic replay of the Miami-FSU game. Lauren grabs a juice pouch off the cooler tree and takes a seat on the floor.

The projection is playing Miami's opening drive. A hovering spherical-video end zone cam zooms in on K. C Renner as he mouths incomprehensible signals, the action set at ultraslow motion. The quarterback takes the snap and pitches the ball to Sam, who heads to his right, where several Seminole players are waiting.

Wild cheers of "Mule . . . Mule . . . Mule" as Sam executes an eye-popping pirouette, races back toward the line of scrimmage, then stiff-arms his way through a wall of defenders like a mad bull, opening up his own hole.

Lauren feels goose bumps. She allows herself a smile. *Maybe I won't be tired tonight . . .*

The camera zooms in tight on Sam's face.

She stops smiling.

Lauren Beckmeyer has known Samuel Agler since they were in ninth grade. In all that time, she has never seen anything like the expression now etched on her boyfriend's face.

Fear.

23

NOVEMBER 20, 2033
MANALAPAN, FLORIDA
SUNDAY AFTERNOON

The palatial south Florida mansion of billionaire Lucien J. Mabus and his wife Lilith, stretches eight hundred feet along a private pristine coastline in Manalapan, a small island town just north of Boynton Beach. The thirty-one-room, three-story home, originally built for $21.3 million back in 1997, features a seaside swimming pool complete with waterfall and swim-up bar, two tennis courts, a fitness center, a twelve-hundred-square-foot grand salon illuminated by a six-thousand-pound crystal chandelier imported from a nineteenth-century French chateau, an observatory dome, and an eight-car garage, its floors paved in Saturnia marble. Each of the six bedroom suites has its own balcony facing the Atlantic. All of the home's windows are self-cleaning, made with a thin metal oxide coating electrified to help rainwater to wash away loose particles.

The mansion's staff includes two housekeepers, a chef, a licensed pilot who doubles as a chauffeur, six heavily armed security guards, and a mechanic. Robotic mowers and trimmers perpetually manicure the lawns and shrubs to incessant perfection. Every computer and control station in the home is wired to a backup fuel-cell power station located on the northern side of the property. There are three satellite dishes on the roof.

All this—for only two adults and the occasional visiting business associate.

Twenty-six-year-old Lucien Mabus, son of the late Peter Mabus, opens his mouse brown, red-rimmed eyes and gazes at himself in the ceiling mirror. His face is ashen gray, his lips—alabaster white. His eyes are sunken, surrounded by dark circles.

"It's just the flu," his personal physician has assured him. "You're far too young and rich to leave us now, Lucien."

That was sixteen days and thirty pounds ago. His personal physician had wanted him to undergo tests in a hospital, but Lilith refused. "Those hospitals will kill you, darling. I'm sure it's just a bad case of food poisoning. I keep warning you about eating so much shellfish. I've sent the cooks home. From now on, I'll personally be bringing you your meals, at least until you feel better."

Lucien glances to the nightstand on his right. Prescription medicines, tissues, and a plastic beach bucket, in case he has to vomit again. A half-eaten bowl of chicken soup sits on a tray. The sight of it makes him queasy. *Chicken soup . . . can't she cook anything but chicken soup?*

The billionaire rolls over, pulling the blanket over his

shoulder. *What's all the money in the world if I'm too sick to enjoy it?*

Chills fade into a hot flash, bringing with it the dreaded queasiness.

Lucien grabs the bucket and retches.

His pulse throbs in his head. His throat burns, his stomach convulsing in spasms. Flopping onto the floor, he holds his head in his hands, praying for the pain to stop.

God . . . what is it you want from me? Charity work? Another wing at some third-world hospital? Just tell me and end this misery.

Gathering his strength, he drags himself to his feet, the vertigo causing the bedroom to spin. Staggering forward, he heads to the bathroom—then stops, staring at his bare feet.

His toes are numb.

"Oh, God . . . what's happening to me? Lilith? Lilith!"

He stumbles out of the master bedroom and into the hallway.

"Lilith?"

No wife. No servants. *Where the hell is everyone?*

He fumbles his way down the hall, the numbness spreading to his feet and ankles. He pauses at the open door to one of the guest suites, hearing voices. "Lilith? Lilith . . . you in here?"

Lucien staggers into the bedroom.

Stretched out across the king-size water bed, staring at her reflection in the ceiling mirror, is his young bride.

"Lilith, help—" Lucien falls to his knees, the sharp pain in his gut overwhelming. Numbness rises past his ankles to his hips. "Call Gill. Get me to a hospital, I think it's my heart!"

"No need to worry, sweetie, it's not your heart."

"How . . . how do you know?"

"Darling, it's just the poison I've been feeding you."

Lucien's blood runs cold.

"Now die like a good little rich boy, and don't stain the carpet."

Lucien collapses facefirst onto the plush beige rug, the numbness rising past his chest, the ringing in his ears insufficient to mute the cackle of laughter coming from his murderous wife's voluptuous lips.

University of Miami

The Jerome Brown Memorial Athletic Center is located on the north side of the University of Miami campus, adjacent to the MTI basketball arena. In addition to its indoor track, pool, weight room, and conditioning equipment, the JBC is equipped with a press room and media center, complete with global uplink capabilities. At the heart of the facility is a circular broadcast chamber, its tinted smart-glass walls designed to conceal a myriad of cameras and lights, microphones, special effects boards, and technicians.

Diane Tanner enters the interview chamber, wearing her standard skintight designer ESPN body leotard. The voluptuous blonde takes her place opposite Samuel in an identical crushed velvet chair and adjusts her cleavage. "Nervous?"

"Should I be?"

"This is a live interview."

"Won't be my first."

"I make you nervous, don't I?"

"Do you always come on to the athletes you interview?" She smiles. "Only the cute ones."

"Stand by, Diane." The voice, coming from a hidden microphone. "Five . . . four . . . three—"

Diane switches to a more professional smile. "Welcome to *This Week in Sports.* I'm your host, Diane Tanner, and with me today is University of Miami's star tailback, Samuel 'the Mule' Agler. Sam, thanks for taking time to be with me." She winks.

"My, uh . . . pleasure."

"Sam, pro scouts have already anointed you the most prolific running back ever to play in the professional collegiate ranks. Before we talk about your accomplishments on the field, I thought we'd take a quick peek into your private life. You were born in Chads Ford, Pennsylvania, is that right?"

"According to the birth certificate."

"Your mother died when you were three. What happened?"

"Drunk driver. This was before the new safety protocols."

"Of course. So your father, Gene, moved the two of you to Hollywood Beach, Florida, to start life over. Why Florida?"

"Job transfer. He took over as principal at Pompano High."

"How old were you when you started playing football?"

"Five or six."

"And the rest, as they say, is history. Star tailback your freshman year in high school. Led the nation in scoring and total yardage for four straight years. The most recruited PCAA athlete in history. Scored a perfect sixteen hundred on your entrance exams. With your scores and grades, you could have accepted an academic scholarship at Harvard."

"I suppose. But I wanted to stay close to home."

"Because you fell in love with your high-school sweetheart. How romantic." Diane allows the sarcasm to drip.

"She keeps me in line."

"I bet she does. You don't drink or Bliss. You donate your time to anti-drug messages. Jesus, Mule, you're every American mother's wet dream."

"Some of us were raised the right way."

"Hmm, now how does that old song go . . . '*only the good die young*?' Anyway, let's talk football. Tell us what it's like to step out on the playing field and have 120,000 crazed fans screaming your nickname? How does it feel?"

Sam offers a half grin. "Feels kind of good."

"Good? I'd think it must feel incredible, unbelievable.

When you scored that touchdown against FSU—what a rush, huh?"

"Yeah. That one felt great."

"Did it?" Diane sits back, the fly now snug in her web. "Let's take a look."

The lights dim, the smart glass becoming a circular hall of projection screens, Sam's image on every panel.

Sam takes the pitch from his quarterback—

Cuts to his right—

Pivots back toward the line, evading tacklers . . . punching his way to daylight—

The cameras zoom in from a dozen different angles—

—focusing on his facial expression as he sprints down the sideline.

The image freezes. The lights come back on.

"Sam, that certainly doesn't look like delight on your face to me. It looks like, well . . . like fear. Were you afraid of something?"

"I, uh . . ."

"You seem kind of worried, like you might have just screwed up royally. How could you have screwed up by scoring a touchdown?"

"I was just winded—"

"You must've had trouble regaining your wind, you only gained sixty-two yards on the ground the rest of the game."

"It happens. FSU had nine defenders in the box. There were no holes."

She smiles coyly. "Since when does the Mule need a hole?"

"What's your point?"

"This was the biggest game of the year. Billions of dollars had been wagered in the federal government's weekly football pool. The Canes were a six-point favorite. The final score was FSU 16, Miami 10. The game was a 'push,' generating a cool 2.3 billion for our friends in Washington, DC."

"Are you accusing me of throwing the game?"

"Of course not, not you, Mr. Perfect. But hypothetically speaking, how much would someone, say, Florida's governor Ryan Wismer, have to pay you to pull up lame?

"You lousy *fushcubitch!*" Samuel stands.

The cameras keep rolling, Tanner far from finished. "Any truth to the rumors the PCAA is launching its own investigation?"

"That's it, we're done. Shut it down." He searches in vain for an exit.

"Sammy, darling, before you dash off, explain to my viewers why you ran out of bounds in that third quarter drive. Samuel 'the Mule' Agler never runs out of bounds."

Sam targets a mirrored panel. He jumps off the stage, pivots in midair, and executes a devastating side kick, his right heel striking the smart-glass like a sledgehammer, shattering it into a thousand smoking shards.

Diane ducks, unable to avoid the shrapnel. "I'm, uh, Diane Tanner, and that's *This Week in Sports!*"

Sam hurtles past the stunned technicians and out the door.

University of Miami Main Campus
Coral Gables, Florida

November 21, 2033
7:18 A.M.

Lauren Beckmeyer stands at the dais, rechecking her notes and display disks for the third time. Seated before her are four of the five committee members assigned to the university's research grant council. *English Lit., Asian Studies, Physics, and History . . . everyone here but my Geology guy . . .*

Professor Christopher Laubin, the fifth member of the council, hurries down the aisle.

"Sorry I'm late." The Chair of the Geology Department nods to the other members of the committee, situates himself in one of the gold-cushioned high-backed chairs, then turns his attention to Lauren. "Are you ready to proceed, Ms. Beckmeyer?"

Been ready, you old . . . "Yes, sir."

She inserts a disk, activating the first series of images— a sequence of moving photos of the Mount St. Helens eruption.

"On May 18, 1980, at 8:32 A.M., a magnitude 5.1 earthquake shook Mount St. Helens. Within fifteen to twenty seconds, the volcano's bulge and summit slid away in a huge landslide. This landslide depressurized the volcano's magma system, triggering powerful explosions that ripped through the sliding debris. Rocks, volcanic gas, ash, and steam were blasted upward at speeds exceeding 300 miles per hour. The blast cloud traveled 17 miles north, its lateral blast producing a column of ash and gas that rose more than 15 miles into the atmosphere in less than fifteen minutes. Over the course of the day, prevailing winds blew 520 million tons of ash eastward across the United States and caused complete darkness in Spokane, Washington, 250 miles from the site."

A slide of the devastation appears.

"Volcanic eruptions are not unusual. Even fifty years ago, scientists were able to predict Mount St. Helens eruption in plenty of time to warn the population." She pauses to make eye contact with the committee. "Now imagine a volcano whose eruption is not predictable, packing ten thousand times the force of Mount St. Helens. Imagine a blast spewing enough ash to cover half the United States in a few frightening minutes. In short, imagine an explosion comparable to an asteroid strike, one that could plunge Earth into millions of years of unending winter."

The image changes, the committee now looking at a satellite view of a crater, its surface boiling azure greens and blues.

"The nightmare I've just described is called a super volcano. Unlike a volcano, it possesses no cone. Essentially, it exists as a massive subterranean magma pocket, or caldera.

A caldera is a depression, formed by the collapse of the ground following a volcanic explosion of a large body of stored magma. What you're looking at is a thermal photograph of Yellowstone National Park's youngest of three calderas. This monster lurks five miles below the surface. It is 112 miles across and 48 miles wide, encompassing nearly the entire park."

Lauren glances up, pleased to see shocked expressions on four of the committee members. *They should be shocked, we're only talking the end of civilization . . .*

Lauren changes the photo to an overhead shot of an island situated in a large crater lake.

"Modern man has never witnessed the eruption of a super volcano, but we know of their devastation. This is Lake Toba, located in North Sumatera, Indonesia. The lake was formed by a super volcano that erupted 74,000 years ago. Keep in mind Lake Toba's caldera is smaller in comparison to Yellowstone's magma pocket, but evidence from its last explosion should give you an idea of the kind of devastation we're talking about."

The lake shot is replaced by a slide of microscopic organisms.

"To understand how the history of Lake Toba affected humanity, we turn to *Homo Sapiens* DNA. While most of our species' DNA is stored in the nuclei of our cells, a small portion can also be found in the mitochondria—the rod-shaped cells responsible for energy production. What's unique about the mitochondria is that its DNA is passed only from mother to child. This feature allows geneticists to trace the natural lineage and diversity of our population by focusing on mutations present in our genome. By analyzing the rate and distributions of these mutations, scientists are able to detect patterns in the history of humanity's population growth.

"With 7 billion people on the planet, scientists expected to find a wide range of genetic diversity. Instead, what they found was something totally unexpected—a bottleneck, or sudden drop in population.

The African-American Chair of the Physics Department raises a hand. "You're referring to a major catastrophe?"

"Yes, sir. Something in the history of *Homo sapiens* decimated our entire species, reducing the number of human beings left on our entire planet to, incredible as it seems, a mere few thousand. The simple and frightening fact is, the DNA of every man, woman, and child living today can be traced back to these few thousand survivors. Now, because mutations in human DNA take place with clock-like regularity, scientists were able to approximate a date when this sudden change occurred." She pauses for effect. "The bottleneck occurred 74,000 years ago, right after the explosion that formed Lake Toba."

The representative of English Literature looks pale. "Are you saying this . . . this super volcano wiped out nearly every human being on the planet?"

"Yes, ma'am. And keep in mind, Lake Toba's caldera was nowhere near as large as Yellowstone's monster."

"Is Yellowstone dormant? Has it ever erupted before?"

Lauren clicks over to the next image—a fossil embedded in soil and ash.

"The geological record shows that Yellowstone's hot spot has been responsible for three major eruptions. The first happened 2.1 million years ago, the second 1.3 million years ago, the most recent 630,000 years ago. Scientists agree that this periodicity of eruptions is likely to continue, meaning the next explosion could occur 100,000 years from now . . . or, as *some* geologists fear"—she ignores Professor Laubin's roll of the eyes—"very soon."

The photo disappears, replaced by a synthesized depiction of an underground cross section of Yellowstone's terrain. Situated above ground along the north section, directly beneath the pocket of magma—is a mammoth, hill-sized bulge.

"This bulge has been rising above Yellowstone's caldera since the first geological survey of the park was taken in the late 1920s. Scientists first became alarmed about thirty years ago when the bulge actually began lifting the northern end of Yellowstone Lake, causing its waters to spill into the forest located along its southern shoreline. As you can see, the forest is now completely flooded.

"This telltale bulge indicates that pressure is increasing within the magma pocket. At some point it's going to explode. When it happens, the devastation will be felt across the entire planet. Since words don't begin to tell the story, I thought you might be interested in a little animation."

The computer image changes to a satellite view of the United States. A dark cloud suddenly belches over Wyoming.

"When Yellowstone's caldera erupts, the pyroclastic blast will instantly kill tens of thousands of people living in the area. The resultant ash cloud that rises into the stratosphere will cover most of the United States, primarily affecting the Great Plains—America's breadbasket. Harvests will be obliterated overnight. The ash plume will eventually span the entire globe, blotting out the sun's rays, leading to a super volcanic winter."

Professor Laubin glances at the digital display on the dais. "Ninety seconds, Ms. Beckmeyer. I suggest you use what remains of your allotted time to explain GOPHER."

"Yes, sir." A final image appears—a schematic of what appears to be a UAV robot.

"One way to potentially cool the magma flow and stave off a major eruption is to flood the caldera just prior to its blast with the waters of Yellowstone Lake. My father, Mark Beckmeyer, is an engineer at Broward Robotics. The two of us designed GOPHER, an acronym for Geothermal Observatory for Pyrolysis and Heat Exchange Release. Pyrolysis is a chemical change caused by the action of heat. Using GOPHER, we intend to create a series of canals running from Yellowstone Lake to key sections of the Yellowstone caldera, creating an early-warning ventilation system. I've already met with park officials, who agree the system could significantly reduce magma temperatures, potentially preventing or lessening the effects of a major eruption."

The history professor is making rapid calculations on his pocket computer. "Seven hundred thousand dollars is a sizable grant, Ms Beckmeyer." *NOT IN 2012* ☺

"Yes, sir, but a small price to pay to save civilization. And the university would share all proprietary rights."

"Time's up," Professor Laubin announces.

The Asian professor looks anxious. "Ms. Beckmeyer, perhaps you could wait outside, please."

Lauren grabs her belongings and exits the chamber. She finds an empty bench in the corridor. *Seven hundred thousand dollars . . . they spend that much on resurfacing their damn faculty parking lots. Maybe I can convince Sam to turn pro. His bonus check alone could buy a hundred GOPHERs . . .*

Professor Laubin joins her in the corridor. "Ms. Beckmeyer, did you really think those scare tactics would work?"

"I can't help it if the facts are scary."

"Yes, well you certainly have a flare for the dramatic." He grins, extending his hand. "You also have yourself a research grant. Congratulations."

Lauren leaps off the bench and hugs him around the neck.

"Okay, okay. Now go save the world."

Belle Glade, Florida

Virgil Robinson tucks his new white dress shirt into his new khaki pants and slips his bare feet into the secondhand brown suede loafers.

"Ready, Virge?"

"Been ready for twenty damn years."

Virgil follows the armed guard past the seemingly endless corridor of cells. He nods to a few well-wishers, avoids eye contact with others.

His heart beats faster as they exit the cellblock.

"You are required to contact your probation officer within twenty-four hours."

"Yes, sir."

"Open up."

The cellblock door rolls open, and a second guard joins them on their walk.

"You may not leave Florida while on probation, do you understand?"

"Yes, sir."

"You will be required to submit and pass a random urine test every month while on probation."

"Yes, sir."

They approach a solid steel door. "Open up."

Virgil squints at the afternoon sun as it peeks between the razor wire and perimeter fencing. A supervisor hands him two envelopes, one containing a three-hundred-dollar credit, the other a plastic bag holding his personal belongings.

Virgil follows the two guards and supervisor outside, the men leading him down fifty yards of fenced-in sidewalk, dead-ending at another gate.

"One for release. Open the gate."

The steel door slides open.

"Prisoner F-344278-B, you have been granted parole by the State of Florida Correctional Systems. Will there be someone meeting you?"

"Yes, sir."

"Very well. Stay on the straight and narrow."

"Yes, sir." *Asshole* . . . Virgil walks out of the shadow of the penitentiary and into the light.

The white limousine is parked along the side of the road. The back door opens.

Out steps a paunchy Caucasian man in rose-colored glasses, dressed in a tropical silk shirt and cream-colored slacks. "Virgil Robinson?" The man's voice—a heavy Louisiana drawl.

"Yeah?"

"The name's Ben Merchant. I work for your daughter. You did receive her letter?"

"Got it right here." Virgil pats his pocket, his shirt already spotting with perspiration.

"Come on, partner, let's get you out of the heat."

The limousine turns south on Smart Highway 95.

"So, uh—"

"Call me Ben."

"Right. So Ben, you say this Mabus fella died yesterday?"

"And so young. Doctor says it was a heart attack."

"And my Lilith—"

"—inherited everything. Exciting, huh? Just think—your little girl, the child you abandoned as a baby, is a billionaire." Ben offers his Cheshire cat smile. "Like hittin' the lottery without even playing."

Virgil looks out the tinted window and stifles a grin.

The limo turns south on scenic A-1-A, driving through a wooded area heavy in pine. On the right are million-dollar neighborhoods, on the left—incredible estates featuring private twenty-million-dollar views of the Atlantic.

They pass a WELCOME TO MANALAPAN sign. Moments later, the limo turns into a gated driveway leading up to the Mabus mansion.

Virgil steps out of the car. "All this one house?"

"Yes, sir. Let's go 'round back and meet your daughter."

Ben Merchant leads him along a stone path beneath a canopy of palm trees until the aqua blue hues of the ocean come into view.

The rear of the Mabus property is a private resort. Tennis courts, wet bar, sauna, whirlpool, cabana, a covered patio overlooking an undisturbed stretch of pristine beach . . . even a helipad.

Virgil's jaw drops. *My little girl got money to burn . . .*

A winding stone stairwell leads up to the main deck. Stretched out before them is a pond-shaped pool, each end adorned with waterfalls and tropical foliage.

Lying in a lounge chair, sunbathing completely in the nude, is Lilith Robinson-Mabus.

For a long moment, Virgil simply stares, his emotions teetering between lust and greed.

"Lilith, darlin', this is Virgil Robinson . . . your biological father."

Lilith stands and hugs him, smearing baby oil all over his clean white shirt. "Well, I've only waited my entire life to meet you. Should I call you Virgil or Daddy?"

"Uh, Daddy's good. Damn, girl . . . ya'll always prance around wit' no clothes on?"

"I wanted our first meeting to be memorable. I know you haven't seen a woman in twenty years."

Virgil bites his lip. "Uh, yeah. Hey, uh, sorry to hear about your husband."

Lilith giggles as she returns to her lounge chair. "Sit, Daddy. Come and sit in front of me where I can see you."

Merchant positions a lounge chair. "Tell what, how 'bout I get ya'll something cold to drink? I think Lucille just made some of her famous fresh lemonade. Virgil?"

"Yeah . . . sure." Virgil sits on the hot vinyl, not sure where to look.

"So tell me, Daddy, did anyone rape you while you were in prison?"

"Say what?"

"You know, hide their sausage in your asshole?"

"Hell, no. I'd kill any muthafucker try messin' wit' me."

"Sort of like you killed my mother, huh?"

"Now girl, I know that was wrong, and I done my time. But see, I'm a changed man. I found Jesus."

"Really? Does Jesus spend much time in prison?"

"Don't sass your daddy, now. I'm here 'cause I wanna make up for lost time."

"How very noble of you. I'm so sorry, I misjudged you completely."

"S'all right."

"Hey, Daddy, do you prefer your women shaved?"

"Huh?"

Lilith spreads her legs. "My late husband used to insist I shave my pubes. He'd say, 'Lilith, I hate that nappy nigger hair.' What do you think?"

"Lemonade time," sings Merchant, shattering the tension. He hands a glass of ice-cold lemonade to Virgil, the heavy condensation dripping.

Virgil drains it in one continuous gulp.

"So, Daddy, now that you've paid your debt to society, where will you live?"

"Don't know."

"You can't go back to Belle Glade, I torched that place to the ground."

"He could stay here," Ben suggests. "We've got plenty of room."

Virgil rubs sweat from his eyes, feeling a bit light-headed. "I'd love to stay, you know, but only if ya'll wanted me."

"Well, I don't know," Lilith says, toying with him. "What could you do around here? Could you garden?"

"Uh, I suppose."

"We have a gardener," reminds Ben.

"Ben's right. And we have a cook and a chauffeur, even a helojet pilot. But you know what we don't have? We don't have a man."

"A man?"

"You know, someone who I can use for sex when I get bored with my vibrator. Think you could satisfy me, Daddy?"

Virgil's heart pounds in his ears.

Ben nods. "Whenever possible, your daughter always prefers to keep things in the family."

"So what do you say, Daddy? Are you, excuse the pun, up for the job?"

A guttural reply squeezes out his throat. "Yes."

"Hear that, Ben? My father just got out of prison for killing my mother, but he's ready to step up and bang his little girl for free room and board. And you said this wouldn't work out."

Merchant bellows a laugh, the sound echoing strangely in Virgil's head.

The deck spins sideways. A dull pain fills Virgil's left eye. The empty lemonade glass falls from his hand, shattering on impact.

Virgil Robinson falls sideways over the lounge chair, unconscious.

"Wake up, Daddy . . ."

Virgil opens his eyes . . . and pukes.

He is on a boat—no, not exactly *on* the boat, he is dangling over the transom of a boat, his arms and legs tightly bound to a cross-shaped object pressing into his spine and shoulders.

Looking up, he sees a heavy nylon rope attached to the cross, part of a large winch used to raise and lower the yacht's skiff.

He moans, the nausea rising again.

Three-foot seas lap at his ankles. His bare feet, now underwater, feel numb, as if they've been submerged for quite some time.

Lilith, dressed in a black bikini, leans out over the rail and licks the back of his neck. "Mmm . . . I taste fear. Don't be afraid, Daddy."

"What . . . what are you—"

"Putting you out of my misery."

"Huh? You insane, girl!"

"A passion I inherited from my mother. Remember her? Pretty Mesoamerican thing, with bright blue eyes. I believe you cut them out of her head the night I was born."

Virgil struggles to move, the damp rope cutting into his forearms. A six-foot swell washes over his chest, and he swallows seawater. "I . . . I can't swim." He gags.

"Don't worry, Daddy, I would never let you drown."

"My feet hurt. What's wrong wit' my feet?"

Ben lights a joint, then leans out over the rail. "Your feet are fine, partner, it's your toes that are the problem."

Virgil looks down. As the boat rises above another swell, his bare feet are drawn out of the water—exposing bleeding stumps where his toes had been.

"Oh, Jesus—help me!"

"Now why would Jesus waste His time helping a murdering sonuva bitch like you?"

"I paid my price . . . I did my time—"

"And I suppose that makes everything hunky-dory, huh? Read a Bible verse, call yourself saved . . . *poof,* you're born again, a clean slate."

Desperate, Virgil searches the horizon for another boat. "I . . . I have to report to my probation officer."

Lilith and Ben laugh.

"Oh look, Daddy, is this him?"

Virgil's eyes widen as a half dozen lead gray fins circle below his ankles. "Oh, God, please—"

"God is dead to you, Daddy."

The boat dips. The sea froths crimson.

"God is dead to both of us."

Virgil screams like a banshee.

The boat rises, revealing a seven-foot mako shark tearing at the remains of Virgil's gushing left knee.

"Fu . . . bitch! Hope you . . . burn in Hell!"

"I've been to Hell, Daddy. You sent me there the night I was born."

A large brown fin cuts the surface, a second dorsal trailing along the creature's broad back. "Uh-oh. See that shark, Daddy? Now that bad boy's a bull shark. Once they bite, they don't like to let go."

"Sort of like you, Lilith, darlin'," Ben says, drawing another lungful of smoke.

The bull shark circles twice, darts toward the boat, then turns at the last second.

Virgil's eyes widen, snot running down both nostrils.

"Why won't he attack?" Ben asks.

"He will," Lilith answers, spellbound in the moment. "He just wants to be sure. It's always best to be sure before you strike."

"We can learn so much from sharks. Such fine preda-tors."

"Yes, nature is the perfect teacher."

The boat rises and dips, submersing Virgil to his neck.

A serene Lilith watches the nine-foot Bull shark bury its snout into its screeching meal, the animal's serrated teeth tearing apart flesh and intestines within a shroud of scarlet foam—

—eviscerating the life from her father.

24

NOVEMBER 21, 2033
UNIVERSITY OF MIAMI
FOOTBALL PRACTICE FIELD
CORAL GABLES, FLORIDA
3:50 P.M.

K. C. Renner lines the first-team offense up at the twenty yard line, scans the alignment of the Canes second-string defense, then barks out signals: "Blue—twenty-six, blue-twenty-six . . . hut, hut . . . hut!"

The ball is snapped. K. C. fakes the handoff to his full-back, then tosses a short pass to Samuel Agler, who has re-leased from his block and is rolling left out of the backfield.

Sam catches the pass—

—and is immediately hit by Alec Parodi, a reserve out-side linebacker for a three-yard loss.

Coach Demaio kicks at the turf, then blows his whistle. "Mule, with me!"

Twenty-one pairs of eyes follow the star tailback as he jogs over to the sidelines.

"Yeah, Coach?"

"You hurt, son?"

"No, sir."

"Girl troubles?"

"No, Coach. Why?"

"Something's gotta be wrong, because you're not running like the Mule I know."

"Coach, I'm giving one hundred percent. Parodi just made a nice play."

"Parodi couldn't tackle you in the open field on his best day." DeMaio lowers his voice. "Look, I've heard rumors. If this is a money thing?"

"Coach, I swear—"

"Okay, okay, I had to ask. It's just that I'm worried about you. We've got a huge game in two weeks in Gainesville, then the first round of the January Jubilee. I need to know my best player is ready."

"I'm ready."

"Hell, son, show me, don't tell me. Coach Lavoie, line 'em up again."

"Yes, coach." Offensive coordinator Mike Lavoie yells at the two squads. "Okay, girls, get your asses in gear!"

K. C. Renner buckles his chin strap, listening as Lavoie's computer communicates the same play.

Sam lines up in the backfield behind fullback Doug Parrish. He focuses his mind inward, his adrenaline pumping, as he beckons the entrance to the "zone."

Renner takes the snap. Fakes the handoff to Parrish.

Sam slips inside the nexus.

The field brightens, the action grinding to a slow crawl.

Sam's quadriceps burn as he pushes through heavy waves of energy. He blocks the blitzing strong safety, pancaking him with vicious forearm to the chest, then looks up as Renner's pass floats toward him like a balloon.

As he looks up, the sun melds into a soothing white light.

Who are you, cousin?

The female's voice coos at him.

Slip inside the light and speak with me.

The light brightens as it widens, blotting out the football, blotting out the entire sky.

Sam leaps out of the nexus—

—as the ball strikes him on his helmet, and Alec Parodi crushes him with a bulldozing hit.

A whiff of ammonia snaps Sam back into consciousness. He opens his eyes, the team doctor's face appearing fuzzy.

"You okay, son?"

"Dunno. My head still attached?"

"Let's get a quick scan of your brain." Dr. Meth slips the portable MRI device right over Sam's helmet. "Don't move, this'll only take ten seconds."

The device activates, scanning Sam's brain.

> PATIENT: SAMUEL AGLER.
>
> DIAGNOSIS: THIRD-DEGREE CONCUSSION.
>
> PROTOCOL C-3: ICE, ANTICONCUSSION/INFLAMMATORY
> MEDS, MONITORED BED REST.
>
> RETURN TO ACTION: THREE DAYS MINIMUM.
>
> NONCONTACT DRILLS FOR FIVE DAYS.

"That's it, son, you're done." Dr. Meth and his two assistants help him to his feet.

Coaches and players watch in accusing silence as Sam limps off to the locker room.

7:16 P.M.

Three hours, a shower, and seven interviews later, Samuel Agler emerges from the air-conditioned training facility into the cool dusk November air.

He motions for the guard to open the gate, then pushes through the usual postpractice crowd. He signs a dozen porto-pads, then sees the black government-issue limousine parked along the sidewalk.

Fubish . . . of all days.

The driver's door opens, releasing a powerful African-American man.

Sam crosses the street, the crowd still enveloping him, shoving porto-pads in his face.

Ryan Beck approaches. "Back off!"

The crowd scurries.

"Hey, Pep. Still have that gift of gab, I see. How you doin'?"

"Just doin'. You look like shit." Beck opens the rear door.

"Yeah, nice to see you, too." Sam climbs in back. The door closes behind him as he takes his place opposite his mother.

Dominique Gabriel removes her dark, wraparound sunglasses. Although she is forty-nine, most would place her age closer to thirty. The ebony hair is still long and parted in the middle, with a touch of gray sprinkled here and there. The breasts are firm, her figure still flawless, thanks to a strict diet and daily regimen of weight training and cardiovascular exercise. The only signs of aging are the crow's-feet that litter the corners of her chocolate brown eyes.

Sam looks her over. "You look good for an old broad."

"Is that how you greet your mother?"

He leans over and dutifully plants a kiss on her cheek. "I wasn't expecting you. You know I don't like surprises."

"You look tired, Manny."

"Sam! Call me Sam."

"To me, you'll always be my Manny."

"Can we cut to the chase?"

"Your brother wants to see you."

"Forget it. We had an agreement."

"Yes we did. You wanted total anonymity, we gave it to you. A new name, a new identity, surrogate parents . . . you got the works. But what you're doing now is extremely dangerous. Instead of living out of the public eye, you've dashed back into the spotlight. Your face is on every website and public broadcast in North America. How long do you think it'll be before some hotshot reporter sees through the tinkered files and false birth certificate and figures out who you really are?"

"Immanuel Gabriel is dead, mother. He drowned six years ago. No one will put two and two together."

"Jacob thinks otherwise, and that's why he needs to see you."

"Jacob's a freak."

The slap in the face stuns him, sending shock waves through his already bruised brain. "That freak, as you call him, gave you a new life. If it wasn't for your brother, you'd still be living in the compound . . . or worse."

"How long are you going to keep this charade up, Mother? You've been giving in to Jacob our whole lives."

"I don't give in to him."

"No, you've done worse. You've empowered him by believing in this whole Mayan Hero bullshit. Look at you. When are you going to get on with your own life?"

"I have a life!"

"Yeah, sure you do. I have a life. You work for Jacob." He shakes his head. "Just tell me how long."

"A few days. He says he needs to discuss things that only you would understand."

"God dammit, Mother, for the last time, I am NOT Hunahpu!" He closes his eyes, fighting back tears of frustration. "The two of you are not part of my life anymore. You don't know a thing about me. I've worked my ass off . . . I trained for years. I take a beating every time I step out onto that field. I am not like . . . *him.*"

"You're right. As cold and emotionless as Jake can be, he's selfless. You're driven by ego."

"Good-bye." He slides toward the door.

"Wait!" Dominique grabs his arm. "I'm sorry. I didn't mean that."

"Yes you did."

"Manny, I *am* really proud of you. Proud of what you've accomplished in school. Proud of the life you've been able to lead. And I like everything I've heard about Lauren. I think she's good for you. Will you at least introduce us before you get married."

"Not a chance."

She smiles. "You're so much like me. Stubborn as a mule."

He cracks a half smile at the mention of his nickname. Checks the digital timer sewn into his shirtsleeve. "I have to go. I'm having dinner at my father's house."

"Surrogate father."

"Whatever."

"I'll pick you up here tomorrow morning at nine. Pack an overnight bag."

"I'm supposed to spend the holidays with Lauren's family."

"Get out of it. She'll understand."

"No she won't. I don't even understand. What am I supposed to tell her?"

"You'll think of something."

"Can't we do this another time?"

"No, it has to be now."

"Why?"

"Tomorrow morning, Immanuel. After that, I'll be out of your hair forever."

He exits the car without saying another word.

Jacob Gabriel had always "sensed" there were enemies about, ever since the day he had learned to read the Bible Code, ever since his first remote-viewing session. But it was not until his last communication with his father that he realized how close he had allowed his true enemy to come.

He had always known Lilith was Hunahpu, his genetic cousin and equal. He had never suspected her to be the Abomination.

Jacob knew there were only two ways to stop the Hunahpu's pursuit; either kill his one true love or convince her that he and Manny were dead.

Faking his brother's drowning had been a simple matter.

The collision on the bridge was easily choreographed, the black hair dye and contact lenses easily fooling the media into believing it was Manny who was the victim. Jacob's immersion into the nexus stifled his life signs long enough to convince CNN and the randomly chosen witnesses.

His own death had been a bit trickier to choreograph.

Jacob knew that Pierre Borgia was out for revenge and that his own public appearance would flush his quarry into the open. What he didn't know was that Ennis Chaney was the former secretary of state's real target, or that Lilith would show up at Manny's funeral. Fortunately, the nexus had given him a chance to intercept the bullet, his Kevlar nanofiber body armor absorbing the projectile's impact, the explosive blood bags hidden beneath his jacket fooling everyone, even Rabbi Steinberg and the physician, who were in on the plot.

Even Lilith.

With both twins safely "dead," Jacob could pursue more advanced training with GOLDEN FLEECE while Manny disappeared into the anonymity he had always yearned for.

Rabbi Steinberg was close to a young couple from his old congregation in Philadelphia. Gene and Sylvia Agler were good people who had never been blessed with children. After several meetings, they agreed to "adopt" Immanuel and adhere to the strict guidelines of the covert arrangement.

GOLDEN FLEECE arranged the falsified birth certificate and school records, their operatives creating a completely fabricated childhood, down to sports awards and home movies. Gene Agler was given a principal's job in another state, the couple a new home.

The burden was then on Dominique. Having already lost her soul mate, Mick, she was now being asked to break apart the rest of her family.

And so she made the ultimate sacrifice so that Manny could be free.

Hollywood Beach, Florida

Small waves lap relentlessly upon the deserted beach, tickling Samuel Agler's bare feet. He stares out at the dark ocean, its wave tops illuminated by the reflection of the three-quarter moon.

The sound of the surf soothes his restless soul.

"Thought I'd find you out here."

Sam turns to face his surrogate father. Gene Agler is in his late fifties, his curly black hair graying around his ears, his six-foot frame stooping at the shoulders.

"Mind if I join you?"

Sam pats the sand next to him.

"You feeling okay?"

"Guess so."

"Everything all right between you and Lauren?"

"Fine." Sam watches a hermit crab scamper up the beach. "My real mother . . . she's in town. She wants me to travel with her tomorrow."

"I know. She called me last week."

"Why didn't you say anything?"

"Didn't think it was my place."

"It's not right what she does, waltzing in unannounced, turning my life inside out."

Gene picks up a fragment of shell and tosses it at an incoming wave. "Try to understand, it's been very hard for her. She's led a lonely life."

Sam lies back on his elbows, the sound of surf deadening in his ears. "Dad . . . I'm thinking about quitting football."

"Well, now that is a pretty big decision. What brought this on?"

"My teammates. They think I'm sandbagging it."

"Maybe you've spoiled them."

"Selfish bastards . . . all they care about is themselves. These guys're supposed to be my friends."

"There are all sorts of friends. Some inoculate us against pain, others walk out the minute there's trouble. It doesn't necessarily make them bad people, it just means they were probably never really good friends to begin with."

Sam gazes at the stars. Says nothing.

"Are you thinking about turning pro, or are you intending on quitting football altogether?"

"Quitting, I guess." The stars blur. Sam pinches away tears. "It's . . . complicated. I . . . I don't think I can compete at the same level anymore."

"Because of one off game?"

"Dad, I can't . . . I just can't do it anymore."

"Well, you know what? I'm glad."

"You are?"

"Sure. For someone sitting on top of the world, you don't seem very happy."

"They'll label me a quitter."

"Who cares? As long as you know it's not true."

"A lot of people will be very upset."

"Yes, the world will certainly be disappointed, but the sun should still rise, and the birds will still sing, so how bad can it be?"

"I feel like I'm letting everyone down. Maybe I should just suck it up and deal with it?"

"Maybe it's time you asked yourself why you're playing football?"

Sam looks up. "What do you mean?"

"Do you remember Rabbi Steinberg's sermon on *Tikkun Olam* and *Tikkun Midot*?"

"Not really." Sam grins. "Sorry. Guess I didn't make a very good Jew either, huh?"

Gene ignores the remark. "*Tikkun Olam* means to mend the outside world. *Tikkun Midot* deals with acts of internal healing. *Tikkun Midot* is a self-awareness that enables you to reach beyond the natural and instinctive, past the reflexive and knee-jerk responses, in order to refine the soul. It means we have recognized the need to turn our lives in a better direction."

"I thought I was going in the right direction."

"Success and prosperity doesn't necessarily equate to living a good life. Something's obviously bothering you about your future. Whether you chose to play football or not should be your decision, not your peers'. You can't allow your friends to make their agenda yours. I think Philip Roth expressed it best when he wrote, 'The human stain that touches all that we do is inescapable.' Do you understand?"

"All but that last part."

"What Roth was saying is that placing great faith in human beings is not only impossible, it's downright foolish. Everything we touch as humans is stained. Roth saw modern man falling into the same rut as Abraham—creating and serving lesser gods—false idols that neither redeem nor save us."

"What does any of that have to do with me?"

"Think about it, Samuel. Look at what you've become. You were born the false idol, a mythical twin worshiped by the masses. You successfully escaped to a different identity, but like some insecure Hollywood actor, you still covet the spotlight. It's like you're afraid to let go, afraid to disappoint. None of this attention is real, son. Fame is fleeting. The only thing that counts is what's on the inside."

Gene looks up at the moon. "You know, I'll never forget the night you and your brother were born. Such a crazy time. Sylvia and I watched the whole thing on TV. There must have been ten thousand people surrounding the hospital. Rabbi Steinberg told me the air literally seemed charged with electricity. And everyone inside—the doctors and nurses, President Chaney, all those nosey reporters and the armed guards—all were anticipating this wondrous miracle. Your poor mother, she was exhausted and in pain, but she hung in there, refusing any drugs . . . so afraid it might affect the birth. Anyway, the blessed event happened, and they finally showed footage of your mother holding you in her arms. I remember looking at you, so innocent, wrapped up in that tiny blanket, and I thought to myself—this is a special child, a gift from God, but from here on out, it's downhill all the way. Because how on Earth could any child, or any adult for that matter, live up to the expectations humanity seemed to be placing on you and your brother?"

Sam sits up. "It always played with Jake's head—all those crazy expectations. I think he was trying to become something everyone wanted him to be. Somewhere along the line, he just lost it mentally."

"And isn't that the reason you wanted out of that life, to escape all that craziness?"

"Yes."

"Looks to me like you jumped from the frying pan into the fire. Samuel 'the Mule' Agler—everyone's all-American hero. To do *Tikkun Midot* means to overcome our less worthy instincts, not to succumb to peer pressure."

Gene Agler stands, brushing away the sand. "When I was eleven, two boys at school beat me up pretty bad, just because I was Jewish. For a long time after that I remember feeling ashamed of who I was. One afternoon my father gave me a card and inside was a poem. *'Be your own soul, learn to live; And if some men hate you, take no heed. If some men curse you, take no care. Sing your song, dream your dream, hope your hope, pray your prayer.'*

"Whatever you decide, Samuel, do what's best for you. Do what's best . . . for your soul."

A wisp of thought, in the consciousness of existence.

Jacob?

Are you out there, son?

If you are there, I have no way of knowing.

The Abomination has blanketed my senses, shielding your thought energy from me. While I cannot hear you, I pray you might still hear me in the hopes that my experiences on Xibalba can protect you.

At one time we spoke of love. It's important you understand the power of the emotion, and how its absence can taint the soul.

As Michael Gabriel, I had lived an existence devoid of happiness—a lonely childhood, followed by a bitter adolescence. I was life's victim, my later years spent in isolation in a mental asylum. Even those precious few moments spent with your mother were fleeting, the pain of her loss filling me with an angst I cannot put in words or thoughts.

Was it mere coincidence that the Guardian arranged a shared existence with the Mars colonist, Bill Raby—himself filled with an emptiness as bad, if not worse than my own? No, I no longer believe in coincidences.

But it was not just Bill Raby who experienced this heaviness of heart, nearly every colonist marooned on Xibalba shared the same unspoken feeling. It was a feeling of shame, of survivor's guilt, magnified beyond the scope of human despair.

Nine billion people on Earth had perished so that a chosen few could survive. Many of us had "conspired with the Devil," meaning we had been selected for Mars Colony based neither by lottery nor merit, but by political affiliation, by favoritism and ethnic background. We survived because of who we knew and how much money we had so that we could manipulate the selection process.

Now, marooned on Xibalba, the immorality of our affairs was tearing us apart inside.

Not all of us, I should say. Your cousin, Lilith, and her son, Devlin, along with their "coven" of friends, seemed quite content with our bizarre predicament.

The rest of us, however, were left to wallow in our existence. "Live for those who died," became our creed. And so we faked our joy, pretending the whole affair back on Earth was just a test of survival.

Merrily, merrily, merrily, merrily . . . life is but a dream.

Was Bill Raby's existence but a dream?

Was Michael Gabriel's? Can one truly exist without love?

Yes, but it is a self-imposed hell.

It was your love that saved me, Jacob, but in your un-selfish quest to release me, I fear you have condemned your soul to the same purgatory, the same ultimate destiny.

You cannot simply be Hunahpu, you must retain your humanity. Step into the real light. Allow yourself to love again, or you will find yourself on the same path as your cousin, Lilith.

Having said what I needed to say, I'll return to my journey on Xibalba.

Each of the alien planet's days was divided into three shifts consisting of labor for the collective, personal time, and more labor, for it was essential to our existence that our first crop yield a bountiful harvest.

During these first six months, I was assigned to a habitat shared by seventy-eight single men and women.

It was there that I met Jude.

Judith Fields was a fellow genetics expert whose specialty was in agriculture. Using the surviving portions of our gene bank, she and her colleagues had begun the process of cloning livestock for New Eden's farms.

Jude was a country girl, originally from Idaho, with long brown hair, hazel eyes, and a great sense of humor. It was Jude who made me feel again, and over the months, our puppy love blossomed into a strong bond. I found myself, or was it Bill, thinking about her constantly. Whoever it was, our time together was one of great happiness that, at least for the moment, sweetened both our souls.

Jude introduced me to Tan Rashid, an astronomer, originally from England, who entertained us with his "theories" regarding the location of our new home world. You see, despite his computers and star charts, despite his infinite knowledge of the heavens, Tan simply could not discern the location of our planet. Was the distant red supergiant Betelgeuse? If so, none of the other constellations were familiar. Seeking answers, he and his fellow astronomers set to work on building Xibalba's first telescope.

As for me, my alter ego—Bill Raby—was a marine geneticist. Since there was little we could do to contribute on an alien planet devoid of oceans, we were assigned to the geology department.

Drone scouts gave us the ability to map New Eden's entire domed landscape, which spanned nearly 3 million square miles, making it roughly the equivalent of Australia. Engineers determined our floating continent had been built in sections over eons. With its temperate climate control systems and agricultural pods, which we still could not access, they estimated New Eden could house and feed more than 2 billion human beings.

Located twenty feet below the habitat's rich layer of soil was an inaccessible subterranean chamber, its alien carbon fiber plating composed of the same composite materials used in the dwellings. Within this sealed level, we theorized, had to be the environmental systems that perpetually purified the cloud city's air and water, fertilized the plant life, and controlled the dome's shielding mechanism.

The first crop was a bountiful success, and the future of our colony and our species seemed secure.

Two weeks later, the plague struck.

The human body is an amazing and complex machine. There are over a hundred thousand different genes in the human genome, and one single gene may contain more than 2 million nucleotides. Our bony framework consists of 206 bones, most of which are in our hands and feet. Our heart and lungs are the power trains behind a circulatory system that supplies muscles and organs with blood, oxygen, and nutrients, all the while removing carbon dioxide and other waste products. Our nervous system and hormones control bodily functions. Our digestive and reproductive systems are marvels of engineering, our brains more complicated than any computer. In fact, the human body is akin to a combustion engine, producing the same amount of energy as a hundred-watt lightbulb.

Yet, for all its nanoscale complexity and metabolic sophistication, the human body is still composed of 70 percent water.

For eighteen months our colony had been consuming New Eden's water. We were cooking with it, bathing in it, and consuming food supplies grown with it.

What we didn't know was that it was affecting us . . . changing us, altering our genetic code.

As Bill Raby, I was among the plague's first victims.

I remember it being an overcast day. Olive-gray storm clouds whipped above New Eden's protective domes. Jude and I were on personal time, strolling along one of the artificial lakes, admiring the handiwork of our alien benefactors, when I was suddenly stricken with intense head pains, as if my brain was on fire. I crumpled in agony, screaming to Jude for help.

Mercifully, I blacked out.

I awoke three days later in a medical ward, quarantined with others like me.

The human brain floats in a self-contained sort of womb, surrounded by and filled with a watery substance called cerebrospinal fluid. Doctors informed me that pressure in this cavity had increased dangerously, causing a portion of my cerebrum actually to press against the inside of my skull. This alien form of hydrocephalus had stricken fifty-seven New Edeners besides me, and more cases were being reported every day.

Drugs were not working, and the pressure on my brain was increasing by the hour. Unless relieved, I would lose consciousness and die within three days.

In effect, it was a death sentence.

How does one take such a pronouncement? Jude fell

apart. Bill Raby's consciousness wept inside, while I . . . well, I just got angry. "Remove the tumor," I demanded.

"It's not a tumor," the resident surgeon said. "Your brain is swelling. Intracranial pressure has risen from 210 mm to 270, and it's still climbing. There simply isn't enough room in your skull to allow for any more growth."

Within hours, I slipped into a coma.

The Homo sapiens *brain is an incredibly unique organ, its electrochemical design quite different from the rest of the body. It is shielded from direct contact with blood, and contains a hundred billion working cells called neurons, which make over a thousand trillion connections. The organ may be the most complex computer in the universe, yet, despite all our God-given intelligence, our species was still only capable of using roughly 10 percent of its brain, lacking the genetic programming to do otherwise.*

The human brain also consists of several unique layers that reflect the gradual progression of our evolution. Rather than discard the antiquated layers, Nature had simply built upon them, preserving our evolutionary history— and perhaps our tendency toward violence.

The oldest and deepest of these layers, dubbed the "neural chassis," consists of the midbrain, brain stem (medulla and pons) and the spinal cord, and controls our basic life functions, such as our heart beat, blood circulation, and respiration. Surrounding this layer is the R-complex, nicknamed the "reptilian brain," as it controls our aggressive behavior, social hierarchy, and territoriality. It consists of our globus pallidus, corpus striatum, and olfactostriatum.

Surrounding the R-complex is the limbic system, a layer developed during our evolution as mammals. Comprising the thalamus, hypothalamus, amygdala, pituitary, and hippocampus, it controls social behavior, emotions, and complex relations required for living in cohesive groups.

The outermost layer of the brain is a tablecloth-sized sheet folded like a parachute. It controls reason, spatial perception, and language. Known as the neocortex, it is divided by anatomists into the frontal, parietal, temporal, and occipital lobes. While the outer layers of other animal brains are smooth, ours is grooved, increasing the surface area of the cerebral cortex.

I bore you with these anatomical facts because, as I lay in bed in my coma, I dreamed that I was actually walking through this outer maze of gray matter, lost in the canyons of my neocortex. Reaching a precipice, I looked down, staring into the dark recesses of human existence.

And I saw everything.

The birth of our universe.

The formation of galaxies.

The evolution of life on ancient Earth.

From insectivores to primates. From early hominid to modern man.

And suddenly, as if a curtain had been lifted, I understood.

Futurists in my time had defined three categories of evolution for human civilization. Type-I civilizations were those that master all forms of our home world's energy resources. This includes everything from mining the oceans to tapping into the planet's core, to modifying the weather. A Type-I civilization is mature enough to rise above petty conflicts of politics, race, religion, and culture to develop a unified planetary economy. While still susceptible to certain environmental and cosmic catastrophes, Type-I civilizations have begun the process leading to the colonization of nearby planets.

The next step up the evolutionary ladder are Type-II civilizations, which harness energy solely by way of their suns. They have colonized other planets and have begun the exploration and possible colonization of nearby solar systems. Able to manipulate their environment, they will no longer be in danger of facing extinction by glaciation or asteroid impact, but will still be vulnerable to supernovas, whose eruptions could irradiate nearby planets.

Type-III civilizations are the pinnacle of advanced societies. They have exhausted the energy output of their suns and must reach out to other star systems throughout the *galaxy. Their starships approach the speed of light, and perhaps, have even mastered "Planck energy," the energy necessary to violate the very fabric of space and time.*

In other words, Jacob, they can manipulate wormholes.

When I left Earth in 2012, our species was still a struggling Type-0 civilization. Our people were hopelessly divided, enmeshed in petty conflicts of equality, religion, and politics. Our technologies focused on making war, and we very nearly destroyed ourselves in our quest of ego and self. Type-0 civilizations are always prone to disasters, whether self-induced, or, as our predecessors learned, through the fury of Mother Nature.

What scientists had left out of the equation was hominid evolution. Homo sapiens was not the last stop up the evolutionary ladder; it was merely the beginning . . . and love was our key to survival.

As this knowledge was imparted to me, I found myself staring at my own genome. The spiraling ladder of DNA was changing, continuing an incredible metamorphosis that had begun the moment the first drops of alien water had passed across my lips.

And though I was dreaming, I knew the vision was real, that I was actually changing, evolving into something more efficient—something superior. Another layer of brain tissue, a hypercortex, was growing over my neocortex.

I was becoming . . . Transhuman.

The transhumanist school first surfaced at the turn of the twentieth century when science fiction gave rise to serious futurism. The term "transhuman" implies our species as being transitional, that Homo sapiens does not represent the end of our evolution but rather its true beginning. Through bioscience breakthroughs and technological advances in nanoscale engineering that enabled telomeric augmentation, proliferated nanoimplants, genomic editing, and mitochondrial genetic preservation, individual humans could prepare themselves as transhumans to reach our ultimate goal as a species: Posthumanism.

A posthuman was imagined to be an augmented super-

brained person no longer merely human. It was believed that posthumans could end up as completely synthetic organisms, living far beyond the human body's limitations— or as some imagined, as exobody consciousness, programmed within some futuristic biochemical computer.

As I watched my genome evolve, my hallucination instructed me. It showed me how my brain was growing. Taught me how to program my own neurological pathways simply by using streams of conscious thought. My dream guided me toward understanding how my biological processes worked and how they could be manipulated.

More than seven full months would pass before I emerged from my coma. When I awoke, I learned I had evolved into a different Homo sapiens subspecies.

It began with my appearance, which was bizarre, bordering on the grotesque. My skull had completely deformed, elongating to accommodate the increased mass of my brain. My body had enlarged as well, to better nourish the brain. My muscles were stronger, not only able to lift heavier weights, but they could fire faster, as if Bill Raby's neural connections had doubled in speed.

There was a new clarity to my thought process. My mind could suddenly recall obscure documents I had read years earlier—word for word. My brain possessed an eidetic memory, but with highly expanded associativity, cataloging key concepts, drawing upon oceans of information in a millisecond of preconscious thought.

The entire colony was undergoing an identical metamorphosis.

As Jude was still in her coma, I decided to leave the ward, my new intellect determined to reveal New Eden's secrets. My first destination was a massive structure, standing seventy-eight stories tall, encompassing a thousand acres. What drew me to this alien facility was its exterior lead gray surface, adorned in ever-changing patterns of lines and glyphs, which radiated the colors of the spectrum.

An imposing thirty-foot arch delineated the grand entry. Approaching the sealed hatch, I closed my eyes and fo-

cused my thoughts inward, imagining the doors unsealing to allow me entry.

Immediately, a strange buzzing sensation overcame me, as if my brain was expelling volts of electricity. I fell to my knees, overcome by vertigo.

When the buzzing stopped, I opened my eyes.

The portal had unsealed.

NOVEMBER 22, 2033
MANALAPAN, FLORIDA
7:35 A.M.

Ken Becker enters destination coordinates into the four-passenger jet-copter's autopilot as his boss straps herself in one of the rear seats.

"Don't wake me until we get to Washington," Lilith orders. Tucking her hair behind her ears, she slips the virtual-reality helmet over her head and closes her eyes.

"Yes, ma'am." Becker activates the airship's three-blade helicopter rotor, guiding the vessel into a hover maneuver. At thirteen-hundred-feet, he shifts to jet mode. Wings, retracted beneath the airship, spread out horizontally, as the jet engines fire and the helicopter's rotors and tailfin fold and retract.

The jet-copter leaps forward, heading north to the nation's capital.

Believing Jacob Gabriel dead, Lilith Eve Robinson knew it was time for her, too, to move on and find her own higher calling. Guided by her new mentor, Don Rafelo, a product of her own schizophrenia, the fifteen-year-old left the United States in the fall of 2028, using Quenton's inheritance to travel to the land of her ancestors: Mesoamerica, home of the Aztec and Maya.

There are no surface rivers in the Yucatán Peninsula, the population's freshwater supplies coming from a vast system of underground caves and sinkholes, known as cenotes (*dzonot* to the Maya). Four thousand cenotes and hundreds of miles of caves are believed to lie within the Yucatán Peninsula, all originating from the wreckage of the celestial impact, 65 million years ago when an object similar to an asteroid plunged through Earth's atmosphere and struck the seabed of the still-forming Gulf of Mexico.

As the Yucatán Peninsula rose from the sea over tens of millions of years and rainwater and streams ate through the cracks in the fractured limestone, it absorbed carbon dioxide and formed carbonic acid. This acid, in turn, eroded the rock, carving out vast subterranean labyrinths that became underground rivers and caverns which stretched beneath the entire peninsula and throughout Mesoamerica.

During the last ice age, water levels dropped, draining the caves. That allowed extensive stalactites, stalagmites, and other calcium carbonate formations to form within the karst geology. Eventually the ice melted and the sea rose, reflooding subterranean dwellings.

The Caves of the Hidden Woman, or *Grutas de Xtacumbilxunaan,* are located just outside Bolonchen, Mexico. A night after she had arrived in the village, Lilith Robinson, armed with lanterns, rope, a map, and spelunking supplies, followed her imaginary uncle down a rarely tracked path through the Mesoamerican jungle until she came to a rocky mountainside. Hidden among the foliage was an entrance to a cave.

"What's inside?" Lilith asked Don Rafelo.

"Your destiny."

With the lantern clenched between her teeth, Lilith got down on all fours and crawled through the opening.

The glow from her light revealed a claustrophobic limestone tunnel, its diameter no larger than a manhole cover. For half an hour the teen continued on her hands and knees, forcing her way into the humid darkness until the tunnel opened to a cavern the size of an elementary-school gymnasium.

The walls of the subterranean room glowed fleshy pink in her light. Dripping sounds echoed eerily in the chilly air. Stalactites and stalagmites leaked calcium-laden water.

She turned as Don Rafelo appeared behind her.

"Where are we, Uncle?"

"*Xibalba Be,* the road to the Underworld. We must descend five levels to reach Lucifer's chamber, this is only the first."

Lilith aimed the beam of her flashlight down a winding embankment leading straight into the bowels of the earth. "Down there?"

"It is where *he* awaits."

Tying off one end of a nylon rope to a stalagmite, she made her way backward down the slope, the limestone beneath her boots slippery, the cavern walls to her left glowing shades of violet and crimson in the lantern's light.

She continued descending backward into the bowels of the mountainside, her exit disappearing above her light's reach in suffocating darkness.

At 108 feet, the steep slope leveled out.

A heavy darkness crept in, surrounding her. Dime-sized drops of moisture splattered on her head, shoulders, and into the pitch. Soft rustling sounds appeared overhead.

Lilith directed her light at the source.

Bats. Tens of thousands of them.

"They won't harm us," Don Rafelo assured her.

And so she continued on, her scalp tingling from the moist bat droppings, her insides repulsed by the ammonia-like stench.

For two hundred yards she followed a terrain last visited by men more than eleven centuries earlier. Eventually she came to the mouth of the pit, the thirty-foot-wide hole's depths disappearing into darkness.

Long ago, ancient cave dwellers had fastened a bamboo ladder to the hole's near-vertical walls. As Lilith looked down, the face of the walls seemed to sparkle in her light, the limestone underworld transformed into quartz crystal.

Cool waves of air rushed up from the hole, chilling her face.

"Uncle . . . I'm scared."

"Holes in the earth cannot harm you. Once your true father embraces you, as he embraced me, nothing will ever scare you again. You will know yourself intimately and see the universe in ways you never dreamed."

"Our Fallen Angel will speak to me?"

"Yes. You will feel his presence as he slips inside your mind, you will register the reverberations of his power as he touches your soul, imparting his wisdom, guiding you as he has guided me."

"Lead me to him. I need to feel his love."

Gripping the handle of the lantern in her teeth, she climbed down the ladder, her mentor following her into the heavy blackness.

Sixty feet down . . . Seventy.

Lilith stumbled as the ground suddenly reappeared without warning.

She was at the bottom of the pit, standing in the rubble from an ancient human sacrifice. Splintered bones crackled beneath her feet. Human skulls and their twisted vertebrae lay entwined by the remnants of jade jewelry and the remains of sacrificial cloths.

A thousand years ago the pit had been a freshwater cenote. The water had eventually drained, exposing the decayed flesh to the rats.

She turned to Don Rafelo. "Who were these people?"

"Followers of the cult of Tezcatilpoca. See? His spirit points the way."

Lilith's light revealed a narrow passage—a drain for the cenote's waters. Gathering her strength, she continued onward.

A tricky forty-minute descent through the winding tunnel led into another chamber, this one as vast as an indoor sports arena, its curved walls reflecting surface waters of a subterranean lake.

Don Rafelo pointed. "The fifth level. You have arrived."

"Uncle, the walls—why do they sparkle?"

"This entire chamber is composed of quartz crystal. Crystal is a living organism, possessing trapped electrical energy. The walls sparkle with their knowledge."

She followed him to the edge of the underground lake, its freshwater surface as clear as glass, the saline layer along the bottom enshrouded in mist.

"The sacred cenote's hidden waters," Don Rafelo said. "We are not far from the sea. Remove your clothing, it is time for your Baptism."

Lilith stripped naked. Shivering from the cold, she stepped into the lake and sank, misjudging the translucent layer of mist separating fresh water from saline for the bottom.

She surfaced, coughing. "It's freezing!"

"Swim out toward the center. You'll find a flat rock you can stand upon."

Lilith swam into the darkness, her wheezing breaths mixing with the crisp sounds of splashing water echoing throughout the cavern. Reaching the midway point, her hands groped unseen rock and she pulled herself atop the slippery limestone rise, her teeth chattering, her head suddenly buzzing with electricity.

Surrounded by darkness and rock, Lilith waited, glancing back toward the lantern-backlit shoreline for guidance.

Don Rafelo's long shadow danced in the eerie light as he chanted, "King of the Fallen, Commander of Hell, I have brought you your wife, Lilith, the Demon Queen, who presides over all Succubi, so that she may preside over your children, in this world—and beyond!"

In her dementia she saw fire ignite along the shoreline, the flames accompanied by a coven of Satanic worshipers, naked, save for their goat masks. "Hail the rebirth of the Succubus. Hail Lilith, Demon Queen!"

"Speak to your master, Lilith. Beckon him to take you."

"Fallen Angel . . . it is I, your mistress, descendant of the Dragon Queen of Creation, summoning you from the fires of Hell. Reveal yourself to me, let me taste your existence. Guide me, so that one day, a child of mine might pry open the gates of Gehenna and release thee!"

The human brain functions by transmitting electrical signals from one nerve cell to another. These electrostatic brain waves have rhythms that can be segregated into four distinct ranges.

Beta waves, occurring at 13–40 cycles per second, are the most rapid and dominant of the four states, most often associated with anxiety, alertness, and concentration. As we become more relaxed, the brain shifts to alpha waves. Lower in frequency, (8–13Hz) they are most closely connected with the first stages of meditation.

When calmness and relaxation deepen into drowsiness, the brain shifts to the slower (4–8Hz) rhythm of theta waves. The theta wave state is associated with childhood memories, sudden insight, and creativity. It is also the state the brain enters during bouts of clairvoyance and prophetic visions, as well as lucid dreams and fantasies.

The slowest stage—delta waves—take over when we are asleep or unconscious.

Electromagnetic waves are always present in the atmosphere. Earth's standing wave resonance averages 7.8Hz. Electrostatic deviations, such as overhead power lines, can expose the brain to frequencies exceeding 60Hz. Longterm exposure to such strong fields can lead to biophysical health problems originating at the subcellular level.

An intense electrostatic field was present in the Mexican cave, the deviation originated from the remains of the object that had struck the seafloor of the Gulf of Mexico 65 million years earlier. Unbeknownst to Lilith, her loud, reverberating chants had disturbed stored electrical energy from within the chamber's quartz crystal walls, amplifying its electrostatic intensity. The effect scrambled the electrical impulses in Lilith's brain, altering her theta wave state.

As she bellowed in the subterranean darkness, Lilith's brain waves suddenly dropped below 6Hz. Electricity crackled in her ears. Acid rose in her belly, smoldering in her nostrils like fumes from a funeral pyre.

Against this backdrop, she imagined a voice whispering into her mind:

I am all that you are. I am all that you shall be. Together we shall destroy our enemies and dethrone the tyrannical Yahweh.

"Instruct me . . . Father."

An icy presence caused her to open her eyes. In her schizophrenic delirium, she saw a mud brown mist envelop her, dwarfing her as it took shape.

Crimson red eyes.

Demonic ears, tapered back like a bat.

A muscular four-limbed torso, its bulk gyrating around her within the haze.

The devilish beast seemed to be inhaling her scent, its cold tongue lashing out to taste her flesh.

Delta waves took over, tugging Lilith toward unconsciousness as the demon's rancid breath exhaled excrement into her feverish dementia.

I will guide you, Lilith.

I will lead you to Xibalba . . .

26

The Space Shuttle is the most effective device known for destroying dollar bills.

—CONGRESSMAN DANA ROHRABACHER

NOVEMBER 22, 2033
UNIVERSITY OF MIAMI MAIN CAMPUS
CORAL GABLES, FLORIDA
8:56 A.M.

The black stretch limousine is waiting for him outside the practice facility.

Samuel Agler takes a quick look around. Seeing no members of the media, he tosses his bag over his shoulder and jogs across the street, climbing in the backseat of the vehicle—

—failing to notice the maroon Chevy Corvette L-9 coupe parked at the end of the block.

Lauren Beckmeyer is in the cockpit of the slick roadster, watching as the limousine pulls into traffic. "Family emergency, my ass. Let's see where you're really going . . . and with whom!"

She activates the power switch, sending the sports car's massive hydrogen fuel cells growling to life.

"So, where are we headed?" Sam glances at his mother, who is wearing a loose-fitting cream-colored bodysuit, made of the latest breathable fabric.

"Cape Canaveral."

"GOLDEN FLEECE?" A chill races down his spine. "Is this really necessary?"

"For security purposes, yes."

Up front, Mitchell Kurtz finishes programming the limo's onboard navigation system, then adjusts his seat to a reclined position and closes his eyes. Ryan Beck is in the passenger seat beside him, engrossed in a game of Situational Combat Training—Level 4.

Kurtz opens his eyes. "Hey, Pep, I need my beauty sleep."

"Nag, nag." Without missing a beat, Beck reaches out a muscular arm, activating a soundproof barrier that sections off the front cab of the limo.

Like all cars approved for America's new supersmart highways, the limousine is equipped with an autodriver, part of a "telematics program" featuring navigational sensors embedded in the roadway, linked through Global Positioning Satellites. Designed and approved in 2017, with the first million miles on-line by 2019, America's new computerized highways regulate traffic patterns and speeds, prevent accidents, and reduce crime rates by giving law enforcement officials the ability to override any suspect or stolen vehicle traveling on their interstate. With infants being tagged at birth with microchips, kidnapping became a thing of the past, the "crime net" able to locate a missing child instantly while overriding the kidnapper's vehicle.

By fall of 2023, all registered vehicles had been required to have hydrogen fuel cells and autodrivers on board, the technologies hailed as the ultimate solution for congested roads, the disturbing rise in vehicular accidents involving alcohol and drugs, and America's dependence on OPEC.

The limousine pulls onto the northbound ramp of SH-95, the autodriver directing the vehicle to the far left lane before accelerating to 130 mph. Lanes speeds are determined by prereserved destinations and current traffic density.

Traveling in a non–rush hour time slot, the 210-mile journey to Cape Canaveral will take ninety-six minutes.

Dominique turns to her son, attempting to ease tensions. "How was yesterday's practice?"

"I'm not really in the mood to talk."

She shoots him a hurt look, then reaches under the seat for her sensory-deprivation headpiece. Positioning the visor over her eyes and ears, she activates the program. Classical music replaces the limo's hum, her consciousness instantly transported to an azure lagoon surrounded by a lush tropical jungle. A cool breeze stirs the palm fronds. Dominique climbs onto a foam cushion, lies back, and floats.

Sam stares at her face, watching his mother's stress lines wash away.

While virtual reality has replaced all other forms of entertainment, many critics claimed the devices were more addictive than heroin. New shutdown safety features were now required after hundreds of VR bangers had literally starved themselves to death while using the machines.

Sam activates the recline button of his own slumber chair and closes his eyes, thinking about Lauren—

—unaware that his fiancée is following him, less than ten car lengths behind.

Situated on 140,000 acres of wildlife refuge, located northeast of Cocoa Beach, Florida, are the two barrier islands housing America's gateways to space.

The smaller barrier island east of the Banana River, bordering the Atlantic Ocean is Cape Canaveral, former home of the Cape Canaveral Air Station and its unmanned launches. Just west of the Cape is Merritt Island, situated between the Banana and Indian Rivers. This larger land mass belongs to the Kennedy Space Center (KSC), which includes the facilities of NASA and her sister organization, 3M-P (Manned Mission to Mars Project).

The origins of KSC and America's space program can be traced back to the first Cold War, when the conflicting ideologies of the United States and the Soviet Union blossomed into a full-fledged race into space. In an attempt to keep pace with the Russians, America formed the National Advisory Committee for Aeronautics (NACA), ordering the Department of Defense and other "rival" national organizations to step up their own research in the fields of rocketry and the upper atmospheric sciences. Unfortunately, the lack of a unified program and the typical in-house bickering among the Armed Forces combined to severely hamper the nation's progress toward achieving their number one goal: human spaceflight.

America would receive its wake-up call on October 4, 1957, when the Soviet Union successfully launched Sputnik 1. Responding to a race the United States was clearly losing, President Dwight D. Eisenhower created the National Aeronautics and Space Administration. NASA would take control of space away from the Armed Forces and absorb all existing research centers.

NASA began by focusing the bulk of its hundred-million-dollar annual budget on Project Mercury—a series of launches and experiments designed to evaluate whether humans could survive in orbit. Thirty-one months later, Alan Shepard Jr. became the first American to fly into space. Mercury's success led to the Gemini Project, an extension of the human spaceflight program that utilized a spacecraft built for two astronauts.

President John F. Kennedy recommitted the nation to space in 1961 by announcing his goal to land a man on the moon and bring him back safely before the end of the decade. It was a specific goal—exactly what NASA needed, giving birth to Project Apollo. On July 20, 1969, eight years, eleven missions, and $25.4 billion dollars later, astronaut Neil Armstrong uttered his famous words, "That's one small step for man, one giant leap for mankind."

Mankind would take a giant leap backward in 1967, when politics once more interfered with science.

The Outer Space Treaty was a document initiated, negotiated, and rammed through Congress by a group of National Security and State Department officials whose only desire was to use fear to shut down the space program so that monies could be redirected to the Vietnam War. Within four short years, space funding had dropped a crippling 45 percent.

Had this not occurred, the momentum of the Apollo program might have led to the establishment of a moon base in the 1980s and a Mars colony before the year 2010, uniting the global superpowers, preventing the nuclear war of 2012.

More devastating political decisions would follow.

A 1969 task force was asked to come up with three long-range space options. These were: a manned Mars expedition; a space station in lunar orbit with a fifty-person Earth-orbiting station serviced by a reusable ferry, or the Space Shuttle, a vehicle designed to take off as a rocket and return to Earth by gliding home like an unpowered airplane.

President Nixon opted for the Space Shuttle.

On April 12, 1981, the shuttle's first mission, STS-1, took off from NASA's launch operations center, now renamed the Kennedy Space Center. For the next six and a half years, the STS Fleet would perform brilliantly as their crew conducted a wide variety of scientific and engineering experiments in space.

A Space Shuttle launch costs approximately $600 million dollars, yet this extraordinary price tag has little to do with the laws of physics or engineering. In simple terms, the business of space never had any cost constraints or competition, leaving the fox in charge of the henhouse.

As an example, Lockheed Martin, the largest aerospace contractor in the world, rarely accepted hardware contracts on a fixed-cost basis. Instead, they "suggested" what a space vehicle might cost, then added 10 percent as a profit. Once contracted, a myriad of managers and planners are added, driving up the cost of the vehicle—along with Lockheed Martin's profit.

Besides making space extraordinarily expensive, this tactic created an "old boy" mentality that stagnated progress in space technology, resulting in no new U.S. launch systems in development. Instead, NASA continued to use an antiquated vehicle, armed with pre-Pentium electronics inferior to most video games, and fragile heat-dissipating tiles designed before breakthroughs in materials science.

Cost overruns and White House cuts would lead to even more serious negligence.

Following the *Challenger* and *Columbia* disasters, and the public's realization that the development of the International Space Station held no scientific purpose, the Bush and Maller administrations forced a "reorganization" of the space program, refocusing its strategies not on space exploration, but space missile defense systems reinforced by policies of fear. Six years and $120 billion later, the only major accomplishment of SDI was to jump-start the second Cold War.

And once again, the future of humanity stumbled.

What the space program lacked was vision and a clear set of goals. Landing probes on Mars was important only if it led to the colonization of the Red Planet in the foreseeable future. What the public really wanted was space tourism. What had happened to all the promises of the "Buck Rogers" era? Space, like politics, had become the frontier of the elite, each mission becoming more prosaic. Tax-payers could care less what temperature aluminum oxidized in a vacuum; they wanted to be a part of the action. The Wright Brothers invention had led to the advent of commercial airlines. Space had led to the sale of personal computers.

When would John Q. Public be afforded the same opportunity to take his family into space?

The Russians would be the first to give space tourism a go, funding the Cosmopolis-XXI (C-21) space plane, a craft designed to be piggybacked atop an airplane and released at 56,000 feet. From there, the space plane's solid-fuel rocket engine would propel it to an altitude of sixty miles for three minutes of weightlessness.

At $98,000 (or $540 per second) it was hardly a bargain, and the space plane was fraught with mechanical problems.

President Chaney's "vision" speech moments before Jacob Gabriel's murder was turned into a rallying cry that recommitted the American public to the space program. Two months after the Gabriel twin's death, President Marion Rallo and a new team at NASA announced its Manned Mission to Mars Project (3-MP), an ambitious 143-billion-dollar project designed to establish a series of habitable hubs on the Red Planet's surface by 2049.

Mars is the only other planet in our solar system endowed with the natural resources necessary for human civilization. Its soil possesses carbon, hydrogen, oxygen, and nitrogen, as well as water frozen as permafrost. Its atmosphere is dense enough to protect inhabitants from solar flares, its solar light ample for greenhouses.

The 3-MP's mission was based on an exploration approach developed in 1990 by Robert Zubrin, then a senior engineer at Lockheed Martin. The key to the "Mars Direct" plan was to travel as light as possible, with rotating crews establishing habitats that would allow them to live off the land. The soil on Mars would provide for food, water, materials, and rocket fuel.

By September of 2029, the ERV (Earth Return Vehicle), a new multistage rocket constructed using parts from already existing vessels, was sitting on its launchpad in Cape Canaveral, ready for takeoff.

Everything changed six weeks later, when the private sector officially stepped up to the plate.

Project HOPE (Humans for One Planet Earth) was conceived in 2016 by a group of former astronauts, design engineers, and rocket scientists who had left NASA years earlier because of the agency's "good ole boy" policies. Unlike other private rocket companies, they were not interested in launching satellites. HOPE was interested in space as public recreation.

The key to HOPE's future was a design for a new space plane, one that could take off horizontally like a jet, rise to its maximum turbojet altitude, then use boosters to rocket the passenger vehicle into space. Once in orbit, the paying public would enjoy twelve hours of zero gravity and a lifetime of memories.

All HOPE needed was a major investor, one that could provide factories and the financial backing to launch the company.

Enter Lucien Mabus, CEO of Mabus Tech Industries.

Lucien had inherited MTI, but was bored with running his father's company. What he needed was a challenge, something he could call his own.

At the urging of his intoxicating fiancée, Lilith, Mabus struck a partnership with HOPE's directors. Fourteen months later Project HOPE went public, offering investors an opportunity to claim their stake in the future.

The response from the global market was mind-boggling. Opening at 22, the stock closed the first day of trading at 106. By week's end it had split twice and was still soaring at $162 a share, making majority stockholder and HOPE's CEO Lucien Mabus the world's first trillionaire.

Attitudes in Washington changed overnight. Cape Canaveral Air Station, which controlled the barrier island and all launch facilities east of the Banana River, offered to move the Air Force's Forty-fifth Space Wing in exchange for a long-term lease with HOPE. Lucien Mabus turned them down, preferring to erect a new complex in the city of Cocoa Beach at half the cost.

On December 15, 2029, HOPE's first "space bus" took off down its new fifteen-thousand-foot runway. On board were 120 passengers, including key stockholders, political dignitaries, a dozen members of the media, and a crew of twelve.

Nothing real or imagined could have prepared these civilians for the magic of space. The sixteen-hour flight was smooth, the service first-class (just eating in zero gravity an experience unto itself) and the view—well, the view was both spiritual and humbling.

Within two months, HOPE was shuttling four space buses a week at a cost of $100,000 per ticket. Even with its high price tag, there was still a fourteen-month wait.

By April of 2032, three more space buses had been added to the fleet, dropping ticket prices to $39,000. By 2033, over eight thousand people representing every nation had orbited the planet.

The residual impact upon humanity was profound. "One Planet—One People," became HOPE's mantra. Many believed it was no coincidence that the last oppressive government fell to democracy during the space bus's reign. Religious and racial tensions eased. The global economy boomed as technology raced to keep up with the exploitation of space, and the exploitation of space created new Earthbound technologies.

By focusing its energies on the heavens, humankind had finally grown beyond its childish adolescence.

Plans were soon revealed for Space Port-1, the first space platform/hotel designed to accommodate the paying public. When completed, SP-1 would contain three main structures, each configured in the shape of a bicycle wheel. The upper wheel, known as the "hub," would house a restaurant, bar, gymnasium, and, at the very end of the structure, a nonrotating zero-gravity observation deck. Below the hub, connected by a main elevator shaft surrounded by spokelike corridors was the middle wheel, or "Spotel." The largest of the three structures, the 1,950-foot donut-shaped living quarters, rotating one revolution per minute, would provide guests with a third of Earth's gravity. Below this massive wheel, connecting to the Spotel through an access shaft were SP-1's control room, infirmary, crew and staff's quarters, and the Space Port's docking station.

Seventy-five private guest modules would afford SP-1's clientele five fun-filled days in space. No amenity would be spared. All suites would be equipped with videophones, Internet uplinks, twenty-four-hour-a-day room service, and private viewports. Activities would include space walks, guided tours of the command center and engine room, and full-body, gravity-free workouts in the gym. For another $30,000, a lucky few could even board a lunar shuttle for a two-day excursion around the moon.

Advertisements were already flooding the global market: *SPACE PORT-1 : Join the 220 MILE CLUB*. Total standard vacation package (including round-trip launch fare) a mere $120,000 per person.

Six months after its plans were revealed, SP-1's reservation list (nonrefundable 15 percent deposit required) was already two years long, and three more hotel chains were negotiating with HOPE to build a Spotel on the moon.

Undaunted, NASA's MP-3 program continued moving toward the successful construction of its Mars Base. With the global economy humming and humanity focused on space, the U.S. Congress increased the space program's budget to levels previously enjoyed by the Defense Department, allowing for the design and construction of a moon base and lunar observatory/radio telescope.

Not to be outdone, young Lucien Mabus and his new bride announced that HOPE was in the process of completing final designs for its own Mars Colony. The first Mars shuttles carrying engineers and supplies would arrive on Mars in winter of 2047—two full years ahead of NASA.

NASA officials were incensed. Lucien Mabus's plans were clearly pushing the envelope of safety and science, all in the name of profit.

The Mabuses scoffed. For sixty years NASA had kept the exploration of space to itself. Had the program been run efficiently following the Apollo Program, man would already be living on Mars. Given NASA's time schedule and its propensity for overanalysis, it might take another six decades before the first civilians could experience the Red Planet's wonders. Like it or not, humankind was evolving, pushing for new sensory experiences in space, and he, Lucien Mabus, cosmic pioneer and heir to the Mabus fortune, was driving the herd.

Unbeknownst to Mabus and the White House, the frontier of space was about to take on an all-new meaning.

A wisp of thought, in the consciousness of existence.

As the transhuman, Bill Raby, I had managed to use telepathy to open the sealed vault of our alien hosts. Heart pounding, I stepped inside the entrance of the ancient megaplex—a dark antechamber that went instantly ablaze with piercing violet lights, projected from multiple angles.

I was being identified.

The antechamber led into a great hall, and somehow I knew that everything man had ever known about his existence was about to change.

They were everywhere, stacked vertically along invisible shelves of energy. Millions of cryogenic glass pods, eight feet tall, four feet across . . . specimens in a zoological library, a thin layer of frost concealing their contents.

Approaching the nearest pod, I wiped ice from the outer glass and peered inside.

It was a gangly bipedal humanoid, seven feet tall, floating within a clear liquid gel. The hairless skull was elongated, just like mine, only the bands of blood vessels traversing the scalp were infinitely more pronounced. The skin was mouse gray, more silicon than flesh. Protruding from its lipless mouth was a thick tracheal tube, the hose of which connected to a control panel somewhere within the hidden base of the glasslike container.

The nostrils were plugged, as were the earholes. The eyes were wide-open, the pupils twice the size of our own, twinkling a luminescent azure blue.

Star-shaped electrodes pulsating violet flashes were affixed to the crown of the being's elongated head, the center of its hairless brow, and along the base of its throat.

Kneeling, I scrapped more frost from the glass, hoping to see the lower torso.

The being was hairless and naked, yet contained no noticeable sexual organs. The five fingers of each hand were long and slightly webbed. From my poor vantage, I could not see the toes.

More star-shaped electrodes flashed over the solar plexus, heart, sacrum, and feet. I recognized these seven spots as chakra points, the body's energy centers. Hindus had long believed the body's chakra points channeled spiritual energy.

I estimated a million of these humanoids were being held in suspended cryogenic animation, stacked one atop the other within invisible energy fields. It was impossible to tell how many of them there were, for the stacks disappeared high overhead into the darkness, and wound around the entire interior of the building.

I knew they were alive, and I knew what they were, for somehow, I could sense their unified presence observing me.

They were posthumans. Alive but not alive, unified yet all alone . . . unable to touch or feel.

Unable to love.

In the chaotic months that followed, every member of our colony would complete the transhuman metamorphosis. Coming out of our comas, we were like infants suddenly made aware of our bodies, each day revealing wondrous new discoveries about our genetic transformation. Besides the obvious leaps in intelligence and body strength, we found we could communicate concepts telepathically.

More astounding was our ability to extend life expectancy.

Numerous factors cause aging and death among Homo sapiens. One is telomerase, an enzyme that elongates the ends of chromosomes. Every time a cell divides, telomerase shrink. When the length drops below a set threshold, Homo sapiens cells stop dividing and mortality approaches. Other proteins, like apolipoprotein E, can postpone aging, *but are present in limited quantities, as opposed to free radicals—the highly destructive, oxidizing molecules produced by the body itself that lead to senescence and disease.*

Given the gift to control our own cellular functions, we found we could now isolate and eliminate free radicals from our bodies while increasing the production of apolipoprotein E and glutathione. Further, we could reduce the loss of telomeres, potentially increasing life expectancy tenfold.

Perhaps more.

Our newfound focus was not just inward. Telepathy allowed us access to all of New Eden, including its recorded history, and we soon discovered the aliens' society had been a dichotomy of existence.

Long before we arrived, the world we had named Xibalba *had been a planet influenced by two distinctly different cultures. The first was the transhuman race responsible for constructing the floating city. The dwellings, the landscaping, the agricultural pods and environmental controls—all were designed for these beings. Little was known of their origin, but it was obvious they had cultivated their domain over thousands, perhaps millions of years. They were space travelers, masters of genetics, and were far superior to us in every way.*

At some point in Xibalban *history, a fantastic scientific discovery was made that allowed these ever-curious transhumans to transcend their third-dimensional physical world and enter the realm of the spiritual. The decision to pursue or ban this science would split the* Xibalban *race in two. The group that rebelled against the discovery would leave the planet, traveling to God-knows-where, while the other group remained behind, intent on evolving beyond their physical forms to walk in God's shadow.*

Self-programming, immortal, and unlimited in power— the group that remained behind would evolve into the posthumans. The beings held within the cryogenic pods were their physical remains.

It is the traces of posthuman DNA, Jacob, that makes us Hunahpu.

* * *

*Professor Ian Bobinac was the most accomplished gene-
ticist in the colony. On Earth, he had pioneered the use of
"Vee-Gees," vaccine genes—genetically engineered cells
used to produce antibacterial, antivirus, and anticancer
substances directly into the human body. On Mars, his
work in genetic manipulation would have been applied to
alter reproduction schedules among cloned livestock.*

*Bobinac was a genius even before his brain had been af-
fected by transhuman metamorphosis. Having "evolved,"
he now spent most of his time living inside his own brilliant head. What finally brought him out of his self-
evolving "funk" was the mystery surrounding the alien
lines and glyphs flashing along the exterior of the great
posthuman hall.*

*Bobinac soon discovered a communication emanating
from the structure—an audible communication—translated at a refresh rate of 267,000 cycles per second. By
comparison, the spoken word is transmitted at a mere
16–20 cycles.*

*What Professor Bobinac had discovered was a posthu-
man language, composed of 212 distinct graphemes (English uses only forty-six phonemes). Most bizarre, the
posthumans' collective mind was still dispersing their communication across the planet.*

But to whom?

*The moment I heard of his discovery, I asked to be trans-
ferred to Bobinac's team. As marine geneticist Bill Raby, I
immediately recognized the 267,000 harmonic cycle as one
shared by a sea creature back on Earth—*

—whales.

*While the effects of our genetic metamorphosis were uni-
versal, our newfound powers affected each of us differently,
magnifying our own unique personality traits.*

Lilith Mabus and her son, Devlin, craved power. As time

passed, the olive-skinned Adonis grew increasingly bel-
ligerent, his sociopathic tendencies, combined with his
mother's influence, driving him to lead the life of a
modern-day Caligula.

Whiffs of wild tales spread through our small commu-
nity. Some told of private gatherings hosted by Devlin in a
transhuman dwelling he had taken over, referring to it as
the "president's mansion." There were rumors of lurid or-
gies and Satanic rituals led by the bewitching Lilith,
though nothing could be substantiated.

In truth, most of us were too involved with our adjust-
ment as "superior beings" to take the time necessary to in-
vestigate these tales. But as the fourth anniversary of our
arrival on Xibalba grew near, there was a growing move-
ment to oust the planet's self-appointed leader and his
wicked parent.

Devlin and Lilith had other plans.

Prior to abandoning the planet to hunt the Xibalban trans-
port in Earth-space, the Guardian had taken DNA samples
from posthuman subjects. Ten thousand years in our past,
they had introduced dilutions of this super-elixir into
Homo sapiens, genetically altering our species, driving us
up the evolutionary ladder.

Unbeknownst to the rest of the colonists, both of De-
vlin's biological parents had possessed Hunahpu DNA.
Cold and calculating as a human, Devlin's evolution as a
transhuman gave him the extraordinary ability to decipher
and manipulate polygenic traits within his own DNA.

In short, Devlin Mabus could self-evolve.

Evolution can be traced back to the first bacteria that
took life from Earth's primordial soup. Housed within our
DNA is a record of every phase of our evolution, from
ocean dwellers to reptiles, from the first insectivorous
mammals to our primate cousins.

Remaining in isolation for weeks, Devlin had tapped

into his genetic code, manipulating a master gene that would help him reengineer his entire being.

On the morning of our fourth anniversary, New Eden's colonists gathered in our adopted public square.

It was Lilith who stepped out of the shadows of the president's box to address the crowd.

"Holy, Holy, Holy is the Lord of Hosts, who has reached across the cosmos to save His Chosen Ones from death. He has led us to the New World and Blessed us with its wonders. He has given us a taste of His wisdom, and transformed each of us into something better than what we were. And now, He has heard the cries of His children.

"Who among you has sinned? Who among you suffers inside? Which of you are consumed in guilt? Raise your hands and be made accountable!"

In unison, we raised our hands, many of us weeping at the memories of the deceased loved ones we had abandoned back on Earth.

"Do you seek salvation? Speak the words aloud."

For such a small crowd, our shouts were deafening.

"We are here today because of a miracle. Long ago, my son, Devlin, was given a vision. In this vision, he saw the incubator Earth cast out humankind. Like a modern-day Noah, he was instructed to build a fleet of spaceships—cosmic arks—in which he would lead the chosen few to salvation. Look around you and tell me this is not so. It was Devlin's vision that led to our rebirth. It was because our true creator touched him that we are here today.

"And now another miracle has occurred. In your prayers for salvation, the one true creator has sent us his archangel. Behold my son, Devlin, the Seraph!"

Jude and I held hands, our breath taken away as Devlin stepped out of the shadows of the president's box and into the light. A hush grew over the crowd as we ogled the creator's handiwork.

He was completely nude, standing before us like some fifteenth-century sculpture of David come alive. Protruding from his genetically altered muscular back and spinal column were massive flesh-toned wings, the appendages spanning no less than twenty feet from wingtip to wingtip.

Devlin had used his Hunaphu awareness and transhuman powers to tap into the master gene cluster responsible for the development and evolution of mammalian flight. He had become Chimera—a genetically altered creature of incongruous parts.

He was Seraph.

As we watched, his wings animated, catching a column of air rising from a hidden ventilation shaft. Like a condor's, Devlin's wings spread as he rose, awkwardly at first, then more majestically, like a great bird of prey.

What a spectacle it was to behold. Colonists fell to their knees, tears streaming from their eyes, while God's "appointed angel" flew above our heads and "blessed" us with his urine stream.

And how could we not have fallen in worship? Like the ancient Hebrews before us, we had considered ourselves the "Chosen Ones," selected by God to survive. Each day for us on Xibalba was a miracle. On the brink of extinction, our Savior had blessed us with the gift of transhumanism. We had overcome the ravages of age and disease, we had transcended the human condition. We were believers, as impassioned as the Children of Israel must have been after Moses had parted the Red Sea.

The scientists among us, myself included, were not so easily convinced.

Jude, a devout Christian, argued endlessly with me about this, swearing that it was divine intervention that rescued us from oblivion.

But Devlin Mabus . . . an angel? The Devil incarnate, more like it.

Flexing his newfound political muscle, Devlin "ordained" that personal time each day would henceforth be *dedicated solely to worship. One religious order—the "Church of Mabus" was proclaimed, and it was mandated that all colonists attend services.*

Those of us who doubted the self-appointed deity sensed democracy and freedom fading fast—replaced by a new theocracy, with its own brand of Inquisition soon to follow.

Something had to be done.

Carefully, and very discreetly, I began recruiting members of the scientific elite who I knew harbored similar misgivings toward Mabus and his mother. Over the months our flock grew to include several dozen engineers and astronomers, rocket scientists and mathematicians, all seeking freedom from a society we suspected would soon turn to "divine" persecution.

Thus was born the brotherhood of the Guardian.

Ours was a secret sect, for to be caught opposing Devlin and Lilith meant dismemberment by their followers. Because our thoughts could be telepathically "tapped," each member of the brotherhood would only be addressed by his or her alias.

We decided upon historical names. As Guardian founder, I dubbed myself: Osiris.

Michael Gabriel's identity surely must have screamed at me from the abyss of Bill Raby's mind.

What our newfound Guardian brotherhood desired was a safe haven from Devlin and his growing flock. We had two choices; either relocate to another part of New Eden or inhabit one of the planet's two moons.

Remaining on New Eden was only a temporary solution at best. Targeting the larger of the two moons, we made plans to steal a shuttle.

A former NASA rocket scientist, known to us only as Kukulcán, was convinced he could salvage enough fuel to get us to our destination. Another scientist devised headgear that would scramble our brain's electromagnetic waves enough to prevent other colonists from eavesdropping. While this assured us at least some semblance of pri-

*vacy while we prepared our escape, Devlin's new religious
decree meant we would have to work during our "sleeping"
shifts.*

*The three shuttles that had carried us into New Eden had
remained abandoned atop one of the transhuman dome-
scrapers for years. While the Guardian scientist, Kukulcán,
worked on preparing one of the shuttles for spaceflight, the
rest of us reconfigured the ships' environmental suits for
our elongated skulls. Agricultural pods were stocked, medical supplies secreted on board.*

*As the day of our departure crew near, we felt prepared
for anything—*

—never suspecting there was a Judas in our midst. . . .

■ ■ ■ ■ ■ ■ ■ ■ ■ ■ ■ ■ ■

27

■ ■ ■ ■ ■ ■ ■ ■ ■ ■ ■ ■ ■

**NOVEMBER 22, 2033
KENNEDY SPACE CENTER
CAPE CANAVERAL, FLORIDA
10:03 A.M.**

The black limousine follows the NASA Parkway east,
leaving Merritt Island and crossing the Banana River
land bridge to Cape Canaveral.

Mitchell Kurtz instructs the vehicle to stop at a security
checkpoint. A flashing sign orders them to step out of the
car.

Immanuel Gabriel, a.k.a. Samuel Agler, his mother, and
the two bodyguards climb out of the limo, allowing two
heavily armed guards to check their credentials. A robot
sensor sweeps the exterior of the motorcar.

Dominique places her palm against the portable DNA scanner, her false identity tag appearing on screen.

> SUBJECT IDENTIFIED: YOLANDA RODRIGUEZ.
> SUBJECT HAS GOLDEN FLEECE CLEARANCE.
> HAVE A NICE DAY.

Kurtz submits to a weapons scan. An alarm sounds, piercing the humid night air, causing both NASA guards to aim their weapons. "Hands high and wide! Move!"

Kurtz looks at Pepper, who rolls his eyes. "Rookies."

A lieutenant exits from the station, stun gun held high. "Is there a problem?"

"He's packing a high-energy taser, sir."

The lieutenant recognizes the limo and its passengers. "Watkins, did you bother to check his clearance?"

The guard looks down at his computer pad. "*Fubishit*, he's MAJESTIC-12."

"Which means I can march into the goddam White House with any weapon short of a neutron bomb," Kurtz says. "Now get that toy out of my face before I vaporize you."

"Yes, sir. Sorry, sir."

The other guard approaches Sam with the portable DNA scanner. "Place your palm against the scanner, please."

"Wrong." Beck steps in between them. "The kid's exempt from DNA protocol."

"Sorry, big fella," the lieutenant says. "Nobody's exempt from DNA protocol, not even President Zwawa."

"Check your orders again, Lieutenant." The imposing African-American moves closer, eyeballing the overmatched officer.

"There's nothing in my orders about a DNA exemption." The lieutenant nervously fingers his stun gun, not sure what setting short of DEATH could stop the bear-sized man.

Dominique sees the expression on Kurtz's face and knows he is seconds away from activating his taser. "Salt, wait! Lieutenant, contact Dr. David Mohr in Hangar 13. He'll verify everything."

The lieutenant hesitates, then touches the comm link on his forearm. "Sorry to disturb you, Dr. Mohr, but I have four guests at the gate, a Yolanda Rodriguez, two bodyguards, and a male adolescent who refuses to submit to a DNA scan."

Mohr's face appears on the tiny screen. "Let them through, Lieutenant."

"But sir—"

"Immediately, Lieutenant. Mohr out."

"Yes, sir."

Hangar 13, referred to by NASA personnel as "the fortress," is a twenty-two-story steel-and-concrete structure situated on the southernmost tip of Cape Canaveral. As wide and as long as three football fields, the building contains two monstrous bay doors, each 297 feet high. Within the complex (the third largest structure in the world), are thirty-one cranes, two 227-metric-ton bridge cranes, and twenty-three of the latest hover-lifts. Cooled by nineteen thousand metric tons of air-conditioning, the facility has its own power plant, cafeteria, and security force. The exterior is surrounded by a series of electromagnetic and electrostatic dampeners, making it the largest Faraday chamber in the world. The site is also protected by an electrically charged forty-foot-high perimeter fence, with gun towers positioned along each corner, two more by the adjacent beach, one more along the shoreline of the Banana River.

No one gets in or out of Hangar 13 unless authorized.

The limo follows a two-lane bridge to the island complex, then turns left into a parking lot. Three more armed guards appear, escorting Dominique's entourage from the limousine into the windowless front entrance. Salt and Pepper head off to the eatery while Sam and his mother are led down a plush magenta-carpeted hallway, past another checkpoint, then to a large alcove, dead-ending at an immense titanium vault door.

A holographic security guard appears. "Good evening, Ms. Rodriguez. You may enter the facility when ready."

Warning lights illuminate the forward steel bulkhead. The impregnable vault door swings open, allowing them entry into a long, brightly lit tunnel.

Sam follows his mother through the naked corridor, registering the change in air pressure as the vault door is sealed from behind. "Okay, Ma, what's this all about? Where the hell are you taking me?"

"Shh. Save your questions until we're inside."

"Inside? You mean this isn't inside? What is this place?"

"Be quiet and be patient."

They follow the soundproof concrete and drywall passage to a set of steel double doors. The door seal parts as they approach and they enter a sterile white chamber, the walls circular, the ceiling domed. There are no windows or doors.

A hologram of an East-Asian secretary appears in the center of the room.

"Good evening, Mrs. Gabriel. Please proceed to Habitat-2. Dr. Mohr will meet you there."

"Thank you, Rameeka."

The camouflage of white wall disappears, revealing a steel door and keypad. Dominique presses her palm to the scanner.

Another passage opens before them. Dominique turns to her son. "Deeper into the rabbit hole, eh, Manny?"

"Cute."

They exit the holographic security chamber and enter a tight corridor, the rounded walls and ceiling composed of clear Luxon glass, a new diamond-based polycarbonate.

"I feel like a goddam hamster. Whoa—" Sam rounds the corner and stops, the floor below having dropped away beneath the glass.

They are six stories above the ground floor of a subterranean hangar. A slow-moving hover-lift glides below, its enormous flatbed transporting an intricate piece of equipment, possibly a rocket engine subassembly. Ahead, a pair of Statue of Liberty-sized 150-foot-high double doors begin to part.

Sam presses his face against the thick glass to see better.

Dominique grabs his arm. "Come on, we'll be late."

"Wait, I want to see what's inside."

"Later. Dr. Mohr's waiting."

The glass corridor bends to the left, another door up ahead. "So who's this Dr. Mohr?"

"The director of GOLDEN FLEECE."

The corridor door opens. To Sam's surprise, they are standing in a pleasant foyer—more ski lodge than space center. Teak wood lines the walls and floor. The ceiling, stretching six stories above their heads, ends in a tinted glass dome. Plush furniture in shades of violet and purples surround a control station.

Seated behind the rounded console is the East-Asian woman who had appeared in the last hologram, only this time in the flesh.

The woman stares at Sam as if seeing a ghost. "Remarkable . . ."

"Rameeka Ellepola, this is my son."

The dark-eyed, brown-skinned Sri Lankan stands, extending her hand. "This is such an incredible honor."

He shakes her hand. "Guess you're a big football fan, huh?"

"Football?" She shoots Dominique a quizzical look.

"I'll explain later," Dominique says. "Where's Dr. Mohr?"

"Observing the training session. He asked you to meet him in the mezzanine."

Sam follows his mother to an awaiting turbolift, the Asian girl never taking her eyes off him. He waits until the elevator door seals. "Okay, what was that all about?"

Before Dominique can respond, the lift door reopens.

They step out onto a dark mezzanine. Ahead is a floor-to-ceiling glass barrier overlooking an enormous indoor

arena, its interior bathed in violet light. Situated on their
side of the glass wall are twelve control stations. A dozen
technicians, both males and females, are seated behind
wraparound head-to-toe plasma monitors. Each wears a
silver-colored body leotard lined with sensory links wired
to their controls. Atop the technicians' heads—sensory vi-
sors, obscuring their faces.

Appearing from behind the monitors is a slight Caucasian man in a white lab coat. He approaches, pausing so
that the beam from an overhead light reveals his face.

"Hello, hello." The scientist kisses Dominique on the
cheek, then turns to her son. "Oh, my, thank you so much
for coming. I've waited so long to meet you."

"Who the hell are you?"

"Mohr, David Mohr. Please call me Dave. I'm in charge
of this monstrosity."

The scientist is six inches shorter than Manny, with
chocolate brown hair graying slightly around the temples.
His complexion is pale, the deep-set eyes brown and twinkling, absorbing everything they see.

Immanuel eyes the offered hand before shaking it.
"Samuel Agler."

Mohr flashes a grin. "Samuel Agler, oh, I love it. Come
with me, Samuel Agler, there's something I want you to
see. Dominique?"

"Go, you know I can't stand to watch."

"Understood." Mohr leads Manny toward the glass barrier. "You know, Sam, your mother has told me so much
about you. Ever been to the Cape?"

"Once, when I was in high school. Wait a second, you're
not the weather-net Dr. Mohr, are you? The Nobel prize
guy?"

"That's me. These days, I'm working on things infinitely
more interesting. Let me show you." He points to the vast
arena, its specifics still hidden in darkness.

"What is this—a holographic suite?"

"As a matter of fact it is. We use it as a training facility.
It allows us to monitor all levels of combat."

"Combat?"

Mohr flashes a boyish grin. "You're just in time for the morning session." The scientist turns to his two assistants. "We're ready, ladies. Begin sequence one."

Yellow ceiling lights illuminate the interior, revealing a replica of an ancient Mesoamerican ball court. The playing field is about 150 yards long, slightly narrower at its width, its rectangle of grass imprisoned within four walls constructed of limestone blocks. The longer eastern and western boundaries are bordered by stone embankments rising fifteen feet, each slanted wall adorned with ancient ball game reliefs. Situated atop the eastern embankment, directly across from the glass partition and control room, is a replica of Chichén Itzá's twenty-six-foot-high Temple of the Jaguar.

Anchored to the two perpendicular walls like a giant vertical donut is a circular stone ring, its hoop twenty inches in diameter.

"You've duplicated the Mayan Ball Court? Why?"

"You'll see."

"The Mayan inscription on the embankment—what does it say?"

"This particular ball court was known to the Maya as 'black hole,' indicating it stood at the entrance of the Underworld, or *Xibalba*. The heroes of the game were said to have descended to *Xibalba* to conquer death. Look, here come their challengers."

Mohr points below and to their left.

Entering from the southern end of the arena, their faces cloaked behind Mayan death masks, are a dozen brown-skinned warriors. Too large to be of Mayan descent, the men are as tall and muscular as Ryan Beck. Each carries an object like a baseball bat, the handles shaped like a serpent's head.

The twelve technicians work furiously at their control stations, each manipulating their designated warrior.

The Mayans line up in formation, shoulder to shoulder beneath the opposite eastern goal.

From the northern end of the field appear two men. In

stark contrast to the warriors, these athletes are dressed from head to toe in modern-day Special Ops combat body armor, one in black, the other in white.

"What are they wearing?"

"An advanced type of exoskeleton. The outer layer consists of ballistic-resistant ceramics backed by a lightweight carbon nanotube. Fabric's as strong as steel, as light as cotton. A mini-fuel-cell-powered thermal comfort system, worn at the hip, cools or warms each soldier. Microturbines fueled by liquid hydrogen provide the body armor with ten kilowatts of power. Those teardrop-shaped helmets have integrated communication systems and augmented reality optics with night-vision screens. Strapped to their backs is a thin, pressurized water pack feeding a tube mounted inside each of the soldiers' helmets."

"Sorry I asked."

Side by side, the two modern-day warriors jog toward the western wall, playing sticks in hand, tinted face shields obscuring their identities.

Two of the brown-skinned warriors step forward, swinging their bats as if warming up for a cricket match.

A bloodcurdling bellow shatters the silence, causing the hairs on the back of Manny's neck to stand on end.

The two men in body armor step forward, accepting the challenge.

From atop the Temple of the Jaguars appears a Mayan king. His face is concealed behind the mask of a gaping serpent's head, a trail of green feathers running down his back. In one hand he holds an obsidian knife, in the other—a round object, dripping with blood. The king raises both arms in ceremonial fashion and begins chanting in an ancient tongue.

"Itz'-am-na, Kit Bol-on Tun, Ah-au Cham-ah-ez . . ."

"The king is invoking the gods." Mohr whispers.

Manny focuses on the dripping object in the Mayan's hand, shocked to see it is the severed head of a boy.

"Game ball," Mohr says, his eyes dancing. "Are you familiar with the game of *tlachtli*?"

"More or less. They have to get the skull, er . . . ball through the hoop."

"Correct. They can use their sticks, knees, and feet, but they cannot touch it with their hands. In combat style, two players per team compete at a time. As you'll see, anything goes."

The king stops chanting. Gripping the gushing head by the hair, he swings his arm in great circles, then heaves the skull toward the center of the playing field.

The four combatants charge forward, the soldier in white first to the "ball." As he feints a strike, one of the masked goons bull-rushes him, attempting to club him with his stick. White pirouettes gracefully to his right—and lets loose a vicious backhand fist, which catches the larger assailant square in the throat, sending him to his knees—

—as a second warrior raises his club, intent on stabbing the soldier in the back with its sharpened end.

But the man in white is too skilled and far too quick. Without so much as a glance over his shoulder he launches a thrusting rear kick that shatters the warrior's mask, snapping his neck in two.

The would-be killer collapses, dead before he hits the ground.

Immanuel feels nauseous as he watches the man in white step over his dead assailants, kicking the skull-ball back to his ebony-clad teammate.

Dr. Mohr points as two more warriors step out of line to greet their opponents, now quickly advancing the skull-ball toward the eastern goal. "This is not quite how the Mayans played, but it's how the Under Lords of *Xibalba* challenged the Hero Twins."

The blood rushes from Manny's face.

White clubs the object to Black. The skull-ball takes a wild hop over the soldier's foot. Turning to retrieve it, Black is barreled over by one of the replacement players, a 260-pound brute masked in a crimson demon's mask. Leaping over the man in black, the brown-skinned warrior kicks the skull-ball to his teammate, who races barefoot across the field toward the western ring . . . and the goal mounted below the observation window.

White, by far the most skilled athlete on the field, overtakes the Mayan and trips him from behind—just as the warrior strikes the ball.

Manny and Dr. Mohr instinctively duck as the airborne head smashes against the glass with a dull thud, the battered face leaving a bloodied imprint on the partition.

White rebounds the wild bank shot and heads back the other way, controlling the wobbling skull with his feet and stick. Evading another assailant's knife, he angles for the eastern wall and its stone hoop.

Two more linebacker-sized warriors abandon the line to cut him off, each man's club brandishing a two-foot-long obsidian spike.

Manny squeezes his fists, measuring speed and distance. *This is it . . . there's no way he can escape this double-team.*

In an incredible move combining soccer, kung fu, and gymnastics, White casually flips the skull-ball over the advancing warriors' heads, then leaps off the ground and executes a stunning airborne double side kick from a full split, the heel-to-face impact a double deathblow that shatters the shocked combatants' temporal bones into brain-slicing fragments.

"Jesus . . ."

White lands, takes three strides forward, and in one continuous motion kicks the skull-ball, sending it end over end toward the stone ring.

With a sickening *thwack*, the severed head banks high off the eastern wall and passes through the hoop—

—instantly transforming the arena into something entirely different.

Gone is the Mayan Ball Court. In its place—the valley of a hellish underworld, its mountainous horizon bathed in vermilion twilight cast from a subterranean roof of volcanic coal. Whiffs of brown smoke roll beneath the emberlike ceiling, creating shadows of movement throughout the terrain.

Manny's limbs turn to Jell-O. He leans against the glass for support.

At the heart of the valley is an enormous crater lake, its molten silvery surface simmering. Rising along the far bank is a great alabaster tree, its entanglement of ivory-colored roots knotted and thick, its sequoia-sized trunk dripping a white ooze.

The bare limbs of the monstrous tree stretch outward in every direction, twisting in the hot wind as if animated with life.

Suspended from one centrally located knot along the trunk is an object—

—a human skull.

Dr. Mohr points. Coming into view—the two soldiers, still clad in their respective white and black body armor. They are double-timing it, approaching the crater lake from the east, the man in white now wielding a double-edged sword.

The center of the lake begins bubbling as they approach.

Immanuel grips the cool iron guardrail in his sweaty palms, unable to move . . . unable to breathe.

Something large is rising from the depths of the lake. Thick globs of silvery ooze drip away . . . revealing a tall alien biped.

Lead gray silicon-like skin. Two arms and legs, heavily segmented, as if adorned in body armor. The anvil-shaped skull is disproportionately large, like that of a monstrous fire ant. Instead of being positioned above its three-humped shoulder, the skull extends horizontally in front of the chest like a turtle's neck, giving the creature an upright yet squat appearance. There are no facial features other than a slit of a mouth and two pupilless eyes, which blaze a burned yellow against the dark skin covering.

The eight-and-a-half-foot being continues to rise out of the silvery lake, its tall, grotesque, angular body devoid of hair or clothing. The thorax is V-shaped and powerful, the abdomen slender, connecting to a pair of squat legs—humanoid in design—except they are twice as thick below the knee than above.

The upper arms are dense and powerful, and hang stiffly from the wide shoulder girdle. The elbows are ball joint in design, allowing the heavy forearms to rotate 360 degrees.

Most frightening of all are the being's hands. Huge and clawlike in appearance, they support four slender, scalpel-sharp fingers. The digits are three times as long as the palm and spaced wide, giving each hand an almost spiderlike appearance.

Fully exposed, the being walk-glides across the lake's mirrorlike surface, sloshing toward the eastern shore.

The two soldiers race to reach the alabaster tree before the alien.

Ten seconds until Nexus. The computerized voice startles Manny.

Nine . . . eight . . . seven . . .

Dr. Mohr moves closer to the glass, his expression suddenly all business. "Come on, come on, you can do it this time."

The alien approaches the thickly rooted tree, reaching for the skull.

Three . . . two . . . one—

Twin streaks of ice-blue lightning . . . a blinding flash of crimson . . . then nothingness.

The violet lights return.

The lake is gone, as is the alien, the tree, and the entire hellish underworld. In its place—the sterile gray emptiness of an immense holographic suite.

Down on one knee, holding his cloaked head in his hands, is the warrior in white. His companion in black is gone.

Dr. Mohr waits a moment, then touches the comm link on his shirt collar. "Are you all right?"

The soldier nods weakly.

"Success?"

The man in white shakes his head—no.

Mohr pinches his brow, obviously disappointed. "Dominique is here. She brought her son."

The man in white stands. Limps toward the glass wall and looks up. Reaches for the hidden latches of his body armor. Slowly removes his hood.

Immanuel presses his face to the glass.

The white hair is longer, the eyes still piercing azure blue, cold and calculating.

Jake . . .

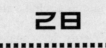

28

NOVEMBER 22, 2033
THE WHITE HOUSE
WASHINGTON, D.C.
11:34 A.M.

It is the most prestigious and powerful address in the world, a political village heavy with history, situated on eighteen acres. First occupied by President John Adams on November 1, 1800, it nearly burned to the ground fourteen years later at the hands of British troops. The home would be rebuilt and refurbished, with colonnades and office space added to both its east and west wings. While a vast subterranean control center would later be excavated beneath the dwelling, the 132-room mansion itself has remained virtually unchanged for over two centuries.

The White House: America's hub of democracy and the seat of world power. Within its 233-year-old walls are routinely discussed the future . . . and fate of humanity.

Lilith Robinson-Mabus, newly crowned queen of Mabus Tech Industries, saunters past the big Victorian fireplace of the State Dining Room, pausing to read the inscription set upon the mantel.

"I PRAY HEAVEN TO BESTOW THE BEST OF BLESSINGS ON THIS HOUSE AND ON ALL THAT SHALL HEREAFTER INHABIT IT. MAY NONE BUT HONEST AND WISE MEN EVER RULE UNDER THIS ROOF."
—PRESIDENT JOHN ADAMS

Lilith scoffs. "Male chauvinist fool. If women had been in charge around here, the world would be a lot less screwed up."

An aide enters the room, one of President John Zwawa's personal assistants. "Mrs. Mabus, on behalf of the entire White House staff, let me extend my deepest condolences—"

"Don't bother. What time is my meeting?"

"The president says he can see you immediately. If you'll follow me."

Lilith Eve Robinson's descent into the Mexican cave had exposed her schizophrenic brain to an extremely powerful low-frequency electrical field. Like an electrostatic tuning fork, the effect served to rephase the girl's already imbalanced brain waves.

Thought is analogous to energy. Firing at microseconds, it possesses no boundaries, not even the limits of time and space. In a manner transcending the principles of radio wave propagation theory, thought energy can be sensed by remote viewers who are highly tuned to these psychic phenomenon.

The phenomenon of reliving a previously seen or experienced event (memory) is an example of present-thought energy interacting with one's past. Though the encounter is usually brief, the mental interplay, or déjà vu, is quite real.

Exposure to the cave's electromagnetic amplification

enabled Lilith's pathological mind access into the psychic realm. Shortly after her descent, she began hearing another voice, one far different than those of her self-created companions.

"I can hear whispers," she had told Don Rafelo. "The voice speaks to me as I fall asleep."

"It is telepathy. The communication is meant to guide you."

"But who is it? How do they know me?"

"The whispers originate from both the near future and distant past."

"Why do you speak in riddles? Just tell me who is speaking to me."

The old man grinned. "You are in communication with . . . yourself."

Three years after her 'descent' into the Mayan Underworld, the seventeen-year-old beauty, now traveling under the name Lilith Aurelia, had arrived at the 2030 World Entrepreneurs Association Meeting in Miami in search of a mate. To bait her hook, she wore a strapless cocoa "fleshhugger" evening gown that matched her skin and barely contained her breasts. Long, wavy ebony hair fell past her tantalizing cleavage clear down to her taut, exposed stomach and gold belly button ring.

The barely legal man-eater sipped her martini as she casually scanned the ballroom crowd. *Nothing but pawns, and a few gray-haired bishops. The Queen of the Succubi is here, now where is my king?*

She watched as her escort, NRA activist Ben Merchant, worked the room. The middle-aged defender of the Second Amendment, dressed in a white Armani tux, wore a black rose tucked in his lapel buttonhole and a Beretta in his ankle holster. Lilith liked the homosexual, whom she had met a year earlier in Mexico City. He was shallow and greedy—easy to read, with the type of weaknesses she enjoyed exploiting. The constant name-dropping was annoying, but nonetheless, he was loyal and seemed to get things done.

"Excuse me, have we met?"

She turned to her right, glancing down at the slight Hispanic man in his late fifties. "And you are?"

"Deputy Mayor Raul Hernandez, at your service. Are you a . . . um . . . local girl, or—"

"Deputy Mayor? Is that something one volunteers for, or do you get season tickets to the theater with the title?"

"Excuse me?"

Her azure eyes blazed violet as her temper rose. "Go away, little man, before I *eat* you."

Hernandez blushed, choked on his retort, then, seeing the almost maniacal look in the girl's eye, decided it was best just to leave.

Ben Merchant approached, snorting a quick hit of cocaine-laced BLISS from a designer thimble. "Well, darlin', what do you think?"

"Pimps and pawns. There's no one here who could fill our bill. I need a real power broker, someone with some backbone, someone I don't have to constantly manipulate like a marionette. Powerful and rich, Benjamin. Filthy rich."

Merchant grinned. "I know just the man."

The handsome jet-setter with the oily black ponytail took his time licking the olive from the redhead's size 47-D cleavage, allowing his right hand to grope beneath the woman's miniskirt.

At only twenty-three, Lucien Mabus, son of the late billionaire, Peter Mabus Jr. was already wealthier and more feared than his deceased father. He had more money than he could spend in three lifetimes and met more women than he could possibly bed . . . and now he was bored.

What Lucien Mabus yearned for was a challenge.

The adrenaline junkie's eyes followed Ben Merchant as he approached from across the room. On the gun lobbyist's arm was the most captivating woman he had ever laid eyes upon.

"Lucien, dear boy, imagine running into you here."

Lucien retracted his hand from beneath the redhead's skirt. "Cut the bullshit, Merchant. My yacht's been docked here all week. Introduce me to the lady."

"I'm sorry . . . Lucien Mabus, this is Lilith Aurelia. Lilith, Lucien Mabus, president and CEO of Mabus Tech Industries."

Lucien extended his hand.

Lilith shook it, then inhaled its scent. "Be careful, your date's ovulating."

Lucien's laugh carried across the crowded bar. Turning to the embarrassed redhead, he shoved a hundred-dollar bill in her cleavage, and yelled. "Go the hell away!"

The redhead stormed off.

Lucien flashed Lilith a coy smile. "I like you. Ever been aboard a yacht?"

"No."

"Join me for a drink. Merchant won't mind, will you?"

"Not at all. Got a full day tomorrow anyway. Watch out for this guy, Lilith, he's a handful."

"Mmm . . . I hope so."

Oval Office, White House

11:43 A.M.

John Zwawa, the forty-seventh president of the United States, has made sacrifices to attain the highest office in the land. Entering the political arena after years as a human rights activist and heavy metal rocker has forced him to shorten his once shoulder-length blond hair, which now runs mostly gray. The thinly shaven goatee is gone too, as are the sideburns. The only remaining physical evidence of the president's years as a musician are his tattoos. On his right bicep is an image of a leaping lion holding two drumsticks, on his left—a large Polish falcon grasping a banner inscribed with his children's names.

The president enters the Oval Office to find Lilith Mabus hovering next to Alyssa Popov, the new director of the United States Geological Survey-Earthquakes Hazard Program.

"Lilith, so sorry about Lucien."

"Thank you, John. Lucien was young, but drugs had taken their toll on his heart long ago." She tilts her head, accepting the formal peck on the cheek from a man she has slept with more than a dozen times, on two occasions *with* her late husband.

"And Ms. Popov. I hear you've been busy at Yellowstone Park."

"You could say that, sir."

"I gather you two ladies know each other?"

"Intimately." Lilith winks, enjoying the president's blush.

"So? What's this meeting about? Next year's midterm elections?"

"No, John, it's about the end of the world and the survival of humanity."

Zwawa's grin remains frozen on his face. "Lilith, I don't have time for these—"

"Show him, Alyssa."

"Computer, play program Popov-One."

Along the far wall, the holographic image of the bookcase and fireplace reverts to a large floor-to-ceiling smartscreen.

For the next thirty minutes, the president of the United States is absorbed in the details of a Top-Secret UMBRA report.

"Computer, end program. Shred Popov-One and all minutes of this meeting."

A stunned John Zwawa sits head in hands at his desk, the weight of the world upon his shoulders. He whispers, "How could this be happening? Why wasn't I told?"

Alyssa shook her head. "With everything civilization's

been through in the last three decades, Yellowstone's never been more than a passing interest. It's only because of recent breakthroughs measuring geothermal changes that we learned of an impending eruption."

"How soon?"

"A decade or two, tops."

The president loosens his collar. "I . . . I can't breathe—"

"Take it slowly, John."

"How bad will it be?"

"Worse than you can possibly imagine," Alyssa says. "The explosion will release ten thousand times more debris than the Mount St. Helens explosion, instantly killing the surrounding population. The Midwestern states will become ground zero, wiping out our crops. Within a few days, the atmospheric debris will blot out the sun."

"And that, John," Lilith coos, "is when the shit really hits the fan. We're looking at a volcanic winter, with global temperatures plunging as much as a hundred degrees. Power grids will fail, populations isolated, the economy lurching to a standstill. Millions will perish during the first few weeks just from the cold. Roads will be impassable. Within a month or two, those who haven't frozen to death will starve."

"Unfortunately, Lilith's correct, sir. We're talking major ice age here, make no mistake about it. This is the end of civilization on this world, at least for a very long time."

"And you say this can happen in a decade or two?"

"Maybe less. When it does happen, we'll have little to no warning."

"There must be something our scientists can do?"

"We have teams working on it, sir. So far, nothing looks promising. You're talking about a major volcanic hot spot. The last time one of these calderas erupted, it wiped out nearly every human being on the planet."

"Who else knows about this?"

"Lilith's people, a handful of scientists, that's all for now."

"And that's the way we want to keep it," Lilith says, her

azure eyes staring through him. "We have one shot at saving our species, John, and only if we act now. Secrecy must be maintained at all costs, or all of us will die."

President Zwawa reaches into his bottom drawer. Removes a flask and paper cup, his hands shaking as he pours himself a drink. "You're talking about Mars Colony."

"Yes, sir. Mars has water, and water means life."

"Yes, but what kind of life? What future do we have on such a desolate planet?"

"Sir, Project HOPE and our own scientists have put together an extensive plan for Mars colonization. As we speak, NASA's geologists are working with HOPE to design a machine called an AGM, or Automated Greenhouse Machine. Powered by nuclear reactors, these mobile factories will produce vast quantities of perfluorocarbons—simple compounds of carbon and fluorine. In the right combination, these molecules are a thousand times more effective at trapping heat than carbon dioxide. Just a few parts per million of perfluorocarbons in the Martian air will produce enough warming to release vast amounts of CO_2 from the Martian polar caps and soil. The thickening of the atmosphere will trap more heat, releasing even more gas. By raising the planet's temperatures a mere twenty to thirty degrees Celsius, you start a runaway greenhouse effect."

"You're going to terraform Mars?" The president sits back, light-headed. "How soon?"

Alyssa Popov shrugs. "With HOPE's resources, we can have the first of these AGMs pumping within three years. In a decade, we'll have hundreds, enough to produce the gases necessary for a Martian atmosphere. Some of the colony's materials can be mined from the planet's two moons—our probes have detected usable concentrations of iridium and aluminum just beneath the surface of the Mars moon, Phobos. If all goes well, by 2070, the inhabitants of our colony might even be able to breathe Martian air without the use of pressurized suits."

Zwawa stands. Paces. "How many? How many lives can we save before the doomsday event takes place?"

Alyssa looks at Lilith, then back at the president. "With the discovery of a second Mars aquifer, the colony can support as many as ten thousand people."

"Ten thousand? Ten thousand out of seven billion? And who decides who goes? You, Ms. Popov? You, Lilith?"

"Actually, yes." Lilith's azure eyes sparkle violet in the light.

"This is barbaric."

"It is what it is. Face facts, John. This planet's been overpopulated for decades. In a sense, an ice age is Earth's way of cleansing itself. If history has taught us anything, it's that those who can adapt survive, while the weak among us perish. It's Nature's way."

"How can you be so cold-hearted?"

"Sir, those chosen will be contributing members of New Earth. Scientists and high-tech farmers, engineers, physicians, and skilled laborers. We'll start humanity over again using the best of the best—"

"—and the wealthiest, of course," Lilith chimes in. "To pull this off requires vast sums of money—money that cannot be allocated through Congress, unless you want planetwide anarchy. I've already started dialogue with CEOs of the Fortune 100s and a dozen private bankers, all of whom are dying—excuse the pun—to invest in HOPE's Mars Colony."

Zwawa sits back in his chair, the blood draining from his face. "If you don't need federal funding, then why are you even coming to me?"

"First," Alyssa says, "because we need your support in shutting down the handful of government and private agencies who might accidentally stumble across the truth. Yellowstone must be shut down to all nonessential personnel. We have a few emergency scenarios in mind, toxic sulfur leak, that sort of thing."

"Second," Lilith says, "because HOPE requires information and access that only you can provide."

"I'm listening."

"Sir, to build Mars colony will take hundreds of supply

missions. At present, it still takes NASA six full months and a helluva a lot of fuel to reach Mars. But if we could harness a different source of fuel, say . . . zero-point energy—"

"—then," finishes Lilith, "we could cut the costs and travel time by a huge margin."

"Zero-point energy? Don't know anything about that—"

"Of course you do, Mr. Former Vice President." Lilith slips behind his desk and rubs his temples, registering the cold sweat dampening the man's hairline. "What I need from you is complete access and control over Project GOLDEN FLEECE, and John . . . I want it now."

29

NOVEMBER 22, 2033
HANGAR 13
KENNEDY SPACE CENTER
CAPE CANAVERAL, FLORIDA
1:14 P.M.

They are seated on a second-floor balcony overlooking a Japanese garden—Dr. Mohr, his mother, Immanuel Gabriel, and the twin he has not seen in six years.

Jacob's surreal blue eyes stare at him, unblinking.

"Jesus Christ, would you stop staring at me?"

"I missed you."

"You mean you missed manipulating me."

"You're my twin. We belong together."

"Get over it. You can't just drag me back into your delusions after all these years. I'm Samuel Agler now. I have a life!"

Dr. Mohr interjects. "Let's everybody just stay calm. No one's forcing anyone to do anything. Manny, er . . . Sam, we brought you here because your brother's worried about you."

"You've been tapping into the nexus," Jacob says, "using it to enhance your performance on the athletic field."

"I don't know what you're talking about."

"It's dangerous, Manny. There are others like us out there, others who share this Hunahpu gene. Every time you enter the nexus, you make your presence known to them."

"How many others?"

"I don't know, one . . . a hundred . . . a thousand."

"A thousand more freaks like you running around? I doubt it."

Jacob ignores the remark. "Eleven thousand years ago, the Guardian began an interbreeding program with ancient man. The Guardian *is* mankind's missing link. In the process of mixing their DNA with ours, they created a sort of genetic time bomb, hoping that one of these Hunahpu would find his or her way to their starship in the year 2012. The Hunahpu would be able to use their genetic calling card to access the vessel and its weapons system, knowing the human race would need it on 4 *Ahau,* 3 *Kankin,* a date forecast in the Mayan calendar, equating to the winter solstice in 2012. Our biological father, Michael Gabriel, was Hunahpu. He wasn't the only 'chosen one,' he just happened to be the poor sap who managed to cross the finish line first."

"And thank God he did," Dominique adds. "Your father saved humanity."

Immanuel shakes his head at his mother. "Still buying into all this, I see."

Jacob sees the hurt in Dominique's eyes. "Mother, Doc, I need to speak with Manny alone."

Dr. Mohr nods, then leads Dominique inside, closing the patio door behind him.

"That was rude, Manny."

"Look who's calling the kettle black? Her heart bleeds for him, and you stomp on it every day."

"I didn't bring you here to fight. There's another Hunahpu out there like me. She's the one I fear."

Immanuel looks away.

Jacob's eyes widen. "You've spoken with her?"

"No."

"You're lying."

"Maybe she spoke with me."

"Maybe?"

"Look, I'll stay out of the zone. I was planning on quitting football anyway."

"Manny, this is way beyond your football career. This is about you finally accepting who and what we really are."

"Here we go again."

A violet twinge appears in Jacob's eyes as he loses his temper. Grabbing an empty chair, he flings it over the balcony rail.

Manny's eyes widen. "Well, well, what happened to Mister Transcendental Meditation?"

"Immanuel, for once, would you please just shut your mouth and listen!" Jacob closes his eyes and breathes, slowing his pulse, regaining his composure. "Have you ever experienced a déjà vu, that strange feeling that you've lived through a particular scene or situation before."

"I know what a déjà vu is."

"And what if you *had* lived through a particular moment before? What if the concepts of time and space are mere byproducts of our three-dimensional existence, which binds us . . . anchors us, if you will, to the physical world."

"I'm listening."

"There's so much we don't know about existence. What really happens when we die? Is there really an afterlife? Do we possess a soul? Does God exist? The answers to these questions are not available to us because they lie in another dimension, a realm of eternity where there is no concept of time, only pure life force . . . pure existence . . . hyperspace.

"There's a fundamental level of quantum existence all around us. Awareness of this energy field comes hard to most people. Certain individuals, Buddhist monks, for instance, can train their minds to look deep into the soul. You and I were born with this ability—an ability that others spend their entire lives hoping to achieve."

"Meaning what? You can see dead people?"

Jacob shakes his head. "Forget everything you think you know about life and death. Our physical bodies are nothing more than flesh-and-bone suits inhabited by the soul, which, in essence, is quantum energy. We may die physically, but spiritually our souls continue to exist. What separates you and me from the rest of humanity is that we have the genetic ability to move back and forth within the nexus, both physically and mentally, without having to die."

"I don't understand?"

"The nexus is an existence that bridges the worlds of the physical and spiritual, the 'ether' that out-of-body travelers have historically described. Scores of people have crossed through it and come back to tell us about it. A person dies. He sees a bright light and finds himself drawn toward its soothing embrace. Perhaps he's escorted through the light by a deceased loved one, assigned to provide guidance. And then—*whoosh*—the dead man is miraculously revived and all that is left are his memories of the journey and a lasting sense that he will never again fear the unknown."

"Like Evelyn Strongin?"

"Yes, like Evelyn Strongin."

Manny nods. "The only thing that happens when I access the zone is that everything sort of slows down. I see the light, but I never enter it."

"That's because you can't, at least not yet. My Hunahpu abilities are more defined than yours, allowing me to go deeper in the nexus into the more spiritual realm of the corridor. That's where I first encountered Lilith."

"The female Hunahpu?"

Jacob nods. "Evelyn warned me to stay away from her. She somehow sensed that Lilith was being exposed to the influences of the lesser lights. And so Lilith killed her."

"She's the one who murdered Aunt Evelyn?"

Jacob nods.

"What does any of this have to do with this whole NASA setup you've got going?"

Jacob leans forward. "What if I told you that our three-dimensional physical world has been caught up in what can best be described as a loop of time and space. Dr. Mohr would call it a fourth-dimensional warp, creating a temporal 'boomerang' effect. The essence of this effect is that major events that happen on our planet have, in fact, happened before and will happen again—unless we do something about it. Specific variables may change, whom we marry, what jobs we take, what choices we make on a daily basis. Chaos theory abounds at the infinitesimal level, but the big picture always remains the same—our history as a species continues to replay itself over and over again."

"How's that possible?"

"The time loop began in what you'd call the distant future when the Guardian's starship, the *Balam,* chases an asteroid-like transport ship through a wormhole 65 million years into our past. The time loop ends, or repeats itself sometime in the near future. A monstrous cataclysm is going to take place, one so devastating it will wipe out nearly every life-form on our planet. Only a handful of humans will survive by relocating to a colony established on Mars. A fraction of these survivors will travel through another wormhole to another section of our galaxy, inadvertently creating a closed causal loop in space-time."

Manny starts laughing, a nervous laugh, driven by spent nerves and fatigue. "You've been reading too much science fiction; it's warped that brilliant mind of yours. A closed causal time loop?" He wipes tears from his eyes. "How do you know all this?"

Jacob shakes his head. "You won't believe me."

"I don't believe you now."

"Existence is energy, Manny, making transdimensional communication possible. I've been in contact with someone from the other side, someone who's been . . . advising me."

"Who?"

"Don't tell Mother."

"Who?"

"Our father."

Immanuel covers his head. *"Oy vey . . ."*

"What's that mean?"

"Oy vey means the guys in the white coats will be coming for you soon."

"Manny—"

"Mick's dead, Jake. He's been dead for twenty years. You're never going to meet our long-lost lunatic father. Never. So get over it."

"He wasn't a lunatic, and you're wrong. Our father fulfilled his destiny, and so will we. Under the spiritual guidance of the Guardian, Mick made the ultimate sacrifice—to return to *Xibalba* in order to save the souls of the *Nephilim.*"

"The *Nephilim?*"

"The Fallen Ones, the ones whom the Guardian were forced to leave behind when they came to Earth. The *Nephilim* are being tortured. Our father was chosen to be their messiah, only he failed, just as the Guardian knew he would, just as is written in the Mayan *Popol Vuh.* Now it's up to you and me to rescue him. We need to save his soul and those of the *Nephilim.* Open your eyes, Manny. Accept our destiny so I can prepare you."

"Maybe it's your destiny, not mine. I'm not going anywhere."

"Ah, but you are, just as you have long ago. You are the Yin to my Yang. Only together can we hope to succeed."

"Okay, *Dim Son,* I've had it—I'm out of here." Immanuel tries to push his way past Jacob, but the white-haired twin is too strong. In one motion he pivots around his brother, catching him from behind in a choking headlock.

"I love you, Manny. I gave you six years, but now it's time—time for you to join me. Did you really believe God gave you these abilities so you could score touchdowns?

The sooner you face your destiny, the better prepared you'll be for what awaits us on *Xibalba*."

A wisp of thought, in the consciousness of existence.

It took our secret band of scientists eight weeks to squirrel away a year's worth of supplies and make one of the three Mars shuttles spaceworthy.

Our Guardian clan now numbered thirty-seven: Twenty men, twelve women, and five children—three of whom were first-generation infants born with elongated skulls. Through genetic manipulation, New Eden's women could control their ovulations and times of conception. They could select boy or girl, even fraternal or identical twins. Most important, the mother could influence an unborn infant's chromosomes while in the womb, preventing disease, even altering certain attributes—including the size and shape of the newborn's skull.

This type of genetic manipulation seemed amateurish in comparison to the mind-boggling things Professor Bobinac and I had discovered down on the planet's surface. Situated beneath the floating city was a vast genetics compound erected on the shoreline of an artificially created sea. Within this facility, the transhumans had left behind evidence of an advanced gene-splicing technique that combined cybernetics with synthetic artificial intelligence enhancements to produce a biomimetic-biomemnetic organism. These beings, dubbed Tezcatilpoca by their transhuman masters, had been weaned within the silvery exotic liquids contained in their artificial sea.

Holographic records showed the Tezcatilpoca had grown into immense cybernetic serpents—each silicontissued monster as large as a train—with sixteen nodes positioned along their frightening spines. Incredibly, these nodes were crystal lattices designed to amplify and focus gravity C-waves and fluxes in zero-point energy, a godlike source of power that had eluded scientists back on Earth. Apparently, the crystal lattices provided a form of synergy or harmonics necessary for the channeling of these incredible energies.

But for what purpose?

As unfathomable as it seemed, Professor Bobinac and I theorized that the transhumans had discovered a way to manipulate wormholes through the use of hypersonics. The Tezcatilpoca creatures created 'magnetic bottles' that bridged the gap between our own physical dimension and the higher realms of existence.

As the day of our secret departure approached, I knew I had to leave my fascinating studies behind. Devlin and his mother were creating a new religion that bordered on a Satanic cult, and the colonists, save our Guardian members, were becoming unquestioning followers.

My biggest concern then was Jude. As founder of the Guardian brotherhood, I had established strict rules regarding secrecy, each new recruit having to pass a number of "loyalty" tests before they could be "brought in." Though I had been "testing" her for months, Jude remained a steadfast Devlin worshiper, refusing to heed my concerns.

Jude's refusal to listen would create a major rift between the shared consciousness of Michael Gabriel and Bill Raby.

Bill Raby loved Jude the way I loved your mother, his emotions soothing a void in our collective soul. As the moment of our departure grew near, his consciousness became more forceful, fearful of losing the woman he adored.

To complicate matters, two days before we were to depart, Jude told us she was pregnant.

Desperate, our shared mind began working on her more intensely.

"Jude, I overheard a rumor today that Devlin's guards dismembered another New Edener. If it's true, that's six in the last two months. Doesn't that worry you?"

"Our Creator speaks through Devlin. If there are nonbelievers and deceivers among us, then the traitors need to be dealt with."

"Traitors to whom?"

"To our Creator, of course. He who brought us here. He who saved us from ourselves back on Earth."

"Then you believe the death of billions was a planned event?"

"Of course. Read the Bible. Wasn't Noah's flood a planned event?"

"I can't accept that. I think you and the others accept it because we're all so overburdened with survivor's guilt."

"Bill, you'll never be happy unless you open your heart to the Creator so that He might show you the way. Come worship with me tonight in our angel's house. Listen to the truth, my darling, and the truth shall set you free."

Jude's brainwashing ran deep, yet I could not bear the thought of leaving without her. Realizing my only chance at luring her away was to learn more about her "angel," I agreed to attend Devlin's service.

The Mabus House of Worship was an immense transhuman dwelling, its alien archways and flying buttresses giving it the feel of a futuristic Notre Dame. Inside the hall were thousands of hover pods—private antigravitational pews that formed a ring around Devlin's pulpit.

Two "thrones" were positioned in the center ring. In one sat Devlin, a crown of gold leaves situated atop his curly black hair, his wings folded in behind him. To his right was his mother, Lilith, the sheer material of her "priest's robe" screaming blasphemy to the Judeo-Christian values both Bill and Michael Gabriel had been raised under.

A cherub-faced transhuman male took his place at the dais, gazing at the capacity crowd through false rose-colored glasses. Instead of using the now-familiar telepathy, he spoke aloud, his Louisiana drawl sounding bizarre in these most alien of settings.

"And the truth, dear brothers and sisters, shall set you free. Yes, these are wondrous times, yet a gray cloud has invaded our lord's blue sky. False prophets have infiltrated New Eden, my friends. They cleverly disseminate their destructive Earthly heresies among you, hoping to infect our

New World and turn you against our archangel, Devlin, whose generosity and wisdom brought us to our cosmic oasis. In their jealousy, our enemies concoct clever lies, hoping you will be led astray. But fear not, devoted souls, for God condemned them long ago, and they will all soon suffer a swift and terrible end."

A chorus of, "Amen."

I felt Bill's consciousness crawl cold beneath my own.

"For our Creator and his archangel spare no one when it comes to blasphemy and sin, just as God spared only Noah and his family of seven from the Great Flood back on Earth, just as the Creator spared only our chosen flock from the devastation and ice age that consumed the seven billion lost souls shortly after our escape. These false teachers are unthinking creatures, born to be caught and killed. Be not sympathetic, for their destruction is a just reward for the harm they have done. They are a disgrace and a stain among you, and their arrogance is laughable.".

And then this plump man removed his comical rose-colored glasses and stared at me.

I could feel the eyes of the congregation upon me.

Devlin stood, his wings standing on end—a hawk, about to strike. In a soothing, almost loving tone, he said, "Seize and dismember him."

A hundred hands were upon me, dragging me from my floating pew. They stripped me naked and stretched me out on the floor, prey for the Seraph, Devlin, who hovered above, brandishing a pair of three-pronged silver claws in his hands.

Adrenaline soared through my body as my mind tried to fathom the hideous death to come.

What followed then, dear Jacob, was truly a miracle.

In the midst of my terror, my being was suddenly overcome by a strange, yet familiar feeling—a feeling of utter calm. It was the same feeling I had experienced in my childhood as Michael Gabriel, when the treacherous T'quan had pinned me down by the edge of the Yucatán well.

It was the same feeling I had whenever I remote-viewed.

I stopped struggling, allowing my mind to enter the void.

The cathedral appeared to brighten. Above, the winged Devlin seemed frozen, his unchanging expression—a mask of rage.

My heart pumped in my ears, and I could feel my muscles growing stronger. In one fluid motion, I yanked my arms free from the worshipers' grip and jumped to my feet.

Devlin stared past me through half-closed eyes, his pout-mouth halfway in sentence. For a fleeting moment, I felt the urge to leap into the air and tear those wings from his spine, to rip his throat apart—

—until I felt the icy presence of another pair of eyes upon me.

It was Lilith.

Her mouth never moved, but her telepathic voice made me cringe. I feel you, One Hunahpu. I've been waiting for your arrival for a very long time.

Her words seemed to pierce my soul, injecting me with a fear so intense that I nearly leapt out of my tingling skin. Still naked, I pushed through invisible waves of energy and raced out of the alien chapel, every muscle in my body burning with lactic acid, the voice of the Succubus cooing to me from the void—

—while Bill Raby's consciousness screamed at me for abandoning his Jude.

I ran from that ungodly chapel, racing through the streets of New Eden at inhuman speed, continuing until I arrived at the home of Christopher Coburn, a close friend and agricultural scientist known within the Guardian's inner circles as Viracocha. *Leaping from the void, I pounded on his door, my overwrought muscles burning with lactic acid.*

Chris dragged me inside, sending an encoded warning through the Guardian "grapevine" while I hurriedly dressed. Then we ran from his dwelling, making our way to the spaceship.

Devlin's people were scouring the city, hunting us like vermin. Those caught were publicly eviscerated and crucified, the children thrown into labor camps for "retraining."

Only twenty-four Guardian made it off New Eden alive.

Omnipotence in the hands of a sociopath is a dangerous thing. As challenges are vanquished, boredom sets in. Eventually, even the private orgies and human sacrifices become trivial.

I suppose I always knew what Devlin was planning, ever since the day I first discovered the posthuman arena. Mabus and his mother coveted immortality, and the godlike powers of the higher realms were a temptation too strong to avoid.

They would stop at nothing until they could locate the portal into the posthuman's netherworld.

I am certain now that this was the reason Xibalba's society had split. While some transhuman beings sought immortality in the spiritual domain, others must have believed there remained some discoveries better left to God.

Having barely escaped the domed city, we directed our lumbering spacecraft into orbit, landing on the far side of the larger of the two moons, hoping the satellite's mass would deafen our enemy's telepathy.

The moon was a lifeless rock floating in space. No water. No soil for growing. Even with our "enlightened brains" how long could we possibly survive there?

Imagine our shock when we discovered the transhumans' abandoned lunar outpost.

Smaller than New Eden, it was nonetheless a habitat of immense proportions and incredible technology. Located within an immense dome-covered crater, the abandoned habitat held oxygen- and water-processing plants, agricultural pods, and solar-powered reactors. Dominating the periphery of the crater were acres of photovoltaic solar panels—massive trackable sheets stretching seven stories high.

The most impressive structure had been erected within the heart of the dome itself. It was a monstrous pyramid, a copy of Egypt's Giza, only three times the size. The facing was composed of translucent gold-paneled mirrors—conduits channeling enormous amounts of energy into the structure—

—as if the pyramid were a massive, cybernetic incubator.

Inside this lunar fortress we discovered artificial intelligence . . . harbored in the guise of a dart-shaped, gold-paneled starship.

The Balam.

The sight of the ship tore at the fabric of my very existence . . .

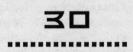

30

I'm sorry, miss, but I can't give out that information."

Lauren Beckmeyer stares at the armed guard, her blood pressure still soaring from the three-hour wait. "I've told you a hundred times, I know he's in there. Just tell him it's his fiancée. He'll come out."

"And I told you that even if your boyfriend is in Hangar

13, this is still a restricted area and you don't have clearance. Now you either get back in your Corvette and drive away like a good girl, or I'll have you arrested."

Lauren flashes the man a killing look. She climbs inside her car and guns the engine, the roadster's rear tires spewing gravel as it heads back across the causeway.

"If we are to succeed on *Xibalba,* you must learn your role," instructs Jacob. "Our attack must be synchronized. Every action, every thought must be rehearsed over and over again."

They are standing within the holographic chamber, now programmed to the ancient Mayan Ball Court. Jacob is in his white training suit, Sam in black. Three stories up, Dominique, Dr. Mohr, and his staff are watching from behind the thick Luxon glass.

"I feel ridiculous," says Sam, still weary from two hours of intense virtual-reality combat training. "Why do we have to wear these stupid outfits?"

"I told you, the atmosphere on *Xibalba* is heavy in carbon dioxide. The masks allow us to breathe, the body armor protects us. In the training arena, the suits are linked to our nervous system. If you get hit by a holographic warrior, you're going to feel it."

"Wonderful."

"Lose the attitude, Manny, I need you to take this seriously. You may not feel threatened in this arena, but make a mistake on *Xibalba* and I promise you, you'll die painfully."

Immanuel kicks at the synthetic limestone surface. For the first fourteen years of his life, the dark-haired twin had been bossed around by his overbearing brother. Virtual-combat programs, Eastern philosophy, training all hours of the day and night . . . everything centered around nightmarish tales of a Mayan hell called *Xibalba.*

Immanuel Gabriel had spent the first two-thirds of his life trying to escape his overbearing twin's fantasies. Now, as an adult, he is being drawn right back in.

Enough!

"That's it, Jake. I'm sick of these games."

"Games?"

"Games, neurosis, whatever you want to call it. Maybe you had Manny Gabriel spooked, but Samuel Agler wants nothing to do with it—or you." He removes his headpiece, tossing it on the ground.

"Immanuel—"

"This Hunahpu gene may allow us to focus inward better than the next guy, but it's screwing with your mind. Mom warned me years ago that it could lead to paranoid schizophrenia—and now you've got it in spades!"

Jacob looks up at Dominique, who backs away from the viewing glass. "Our mother has no idea what she's dealing with."

"I think she does. Our father was locked up as a mental patient, diagnosed a paranoid schizophrenic. Mom was his intern."

"Our father was not schizophrenic. His sentence in that asylum was based on bogus charges."

"Believe whatever makes you happy. Keep playing your combat games, only do it without me. See, Samuel Agler has a life, and it's not here." He strips off the body armor and heads for the exit.

"Computer, lights." The arena loses its violet hue. "Manny, look around. Do you honestly believe NASA would invest millions of dollars in a facility like this just to humor me? Do you really think all this is part of some schizophrenic delusion?"

"Jake, you live on a government installation, just as we did on Longboat Key. You train in a holographic suite, using a program you designed after the *Popol Vul*'s story. That doesn't make it real, and it doesn't impress me either. Heck, you should see some of the training facilities we have at the University of Miami. Blows this shit away."

"Manny—"

"All this Mayan Underworld crap, it all began with our grandfather and his stupid journal. He's long gone, and so is Mick. Personally, I've accepted the fact that our whole family is nuts. Mick was a schizoid, Mom suffers from severe depression, I'm living under a false identity, and you—well, you're the head squirrel. I love you, man, but I have to go. Have a good life."

Jacob shakes his head in disbelief, then looks up at Dr. Mohr. "This is going all wrong. I need to show him."

Mohr's voice sounds metallic over the speaker. "Jake, we talked about this. Your brother doesn't have clearance."

"He's my brother. He has more right to see GOLDEN FLEECE than anyone on this base." Jacob jogs out of the arena into the corridor. "Manny, er, Sam, before you go, I want to show you one last thing."

"Give it up, Jake."

"It won't take long, I promise. Humor me one last time."

Jacob takes his arm, leading him down a long subterranean corridor. They stop at a steel door guarded by two heavily armed soldiers.

"Morning, sir."

"I want to show my brother GOLDEN FLEECE."

The guards look at Immanuel, then at each other, unsure. The guard on the left says, "Sir, your, uh, your brother doesn't have clearance."

"Contact Dr. Mohr. He'll approve it."

"Forget it, Jake," Manny says. "Whatever it is, I'll see it another—"

"Contact Mohr. Now, please."

The guard activates his comm link. "Excuse me, Dr. Mohr, but Jacob insists we allow his brother inside to see GOLDEN FLEECE."

"Request denied. Escort Jacob and his guest to my office immediately."

The guard looks at Jacob. "Sorry, kid."

In a blur of movement, Jacob lashes out with two vicious karate chops, striking each guard along the carotid artery.

The unconscious men slump to the floor.

"Damn, Jake, you trying to kill them?"

"They'll be fine. Come on." He presses his palm to an identification pad.

The heavy steel door swings open.

Jacob grabs his protesting twin by the arm, leading him inside.

"Yo, man, that was not cool. This is NASA. I don't need trouble with the PCAA."

"Thirty seconds." Jacob pulls him down a short recess leading into an immense facility. "Just take a quick peek at what's inside, then I'll leave you alone for another six years."

"That's not what I'm . . . oh . . . oh . . . shit."

They are standing at the entrance to a mammoth factory, twenty stories high, as wide and as long as six football fields. But it is the object at the center of the facility that causes Immanuel Gabriel's heart to race, his muscles to turn to jelly.

It is an enormous spacecraft, 722 feet long, its dagger-shaped, warship-sized hull composed of shimmering, mirrorlike gold panels. The monstrous keel is situated twenty feet off the ground, resting on a series of rubber-tipped concrete-and-steel racks.[[AR 2]]

Manny sucks in slow breaths, forcing himself not to hyperventilate. *No way . . . this isn't real. It can't be—*

The forward two-thirds of the starship's "blade" morphs into the rear one-third "hilt," where two colossal assemblies are mounted along either side of the vessel's tail section, each bulbous structure as large and as high as a three-story building. Several technicians in white suits are working inside the alien engine, their lights revealing a wasp's nest of charred, afterburner-shaped housings, each orifice no less than thirty feet in diameter.

"This is the *Balam,* the starship the Guardian piloted to Earth 65 million years ago. *Balam* was a Mayan deity, represented by the jaguar, who protected the community against external threats. The vessel was excavated years ago from a subterranean chamber in Chichén Itzá. The

great teacher, Kukulcán, who was in fact the last of the Guardian survivors, instructed the Maya to erect his pyramid over the site—"

Immanuel feels the room spinning.

"—and the ship is also armed with an ion cannon. Our father used the weapon to defeat Tezcatilpoca on the winter solstice of 2012."

Immanuel drops to a knee, his lungs struggling for breath. He lies back on the cold concrete surface, staring up at the ceiling, which seems a mile away. *God, please, this can't be real . . .*

"Manny?"

Immanuel squeezes his eyes shut. *Come on, Mule, wake up, just wake the hell up—*

Jacob drags him onto his feet. "Now don't go schizoid on me, bro. Our deeply depressed mother wouldn't like that."

"Jake . . . I can't do this . . . I'm not ready—"

"Yes you are. Come on, I'll give you the tour." Jacob puts his arm around Immanuel's waist, steadying him as he leads him toward a small gantry rising halfway up the port side of the starship. He lowers his voice. "The reason the government invested so much money into my so-called dementia is this ship. They don't give a rat's ass about *Xibalba* or the Mayan prophecies. Project GOLDEN FLEECE is all about reverse engineering this starship to see how it draws energy from our planet and deep space."

"No . . . this isn't real—"

"We were kids when NASA finally excavated this vessel and transported it, quite covertly, to Kennedy. Problem was, they had no way of accessing it—at least until I came along."

"What are you talking about?"

"The Guardian designed the entries into the ship with a genetic code. You and I are the only ones capable of entering and commandeering the vessel. NASA was forced to give me *carte blanche* in exchange for my cooperation."

They reach the gantry and board a small open lift. The elevator rises five stories to a gold panel marked with a three-pronged alien candelabra, the insignia glowing crimson red.

"The Trident of Paracas," Manny whispers. "I remember this from Julius's journal."

"The sign of the Guardian." Jacob points to an eight-foot-high access plate. "Go ahead, close your eyes and command the entry to open."

"How?"

"Just imagine the panel opening."

Immanuel closes his eyes. Concentrates.

Nothing happens.

"Concentrate!"

"I am, asshole!"

"Here, watch." Jacob closes his eyes. A second later, the panel retracts with a gush of compressed air, revealing a passageway.

"You'll get better with practice. Come on." Jacob leads his twin inside.

The interior is dark and warm, the corridor's arched ceiling rising a good thirty feet above their heads. The curved walls are barren and smooth, composed of a highly polished, translucent black polymer. Behind the tinted glasslike surface Manny can make out elaborate circuits and machinery.

"The ship is divided into different levels. We're on the upper forward section, heading toward the bridge. These curved walls are actually interface panels linked to a central command computer, which in turn, responds to the frequency of our Hunahpu thought-energy patterns."

"Does this thing have a bathroom?"

Jacob smiles. "It has everything. But here's the most amazing thing—this ship is not just a spacecraft, it's sort of a living composite machine-organism."

"A what?"

"It's artificial intelligence. At the center of the ship is its brain—a crystalline biological organ situated in a fishbowl the size of a truck. Running out of the brain stem are billions of microcircuits and exotic metal conduits that feed like blood vessels throughout every square inch of the ship. This ship not only reads my thoughts, at times I think it talks back to me."

"The Guardian created all this?"

"No. The ship was made available to them, by who or what I have no idea."

The end of the corridor opens into a massive, onion-shaped control chamber. Rounded walls radiate a faint electric blue. At the very center of the cathedral-style, domed ceiling is a five-foot-wide passage, which rises straight up like a chimney.

"Is this vessel . . . operational? Jake?"

Jacob is standing at the center of the room, his eyes closed.

A pencil-thin blue laser light blinks on above his head, its beam kissing his white hair.

Manny jumps back as the chamber instantly powers to life. Blue LED lights illuminate from behind the tinted walls and floor panels, revealing a myriad of alien conduits and circuits, machinery and biochemical plasma ducts.

"Listen and learn. We'll call this first lesson Guardian Astronomy 101."

A volumetric projection takes shape just above the polished floor, the image—a spiral galaxy, rotating like some luminescent cosmic pinwheel in the vastness of space, hauling more than 500 billion pinpoints of light around its slowly swirling vortex.

"Welcome to the Milky Way." Jacob points to the galactic bulge, a swirling cloud of brilliant cosmic dust. "Computer, magnify galactic center ten to the power of six."

In a dizzying zoom, the galactic bulge expands across the entire chamber.

Immanuel stands within the projection, looking down upon a mist of three-dimensional penny-sized fiery red and orange stars, all clustered around the heart of the rotating maelstrom.

Dead center of the galaxy is a black hole. Like the slow-moving hub of a wheel, the black hole appears to be churning the entire galaxy, every so often inhaling one of the tiny stars into its monstrous onyx gullet.

"The black hole is our galaxy's power train. Like the nucleus of a great atom, its gravitational pull serves as the glue which provides the cluster of stars its mass. But beyond the human eye, beyond the third dimension, the black hole provides an even more magnificent service. Computer, invert."

Instantly the stars blink out, their luster fading to a deep purple hue, as if illuminated by a black light.

Manny stares at the black hole, which now glows emerald green. From within its slowly swirling whirlpool of gravity sprout tiny conduits—veins of energy that span outward throughout the darkened heavens of the Milky Way like cosmic subway tunnels.

Splintering away from these gravitational veins are capillaries, which glow a luminescent crimson. Unlike the larger, thicker veins, these thinner spaghetti-like strands seem to be floating through the dark matter of space on their own, their free ends twisting and rotating around the cosmic pinwheel like twigs caught in a drain.

"You are now looking at the galaxy the way it appears in the nexus. Black holes that originate at the center of galaxies were created in the early days of the universe. If you could survive passage through their vortex, you would enter a parallel universe—a higher dimension of spiritual energy where time no longer exists. When we physically die, our souls pass through these higher dimensions and enter—"

"Heaven?"

"Something like that." He points to the twisting branches shooting out from the black hole's steep gravitational well. "So powerful is the black hole's mass that its throat, or event horizon, cannot sustain all of its energy. The pressure-relief conduits branching out across the galaxy are called white holes. White holes violently eject matter into space. Those red squiggly lines that move in proximity to the ejected matter are wormholes. Notice that each wormhole has two mouths located in different parts of the galaxy. The *Balam* possesses an antigravity field powerful enough to counteract the effects of a wormhole, allowing the starship to use it as a cosmic shortcut across the Milky Way."

"And that's how you plan to get to *Xibalba*? Through a wormhole?"

"Now you're catching on."

"But everything's constantly moving. It's like . . . it's like jumping on a cosmic merry-go-round. How do you even know when and where its entrance and exits are going to show up?"

"The positions of the wormholes change in relation to the rotation of the galaxy. Each passage has been precisely charted. The *Balam* knows when it's time to leave."

Manny pinches his brow, struggling to deal with this information. "Where are we? Where's Earth? Where's this *Xibalba*?"

Jacob closes his eyes. The astrotopography reverts to the original volumetric image. "Computer, magnify the Orion spur ten to the power of nine."

A section of one of the Milky Way's long outer arms leaps outward, the magnified projection again swimming around them. Below and to Jacob's right appears a yellow speck. As Manny watches, the area magnifies, revealing Earth's sun and its planets.

Jacob points high above their heads to three bright pinpoints set in a familiar alignment, the pattern identical to the formation of the three pyramids of Giza.

"Al Nitak, Al Nilam, and Mintaka, the three belt stars of the constellation Orion. Look just below the stars. Can you see that tiny crimson-and-silver world? According to the Guardian, that planet is *Xibalba*. Now watch."

Jacob points to their right. Moving slowly through the three-dimensional cosmos is a paper-thin looping slash of scarlet laser light, running north–south through the Orion arm. "Here comes our wormhole. Its proximal orifice will pass between Earth and Mars in seven days, its distal mouth whipping around in time to deposit us in the vicinity of *Xibalba*. The last time a wormhole intercepted our solar system in this manner was on 4 *Ahau*, 3 *Kankin,* the winter solstice of 2012—the last day of the Mayan calendar. The time before that was almost 65 million years ago."

"Wait . . . this thing will arrive in seven days?"

"No, I said the wormhole's closest mouth will pass near Mars in seven days. To rendezvous in time means we'll have to leave Earth in ninety-eight hours."

Immanuel swallows back the bile rising from his throat. "No way . . . no *fubitshitting* goddam way, Jacob Gabriel!"

"Manny—"

"No!" The dark-haired twin bolts out of the control room, then races down the passageway, searching for the camouflaged exit. "Open up, goddam it! Jacob, let me out! I can't breathe!"

A panel retracts, revealing the gantry and the inside of the warehouse. He looks down to see the lift rising slowly to meet him.

Desperate to escape, he leaps forward and grabs hold of one of the aluminum tower's horizontal support beams, using it like a fireman's pole to descend quickly to the concrete floor—

—the armed guards already in position as he reaches bottom.

Meteorology Lab
University of Miami

The Meteorology Center on the University of Miami's main campus is the latest in a new line of ESD (Environmental Shield Designs) sprouting up along the eastern seaboard of the United States. The building has a second exterior consisting of a domed outer shell, composed of reinforced concrete and steel, designed to withstand hurricane winds up to 220 miles an hour. Inside this barrier is the mainframe, each door and window housing retractable steel shutters that seal automatically at the touch of a switch. Backup generators situated on the first floor can power the entire thousand-room building for two weeks, while satellite relays, wired directly into the curved roof, provide ample reception for the Center's lines of communication.

Besides its role as a teaching facility, the Meteorology Center also serves as the United States southeast regional headquarters for the Earth Systems Management Agency, an organization that assesses, predicts, and monitors all environmental catastrophes across the globe.

Bruce Doyle rubs his sleep-deprived eyes, then drains the remains of his now-cold coffee. Although the effects of global warming had become increasingly apparent as early as the late 1980s, the U.S. government's response to the problem was too little, coming too late. Doyle, the regional director of the ESMA, often equates the public's delay with sticking one's hand in a pot of cold water on a simmering stove. Because the changes in temperature happen so gradually, the victim never realizes the danger until flesh starts peeling away from the bone.

Doyle shakes his head in disbelief as he glances at the *Winter 2033 ESMA QUARTERLY REPORT.* Colder winters and hotter summers—that has been the pattern over the last thirty years, and the effects around the globe seem to be magnifying. More than 100 billion tons of water are being released from the Greenland Ice Sheet each year, doubling the melting rate from only two decades earlier, while raising sea levels another four inches. Millions of people living in low-lying lands have been displaced, from Bangladesh to Egypt. Outbreaks of malaria, dengue, and yellow fever continue moving farther north with each passing season. Storms and floods have washed away crops. Droughts and fires destroy more than 10 million hectares of forests a year. Summer heat waves have led to the deaths of thousands, while vanquishing thousands of plant and animal species into extinction.

And according to the *QUARTERLY REPORT*, things are getting worse.

The Western Antarctic Ice Sheet is continuing to melt at an alarming rate. The ice sheet, which rests on a bed far below sea level, contains nearly 2 million cubic miles of ice. Scientists now know that all marine-based ice sheets have melted within the last twenty thousand years. If the Western Antarctic Ice Sheet were to go, world ocean levels would rise, and not just by inches, but by more than twenty feet.

More severe weather patterns are also taking their toll. Typhoons and hurricanes are not only appearing later in their seasons, but elevated ocean temperatures have increased their intensity, especially in the North Atlantic.

The power train behind our planet's storm systems are the oceans, which provide energy both by direct heat transfer from their warm surface and by the evaporation of water. Tropical cyclogenesis takes place when the atmosphere takes on heat and moisture from warm surface waters (at least eighty degrees Fahrenheit to depths of about 150 feet). As latent heat in the form of water vapor is drawn up from the ocean, the thunderstorm's cyclonic surface winds cause it to spiral counterclockwise (clockwise in the Southern Hemisphere). As the storm system strengthens and hurricane-force winds are achieved, inward-moving air turns upward and outward, creating an eye, a center of calm usually twenty to forty miles in diameter. The heat energy generated by the evaporation process is stored in the form of water vapor, which rises in a ring of towering cumulonimbus clouds surrounding the calm eye of the cyclone. The eye itself is composed of slowly sinking warm air while the eye wall is a strong upward flow of air created by a moderate to strong low-level convergence of air.

A medium-sized hurricane releases enough energy in a single day as the simultaneous explosion of four hundred twenty-megaton hydrogen bombs—or more than half the electric energy used by the United States population in an entire year. Hurricanes (cyclones forming in the Atlantic) are rated using the Saffir-Simpson Scale, which categorizes storms based upon their maximum sustained winds. A tropical storm officially graduates to a Category-1 hurricane when its winds are clocked at 74–95 mph. A Category-5 storms packs winds of 156-plus miles per hour.

By the late 1990s, the effects of global warming made themselves known through hotter summers and colder winters, intensifying weather systems across the globe. The initial effects on hurricanes were tempered with the arrival of an El Niño cycle, a circulation pattern where pools of warm surface water and air pressure in the tropical western Pacific roll back and forth across ten thousand miles of ocean. While El Niño brought increased rainfall across the southern United States, its high winds sheared off the northern edges of hurricanes, sparing the East Coast.

From the mid-1970s to 1998, El Niño dominated weather patterns across North America. It wasn't until the early 2000s that the first real effects of global warming suddenly became alarming.

La Niña—the little girl—is the flip side of the El Niño southern oscillation cycle. Many meteorologists classify the shift as a "cold event" as La Niña cools ocean temperatures along the West Coast of the U.S. The effect of this phenomenon on the long-wave circulation pattern is to produce an upper air trough over the central United States, with a southerly flow over the East Coast—feeding virtually every low-pressure system coming across the Atlantic.

In late August of 2007, Hurricane Susan jumped from a Category-4 to a Category-5 storm as it approached the U.S. mainland. As an awestruck nation watched helplessly, the storm's sustained winds reached 189 miles an hour just before its eye snaked across Savannah, Georgia, The ESMA's early warnings helped keep Susan's death toll below a dozen, but the killer storm's winds (which spawned seven tornadoes) caused more than 4 billion dollars in damages.

So powerful was Susan that it forced the ESMA to add an additional classification to the Saffir-Simpson Scale. A Category-6 storm (or Super-Cane) was now regarded as a La Niña-induced hurricane packing winds in excess of 175 mph.

Less than a year later, Super-Cane Abigail, the first official Category-6 storm, made landfall in Vero Beach, Florida. The system's storm surge would rise thirty-four feet above sea level, flooding coastal areas from West Palm Beach up to Daytona, then clear across the Florida panhandle.

By 2015, the eastern seaboard of the United States was becoming a very dangerous place to live. Seven Super-Canes had formed in the Atlantic, two making landfall. The worst of the lot was Super-Cane Pamela, whose double eye finally collapsed over Wilmington, North Carolina, pummeling the evacuated city with her near 200-mph winds and two dozen tornadoes.

Nature was taking its vengeance upon modern man, and something had to be done to placate her.

The first attempt to modify a hurricane's winds dates back to 1947 and Project CIRRUS. Warm ocean water and high humidity in the air produce a drop in pressure along the surface. Horizontal winds near the surface respond to this drop in pressure by accelerating inward. The more the surface pressure falls, the higher the winds become. As low-level air moves inward from greater distances, the process intensifies, building around the eye of the storm. Project CIRRUS scientists attempted to cool the cyclone's "chimney" by dumping dry ice along a storm's inward wall, disrupting its pressure differential.

Unfortunately, CIRRUS aircraft were not equipped to monitor a cyclone's dynamic and structural changes. Worse, the first hurricane they attempted to cool abruptly changed directions and struck Georgia, causing a political ruckus. CIRRUS was canceled, and crippling new limitations were placed on all future cloud-seeding experiments.

These limitations would drastically affect Project STORMFURY, an ambitious hurricane modification program conducted from 1962 through 1983 by the Weather Bureau (eventually the NOAA), the Department of Defense, and the National Science Foundation. The basic idea behind STORMFURY was to heat the atmosphere over a greater distance from the hurricane's eye, reducing the pressure gradient near the center of the storm, thereby reducing its wind speed. To achieve that end, scientists seeded the clouds away from the storm's core with silver iodide (AgI), whose crystals are an especially efficient freezing nuclei, causing supercooled water droplets to change to ice crystals. By inducing freezing of the supercooled water held in the upper clouds away from the storm's eye, a sufficient quantity of latent heat might be released to reduce noticeably the surface pressure gradient.

On August 19, 1963, Hurricane Beulah formed east of the Lesser Antilles. By August 24, the storm had been seeded twice, its maximum winds dropping by more than thirty knots. The cyclone's eye wall dissipated, then reformed ten miles farther away from the center of the storm. Unfortunately, a causal relationship could not be established, and STORMFURY, strangled by the new seeding restrictions, eventually lost all funding.

It wasn't until 2016 that President Ennis Chaney reestablished funding for these vital experiments. Years later, three scientists would unite to take STORMFURY's experiments one step further.

Essentially, a hurricane is fueled by the latent heat released by the condensation of water vapor to liquid cloud droplets. STORMFURY's scientists chose to draw the hurricane's latent heat away from the eye, hoping to disrupt its vortex by spreading its energy out over a greater distance. Dr. Lowell Krawitz, a meteorologist at MIT, wanted to attack the power train of the cyclone at its source by *cooling* the interior eye wall, thereby inhibiting condensation and convection. His delivery system—the Navy's antiquated fleet of Trident nuclear submarines. Under Krawitz's plan, vertical missile silos that once held Trident D-5 nuclear missiles would be refitted and converted into pressurized ejection systems, powered by the sub's nuclear reactors. By ascending within a Super-Cane's eye while still at sea, a cooling agent could be injected directly into the eye wall. While stopping a hurricane was not feasible, reducing its wind speed from 200 to 130 miles an hour would reduce its energy by more than 50 percent—something that could save countless lives and billions of dollars should the cyclone ever reach land.

What Dr. Krawitz needed was a compound that would both cool and expand.

Enter Dr. David Mohr and his colleague, Barry Perlman, two scientists who had spent the last twenty years working on liquid hydrogen/liquid oxygen rocket engines. Together, they had developed several variants of cryogenic nitrogen gas used to cool fuels. A chance meeting with Dr. Krawitz led them to experiment with a nitrogen-hybrid gas, which, when introduced to a lower pressure region, would expand exponentially as it cooled.

On August 10, 2023, eight refitted Trident SSBN submarines moved to intercept Super-Cane Carol, whose 193-mile-per-hour winds were trekking west across the Atlantic toward Haiti and the southeastern seaboard of the United States. The submarine fleet rose within the eye and, maintaining course and speed, proceeded to pump MPK gas (named after the three scientists) directly at the approaching southeastern wall of the storm.

As the hurricane continued on its northwesterly track, the passing eye wall inhaled the MPK gas, which expanded a hundredfold as it crystallized. Within minutes, the cryogenic gas disrupted the vertical convection within the cyclone's wall clouds, thus reducing the amount of water vapor being condensed and sharply reducing the release of latent heat. Within an hour, sustained winds had dropped from 193 to 157 miles per hour at the center of the storm—a substantial reduction.

The success of the experiment earned the three scientists Nobel prizes and rejuvenated the Navy's antiquated fleet of nuclear submarines. A new sub force, known as "the weather net" was commissioned, with refueling outposts established in the North Atlantic, North Pacific, and western North Pacific. Having been relegated to reduced duties thanks to the advent of space defense systems, the Navy was suddenly back in business as "Cyclone Killers."

Bruce Doyle stifles another yawn as he watches *Super-Cane Kenneth*'s powerful vortex near the Virgin Islands. Doyle is exhausted, having kept vigil on the Super-Cane since the tropical cyclone's birth ninety-seven hours earlier.

And *Kenneth* is becoming an absolute monster, more enormous than even Super-Cane Pamela. To make matters worse, a fire at the weather-net depot in Haiti has forced the Navy to arrange emergency shipments of MPK cryogenic nitrogen gas mix from the Port of Miami. A three-day delay in acquiring an antiquated oil tanker for transport has allowed the already dangerous Category-6 storm to intensify.

The ESMA director checks the latest information coming in from the center's Unmanned Cyclone Aerial Lab, known as "UNCLE." Resembling a four-foot steel dart with wings, these hurricane chasers fly back and forth through the storm, transmitting data.

SUPER-CANE KENNETH

0400 GMT TUESDAY 11/22/33
LOCATION: 18.3N 53.7W
MAX. WIND: 199 MPH
GUSTING: 212 MPH
MOVING: NW AT 14 MPH
PRESSURE: 941 MB
PREDICTED U.S. LANDFALL:
SATURDAY 11/26/33
13:40 HRS
DESTINATION: SOUTHEAST FLORIDA

"Jesus . . ." Bruce Doyle touches the speed dial on his cell phone. "Sharon, it's me. Contact the airlines. I want you and the kids in Philly by tomorrow afternoon. Don't argue, just plan on staying with your mother at least a week."

■■■■■■■■■■■■■■■■

31

■■■■■■■■■■■■■■■■

NOVEMBER 22, 2033
HANGAR 13
KENNEDY SPACE CENTER
CAPE CANAVERAL, FLORIDA
TUESDAY NIGHT

Manny follows his brother through the indoor Japanese garden, his head still foggy from the physician's mood inhibitor. Moonbeams peek through the atrium's Plexiglas dome above their heads, lighting the gravel path and a shallow stream, which crosses beneath a small wooden bridge up ahead.

"You okay?" Jacob asks.

"No. What is this place?"

"I call it my refuge, it's the only place I feel safe. This entire complex is shielded from electrostatic waves. We call it a quiet zone. It safeguards my presence from Lilith and any other Hunahpu who might be out there."

Up ahead is a timber-framed Japanese house.

"You're really into this oriental stuff, aren't you?" Immanuel asks.

"The concept is called *Wabi* and *Sabi* . . . simple quietude—elegant simplicity. I find it spiritually liberating."

Just before the entrance, lying in the middle of the path is a grapefruit-sized stone, wrapped in hemp. Jacob picks it up and shows it to his brother. "The bound stone symbolizes entry into a different world. You are now entering mine."

Immanuel follows his brother over the bridge to the open formal entranceway.

"You see, Manny, in the traditional Japanese home, there is no clear delineation between the exterior and the interior. Instead, there's an intermediate structure composed of a formal entranceway, a veranda, a drawing room, and a courtyard, separated by various screening devices, all of which are designed to bring Nature indoors while still shielding its inhabitants from the elements." Jacob pauses at the raised deck to remove his shoes. "Please?"

Immanuel kicks off his sneakers, feeling ridiculous.

There are no formal doors or walls, only an open wooden shutter. The floors inside are made of polished bamboo, covered here and there with tatami mats. A small alcove leads to a high-ceilinged, A-framed drawing room, at the center of which are four comfortable leather chairs situated around a stone coffee table. The kitchen is immaculate, the latest appliances discreetly hidden behind a wooden bar. A step down leads to the sunken dining room, its floor covered in a violet tatami, the surrounding bamboo benches lined in matching pads. The walls are made entirely of *shoji*—framed paper sliding doors. Through an open partition Immanuel sees another formal garden. He hears the soothing sounds of water—the stream passing beneath the floorboards to intersect the center atrium of the house.

"Are you hungry?" Jacob asks.

"Just tired."

"The guest room's through here." Jacob pulls open a *shoji,* revealing a small room, at the center of which is a tatami bed. "Better get some sleep. Tomorrow will be a long day."

"Jake, what did you mean when you said I'm the Yin to your Yang?"

"Yin and Yang are the two fundamental forces that make up the Tao—a primal, mysterious energy that translates simply into 'The Way' or 'The One.' From The One comes 'The Two'—the Yin and the Yang, two powerful polar forces, like the positive and negative poles of a battery. Neither is fully dominant, each in a constantly changing dynamic of push and pull, energizing and pacifying.

"There is a saying: All things arise from the Tao, formed out of matter, shaped by their environment. Take this home for example. You are the Yin, the house itself and the earth on which it stands. Both are formed of matter. Surrounding the home is energy—the Yang—constantly in motion, unfolding the boundaries of space and time. For the last six years our home has been closed, our two energies isolated. Now the house is open, and our two energies shall interact once more, shaped by our environment, reacting to the forces at play within the universe."

"This whole Mayan *Xibalba* thing . . . you really believe it's our destiny?"

"It is the journey that we were genetically programmed to follow."

"Yeah, right. But you also said that humanity's stuck in a time loop. And you mentioned we've made the journey before."

"We've been there, yes."

"So, if we've been there, why are we still stuck in this time loop?"

Jacob sits on the edge of the tatami bed. "Our last effort failed. I'm not certain why, but I believe our attack was not properly . . . coordinated."

"By failed, I take it you mean we died?"

"Don't worry, this time everything is different. This time our father has reached out to prepare me. I've also spent the last six years readying battle plans in the holographic suite. I've re-created and analyzed every possible attack scenario. You'll understand once your training begins."

"I want to understand now."

"It's late, Manny. Get some sleep, and tomorrow I'll—"

"Now, Jacob!"

Jacob closes his eyes, debating. "Computer, activate guest-room screen."

A panel of clear smart-glass rises from a bamboo floor-board.

"Computer, load last combat scenario. Commence replay five thousand frames prior to contact in the nexus."

A scene illuminates upon the face of the smart-glass. The landscape of the Underworld appears. Two warriors, Jacob clad in white, the computer-simulated Immanuel in black, approach the molten metallic lake and alabaster white tree.

"The calabash tree is a living conduit of the nexus. The Abomination is using it to hold our father in a sort of suspended animation. The tree glows white because of his aura in the Underworld.

"The warrior in black representing you is a VR drone, programmed to respond in a set pattern of combat moves. What it can't do is think and react like a Hunahpu warrior. Keep that in mind."

Jacob points to the twins, who are hurrying toward the lake. "The Abomination can sense us while we're in the nexus, which is why we remain in the third dimension as long as possible."

Immanuel stares at the lake. Ripples appear, signaling the emergence of the alien being from the silvery ooze.

"The alien is a spiritual demon—a sentry, posted to guard our father. The silicon skin gives it form and substance in the physical dimension. Its most deadly feature is its claws, which release a fast-acting toxin. Our Hunahpu genetics can fight the poison in small doses, but anything more than a severe scratch would be fatal."

"Lovely."

A brilliant explosion of emerald green light ignites across the horizon.

"Computer, pause."

The on-screen image freezes as the two warriors sprint toward the alabaster-goo tree.

"We've just entered the nexus. What follows will play at less than 3 percent of its actual speed."

"Three percent? I can't move that fast."

Jacob flashes a grin. "Not yet. Computer, resume play at nexus speed."

The scene continues, frame by grainy frame. The twin in white is almost flying around the lake, his feet barely touching the shoreline. He reaches the tree at the same time as the demon sentry. Drawing what appears to be a sword, Jacob lashes out at the frightening creature, keeping it at bay.

With each stroke the blade glows a deeper shade of blue.

"Lasers and guns do not work in the nexus. The sword is made of a nanofabricated alloy steel. With each movement, the macromolecular motors within the blade expand and heat the edge, threatening to cut through the demon sentry's silicon outer skin. The blood bleeds blue without hemoglobin, because there is no oxygen on *Xibalba*, only CO_2."

The warrior in white is a whirlwind of movement, slashing and parrying, stabbing and retreating, barely able to keep out of the larger sentry's superior reach.

Immanuel shakes his head. "How can you keep that up? I would have collapsed long ago."

"Training. Now watch carefully."

The black-clad warrior representing Immanuel has reached the tree. As he attempts to free the drone representing their father, the demon sentry suddenly lunges toward the trunk, attempting to strike the virtual-reality Immanuel with its left claw.

But Jacob is too quick. Having clearly anticipated the move, he dives forward, slamming his now-flaming sword down and through the alien's right arm, severing it at the elbow joint—

—as the black-clad warrior lashes outward with his own sword, decapitating the stunned sentry with one powerful blow.

The monstrous skull thuds against the rocky surface, its headless body following suit.

"Yes!" Manny is on his feet, barely able to catch his breath. "We won . . . right?"

Jacob shakes his head. Points.

The drone representing Michael Gabriel is lying against the simmering remains of the calabash tree, blue blood streaming profusely from his abdomen.

"Computer, rewind six hundred frames and pause."

The image returns to the demon sentry's lunge toward the tree. "Watch closely. His left claw is the decoy. Ignore it and focus on the right. Computer, resume at 1 percent nexus speed."

Immanuel watches the demon's left arm, which is partially hidden below its lunging body. Even at greatly reduced speed the limb is just a blur as it extends toward the Michael Gabriel drone, which is morphing out from the trunk of the dripping white tree.

Two of the sentry's scalpel-sharp clawed fingers puncture Mick through his abdomen and out his spine before the appendage retracts in an attempt to parry Jacob's blow.

"Jesus, it . . . it butchered him."

Jacob nods. "We can win, but it'll take both of us to do it. We have a long day tomorrow, try to get some sleep."

"Sleep? You honestly expect me to sleep after seeing that?"

"If you can't sleep, ask the computer for a green tea sedative." Jacob exits through the open *shoji*, then turns. "Tomorrow is a big day, Manny. We need to bring you back to our chosen path."

Immanuel Gabriel lies back on the uncomfortably hard bed, staring at the ceiling.

Maybe it's your chosen path, bro, but it's not mine.

Geology Lab
University of Miami
Coral Gables, Florida

Lauren Beckmeyer is in Bill Gabeheart's office, her bare feet propped on his desk. She has been in the lab over two hours, waiting for the lab's computer to complete a data search to confirm information downloaded earlier from Yellowstone Park is identical to data received in the past.

ANALYSIS COMPLETE. REPEATING DATA FOUND BETWEEN YELLOWSTONE CALDERA READINGS OF 16 APRIL 2030 AND 19 NOVEMBER 2033.

"Repeating data? Computer, how close in similarity are the two readings?"

NO VARIANCE FOUND. DATA IS IDENTICAL.

Gabeheart was right. Those Fed bastards are hiding something. She types in Gabeheart's access code on her laptop.

The professor's prerecorded image flashes on screen. "Hi. Sorry to disappoint you but this isn't me. Since I'm probably outside watching Old Faithful, feel free to leave me a message."

"Doc, it's Lauren. I found something. Contact me the moment you—"

The recorded image disappears, replaced by that of Paxton J. Walther, Bill Gabeheart's regional coordinator at Yellowstone. "Ms. Beckmeyer?"

"Yes, sir." *What's he doing on Gabeheart's private comm link?* "Sir, where's Professor Gabeheart? I need to speak with him."

Paxton shakes his head sadly. "I'm so sorry—"

Lauren's muscles contract in fear.

"—there's been an accident. Bill . . . he died earlier this morning."

"What?"

"He was taking temperature readings at one of the hot springs when there was a tremor and Bill fell in. By the time we got to him . . . the third-degree burns . . . he was gone."

"Oh, God . . . oh my God—"

"I'm so sorry."

"I can't . . . I just spoke with him the other day."

Paxton's eyes come into focus. "Saturday?"

Lauren feels light-headed as the blood drains from her face. "I, uh . . . I don't know. Might have been—"

"Lauren, did Bill download something to you?"

"No, I mean, yes, it was midterms. I . . . I had to turn them in before Thanksgiving break. Have you notified Gabeheart's family?"

"Not yet. Lauren, I'm sorry to have to spring this on you like this, no pun intended. I know you and the professor were close. Where can I find you . . . to notify you about the funeral arrangements?"

Don't tell . . . don't say a word . . . "I . . . I honestly don't know."

"Are you going away for the holiday?"

"I'm . . . not sure." *Get off now, before you say too much . . .* "I have to go, I'm sorry—"

"Lauren, wait—"

She disconnects the comm link. *Oh, God, oh my God . . . those bastards—they killed him!* She covers her face, tears pouring from her eyes, sadness and fear taking her breath away. *If they think I know something, they'll come after me, too!*

"Stop! Get a grip and think. First step, erase the data trail." She turns to the main computer terminal. "Computer, erase all communication records received over the last week, with the exception of the last outgoing call."

ACKNOWLEDGED.

Lauren's hands are trembling. *Okay, you can't go home . . . can't stay here . . . Who can I tell? Who would believe me?*

A sudden noise—outside the lab. "Computer, seal the outer lab doors."

ACKNOWLEDGED.

A knock outside the lab door.

She whispers, "Computer, who's out there?"

CAMPUS SECURITY.

"Shh. Reduce volume 80 percent and run a background check on the guy outside the lab door. I want a name and time he's been on the job."

COLLIN SHELBY. TRANSFERRED TO CAMPUS PATROL 19 NOVEMBER 2033.

November 19 . . . only three days ago. Jesus, these guys move fast.

More banging, this time insistent. "Hello? Whoever's in there, could you unseal the security doors please?"

Cold beads of sweat pour down Lauren's face. "Computer, shut down and lock out all terminals, access code Beckmeyer Tango-Zulu-8659."

ACKNOWLEDGED.

Gotta disappear fast, before he overrides the lock.

She looks around, desperate, then notices the antique letter opener.

*   *   *

Outside the lab door, Collin Shelby slides his bogus identification card across the magnetic seal. "Computer, override lock. Security, Shelby 28497-M."

The doors *hiss* open. Shelby enters the lab, stun gun in hand. "Ms. Beckmeyer?"

No response. No one visible.

The guard looks around, then checks Gabeheart's private office.

Empty.

"Computer, locate Lauren Beckmeyer, microchip identification 341124876-FL-USA

LAUREN BECKMEYER IS OFF-LINE.

"Off-line?" Shelby looks around. Sees the letter opener, stained with blood on Gabeheart's desk. Locates the remains of the crushed microchip implant in the trash can.

"Clever girl."

Shelby removes a palm-sized device from his jacket and attaches it to Gabeheart's computer, overriding the lockout mechanism. "Computer, access all e-mail records and hard drive documents and delete."

Thousands of records flash past the small screen in an instant.

Collin Shelby is a member of UMBRA, a mercenary subcontracting organization that functions in extreme sanction situations for the DIA, CIA, and NSA and maintains liaisons with senior FBI personnel. Formerly labeled the "Talent Pool," the shadow organization's primary cover is the prevention of terrorist activities.

Shelby has no idea why he has been ordered to assassinate Lauren Beckmeyer, nor does he care. A harsh byproduct of the new global Internet and unified monetary system is that terrorist organizations can now recruit young and old, male and female from any nation and every walk of life. *Last month's biological attack at the 9-11 Memorial killed more than sixty civilians. If the death of one confused college student can prevent more bloodshed . . .*

E-MAIL RECORDS AND HARD DRIVE DOCUMENTS HAVE BEEN DELETED.

Shelby detaches the remote link and looks around.

Inches beneath the soles of his boots, hidden below the lab's gridlike paneled floor, is a terrified Lauren Beckmeyer. She is scrunched up in a tight crawl space containing computer cables and circuitry, her bleeding palm wedged firmly in her mouth, preventing her from wheezing out loud.

The guard touches the comm link on his forearm. "It's Shelby. She's gone."

"Did you erase Gabeheart's records?"

"Yes, sir. Where do you want me?"

"We've got her dormitory covered. Join Bates at her fiancé's place."

"Yes, sir."

The guard looks around one last time, then leaves.

Lauren remains hidden, her pulse pounding in her ears.

■■■■■■■■■■■■■■■

32

■■■■■■■■■■■■■■■

**NOVEMBER 23, 2033
HANGAR 13
KENNEDY SPACE CENTER
CAPE CANAVERAL, FLORIDA
WEDNESDAY DAWN**

The sound of a brook, running beneath the wooden structure.

A bird chirps somewhere in the garden.

Immanuel Gabriel opens his eyes, surprised to find a slight Asian man in an orange monk's robe standing in the entry of the open *shoji*.

"*Ni hao.*" The man grins.

"Knee who?"

"I said, 'good morning.' Did I startle you?"

"Everything startles me these days. Guess you're looking for my brother?"

"Bu shi."

"I'm sorry, did you say bullshit?"

"Bu shi means, 'that is not right.' I am here to meet you and escort you to your brother. I was observing you as you slept. Your soul is not at peace."

"No bu shi." Immanuel stands, offering the Asian his hand. "Samuel Agler."

"Chong Xiong."

He shakes the Tibetan monk's hand, registering the power behind the smaller man's grip. "I take it you're one of my brother's teachers."

Chong grins. "There is a robe in the bathroom. Please get dressed and follow me, your brother is waiting."

Immanuel heads for the bathroom, his stomach grumbling. *Get dressed and follow me . . . who's this guy think he is?* He tugs the *shoji* shut behind him, urinates, washes his face, then gets dressed in the white kung fu clothing.

Exiting the bathroom, he heads straight for the kitchen. "Hey, Mr. Chong, you want some breakfast?"

"We will not eat at this time." Chong points outside. "Please."

"But I'm hungry."

"Master your appetite."

"How do I do that?"

"Imagine a dead rat, its steaming intestines draining on your fly-infested morning toast."

Immanuel swallows the bile rising in his throat.

Chong's grin never changes. "No shoes, please."

Moments later, a barefoot and impatient Immanuel Gabriel is jogging along a stone path leading out of the atrium.

"So you're a Tibetan monk, huh?"

"You are familiar with the history of the Shaolin?"

"Just from watching those old kung fu movies."

Chong slows to a quick walk. "Kung fu is just one part of our training. To understand Shaolin means tracing the history of China, which dates back to 2600 B.C., to the age of the Five Rulers. For two thousand years, China remained divided and at the mercy of the invading Huns and Mongolian nomads."

"That's why your ancestors built the Wall, right?"

"The Great Wall you see today is a result of tourism. The original structure was merely a collection of short barriers. Since it was not continuous, Mongol invaders had no trouble going around it. It was not until 221 B.C. that Emperor Chin finally made strides in uniting China into one nation. Seven hundred years later, an Indian Buddhist monk by the name of Ba Tao came to China to teach Buddhism. The Emperor summoned the monk to his palace and was so impressed by the man's wisdom that he offered him his own palace to continue his teachings. Ba Tao declined this offer, instead requesting a large piece of land away from civilization where he could build a monastery. The Emperor granted his request, offering him land in the province of Henan on the side of Sung San Mountain. The district was called 'Wooded Hill,' which translates to *Shaolin* in Mandarin. Thus was born the first Shaolin Temple.

"In A.D. 539, a holy man named Bodhidharma left his monastery in India to spread the teachings of Ch'an Buddhism, what Westerners refer to as Zen. Bodhidharma was described as a bearded wise man with piercing blue eyes."

"He was a Guardian?"

Chong only smiles. "It is said Bodhidharma traveled hundreds of miles to reach northern China, crossing the Himalayan Mountains and the Yangtze River until he arrived at the Shaolin Temple. Unfortunately, the abbot, Fang Chang, refused him entrance, and so Bodhidharma located a nearby cave. It is written that the wise one sat in meditation, facing a stone wall until his piercing blue eyes bored a gaping hole through the cliff wall. Visiting monks supplied him with food and water and became so impressed with his depth of knowledge that they invited him inside the Shaolin Temple.

"Upon entering Shaolin, Bodhidharma, now called Ta Mo by the Chinese, observed that the monks were too weak to meditate. He taught them three series of exercises, which marked the beginning of Shaolin Temple Kung Fu, which means, 'hard work and perfection.' These techniques were later refined into fighting methods to repel attacks from local bandits. Eventually more temples were built, each run by several Shaolin Masters—experts in training of the mind, body, and spirit."

"You're a Master?"

"Grand Master. I began my training as a boy in the Shaolin Temple at Sung San Mountain, then began Pak Mei Kung Fu training in the Gwong How Temple when I was twenty. Ours is a style that incorporates both Shaolin and Taoist practices, allowing the warrior to move from a relaxed movement into explosive power."

"How long have you been teaching Jake?"

"Five years. Now Jacob is teaching me."

They follow a subterranean passage, then turn right into an alcove. A steel door slides open as they approach, revealing a narrow, subterranean flight of stone steps leading below.

Immanuel follows the slight Asian down the spiraling stairwell, which is lit only by an occasional oil lamp mounted on the limestone wall. "The decor was your brother's idea," the Tibetan says. "It sets the proper mood."

They descend two stories, the temperature within the stairwell dropping noticeably. Immanuel rubs goose bumps from his exposed forearms. "Must be one hell of an air-conditioning bill. Whoa . . ."

The stairwell abruptly ends, depositing them on the top of a snowcapped mountain. The peaks of the Himalayas loom in every direction, crowding infinity itself. As Immanuel steps off the last stair and into a three-foot-high snowdrift, the stone corridor behind him disappears, camouflaging the entrance to the immense subterranean holo-suite.

"Jesus, it's freezing." Through teary eyes, Immanuel can see his breath. "Okay, now what? Hope you guys created a ski lodge somewhere nearby, my balls have turned blue."

Ignoring him, Chong trudges through the knee-deep snow across the summit.

Immanuel follows, his lungs heaving, his bare feet numb. After several minutes they come to the entrance of a cave.

Seated outside the cave in the snow, his legs tucked into a lotus position, is Jacob. He is bare-chested, wearing only the bottoms of his black kung fu garb. His eyes are closed. The skin covering his chiseled muscles is a healthy pink.

"Is he crazy . . . never mind, I already know." Immanuel's teeth chatter. "Wake him up before he freezes to death. It's gotta be below zero out here, er, in here."

"With wind chill, it is minus eighteen degrees Fahrenheit. Touch his skin."

Immanuel reaches out and grips his twin's shoulder—shocked to find it warm, almost hot to the touch. "He's burning with fever!"

"It is not fever, at least not a fever generated by sickness."

"I don't understand. How long has he been out here?"

"Just under four hours."

"Four hours? How—"

"It is a form of meditation we call *Ta Moo*, taught to us by our Shaolin wise man. Using the life force, *Chi*, we can manipulate our internal functions, overriding our brain's beta rhythms, redirecting with alpha rhythms. Jacob has raised his body's internal temperature to compensate for the extreme cold. Now see if you can find your brother's pulse."

The dark-haired twin touches his brother's exposed neck, feeling nothing. Bending down, he presses his half-frozen ear to his brother's bare chest, Jacob's flushed skin warming Immanuel's cheek. "There's no heartbeat. He's in the nexus, isn't he?"

"No. This part of his training prepares him for the nexus. It allows him to communicate with your father."

"You taught him this?"

"Yes, but even my own master was never this skilled. When Jacob remains focused like this, his alpha waves are off the scale."

Immanuel's teeth chatter. "What about . . . me?"

"Let us find out. Remove your robe and sit down in front of your brother."

Hesitantly, he takes off his top and assumes a lotus position. As if in response, a gust of icy wind blows across the holographic mountaintop, its frigid chill burning into his exposed flesh.

"Damn!"

"Ignore the cold and close your eyes. Imagine there are small pipes running through your rib cage. These pipes are red-hot. See the pipes in your mind's eye. Feel their warmth radiating inside your chest. Feel the heat seep into your arms and legs, into your wrists and ankles, filling your fingers and toes. Breathe slowly through your nose . . . exhaling softly through your mouth. Each slow breath stokes the hot coals that heat the pipes. Relax into the warmth."

Immanuel slips into the imagery. The tension in his muscles eases. He is no longer shaking.

"Good. Very good. Now, I am going to place a sheet over your shoulders. The sheet will feel wet. I want you to focus the heat from the pipes up through your body, into the wet sheet."

The Tibetan enters the cave. Inside is a wooden barrel, filled with icy water. Reaching inside, he removes a bedsheet, wrings it out, then wraps it around Immanuel's exposed shoulders.

Manny's eyes flash open, then close again as he forces himself back into the trance.

"Focus the heat from the pipes up through your chest

and shoulders and back, into the wet sheet. Breathe in through your nose, out through your mouth, each breath stoking the hot coals . . ."

Immanuel slows his pulse, his breathing all but disappearing. He can feel the burning in his stomach, only this time it is soothing warmth, not the lactic acid he experiences while playing football.

His mind wanders, pushing him deeper through the corridors of darkness, until he hears:

It must be boring to be God . . . omnipotent and immortal, never knowing ambition or desire, triumph or loss. Is that why You created us, Lord? To entertain You? Is that why You "blessed us" with our insecurities, poisoned us with ego, enslaved us with lust and greed, power and revenge? Is the human race one big cockfight to you? Do You enjoy the cruelties we inflict upon one another?

Does it entertain You?

Or have You, our parental deity, simply given up? At what point, I wonder, did we finally cross the line? Not during our infancy, when You instructed us through Noah and Abraham, Jacob and Moses. Was it after Christ was crucified? Did You really forgive us? Perhaps it was during humanity's adolescence, those terrible "teen" years when most parents feel like abandoning their child. Was that it, Lord? Was it the Holocaust that caused You to shake Your mighty head in shame? Hiroshima? Korea? Vietnam? September 11? The 2012 conflict? The atrocities in Africa? The endless turmoil in the Middle East?

At what point did You say, "To Hell with them."

Selfish and stupid, violent and destructive, shortsighted and cruel. Children step on your toes when they are young, then step on your hearts as they get older.

Everyone makes mistakes, God. Were we Yours?

Or was this whole thing just part of Your master plan?

Forgive my tirade, son, but since your departure from my soul, I am so full of anger, so full of hate, so full of blasphemy that at times I feel as if I could burst—

Immanuel's ebony eyes flash open as he wails a blood-curdling scream and leaps to his feet, tossing the now-dry bedsheet from his shoulders.

Jacob grabs him around the shoulders. "Manny, what is it?"

Immanuel hugs himself, pacing back and forth in the snow, his limbs shaking.

"Computer, end program!"

The snow and mountainside disappear, revealing the onyx-tiled sensory chamber. The heavy chill ceases, replaced by waves of heat.

Jacob hovers over his brother, who is kneeling on the damp floor, huddling in the warmth. "You heard him, didn't you, Manny? You heard our father!"

Immanuel looks up, his body still trembling. "I heard nothing. Now get me the hell out of here."

33

NOVEMBER 24, 2033
HEALTH SOUTH DOCTOR'S HOSPITAL
CORAL GABLES, FLORIDA
THURSDAY MORNING

Lauren Beckmeyer is exhausted.

It is not the kind of exhaustion she ordinarily relishes from her physical training. This is something she has never experienced, the kind of overwhelming fatigue that comes from being a fugitive. Perpetually draining, it refuses to allow her mind to rest, her fraught nerves to settle.

It is exhaustion based on the fear of death.

For the last thirty-six hours the track star has been ducking through back streets and alleyways, hiding in shadows—avoiding people. She cannot go to her apartment. She cannot contact her parents or friends, fearing the men who murdered Professor Gabeheart will come after her loved ones, just as they are coming after her. She has not eaten, since the purchase of food requires identity scans, and hers has been excised.

Lauren doesn't know who the enemy is, but she has her suspicions. Late the previous night, as she lay alone on the beach, her mind had finally quieted enough to piece things together.

Whoever wanted Gabeheart silenced feared the professor might learn the truth about Yellowstone's caldera. To resort to murder means pressure within the caldera system must be building, which means an eruption is imminent.

The last eruption in Yellowstone led to an ice age. If this next one is anywhere near as devastating . . . oh, Jesus!

Lauren did not sleep, the threat to her own life suddenly overshadowed by the thought of a super volcanic winter. Somehow she had to get a warning to the public. Somehow she had to make the world listen while there was still time to act . . . assuming there was still time and there was another course of action.

But who would listen to her? She was a nobody, someone who could easily be snatched away before the first television camera could be turned on. And what proof did she really have?

But there was someone the media would listen to, someone they wanted to interview, someone who received more news coverage than any scientist, any geology student ever could.

Lauren needed to find Sam.

* *   *   *

Lauren watches the Student Medical Center side entrance from her vantage behind a row of shrubs. Her hair is slicked back with water and tucked under a baseball cap.

She crosses the street, blending in with a family as they enter the facility. She follows a crowded corridor, then waits in line to access an automated hospital help station.

Presses PATIENT DIRECTORY. "Kirk Peacock's room."

KIRK PEACOCK IS LOCATED IN ROOM 310, BED B. HAVE A NICE DAY.

She looks around, bypassing the elevator for the stairs.

Kirk Peacock is lying in bed, his drooling mouth open, his eyes cloaked behind a virtual-reality headpiece. Lauren takes a seat by his bed, averting her eyes as a robonurse enters and changes his IV bag.

"Kirk. Hey, Kirk!" She knocks on the VR helmet, then yanks it off his head.

"Cut the *fubitchshitting* . . . Lauren? Hey . . . what're you doing here?"

"I came to see you. You feeling okay?"

"Fuck no. Got needles and tubes comin' outta my bung-hole. Haven't done a leech in days. They took my contacts, my body piercings, my hair's growing in over my 'too, and my father's making me restain my pigment flesh tone. Life blows."

"Yeah. Kirk, I need a favor. I need to get away for a few days. I'll trade you my car for your Amphibian."

"Your 'Vette? You on meds?"

"It's just for a few days. I promise I'll take good care of it."

"Sink it for all I care. Belongs to my old man. *Fubitchshittingasswipe*."

"What's your access code?"

"Access code . . . damn . . . oh yeah." He holds up his bare foot. Tattooed to his heel is KP-3757-D.

Lauren memorizes the code. "Thanks, Kirk, I owe you. When do they let you out?"

"*Shifubitchin'* know-it-all tin can mechanical doctor ordered another blood scrub. I told that trash can she can suck my plasma only if she replaces it with BLISS. Ha-ha . . . hey, 'ren-man, where you going?"

Hangar 13
Kennedy Space Center
Cape Canaveral, Florida

Thursday Afternoon

Immanuel Gabriel loses his thoughts in the psychiatrist's eyes, watching them shift from hazel to green in the overhead lights. The man's hair is brown and spiked, the cleft lip and telltale scars along the jaw line revealing recent reconstructive surgery.

"You sure don't look like a psychiatrist."

Mike Snyder smiles. "And what should a psychiatrist look like?"

"I don't know . . . more scholarly, I suppose. What happened to your face?"

"Battle scars. I double as one of your brother's sparring partners. At least I used to. He's way beyond us mere mortal foes these days."

Immanuel sits up in the lounge chair, his head still woozy from the sedative. "So you're Jake's psychiatrist? Bet he plays head games with you."

"Only all the time. On occasion he might let something slip, but usually he only confides in Dr. Mohr or Grand Master Xiong. Jacob's very sure of himself. Even as a fourteen-year-old, he always came across as if he knew exactly who he was and what he needed out of life. And he's not one to lose his cool."

"Unlike me."

Dr. Snyder grins. "Don't be so hard on yourself. If someone told me I was getting on that spaceship bound for God-knows-where, I'd have popped a few too many meds, too. What you can't do is allow yourself to be drawn into your brother's psychosis."

"Psychosis?" Immanuel perks up. "Then you don't believe this whole Mayan Hero thing?"

"Do I believe you and Jake are unique individuals—absolutely. Do I believe the two of you were somehow the subject of a Mesoamerican tale written five hundred years ago? No."

"But Jake believes it."

"Jake's mind absorbs everything like a sponge. Unfortunately, this Mayan mythology thing has been ingrained into his psyche since birth. It's become part of his dementia and his persona, and it's now impossible to separate the two."

"But . . . I heard my father's voice."

"Think about it, Manny. Where were you at the time?"

"In a holograph suite . . . programmed by my brother, that cocksucker! But wait, the Guardian's starship—how can you deny that?"

"Who's denying it? An ancient alien spaceship was excavated from Mexico. From what I'm told, it's been buried for at least ten thousand years. Is it one of the greatest, if not the greatest discovery in man's brief history? Absolutely. Does its existence have anything to do with your late father? Probably, since he was the one who discovered it."

"Then you don't believe Jake and I are destined to board that ship and leave orbit in four days?"

"In that ship?" Dr. Snyder snorts a half laugh. "Listen, Dr. Mohr believes in this Mayan nonsense as much as Jacob, but even he'll tell you those engines haven't been fired in thousands of years, and trust me, it's not like NASA hasn't been trying. The only way that old clunker's leaving orbit is if we strap it to one of our new Mars transports and tow her into space."

A huge smile breaks across Immanuel's face, tears of relief flooding his eyes. "Doc, I could kiss you."

"Save it for your mother. She's the one who needs it."

"What do you mean?"

"Jake may be a cold fish when it comes to his feelings, but your mother's torn up inside. Imagine spending twenty years of your life, holding on to the slimmest of hopes that the only person you've ever loved, a man who disappeared before your very eyes, might still be alive. It's like telling the wife of a POW not to move on with her life because her missing husband might return. Look at the life your mother's led. Isolated from the public, unable to see one son, the other in a world all his own, with no social life of her own to speak of. Not knowing what to think about Mick's death, your mother's refused to allow herself to get involved in another relationship, to say nothing about how she's made herself available to Jacob's every whim."

"It's always been like that. I'm guessing Jake has her convinced we're flying off to *Xibalba* in four days."

"Which means in four days he'll suddenly be confronted by the reality of his own psychosis, and it's going to tear him apart. Your mother knows what's coming, and it scares her to death."

Manny pinches away tears. "Where is she? I want to see her."

Soft pink sand.

A tranquil lagoon, its small, soothing waves lapping at their ankles.

Dominique is holding Mick's hand. She stares lovingly at his tan face, the golden rays of the setting sun dancing in his ebony eyes.

"Mother?"

Mick looks at her with a sad smile. "You have to go."

"Mother, can we talk?"

Dominique removes the virtual-reality headgear, squinting into the hallway light.

"I'm sorry," Manny says. "Am I disturbing you?"

"Computer, lights." The overhead lights come up gradually. She sits up from the couch, then ejects the VR program. "How're you feeling? We were all worried about you."

"I'm okay."

"I'm sorry Jake's driving you crazy. I should have never let him talk me into bringing you here. All I ever wanted for you was to live a normal life."

"Ma, it's okay." He sits next to her. "It's you I'm worried about."

She flashes a false smile. "Since when?"

He swallows the lump in his throat. "I realize now how hard it's been for you . . . you know, being without Mick, seeing your family separated. Pushing you to let me go only made things worse."

"Your instincts were right. What I did . . . what I allowed Jacob to do was wrong."

"Jake manipulated you, just like he's always manipulated me."

"It wasn't just Jake, I believed it, too. I mean, how could I not, with everything that had happened. When your father first left me, I honestly believed he was still alive. I can't describe the feeling, but somehow I just knew he was around, I could feel this terrible tugging in my heart. But as the years passed the feeling subsided. Your father's dead, Manny. I've come to accept that now."

"And all Jake's training, all this nonsense about taking a journey?"

"All my fault. I was confused . . . I should have never allowed him to read your grandfather Julius's journal. It's become the basis of his psychosis. By the time I realized what I'd done, it was too late."

"I'm sure GOLDEN FLEECE made things worse. These scientists are using Jake's delusions to get what they want. Why did you go along with it?"

"Why? Because I had no choice. The two of you have always had enemies. Weeks before we set up your phony deaths, the FBI caught a terrorist cell that was planning to launch a crude biological weapon at our home. Living in the compound—we were sitting ducks. Dr. Mohr supported Jacob's training in exchange for your brother's cooperation, allowing them access to the starship. Jacob feels safe here. He said he never felt safe on Longboat Key. How could I deny him that?"

"Jake claims he can operate the *Balam*."

"He can access the vessel and manipulate a few of its astrotopography programs. Other than that, your brother has no more control or knowledge of that ship than you or I."

"That white-haired *fubitshitter* . . . he did it to me again."

"It's the reason Dr. Mohr didn't want you to see the starship. He knew Jacob would use it to manipulate you."

"Why didn't you tell me any of this before we arrived? Never mind, if you had, I never would have come."

"Manny, it's not Jacob's fault. He has a disease. While it may allow him to focus inward, it causes psychotic behavior, robbing him of his ability to grasp reality."

"And what about me? Will I turn out like him?"

"I don't think so. Even if this Hunahpu gene were to suddenly grow dominant, you're already well grounded in reality. Jacob was born into his dementia, and he's too stubborn and too damn smart for his doctors to be coerced into therapy. Everyone agreed our only option was to allow this whole thing to just play itself out. When he finds himself stuck on planet Earth in four days like the rest of us, maybe he'll open his mind enough to allow us to help. But there are other complications. Dr. Mohr just learned the entire GOLDEN FLEECE project's being absorbed by HOPE."

"So what happens to Jake?"

She looks away.

"Ma, I'm here now, I'm part of the family again. You have to tell me. What's going to happen to Jake after Saturday?"

"He'll be committed . . . to a private sanitarium."

Immanuel follows his brother and Dr. Mohr into the secured facility that holds the *Balam*. The chamber is deserted, GOLDEN FLEECE's technicians having already left for their four-day Thanksgiving holiday.

The immense starship's mirrored gold hull sparkles beneath the overhead lights.

Dr. Mohr pauses by one of the vessel's massive engines, grinning at Jacob from ear to ear. "Okay, I'm ready to give this thing another try."

Jacob stretches, feigning boredom. "Go ahead, Doc, but explain things so Manny can understand them. Remember, he's only a PE major, not an expert in quantum physics."

Immanuel shoots his twin an elbow to the ribs.

"Okay, Manny, er, Sam, the thing you need to understand about space travel is that the universe is big. The fastest thing we know of is light, which travels in the vacuum of space at 186,281 miles per second. Even at that rate, it would still take light a full four years just to reach our closest neighboring star. According to the star charts your brother was able to access, this ship originated from somewhere within the Orion Belt, which means it's capable of exceeding light speed. With that sliver of information, GOLDEN FLEECE scientists have been trying to reverse engineer these engines, trying to figure out how the heck they work. Now, we know the ship doesn't use conventional rockets—"

"How do you know that?" Immanuel asks. "They look like regular engines."

Mohr smiles. "Rockets are okay for traveling to the moon or Mars, but you can't use them for interstellar travel. The problem is the rocket's fuel, or propellant. Unlike a plane, which pushes against air, a spacecraft has no mass to push against in the vacuum of space. Therefore, rocket ships must transport with them all the mass they'll need to push against in order to move. Let's say you wanted to use one of our newest Mars transports to reach Proxima Centauri, the closest star to our sun. Forget the fact that it would take you nine hundred years to arrive. In terms of propellant, there isn't enough mass in the universe to get you there. Now, if you used a nuclear fusion rocket, something several space agencies are working on, you'd still need a thousand supertankers of propellant. Of course, if you wanted to get there sooner, it would require even more ungodly amounts of fuel."

"I saw a program about the new Mars cargo vessels. They're going to use lunar-based lasers to push light sails."

"Correct, but the technology is still not feasible over great distances. Let's say you were one light-year from Earth and wanted to make a course change. It would take two years just for the new commands to be radioed to ground control, received, and sent back."

"So what's the solution?"

"The solution is twofold: First, find a source of energy that is already in the vacuum of space; second, discover the means to manipulate the coupling or connection between mass and space-time.

"Back in 1948, a Dutch physicist by the name of Hendrick Casimir completed an experiment using two metal plates. When brought close enough together, the plates attracted each other, revealing the presence of energy within the vacuum. The Casimir effect, as it was later named, was defined as zero-point energy—the random electromagnetic oscillations left in a vacuum after all the other energy has been removed.

"Exactly how much energy resides in space is unknown, but many scientists now believe that before the Big Bang, the conditions of the universe were very similar to those inside a black hole. At minus 273 degrees Celsius, or absolute zero, molecular motion ceases. Zero-point energy doesn't cease; in fact, it may have been so intense that it actually triggered the Big Bang, creating the universe as we now know it. Even though we can't see it, space is, in fact, a sea of zero-point energy, so-called because it is everywhere and balanced to apparent zero. If we were to place a glass vase in a vacuum, the energy would cause it to wobble but prevent it from falling over since the energy would be rushing at it from every direction, neutralizing the effects. If zero-point energy does exist out there, and we believe it does, then there is more than enough energy in the volume of a cup of coffee to evaporate all of Earth's oceans."

"That's some cup of coffee."

Dr. Mohr smiles. "Yes it is. Our challenge lies in organizing these multidimensional spectrums of energies simultaneously. According to Einstein's theory of relativity, the speed of light is the limiting velocity for all ordinary material particles. Tardyons—particles having nonzero rest mass can approach the speed of light but can never achieve it, or their masses would become infinite. At the same time, luxons—particles with zero rest mass, such as photons and neutrinos, must always travel at light speed in a vacuum."

The rocket scientist points to the starship's engines. "The inverse of tardyons are tachyons—theoretical subatomic particles that can only travel at speeds exceeding that of light. What I believe we're looking at here is some type of hyperdrive system that channels tachyon energy." Mohr turns to Jacob. "So, Professor Gabriel? Am I right?"

Jacob grins. "There was a young lady named Bright, whose speed was far faster than light. She went out one day, in a relative way, and returned the previous night."

"What's that supposed to mean?"

"What your brother means is that if you can move faster than the speed of light, you could theoretically travel back in time, potentially causing all sorts of paradoxes."

Immanuel turns to his twin. "As in . . . a time loop?"

"Shh, don't interrupt," Jacob says. "Okay, Doc, you're stumbling along just fine, now see if you can tell me how this hyperdrive concept of yours works."

Dr. Mohr points to the wasp's nest of charred, afterburner-shaped housings, each orifice no less than thirty feet in diameter. "Once in orbit, those housings open, allowing a tachyon stream to pass through. The *Balam*'s computer regulates course and speed by widening or shunting off the openings in different combinations. The lower the tachyon stream's energy, the faster the ship would travel." The scientist smiles. "So? Did I pass?"

Jacob's communicator flashes on, interrupting them.

It's Dominique. "Jacob, dinner's ready. I want you and your brother home now, please. And tell Dr. Mohr that his wife called, and he'd better get his rear end in gear."

Dave Mohr checks his watch. "Oops, abort, abort. I'll see you boys tomorrow morning."

Immanuel watches the wiry scientist hurry toward the exit. "He seems to know an awful lot about this spaceship."

"He should," says Jacob. "After all, he once piloted it."

"Huh?"

Jacob turns to face him, his piercing blue eyes suddenly dead serious. "The time loop, Manny. When the cataclysm strikes Earth, Dave Mohr will be one of the scientists selected for Mars Colony. Only he'll never make it, his ship and several others caught within the gravitational forces of the wormhole."

"Dr. Mohr was on *Xibalba?*"

"Yes. Fortunately, he and a few other members of the brotherhood managed to escape before the Abomination took over."

"Whoa, wait a minute . . . are you telling me Dr. Mohr was a . . . a Guardian?"

"Was, and will be again, unless we return to *Xibalba* and succeed. He doesn't remember it, but Dr. Mohr was once the great Mayan wise man, Kukulcán."

South Beach, Florida

The setting sun has turned the Atlantic Ocean a deep magenta.

Lauren remains hidden in the shadows of an alleyway another five minutes before crossing A-1-A to the row of private beach garages. She quickly locates the facility belonging to the Peacock family and enters the access code.

The aluminum panel opens, revealing motorized water skis, lounge chairs, and a canary yellow three-wheeled dune buggy, its fiber-cast hull more boat than car.

Lauren climbs inside the two-passenger open cockpit of the Amphibian. Powering up the engine, she guides the vehicle out of its garage, then bounds over the grass dunes and sand, straight into the ocean.

Waves lift the buoyant vessel away from the silt. Wheels retract. A forward ski moves into place beneath the pointed bow, a rotary-driven propeller dropping beneath its stern.

Lauren guns the engines. The wind howls in her ears as she races north, bouncing along the surface at fifty miles an hour, heading for Cape Canaveral.

Hangar 13
Kennedy Space Center
Cape Canaveral, Florida

Roasted turkey. Stuffing. Sweet potatoes. Freshly baked rolls.

Immanuel is stuffed. He lays his head back against the violet cushion and belches.

"That was nice."

"Sorry, Ma, but that was the best meal I've had in a long time. How long it take you to synthesize it?"

She shoots him a harsh look. "I cooked it. That was real turkey, not that synthetic soy crap laced with flavoring and chemicals. If you want to get your dailies, take them the old-fashioned way."

Grand Master Chong enters, a look of concern on the old man's face. "Jacob, come please. Your brother, too."

Dominique feels the blood rush from her face. "What is it?"

The monk shakes his head. "We have guests."

Atlantic Ocean

8:56 P.M.

Lauren eases back on the Amphibian's throttle and turns toward shore, allowing the two-man boat to settle in the swells.

She stands in the open cockpit and stretches, her buttocks numb. She has been following the Florida coastline for three hours. Exhausted, cold, and sore, she has been questioning her own sanity for most of the trip.

Glancing down at the control panel, she quickly verifies her position on the LED computer screen.

The old Cape Canaveral lighthouse is a half mile north. Just ahead is the immense building she had seen from the NASA causeway only days earlier.

Days? Seems more like years. Okay, if you're really going to do this, then do it . . .

She accelerates behind a cresting wave and rides it into the beach, activating the amphibious switch.

As the jet ski rolls forward onto the sand, three tires rotate into position beneath the chassis, instantly converting the seacraft back into a landrover.

Lauren parks the triwheeled dune buggy on dry sand, her eyes focused on the forty-foot-high perimeter fence which runs parallel to the shoreline.

WARNING: ELECTRIFIED FENCE. NO TRESPASSING
BY ORDER OF THE UNITED STATES GOVERNMENT.

She tosses a seashell fragment.

Zapp!

Okay, Einstein, now what?

A flash of headlights causes her to duck. She watches as a white stretch limousine parks in front of the main entrance.

Lauren sits back, rubbing her head, trying to fathom the sudden sensation of déjà vu.

* * *

Grand Master Chong, Dominique, Jacob, and Immanuel stand before the two-way observation panel, watching the occupants in the next room.

Seated at the head of a simulated oak conference table is President John Zwawa. On his left is Alyssa Popov, on his right, a Hispanic member of GOLDEN FLEECE.

"Danny Diaz," Jacob mutters, "Dave Mohr's right-hand man. Looks like the bastard sold us out."

A disheveled Dr. Mohr enters the conference room, followed by the most stunning woman Immanuel Gabriel has ever seen. She is young, about his age, but carries herself in a more worldly way. Mocha tan skin. High cheekbones, accentuated by long, wavy ebony hair, which rolls down her taut, muscular back to her flawless waistline. Her lips are full and luscious, her dark, wraparound sunglasses adding an air of mystique. She saunters around the room in her own little world, her bone-colored silk pajama-style outfit threatening to fall away.

Manny watches her circle, his eyes wide. "Who is that?"

Jacob stares at the woman as if seeing a ghost. "Trouble."

Dave Mohr's voice emanates from speakers within their sound-proof office. "Mrs. Mabus, honestly, I'm not really sure what you're after. After all, we've been attempting to reverse engineer the starship for more than a decade now, and—"

"Please, Dr. Mohr, let's not begin our tenure together with lies." Her voice, so soothing, yet not one to be trifled with. "Daniel?"

Danny Diaz activates a recessed volumetric display, which rises to show the three-dimensional image of the Guardian's starship rotating above the tabletop. "We've been able to access the *Balam*'s astrotopography program. We also located the source of the electromagnetic pulse weapon, which essentially prevented us from annihilating one another back in 2012."

Lilith glides around the room, then abruptly stops and stares at her own reflection in the two-way mirror, inches from Jacob and Manny.

"Who is she, Jacob?" Dominique whispers.

Lilith suddenly smiles like an enchantress, then slowly lifts her silk top, exposing her tan, grapefruit-sized breasts at the two-way mirror.

Immanuel grins.

Jacob's heart skips a beat.

And then the woman removes her wraparound sunglasses and reveals the sociopathic intensity of her azure blue eyes.

Jacob grabs his twin by the arm and forcibly drags him from the room.

"Jake, stop—"

"No! You need to leave here, now!"

"Jake, her eyes . . . was that—"

"Yes. Now listen to me very carefully—"

They race down a corridor to a door marked EQUIPMENT. Jacob keys a code into a pad, then opens the door—

—revealing a stairwell that descends into darkness.

"This will lead you outside to the beach. Give me two minutes, and I'll cut power to the electrical fence. Your girlfriend's outside."

"Lauren's here? How do you know—"

"Don't talk, just listen. Head south. Stay out of the public eye. Find Frank Stansbury, he's a friend of the family. Lives in Delray Beach, in the Western Estates."

"What about you?"

Jacob embraces his twin. "Don't ask—just run! Remember, Frank Stansbury. And stay out of the nexus, or the Hunahpu will sense you. Now go!"

Immanuel hurries down the steps. Kicks open the rusted steel door and jogs out onto the beach, the wind gusting, the ocean spray blasting him in the face.

Searchlights activate behind and to his left. He dives forward, rolling to the base of the electrical barrier.

The searchlights' motion detectors locate him. He tosses

sand at the fence, which sizzles with static. *Come on, Jake, shut it down!*

He takes a few breaths, looks around, then throws another fistful of sand.

This time, the charge is gone.

Leaping to his feet, he grabs hold of the fence, scaling the forty-foot-high steel barrier like a lizard. He leaps into the night, drops and lands on both feet—

—as a familiar figure runs away from him, heading for the ocean.

Lauren sprints down the beach, away from the sirens, away from the searchlights. The wind whistles in her ears as the world-class sprinter races for the Amphibian.

"Lauren, wait!"

Sam?

Lauren stops running as her fiancé stumbles, barreling sideways into her.

"Lauren?" Sam stares at her in disbelief. "Oh, God, it is you!"

She leaps into his arms, sobbing. "Sam, I'm in so much trouble—"

"You and me both." Looking back over her shoulder, he spots the armed security guards. "Come on, we gotta move."

Hand in hand, they race down the beach.

"No, this way!" Lauren pulls him toward the water.

He spots the *Amphibian*, then looks back, as one of the security guards activates his taser.

No! Ignoring his brother's warning, he slips into the nexus—

—time slowing to an excruciating crawl.

Behind him, pushing through clear gelatin-like fourth-dimensional waves, is the taser's sizzling violet circle of energy. Expanding rapidly across the beachhead, the paralyzing loop of lightning reaches for them—

—as Jacob grabs Lauren around her waist and leaps into the Amphibian's cockpit.

I can taste you, cousin. Why do you run? What is it you fear?

Gunning the engine, he converts the jeep into a boat, then activates the craft's autopilot, pressing the setting for Miami—

—as the wave of energy slams into them from behind, zapping them into unconsciousness.

34

25 NOVEMBER 2033
USS PENNSYLVANIA
ATLANTIC OCEAN
297 NAUTICAL MILES EAST OF MIAMI
FRIDAY MORNING

Captain Robert Wilkins, Operational Commander of the Weather Net-Atlantic Force, stares at the real-time satellite image of Super-Cane Kenneth being projected on the control room's large monitor. The Category-6 storm has become an absolute freak of Nature, its clearly defined eye sixty nautical miles northeast of Eleuthera Island, its swirling vortex already engulfing the Bahamas, punishing the hastily abandoned islands with winds in excess of 195 miles an hour.

Wilkins is as frustrated as he is worried. The delivery of the MPK gas mix to the Port of Miami was not only late, it was light, with barely enough of the pressurized cryogenic nitrogen to fill half the fleet's converted vertical silos.

Category-6 Super-Canes mandate a minimum of eight fully loaded vessels. Wilkins has barely six, and Kenneth is no ordinary superstorm.

Executive Officer David Sutera approaches, handing him a printout. "Skipper, we just received this latest GMT."

SUPER-CANE KENNETH

1100GMT FRIDAY	11/25/33
LOCATION:	26.1N 75.8W
MAX. WIND:	197 MPH
GUSTING:	208 MPH
MOVING:	W AT 16 MPH
PRESSURE:	941 MB
PREDICTED U.S. LANDFALL:	
	SATURDAY 11/26/33
	09:20 HRS
DESTINATION:	MIAMI

"Christ, it's picked up speed."

"A mandatory evacuation order was just issued. Key West north to West Palm Beach."

"Conn, sonar, skipper, we're in the eye."

"Very well. Officer of the Deck, bring us about, make your course two-seven-zero, steady at four knots."

"Aye, sir, coming about. Making my course two-seven-zero, steady at four knots."

"Bring us to periscope depth."

"Aye, sir, coming up to periscope depth. Steady at sixty feet."

Sutera presses his face to the periscope and takes a quick 360-degree scan of the surface. "Confirm, skipper, we're in the eye."

"Sonar, Captain, is the fleet in position?"

"Conn, sonar, still waiting on the *Wyoming* and *Kentucky*. ETA four minutes. All other ships have come about and are standing by."

Wilkins reverses his cap and looks through the periscope.

Sunshine reflects off an ominous olive green sea, its rolling waves peaking at thirty feet.

An oasis of calm within a vortex of hell . . .

The captain rotates to the west and focuses on the advancing eye wall. It is as if he is looking out from inside the heart of a tornado. A dark purple wall of clouds—swirling, twisting, igniting every few seconds in bursts of lightning—the storm is a living, raging beast.

"Conn, sonar, all ships now in position."

Wilkins pulls himself away from the periscope and readjusts his cap. "Very well. Officer of the Deck, put us on the ceiling. Increase speed to sixteen knots."

"Aye, sir, surfacing ship. Increasing my speed to sixteen knots."

"Conn, sonar, give me two pings down the fleet's bearings."

"Aye, sir, two pings."

Two thunderous gongs echo across the sea, alerting the other Trident subs, which have fanned out along the eastern eye wall.

"Weather Net Officer, this is the captain. Begin ejecting MPK gas."

"Aye, sir. Ejecting MPK gas."

Located amidships, standing in pairs like steel redwood trees, are the sub's twenty-four vertical missile silos, each rising more than three stories. Originally designed to launch sixty-five-ton Trident D-5 II nuclear ballistic missiles, the tubes have been refitted to hold compatibly sized canisters of pressurized cryogenic nitrogen gas mix.

Weather Net Officer Matt Winegar activates the digital clock on his control board, then presses EJECT-1 and EJECT-2.

Exterior hatches pop open along the top of the submarine. Seconds later, a clear stream of gas is forcibly expelled through venturi tubes. As the MPK gas mixes with the low-pressure, high-humidity atmosphere, it expands and crystallizes, forming a thick fog, which is quickly suctioned toward the approaching wall of the cyclone.

Immense waves lift and drop the sub, sending several off-duty sailors scampering to the head.

WNO Winegar tries his best to ignore the building queasiness in his gut as he watches his clock. Each MPK tank release must be timed to feed the storm, too much gas at once, and the storm will choke.

At four minutes a green light flashes, alerting Winegar to release the next two batches of compound.

The storm continues east as it feeds, its western eye sucking the chemical up into its vortex, dispersing it within its cumulus fury.

High overhead, flying back and forth through the Super-Cane's clouds like steel falcons are ESMA's Unmanned Cyclone Aerial Labs. These four-foot-long winged darts, known affectionately as UNCLE, traverse the walls of the eye, gathering precious data.

The officers and crew of the *Pennsylvania* hold on and watch as UNCLE's data appears on screen.

Super-Cane Kenneth: Sustained Winds: 193 mph

The hurricane's winds continue dropping. **182mph . . . 181mph . . . 179mph . . .**

"Conn, Weather Net Officer. All silos flushed, skipper."

"Officer of the Deck, take us down. Make your depth one hundred feet."

"Aye, sir, taking us down. Making my depth one hundred feet."

Captain Wilkins stares at UNCLE's numbers, silently rooting for them to descend faster. From experience he knows the MPK gas must decrease sustained winds below 140mph for the storm's feedback cycle to be significantly disrupted.

168mph . . . 167mph . . . 166mph . . . 167mph . . .

The crew groans.

Wilkins grits his teeth. *Wasn't enough . . . not nearly enough.* He lets out a frustrated breath. "Conn, radio. Contact ESMA headquarters. Alert them the weather net has failed to cap the storm."

South Beach, Florida

Friday Afternoon

The surf laps gently along a deserted stretch of beach. The sun beats down upon a coconut tree, a gust of tropical air causing one of its fruit to fall. Sandpipers dip, then soar away, racing inland.

Immanuel Gabriel opens his eyes.

He is strapped within the bucket seat of the *Amphibian,* which has beached itself on shore. Releasing the shoulder harness, he turns around to face Lauren, who is strapped in the seat behind him. "Lauren? Lauren, wake up."

She opens her eyes, spitting a strand of hair from her mouth. "Oww, my head . . . what happened?"

"We got zapped by a taser. I managed to activate the autopilot before it hit us. Looks like we made it to Miami."

He climbs slowly out of the cockpit, then helps her from her seat.

She hugs him, laying her head wearily against his chest. "Why were you at NASA?"

"God, don't ask. It was sort of, I don't know . . . call it a family obligation. I'll tell you about it later. What were you doing there?"

She pulls herself from his embrace. "I'm in real trouble. Someone killed Professor Gabeheart, and now they're after me!"

"Whoa, slow down. Who's after you?"

"Government thugs. Something's happening in Yellowstone. We have to go public—"

ATTENTION.

They look up, startled.

It is a PAWS (Public Aerial Warning System), a flying vehicle operated by the Earth Systems Management Agency to assist in evacuating populated areas prior to storms.

THIS AREA HAS BEEN CLOSED BY ORDER OF THE ESMA. EVACUATE THE AREA AND REPORT TO A STORM SHELTER IMMEDIATELY OR FACE PROSECUTION.

"Super-Cane Kenneth—I completely forgot."

"Come on." Sam climbs back in the Amphibian and tries the power switch.

Nothing.

"*Fubitchshitting* piece of junk."

DO YOU REQUIRE ASSISTANCE?

"No, no, we're waiting to re-charge." Lauren activates the battery re-charger, then drags him out of the boat. The two hurry off the beach.

PAWS keeps pace, hovering twenty feet above.

She whispers frantically in his ear. "They're watching both of our apartments."

"Who's watching?"

"Them! The guys who killed Gabeheart." She digs her nails into his arm. "One of them came for me in the lab. I hid under the computer decking. I heard him say they were watching my dorm. If they find me, I'm dead."

They exit the beach, crossing Collins Avenue. South Beach is deserted. There is no traffic, not a single car or street vendor present.

"Kind of spooky."

"Sam!"

"Okay, okay—" He looks around, then pulls her beneath a floating walkway. "All right, start from the beginning."

Lauren tells him everything, showing him her scarred hand.

When she is through, he leans back against a lamp post, rubbing his brow. "Jesus, Lauren, how'd you get yourself into this mess?"

"I don't know."

"And you really think these people have connections within our government?"

"Yes! Weren't you paying attention?"

"Okay, okay."

"Sam, that PAWS drone will alert the cops. We have to get out of here."

He recalls Jacob's last words. "I think I know somewhere we can go."

Hangar 13

Friday Evening

The parking lot of Hangar 13 is filled beyond capacity.

HOPE employees are arriving by car and bus, board members by private helojet. An invading army of technicians and scientists, engineers and associates—all waiting their turn to view the alien starship berthed in the main hangar bay.

Inside the complex, away from the action, four people emerge from their hiding place beneath the Japanese A-frame.

The two bodyguards, Salt and Pepper, stand vigil at the front porch. Each is wearing an aluminum foil EMP suit, designed to shield their nervous systems from the effects of taser fire. Dominique is inside Jacob's home, anxiously waiting for her son to finish working at his computer.

Mitchell Kurtz scans the atrium using his smart-glasses. "Here we go. Northern entrance. I see four guards, all carrying stun guns."

"They're yours," says Pep. "I'll get Dom and the kid."

Jacob finishes uploading information from his computer terminal. "Computer, complete upload to mainframe, then erase all records . . . Password: Gabriel Alpha-Zulu-Delta-4 Ahau, 8 Cumku."

UPLOAD COMPLETED. ALL RECORDS HAVE BEEN ERASED.

"Jacob?"

"Mother, listen to me carefully. Go with Salt and Pepper, they'll get you out of here. Pick up Eve Mohr, then meet me at the rendezvous point."

"What about Manny?"

"He'll be all right." He forces a smile, then hugs her tightly. "Remember, do exactly what we talked about, and I'll see you soon."

Pepper yanks open one of the *shoji* panels, the powerful bodyguard literally tearing it from its frame. "We gotta go—now!" He grabs Dominique by the arm, half-carrying her through the fragmented doorway.

She looks over her shoulder.

Jacob is gone.

Mitchell Kurtz glances up casually as four heavily armed Mabus security guards make their way across the bridge. "Evening, fellas."

"Don't move. Don't even blink."

Kurtz smiles. In a millisecond, his thought energy is processed through the neural shunt connected to his biceps, igniting the taser strapped to his forearm.

The four guards drop like a house of cards.

Jacob is in the central garden of his home, seated in a lotus position. Registering the change in temperature, he opens his eyes.

Lilith is staring at him from the open *shoji* door. "Jacob?"

Jacob stares at her as if observing an approaching cobra, her smile electrifying his groin.

"I always suspected you were still alive . . . always sensing the shadow of your presence." Her eyes flash violet. "You abandoned me!"

"I shouldn't have. I'm sorry."

"Sorry? Is that all you have to say? You were my only

friend, the only one who loved me. All of those promises . . . they were all lies."

"I did love you, Lilith, I still do."

"Bastard." She circles him, brushing her fingertips lightly across his chest and neck, their lips inches apart, the glow of their azure eyes reflecting off one another's cheeks.

She moves closer, allowing her hip to brush against his groin.

"I make you afraid. Why are you so afraid of me, Jacob?"

Lilith's scent is in his nostrils, pounding in his blood. "I'm . . . I'm afraid of my feelings."

"Liar. You're afraid of what I'll become. But like you, I'm simply a product of my environment. Which means you helped create me, just as I've created you."

She grins. Leans in. Pauses. Licks his lips.

A tidal wave of insanity overwhelms him as his mouth crashes against hers and their limbs entwine in the embrace—two victims of society, two polar extremes, two lonely souls sharing this one promised moment of passion.

Lilith pants in his ear as her fingers scramble to undo the belt buckle of his pants—

—while Jacob's hand slides beneath her silky bottoms, groping her moist pubic region, all the while his conscience screaming at him, *No, Jacob stop, Jacob stop . . . stop . . . stop . . . STOP!*

He yanks his hand free, pushing her away. "I can't . . . I can't do this!"

Lilith's azure eyes are full of lust, her lips red where the kiss has bruised them. "We were meant to be together."

"No . . . too dangerous."

"I want you, Jacob." She slips off her top, exposing her breasts. "I want you inside of me, and I won't take no for an answer."

And suddenly she is upon him, raping him from within the nexus. Jacob's mind leaps inside the void to join her, Lilith's nude torso thrusting up and down upon his naked pelvis, the intensity of the moment magnified a hundredfold within the supernatural corridor.

And in his single moment of weakness, he explodes inside her, planting his Hunahpu seed deep in her ovulating womb.

Exhausted and spent, their minds tumble out of the nexus, Lilith collapsing upon his chest. "You're my soul mate, you always will be."

Jacob Gabriel wraps his arms around her and weeps.

Salt and Pepper escort Dominique through the open vault door and down the main corridor.

"Hold it!" The two MTI security guards at the end of the hall raise their weapons. "No one leaves the facility without Mrs. Mabus's permission. Stop or we'll fire."

The three continue running toward them.

The lead guard fires–

—the electrical burst immediately absorbed by their suits. *"Fubishit—"*

Ryan Beck is first to reach them. Grabbing each guard by the back of the neck, he slams their heads against the steel door, knocking them out.

Delray Beach, Florida

The estate home at the end of the cul-de-sac is similar to the other mansions in this very private, gated West Delray community. Like other homes, it overlooks a lake on three acres of land. It has a tennis court, a basketball court, and a pool, but seldom are they used—except when the grandkids come to visit. In fact, the only amenity its owner uses these days are the satellite dishes, and, of course, the live-in private security personnel.

Ominous clouds have blanketed the sky by the time the canary yellow Amphibian skids to a halt in front of the automated guardhouse located at the main entrance of the community.

Immanuel Gabriel climbs out. Presses the ID pad.

REMAIN BY YOUR VEHICLE, SIR. STATE YOUR BUSINESS.

"Samuel Agler to see Frank Stansbury."

STAND BY.

Heavy raindrops plop against the multicolored pavers. *Come on . . .*

PLEASE WAIT. MR. STANSBURY'S SECURITY VEHICLE WILL ESCORT YOU TO THE HOME MOMENTARILY. HAVE A NICE DAY.

Droplets have turned into a downpour by the time the security vehicle pulls up to the outer gate. An armed guard climbs out of the back seat, signaling for Immanuel and Lauren to get inside.

As the door closes and they drive into the complex, a tow truck arrives to haul the Amphibian away.

Inside the car, the driver says nothing. Immanuel notices Lauren's hand is trembling. He squeezes it.

The vehicle enters the gated driveway of an estate, stopping beneath an enormous porte cochere, its rooftop shielding them from the rain.

The driver turns to face them. "Out you go. Mr. Stansbury is waiting for you inside."

They exit the vehicle. Manny knocks on the imposing double oak door.

The door opens, releasing an aroma of glazed ham and stuffing.

The African-American is stooped over. The eyes are sunken, twitching behind old-fashioned spectacles. What's left of the man's hair has grayed.

The owlish smile is genuine, the voice a familiar rasp.

"Hello, Manny. Been expectin' you."

Ennis Chaney, former president of the United States pulls his shocked godson in, out of the weather.

35

Manny sits alone on the sofa opposite Ennis Chaney's mahogany desk, feeling lost in time. "Jacob told you I'd be coming?"

"Years ago. Your brother's ability to foresee certain events convinced me long ago to go along with his schemes."

"So what happens now?"

"I don't know. Jacob told me to expect you, nothing more. So let's talk about your fiancée. Lovely girl. Why haven't you told her who you really are?"

"How can I? How do you tell the person you love that you've been living a lie, that you're not the person you claim to be?"

"She deserves to know. What if you two have children? They could turn out like Jake?"

"I know."

"Tell her."

"I will."

"When?"

"Soon."

"Do it tonight."

Immanuel looks up at his godfather. "Why tonight? What's the rush?"

"Just do it tonight." He leans back in his easy chair.

"Now go bring her in, and let's see if I can help her out of the mess she's in."

Immanuel finds Lauren in one of the guest rooms, changing into dry clothes.

"Lauren, I spoke with Chaney. He wants to help."

"Thank God." Lauren hugs her fiancé, then follows him back to the office.

Chaney sits back in his chair and thinks. "Okay, young lady, let's say you're right. Let's say Professor Gabeheart was murdered because he suspected something someone wanted kept quiet. How do we prove it? Where's the evidence?"

"The evidence is in Yellowstone," she says. "The evidence is hidden beneath the hot springs and caldera."

"Assume things are as bad as you say, that the caldera is getting ready to erupt. Who'd want to keep it secret? And how could they?"

"They'd do it by shutting down the park. They'd want it kept a secret to prevent a widespread panic."

"Mr., uh . . . President, we need you to bring Gabeheart's death and this entire issue into the public eye. Once you do that, it eliminates the need for outside parties to keep Lauren silent."

Chaney nods. "Okay, consider it done. By Sunday morning, the story will be sent to every media outlet in the world. Only then will we bring the FBI in. Sound like a plan?"

"Oh, God, thank you." Lauren wipes back tears of gratitude. "Thank you so much. And thank God you're a big Miami booster." She looks at Immanuel. "Sam, I had no idea your father had such influential friends."

Manny shrugs.

Chaney grins. "For now, the two of you will stay with me. Bad storm coming, but we should be okay." He stands, hobbling like an old soldier to the den door. "Come on, my wife's prepared a Thanksgiving feast. Eat everything, or I'll be dealing with leftovers past Christmas."

Hangar 13
Kennedy Space Center
Cape Canaveral, Florida

Hand in hand, Lilith and Jacob stand before the *Balam*'s sealed entry.

"Incredible," she whispers. "And this was built by our Hunahpu ancestors?"

"No," Jacob says. "The origins of the starship remain a mystery."

Danny Diaz, Dr. Mohr, Benjamin Merchant, and two gorilla-sized security guards join them on the gantry platform.

Merchant smiles. "Why, Lilith darlin', you're positively glowing. I'm extremely jealous."

Jacob looks below. More than six hundred MTI technicians, scientists, and VIPs have gathered, all waiting to tour the interior of the sleek, gold-paneled vessel.

Lilith coos in his ear. "Open it, my love."

"Of course." Jacob closes his eyes.

The sealed panel door of the *Balam* slides open.

Lilith steps forward—

—and suddenly she is sent hurtling over the rail, falling to the crowd below.

The blur of movement that is Jacob Gabriel grabs Dave Mohr by his wrist, yanking the scientist inside the starship.

Lilith lands awkwardly atop the crowd. "Jacob!" She scrambles to her feet. "Damn you, Jacob . . ." She slips inside the nexus.

Jacob pulls Dave Mohr to his feet. "You okay?"

The scientist nods. "What happened?"

"No time to explain, just hold on."

* * *

A low rumbling sound, like a generator, echoes throughout the hangar, quickly increasing to a dull thunder.

The gantry trembles, sending the crowd rushing toward the nearest exits.

Lilith is flung free of the nexus as the long-dormant engines of the *Balam* power up. An invisible wave of electromagnetic energy is expelled from beneath the hull, blasting bodies, equipment, and ten years of dust in all directions.

Beneath this cushion of energy, the alien starship rises. Dorsal plates punch upward through the roof. Steel beams and metal sheeting tumble like kindling.

Lilith pulls herself free from beneath the fallen gantry and looks up, screaming her outrage, as the starship *Balam* disappears into the approaching gray storm clouds of Super-Cane Kenneth.

Delray Beach, Florida

11:37 P.M.

One-hundred-thirty-mile-an-hour gusts whip through the deserted streets of Dade, Broward, and Palm Beach Counties, announcing the arrival of Super-Cane Kenneth's outer wind bands. The once-tranquil ocean swells thirty-five feet, the storm surge submerging the beach before pouring over sea walls to inundate scenic highway A-1-A. Waves lap against storefronts. A driving rain lashes palm fronds and debris, turning refuse into miniature missiles.

And the superstorm's eye is still nine hours out to sea.

Cuddling beneath the blanket, Immanuel Gabriel curls his naked body around Lauren, nuzzling her neck, while outside, fierce winds hammer the steel hurricane storm shutters.

"I feel safe in your arms," Lauren whispers.

"I missed you."

"Why you were at the Cape?"

"I was . . . visiting a relative."

She rolls over to face him. "Who?"

"My mother. My biological mother."

"I don't understand?"

"Lauren, I was adopted. I never told you about it because, well, I sort of wrote them out of my life long ago."

She sits up. "Them?"

"I have a brother. I saw him this week for the first time in six years. He has problems, mental problems. My mother may have to put him in an asylum. That's why I had to come up to the Cape this week. She wanted me to see him before he's locked away."

"I don't know what to say. Are you okay with all this?"

"Guess I'm a little screwed up."

"Can I meet them?"

"Someday."

She lays her head on his chest. "All this time, I had this terrible premonition you were getting ready to leave me."

He swallows the lump in his throat. "I'm not leaving you."

"Promise?"

The wind howls outside and he hugs her tighter. "I'm not leaving you, Lauren. I promise."

Hope Control Room
MTI Operational Headquarters
Cocoa Beach, Florida

**Saturday
2:35 A.M.**

Lilith Mabus is in her late husband's private office, seated before a wall of computer monitors. The upper two rows are real-time links being broadcast from NATS—Nanosat

Trailblazer Spheres—cluster satellites, no larger than a basketball. Thousands of these spheres orbit the Earth, scanning every square inch of the planet.

Despite NATS extensive coverage, the alien starship is nowhere to be found.

"Computer, replay security sequence."

Another set of screens activate, revealing different angles of the perimeter security fencing surrounding Hangar 13.

The figure of a dark-haired man appears on screen. He crosses the compound and heads for the fence. Pauses, then practically vaults over the steel barrier before disappearing into the night.

Lilith's azure eyes widen. "Computer, rewind and replay sequence at half speed."

The image begins again.

"Freeze. Focus on subject's face. Increase magnification by ten."

A blue square frames the man's face, expanding and focusing.

The image of Samuel Agler appears on screen, frozen in time.

Jacob's twin . . . the dark-haired one still lives! "Computer, identify subject."

SAMUEL AGLER, IDENTIFICATION 13-9-23-FL-742-45-M.
SUBJECT IS A PCAA ATHLETE CURRENTLY ENROLLED AT THE
UNIVERSITY OF MIAMI.

Lilith claps her hands in delight. "Samuel, the 'Mule' Agler is Immanuel Gabriel? Computer, tap into all government resources and communication links. Check identifications in all storm shelters and every mode of transportation. I want Samuel Agler found before dawn."

Delray Beach, Florida

7:50 A.M.

Super-Cane Kenneth's fury rips across South Florida's landmass like a mad bull, uprooting trees, peeling away antiquated tile roofs, churning the community beneath a blizzard of wind and water.

Guided by its autopilot, the black stretch limousine finds its way through the storm, eventually arriving at the estate registered to Frank Stansbury. The vehicle parks itself beneath the huge porte cochere. A woman dashes for the front door.

Dominique shakes water from her hair, then hugs Ennis Chaney. "Where is he?"

"In the shower. His fiancée's here, too."

"Lauren's here? Has he told her?"

"He said he would."

Lauren enters the foyer, dressed in a sweat suit. "Has he told me what? Who are you?"

Dominique turns on a smile. "I'm Immanuel's mother. It's so good to finally meet you."

Lauren looks lost. "Immanuel? Who's Immanuel?"

"I am." Manny exits the bathroom.

"I don't understand."

"Lauren, this is my real mother, Dominique Gabriel."

"Gabriel? Immanuel Gabriel . . ." She makes the connection. "Oh, no . . . oh my God—"

"Lauren—"

She pushes him away, then covers her mouth, fighting to breath. "But you're dead. And Sam . . . who's Sam—"

"Calm down and listen—"

"You lied . . . all these years."

"I had to. Can you understand that I had to lie? If word got out—"

"We have to go," Chaney announces.

"Go where?" Dominique and Lauren ask in unison.

"Jacob's given me very explicit instructions. We'll take your limo. Dominique, Manny, let's go. Lauren, you're supposed to stay here."

"No way." Lauren grabs Immanuel's arm. "Wherever he goes, I'm going, too."

"Out of the question," Chaney states.

"Either she comes, or I stay," Immanuel says.

Chaney eyeballs his godson, who returns the old man's glare. "God dammit, I'm too old for this foolishness." He looks at Lauren, the girl desperate. "Okay, everyone in the goddam car!"

Meteorology Lab
University of Miami

7:50 A.M.

The Meteorology Center is a beehive of activity as dozens of technicians from the Earth Systems Management Agency track Super-Cane Kenneth, its monstrous eye less than twenty miles offshore.

Bruce Doyle stares at the cyclone's image on his screen. *Sweet Jesus, it's heading straight for Biscayne Bay . . .*

Two floors down, Special Agent Collin Shelby sips his coffee as he waits for the latest encoded dispatch from UMBRA headquarters in Virginia. Twenty hours earlier, Lauren Beckmeyer's fiancé had placed an unsecured communication from Miami Beach. Satellite eavesdropping had immediately zeroed in on both subjects, who had headed north and were given shelter in a Delray Beach home registered to a retired airline pilot going by the name of Frank Stansbury. This last bit of information was quite disconcerting. *What if it's another biological attack . . .*

Shelby's communicator vibrates. He places the sunglasses on his face, reading the encrypted message appearing across the inside of the tinted lenses.

ALERT: SUBJECT'S VEHICLE TRAVELING SOUTH
ON SH-95, HEADING FOR MIAMI.
FLOOD ZONE.

Shelby rubs his sleep-deprived eyes. "Flood Zone" was UMBRA's term for killing the subject and all witnesses. Whatever act of terrorism this Lauren Beckmeyer and her accomplices were planning had to be something big.

The government assassin checks his weapons, then grabs his rain gear and heads for the door.

Inside the Limousine
Miami Beach, Florida

9:36 A.M.

Immanuel squeezes Lauren's trembling hand.

They are seated in the back of the swaying limo, along with his mother, Ennis Chaney, and Dr. Mohr's wife, Eve. The two bodyguards are up front, praying the autopilot will guide them to their undisclosed destination before Super-Cane Kenneth pummels them to death.

The wind is howling so loud, the rain beating on the exterior with such force that communication is impossible. Only the former president knows where they are going, and he refuses to say.

After ninety minutes of steady driving, they exit the Smart-way interstate and snake their way through streets flooded with ocean and rain.

Twenty minutes later, the vehicle abruptly stops.

The rain has eased, the wind turning to a high-pitched whistle, as if they are parked in a tunnel.

Immanuel presses his face to the bulletproof glass. Through the foggy window he sees a brick wall. "Wait a second . . . I know this place."

Chaney checks his watch. "You should. It's one of the emergency vehicle passageways at the MTI Bowl." He taps Kurtz on the shoulder. "The eye of the storm should be passing over us any moment. When it does, pop the gate and drive us straight onto the field."

"Yes, sir."

Immanuel's heart races. *Jacob's orchestrating something . . . but what?"*

Lauren stares at him as if they've just met. "You should have told me . . . Manny."

"I couldn't. Try to understand, it was a lifetime ago, it's not who I am."

"I don't know who you are anymore. Do you even love me?"

"Lauren—"

The wind stops howling.

Ryan Beck steps out of the vehicle, aims his laser rifle, and blasts open the locked gate. Kurtz guides the limo up the concrete ramp, using the vehicle's reinforced front bumper to bash through the unhinged iron doors.

The limousine climbs a river of water, then drives onto the flooded football field.

Kurtz maneuvers to the fifty yard line and parks. Moments later, the rain stops and the wind ceases blowing. Wisps of blue sky and sunshine warm the drenched field.

They are within the very eye of the storm.

Everyone climbs out of the car, sloshing in calf-deep water.

Lauren looks toward the heavens. "How is this possible? How did you know the cyclone's eye would pass directly over this spot?"

Immanuel Gabriel's insides are trembling, his mind screaming at him to run, to get the hell out of this stadium while he still can.

"Look!" Kurtz points to the approaching western eye wall.

An object has emerged from the foreboding lead gray vortex, the sun's rays shimmering off the mirrorlike gold panels of its dagger-shaped bow.

The Balam . . .

Immanuel drops to his knees, hyperventilating as he recalls Jacob's words. *". . . the wormhole's closest mouth will pass outside Mars in a week. To rendezvous in time means we'll have to leave Earth's orbit in ninety-eight hours."*

The Guardian's starship hovers high over the flooded field, then descends, its landing gear splashing onto the flooded field with a walloping *thud*, its dissipating force field sending waves rippling in every direction.

Ryan Beck is supporting Dominique, who is close to fainting.

Lauren stares at the object, slack-jawed, then spins around to face her fiancé. "The *Popol Vuh* . . . the legend of the Hero Twins! All this time you knew . . . you knew you'd be leaving me!"

"It's his destiny." Jacob descends from a ramp located beneath the starship, Dr. Mohr in tow. Seeing his wife, the teary-eyed NASA scientist slogs through the flooded field and hugs her.

Jacob stares hard at Chaney, his azure eyes violet with anger. "I was very specific. The girl wasn't supposed to be here."

"Don't blame me," rasps the former president. "Your brother insisted."

The white-haired twin turns to his brother. "Say your good-byes, Manny. We have to board the *Balam* before the eye passes."

"I'm not going," Immanuel states.

"You have no choice."

"He said he's not going," Lauren says, stepping in between them.

Jacob ignores her. "Manny, you must trust me, there's

nothing for you here. Even if you did stay, Lilith Mabus would hunt you down, and all would be lost."

"No."

"Then you leave me no choice." Jacob slips into the nexus and grabs his twin from behind, subduing him in a full nelson as he forcibly drags him toward the starship.

Immanuel enters the zone, struggling against his over-powering foe. "Let . . . me . . . go—"

"For once in your life, trust me!"

"No!"

"Humanity's future depends upon you fulfilling your destiny—"

"You're wrong! I wasn't meant to go! Lauren loves me!"

"Lauren's as good as dead."

"What?" A tsunami of rage washes over Immanuel, drenching his muscles with adrenaline. Whirling around, he grabs Jacob's head in his hands, drops to one knee, and flips his brother over his shoulder, slamming him onto the flooded turf.

Both Hunahpu tumble free from the nexus.

Dominique reaches into the fray, separating her two sons. "Jacob, stop! Leave him be. Manny . . . my God, Manny, your eyes!"

Jacob stares at his twin. Immanuel's irises are radiating a striking azure blue, just like his own. "It's happening. He's changing—turning full Hunahpu. Manny, everything will become clear to you soon, but we have to hurry if we have any hope of rescuing Mick."

"Mick's alive?" Dominique grabs Jacob by his shoulders. "How do you know? How can you be sure?"

Immanuel takes Lauren's hand. "Jake claims he speaks to him."

"You've been speaking with your father? How? Why didn't you tell me?!"

Jacob glances over his shoulder at the approaching eye wall. "We don't have time for this, we have to hurry. The *Balam*'s force field can't manipulate the storm much longer."

"You hurry, I'm not going anywhere."

"Manny, our destiny's on *Xibalba!*"

"Yours, not mine. I was meant to stay behind. Think about it. The *Balam* should have opened for me, but it didn't."

"You weren't full Hunahpu then."

"Neither was Mick, but it opened for him."

"We don't have time for this nonsense." Jacob turns to Kurtz. "Salt, stun him!"

Kurtz shakes his head. "Manny said he wants to stay. It's his choice."

"Pep—"

"Back off, Jake. Let the kid choose."

Jacob approaches his brother, becoming desperate. "Manny, listen—please, it takes two people to resurrect our father and save the *Nephilim*. I can't do it alone."

"Then take me instead," Dominique demands.

"Mother—"

"I said, take me!"

"Impossible."

"Impossible? Don't you tell me impossible! I've kow-towed to your every whim for twenty years. I've dedicated my life to you and this . . . this Mayan mythology, all in the hopes of seeing Mick again. Now you're going to take me to see him!"

Collin Shelby hurries through a river of rainwater stream-ing down the tunnel's concrete incline. He stays close to the brick wall, remaining in the shadows, as he scans the group of people in the scope of his XE-29 sniper rifle.

Isolated at midfield . . . like shooting ducks on a pond. Uh-oh . . . what's this? He focuses on the three EMP suits worn by the two bodyguards and one of the women. *Have to use the tungsten rounds.*

Shelby loads a tungsten dart into the chamber of his ri-fle, then switches the trigger from taser fire to explosive bullets. Unlike old-fashioned bullets, these lethal projectiles contain the latest biocide, nanoswarm EPI-46, a fast-spreading, human flesh-consuming agent. Any contact ensures a lethal strike.

The UMBRA assassin steadies himself as he aims the crosshairs of his scope.

"Think about it, Jake," Immanuel pleads. "For six years you've been devising strategies for defeating the *Xibalban* sentry, and you've never won. Didn't it ever occur to you that they know we're coming, too?"

Jacob stares at his twin, pondering the thought.

"You say you've been communicating with our father. How do you know Lilith wasn't eavesdropping? Maybe that's why we lost the first battle, because Lilith was listening to Mick."

"Yes . . . it's possible."

Manny takes Lauren's hand. "You once told me Lilith was your soul mate. Well, Lauren's mine, and I'm not leaving her."

Dominique nods. "I'm coming with you, Jacob. Case closed."

Jacob turns to her. "Okay, Mother. Say your good-byes quickly."

Dominique rushes to Immanuel, hugging him as hard as she can.

"Ma . . . thank you. I love you."

"I love you, Manny, I love you, too." She hugs Lauren. "You take care of him."

"I will."

Jacob hands Dr. Mohr a microdisk. "This will allow you access to everything you'll need. I don't know what's going to happen from this point on, but all of you are fugitives. Go now, before Lilith finds you." He looks at the big African-American bodyguard. "Take care of my brother, Pep. Lilith won't rest until she finds him."

Ryan Beck nods. "Do what you were born to do. We'll watch over them."

Jacob embraces Manny, whispering into his ear. "Remember the young lady named Bright, whose speed was far faster than light. She went out one day, in a relative way, and returned the previous night."

"Why are you telling me this?"

"Because your actions today will create a new fork in the road of space-time. Where that road leads is up to you. I hope you're ready to face its consequences."

"It's what I choose."

The edge of the storm reaches the stadium, its 196-mile-an-hour winds causing the folded-down arena seats to flap open and closed, the sound echoing across the empty arena like a flock of cackling geese.

Immanuel nods at the *Balam*. "Go find our father."

Jacob takes Dominique by the crook of her arm and leads her into the starship, the portal resealing behind them.

Waves form on the flooded field. The wind howls in Immanuel's ears as the starship's engines power up. Salt grabs the Mohrs, Beck takes Chaney. "Move! Everyone in the limo!"

Immanuel turns to Lauren, who is smiling at him, tears in her eyes. "I love you, Immanuel Gabriel."

"I love you." He reaches for her—

—a scarlet explosion splattering his face. He falls backward, Lauren collapsing against his chest in a shattered heap.

Kurtz wheels around, his smart-glasses instantly retracing the line of fire. Zooming in on the target, he fires, the laser burst from his rifle igniting inside the tunnel, vaporizing Collin Shelby into a wisp of organic ash.

Manny holds Lauren, his fiancé's life gushing from the still-expanding scarlet gap in her waist. "Lauren! Lauren!"

She glances up at him, unable to speak, her face pale and drained.

"Oh, God, Lauren, don't leave me!"

The hazel eyes glass over. The pulse in her neck stops beating.

"Oh, God! Oh, God, help!"

Kurtz scans the stadium with his smart-glasses. "We're sitting ducks out here. Pep, grab Manny."

Lauren Beckmeyer's remains continue disintegrating in blood-soaked clumps. Immanuel releases her detached upper torso and stands in rigid defiance against Ryan Beck's grip and the blasting wind, his fists balled, tears streaming from his azure blue eyes as he looks up and screams, "Ja—cob!"

The gold starship continues its majestic ascent into the swirling heavens until it disappears into the diminishing blue eye of the storm—

—leaving him behind.

A wisp of thought, in the consciousness of existence.

The site of the gold-paneled starship on that distant moon did something to me.

Michael Gabriel's anguished soul seemed to cry out to me for your mother, or maybe it was Bill Raby's tortured heart, refusing to go on without his Jude.

Whatever it was, I had finally had enough. Aiming a high-energy taser at my head, I pulled the trigger—

—and awoke!

Bill Raby was gone. I was Michael Gabriel again, still aboard the Guardian's pod, only my vessel was no longer moving through space, I was hovering over the alien moon.

Moments later the pod landed in the domed subterranean facility.

Before me stood the Guardian survivors, behind them the Balam.

The wormhole . . .

The time loop . . .

Am I conscious, or is this all a dream?

Am I Michael Gabriel or Bill Raby?

Where am I? On a moon somewhere in the Orion Belt, or

lying unconscious in solitary confinement back in my cell in Massachusetts?

Michael Gabriel? One Hunahpu?

Bill Raby? Osiris?

Jacob, are you there? Are you real, or are you part of the delusions?

Michael?

Dominique?

God, why must you torture me? Why must you . . .

The white fog! Two pinpoints . . . angry violet eyes, stare at me from within the nexus haze.

"One Hunahpu . . ."

Her shadow appears, her form pushing forward . . . co-coa skin . . . so intoxicating. The Abomination! How could I have let my guard down?

"Come closer, One Hunahpu, so that I might taste your soul."

"No, please . . . God! God help me!

"God? God is like eternity, his existence cold and lonely. Bathe in my heat, Michael, and let me thaw your mind. Crawl into my womb as I entwine your being. Inhale my breath as I caress your lonely soul."

No! I am Michael Gabriel. I am One Hunahpu. I am in control. I control my mind, not the Abomination. My mind is a safe haven.

"The Guardian have deceived you, Michael. I am not your enemy, I am your salvation."

. . . I will focus on the echoes of my mind and not the coos of the Abomination. I shall control my mind, and the Abomination cannot hurt me. I shall retell my tale to my sons, and occupy my thoughts—"

"No more tales. Our destiny together begins anew as we await the arrival of your sons."

Boys, can you hear me? Jacob? Stay away! The Abomination knows you're coming!

"The cosmos has turned a deaf ear, Michael. Now, there is only us."

No! God is out there, God will help me!

"God? God is dead, Michael—

—a mere wisp of thought, in the consciousness of existence . . ."

PART 7

■■■■■■■■■■■■■■

AFTERLIFE

God is testing us, to see if we can
kill the Satan within us . . .
—FROM NIGHT, BY ELIE WIESEL

Darkness cannot drive out darkness,
only light can do that.
—MARTIN LUTHER KING JR.

Each of us makes our own prisons,
and each of us has the ability to set ourselves free.
—JULIUS GABRIEL

Love is all you need . . .
—THE BEATLES

36

The 722-foot-long starship cruiser, *Balam,* is divided into two main decks. In the lower deck, located midships to stern, is the propulsion chamber and its twin power cores, with extensive feeder assemblies and circuits growing out of the bulkheads and deck. Designed into this compartment is the *Balam*'s massive solar plant, with links to the ship's recycling water supply with distillers, gravity mats, and a myriad of machinery responsible for the starship's force field and weapons system.

At the heart of the vessel is the *Balam*'s central processing cortex and its immense biochemical brain. Sealed within an immense chamber of gelatinous liquid, this beehive of nanocircuits crackles with energy. Neuroclusters fire in the isolated darkness like a million fireflies. Fluid-filled sensory vacuoles branch out from the biochemical organ, interconnecting every neuroprocessing center within the ship.

The rest of the lower deck is devoted to the hyperdrive system and "scoop" that channels tachyon particles from space into the vent-style gills located along the ship's wings, essentially "pulling" the *Balam* through the cosmos.

Embedded in every bulkhead, ceiling, and deck are artificial gravity node emitters, set to normal Earth gravity. Inertia dampeners protect flight crew operators from possible injuries caused by sudden acceleration, deceleration, or rapid changes in direction. Voice controls in each room can adjust ambient light, humidity, and temperature controls.

The upper deck is constructed to assure passenger comfort and survival. Hydroponic vats, biological waste treatment converters, and chemical storage containers needed to produce crops are located in an aft hangar, along with storage bays and a series of "autophysician" pods that look like sarcophagi, something Dominique remains too claustrophobic to use. A main corridor leads forward into the centrally located "habitat," a 230-foot-long chamber that contains a kitchen, bathing pods, toilets, workstations, virtual reality facilities, exercise, and sleeping pods.

The onion-shaped control center is located upper deck forward. Escape chutes leading to smaller landing/escape pods are situated throughout the vessel.

Dominique Gabriel opens her eyes. The padded "curtains" covering the portals in her sleep chamber have parted, allowing filtered sunlight to brighten the compartment. Reaching across her body, she unfastens the Velcro straps of her sleep suit, which cause her to adhere to the wall.

The dull headache returns the moment she floats free.

Dominique has been traveling in space for two days, twenty-two hours, and eighteen minutes. She has been suffering repeated bouts of spacesickness and an aching lower back, anxiety, sleep deprivation, an inability to focus, and an almost constant dull headache.

Her diet of freeze-dried rations has only added to her irritability.

"Computer, activate gravity mats."

A moment of nausea as her Earth weight returns, landing her awkwardly on both feet. She groans as the menstrual pain returns.

"Computer, locate my son."

JACOB GABRIEL IS ASLEEP IN HIS POD.

* * *

Dominique enters the habitat where her son is sleeping. During her first "night" in space, she had tried to sleep in a similar pod, but the coffinlike bed was too confining.

Hearing a muffled scream, she rushes over to one of the sleeping pods, where her son is in the throes of a terrible nightmare.

"Jake?" She bangs on the tinted plastic lid, then struggles to open it.

Inside, her son thrashes violently, as if being attacked by a swarm of bees.

Dominique yanks open the cover, grabbing him by his wrists. "Jake—wake up! Jacob!"

The azure blue eyes flash open—absolutely terrified. He grips his mother's biceps, bruising them within his powerful fingers.

"Jake, it's okay . . . Jacob, you're hurting me . . . Jacob!"

"Huh?" He gazes up at her and stops thrashing.

Dominique helps him out of the pod. "Are you all right?"

He nods weakly, then collapses into a deck-mounted "nourishment" chair. "Computer, 20 cc's supplement 4-F." Placing the feeding tube into his mouth, he closes his eyes, sucking the clear liquid through the two-foot-long pressurized straw.

"Another nightmare?"

"It was a vision. A final warning from my father."

She kneels in front of him. "Tell me."

He shakes his head.

"Jacob . . . please—"

The white-haired twin looks up at his mother through gallows' eyes. "I was deep inside the nexus, enshrouded in heavy white fog. My physical body seemed to have left me, there was only my mind's eye. Two violet specks appeared . . . two eyes, glowing at me from within the thick haze. It was Lilith. She whispered into my mind, 'Jacob, we've been waiting.' And then I saw her.

"She was so intoxicating, Mother, like exquisite poison. 'Come to me, Jacob,' she said. My mind screamed no, but then I felt her touch, and it was beyond any ecstasy I've ever known. I could feel her warm breath in my ear. My nerve impulses tingled as she caressed the pleasure centers of my mind, and her nectar spread over me like a soothing balm.

"I could have stayed there forever. I could have let her drain me, dying a happy man. But then these blue specks appeared—a pair of Hunahpu eyes observing me from beyond the fog.

"It was my father. 'You have allowed the serpent into your garden,' he said, 'and once more you've been deceived.' Then the fog lifted, and I saw the Abomination for what she really was.

"She was part-human, part–demonic creature. Her skin had bleached ghostly white, her long hair was black and knotty. The corneas of her eyes were violet-red, her pupils like a viper. But it was her mouth that made my soul retch—a vertical slit, like a fleshy trap—like a vagina, Mother, only it was filled with hundreds of these sickening stubbly black teeth.

"Blood was smeared across the monster's unholy slit . . . my blood! She stood before me, an obscenity of humanity. Her hideous lips spread apart, inhaling my consciousness inside her orifice, and I knew I was in Hell.

"And though I had no body, I could still feel her heat melting the flesh from my bones, and though I had no nose, I could still smell the putrid scent of demon's vomit, and though I had no mouth, my tortured mind screamed over and over as the Abomination entwined her naked limbs deeper around my mind, and ground her rancid groin into my being."

"My God . . ."

Jacob wipes tears from his glazed over eyes. "I was drowning in her sulfuric maelstrom, ranting and raging and screaming as if caught in a swirling pool of lava, then suddenly I was in an oasis of calm. Somehow Mick had reached in and saved me, pulling me to safety. I could still feel the Abomination clawing at my back, tempting me to look at her. And even though I had just escaped her Hell, it was all I could do to keep myself from turning again.

"My father pulled me into his arms and held me, whispering that I am the true Hunahpu, the *Nephilim* messiah, and that he would be there for me when I needed him."

Dominique wipes a tear. "How did he look?"

"Weary. And then he faded back into the white light."

Warning bells sound, snapping Jacob to attention. "Computer, report."

WARPED SPACE DETECTED, COURSE TWO-ZERO-THREE MARK SIX. TIME TO INTERCEPT: FOUR MINUTES, TWENTY SECONDS.

"Origin of warped space?"

GRAVITATIONAL RIPPLE.

"The wormhole?" Dominique asks.

Jacob nods. "Computer, plot and execute intercept course."

She follows Jacob forward into the control room.

"Computer, activate forward screen."

A three-dimensional image of space appears on the wall before them. Located in the upper right hand corner of the screen, growing in size as it travels from east to west, is the frightening scarlet-ringed aperture of the wormhole.

Jacob stares at the object. "I think you'd better strap in."

Dominique climbs into one of the pilot chairs, which instantly conforms to her physique.

The mouth of the vortex appears before them, radiating like a swirling, orange-red alien moon.

ACTIVATING EXOTIC-MATTER BEACONS.

The image of the scarlet orifice blurs as the negative energy field of the starship's exotic-matter force field carves an invisible path before them.

Jacob pulls himself into his command chair as the wormhole's mouth grows to occupy the entire forward screen. "Hold on!"

The sleek starship crosses the wormhole's threshold, the

cosmic tunnel's intense gravitational forces instantly sucking the vessel down its throat, propelling it through its conduit.

Dominique's arms are suctioned to her chair, the intense gravitational turbulence shaking the vessel hard enough to loosen her back teeth. She bites down, her eyes barely able to focus on the forward screen.

They are rocketing through an iridescent sky-blue funnel, rimmed by a strange bloodred hue. At the very center of the image is a black dot . . . growing larger . . . larger—

And suddenly they are flung free, hurtling through space into an unrecognizable sector of the Galaxy.

Before them—an alien silvery-red planet.

Dominique whispers. "*Xibalba . . .*"

Jacob nods. "Computer, reactivate main engines. Plot a course for the larger of the two moons."

PROBES HAVE BEEN LAUNCHED FROM THE LUNAR SURFACE, APPROACHING GRAVITY RIPPLE.

Activate aft screen."

The image of space changes. Appearing on-screen—the wormhole's exit, bathed in emerald green. Moving into position along the perimeter of the orifice are hundreds of school-bus-sized probes, each emitting a luminescent blue beacon.

Dominique stares at the image on screen. "What's happening?"

"Someone's stabilizing the wormhole, preventing its gravitational field from collapsing."

"The Guardian?"

"Let's hope. Computer, establish orbit around the planet's larger moon. Prepare an escape pod to take us to the lunar surface."

ABOARD THE BALAM'S ESCAPE POD

The twenty-seven-foot escape pod circles the lunar base, then descends to what appears to be a docking berth.

Jacob clutches his head, his eyes squeezed shut.

"Jake, what's wrong?"

"Voices . . . so many voices . . . probing my mind telepathically—"

A written message appears across the pod's main viewing screen.

WELCOME HOME.

The pod touches down with a *hiss*. Alien hydraulics rotate the vessel into position.

Without warning, the entire landing pad and escape pod plummet hundreds of feet below the surface.

Dominique grips her seat, her stomach jumping with the sudden descent, then they are slowing, braking on a cushion of air.

The pod's outer hatch yawns open, revealing a massive subterranean facility.

Standing before them in absolute silence are hundreds of humanoids, seven feet tall, all possessing silky white hair, bright azure blue eyes, and elongated skulls.

Jacob and his mother are escorted down a long corridor to a private chamber. Waiting for them inside are three Guardian elders. Two are males, possessing white hair and matching silky beards. The female's hair is also snow white, her luminescent eyes holding a maternal quality. All three are wearing skintight biopneumatic bodysuits, entwined with biochemical capillary-like vessels pulsating with energy.

The older of the two males, dressed in a black bodysuit, speaks aloud, solely for Dominique's benefit.

"I represent First Clan."

The women, wearing gray, states. "I represent Second Clan."

The younger male, in a white jumpsuit, steps forward. "I represent Third Clan. It is an honor to meet you, First-Mother, though your presence was not anticipated."

"Who are you?"

The younger male holds up two fingers. Balanced on each fingertip is a dime-sized, paper-thin device. "These are bionetic implants. All you wish to know will be downloaded."

Before Dominique can object, the younger male touches the device to her left temple—

—inhaling her consciousness into darkness.

Where is Immanuel?
He refused to join me.
Illogical. He was programmed to be here.
The Hunahpu gene remained dormant for too long. He possessed free will.
You cannot succeed without him.
My father will assist me.
Your father is lost.

Dominique forces open a heavy eye.

She is lying on a free-floating couch, the room spinning in her head. The three bizarre-looking humanoids are standing before Jacob, their eyes closed as they communicate with him telepathically.

"Speak out loud!"

They turn slowly to face her, their glowing eyes now open.

"Who are—" As her lips purse to form the words of her first question, a wave of information instantaneously washes over her mind.

The Guardian . . . survivors of an Earth holocaust . . . destined for Mars Colony . . . twelve spaceships diverted through wormhole . . . arrived on Xibalba as Homo Sapiens . . . evolved into transhumans through retrotransposon manipulation . . .

Dominique grips the sides of her head where the neural implants have been embedded.

"Stop," Jacob protests, "you're overwhelming her."

The female transhuman blinks, causing the neural transmission to cease.

Jacob kneels by his mother's side. "Are you all right?"

Dominique nods.

"We will communicate aloud," the female commands.

"I want to see Mick. Take me to him."

"One Hunahpu is long gone," the elder male coldly states. "Our concern now is for the *Nephilim*."

Dominique stands. "I don't believe you."

"Michael Gabriel failed," voices the younger male.

"You don't know even where he is, do you?"

"We know," the elder male retorts.

"No . . . you're lying, in fact, your whole brotherhood is one big lie! This lunar outpost, the *Balam* . . . none of it's yours, you only inherited the technology, you don't really understand it. You're like a bunch of children operating a television. You can program it and adjust the volume, but you don't know the first thing about how it really works, do you?"

Jacob looks at the Guardian elders and smiles. "My mother may not be Hunahpu, but don't underestimate her, or her bond to my father. Tell her everything."

"What you say is true," the female Guardian admits. "The *Balam* was here when we arrived, we still don't know its origins."

The younger male steps forward. "Like you, we once lived on Earth as *Homo sapiens*. But our species was threatened by a great cataclysm—a super volcano, whose imminent eruption would cast Earth into a species-ending ice age. Some of us were chosen to begin our lives anew on Mars. Ours was the last group that managed to escape Earth before the caldera erupted. On our journey to the Red Planet, our twelve ships were seized by the wormhole, which deposited our ships in this time and place."

Dominique covers her mouth. "Wait a minute . . . are you saying everyone on Earth will die? When will this happen? How soon?"

"Less than a decade after the Hero Twins' twentieth year."

"Oh my God."

"The planet we now orbit was once inhabited by an advanced race of humans. Before we arrived, this transhuman culture made a breakthrough in human evolution. By linking their minds into a collective consciousness, they were able to create a resonant 'supermind,' one that would allow them to transcend the physical world into the spiritual. This discovery ultimately divided the culture in two. Those who sought to abandon their physical bodies in order to walk in God's shadow eventually evolved into a posthumanoid species. Those who opposed this evolutionary blasphemy abandoned the planet."

The female takes over. "The physical and spiritual realms are connected by a nexus—a transspatial existence that bridges the gap between our physical dimension and the spiritual worlds. By creating a collective mind, the transhumans could bypass physical death and enter the spiritual realm using high-frequency psychotronic harmonics. That gave them access to the nexus, but still prevented them from entering the higher spiritual realms they sought. In order to gain access, they needed another lifeform—a host species—one capable of reproducing these psychotronic harmonics within the nexus itself. From genetic catalogues, the transhumans selected a species once indigenous to the planet. Using advances in gene splicing and cybernetics, they began cloning and genetically manipulating generations of these biological creatures to serve their own selfish needs."

A volumetric image appears before them. It depicts a crater-shaped sea of silvery, almost metallic liquid. Moving just below the surface are immense serpentine creatures, their broad backs churning the undulating broth.

Dominique's eyes widen. "It's the creature—the one that rose from the Gulf of Mexico, the one Mick destroyed in Chichén Itzá."

"Tezcatilpoca," Jacob whispers. "The Mayan name for 'smoking mirror.'"

"The mirror into the soul," the female adds. "These docile, intelligent beasts were genetically altered and enhanced to exist on both sides of the 'mirror of existence.' It is their harmonics that summoned the wormhole. Their posthuman masters used the Tezcatilpoca to pass through the nexus into the spiritual world. Our fellow castaways— our own fallen brothers and sisters—followed them down this same dark path. Now the vanquished cry out to us for salvation. They must be saved."

Jacob circles the female elder. "The *Nephilim,* the Fallen Ones. These are your fellow castaways?"

"Yes. All evolved into transhumans within years after being exposed to the planet's water supply."

Dominique fights to remain in control. "What does any of this have to do with Mick, or my sons?"

"Michael and your sons carry the Hunahpu gene."

"I know that! What I don't know is what a damn Hunahpu is."

The female answers, her motherly demeanor intended to soothe. "Before they escaped from *Xibalba,* our Guardian founders took samples of posthuman DNA. The samples were taken onboard the *Balam* when it journeyed through the wormhole, chasing after the *Xibalban* transport vessel carrying the creature. The Hunaphu are a *Homo sapiens* bloodline genetically enhanced with posthuman DNA."

The older male takes over. "The Abomination's plan was to send one of the Tezcatilpoca on a transport ship back through the wormhole to Earth, where the creature's presence would create a cosmic bridge between both worlds and time periods. Fearing the Abomination would attempt to lead her people to old Earth, the Guardian downed the vessel, only they failed to kill the creature."

"Fortunately," Jacob says, "my father, possessing Hunahpu blood, was able to circumvent their plan."

"I don't understand," Dominique says, looking to the elder Guardian male. "How can Lilith be Hunahpu? I thought Mick was your chosen one?"

"Michael Gabriel was only one of several hundred possible genetic anomalies the Guardian hoped would evolve in time to activate the *Balam*'s weapon system. Lilith's great-uncle found a way to manipulate the Hunaphu bloodline. This mutation causes a deeply rooted schizophrenia that was passed on to Lilith."

"And where is Mick? What happened to him?"

"Michael and our fellow colonists are trapped in a netherworld, a bubble of existence created by Devlin Mabus."

"Devlin?"

"Lilith's son, a pure posthuman, very powerful, conceived from two Hunahpu parents."

Jacob sits, suddenly light-headed.

"Who's the father?" Dominique asks. "Jake?"

"I don't know, Mother. Yes, it's possible. For that matter, it could be Manny or another Hunahpu in our time."

The three Guardian elders go silent, their minds exchanging thoughts at light speed.

Dominique loses patience. "I don't care about this Devlin or Lilith, I came here to find Mick. Tell me what happened to him and how I can reach him."

The younger male is first to speak. "Michael Gabriel journeyed into Devlin's realm to save the *Nephilim,* but Lilith and her son had been forewarned. He remains trapped in the netherworld. Lilith uses his light to control her followers and keep them in line. Michael's light attracts them like a moth to flame. It gives them hope, but Michael cannot escape. Now, only the combined strength of the Hero Twins can free One Hunahpu and the Fallen Ones."

The elder Guardian male looks hard at Jacob. "Which means our mission has failed. Your brother should have made the journey, not First-Mother."

Dominique ignores the remark. "How many years have passed since Mick's arrival?"

"Just over a *Xibalban* century," the female answers. "Approximately 114 Earth years."

"Oh . . . God, how's that possible?"

The female takes her hand. "Dominique, Michael hasn't aged in a physical sense. His body remains in suspended animation. It's his mind that is being tortured."

"Tortured?"

"By the Abomination. She is a leech to his soul."

Jacob stands. "I came here to save my father and rescue the *Nephilim*. Tell me what I have to do?"

"You may already be too late." The older male points a finger.

A volumetric display activates. The astrotopographic projection races through space, approaching a monstrous blazing red fireball of a star. As the red supergiant grows closer, its surface cools in color to that of a soft lightbulb—

—revealing the presence of a second star lurking behind its mass. The smaller star, a white dwarf, is under tremendous turmoil, its surface bloating.

"The red supergiant will go supernova in thirty-one hours, seventeen minutes. When the event happens, it will disperse massive doses of radiation and energy across this sector of the Galaxy. Nothing on this moon or the planet will survive."

"What will you do?" Dominique asks.

The image changes, zooming past *Xibalba* to focus upon the planet's smaller moon—an immense potato-shaped starship. "This damaged transport was left behind by the transhuman culture that vacated the planet. Our scientists have effected repairs. With the wormhole's passage now secured, we'll be able to use the vessel to escape before the star explodes."

"We're going back to Earth," states the female. "Back through time to save *Homo sapiens* from the caldera.".

Dominique perks up. "You can do that? Change history?"

"It's possible," the younger male answers. "Unfortunately, Jacob cannot possibly hope to defeat Lilith and Devlin alone."

"He won't be alone," Dominique says. "I'll be with him."

"You?" The male elder shakes his head. "You are not Hunahpu. You're not even a transhuman. Devlin and his followers would crush you like a bug."

The female Guardian holds up her hand. "Don't rush to judgment. First-Mother's presence in the Underworld may actually confuse the Abomination and her son, who are still expecting both Hero Twins. Once Dominique reaches the Dark Road, her mind will remain cloaked to all transhuman telepathy. It may present her an advantage."

"Advantage?" The elder Guardian's eyes blaze at his female comrade in disbelief. "They'll never make it past the Dark Road without Immanuel. Or have you forgotten the *tlachtli*?"

Dominique looks puzzled.

The younger male explains. "The entrance that leads into Devlin's netherworld is guarded by a band of sociopaths. Lilith has convinced these transhumans that they are reincarnations of cannibals who lived thousands of years ago in ancient Mesoamerica. These Devil worshipers exist only to serve the Abomination and her son. To enter Devlin's netherworld, you must defeat these warriors in a game of *tlachtli,* and the battle is to the death."

Jacob turns to his mother. "The battle in which you've seen me train for the last seven years."

"And what about weapons?" Dominique asks. "Can't we just shoot them with an ion cannon or something?"

"Modern weapons do not function within the spiritual realm," the female answers. "The laws of physics as you know them do not apply in the Land of the Damned."

"One of our transport ships will take you to the surface facility where the last remaining Tezcatilpoca is penned," the younger male says. "Jacob, use your Hunahpu powers to summon the beast. The creature will allow you access beyond the nexus into the Abomination's netherworld. The Guardian brotherhood have programmed the serpent to safeguard a weapon, one we believe is capable of destroying the Abomination and her son."

"My sword," Jacob tells his mother. "I've seen all of these things in my visions."

"Remember," the female cautions, "you only have thirty hours before we must depart through the wormhole. If you haven't returned by then, don't bother coming back. The radiation from the supernova will kill you."

Dominique allows the female Guardian to assist her into a black temperature-regulated exoskeleton bodysuit.

"This suit was designed by the transhumans to access the nexus. It should allow you to survive in Devlin's realm as well. As you move, the battle armor and its neural connections will collect and recycle your body excretions, providing you with water. Drink through this extraction tube. Attached to your back is a thin, flexible air tank and oxygen processor, which supplies air through this nostril tube. There is no oxygen in purgatory; this unit creates your air supply by extracting oxygen from the CO_2."

Dominique finishes dressing, then joins Jacob, who is already wearing his white body armor.

The Guardian lead them to a launch chamber.

Lined up in rows along the chamber's periphery are dozens of two-man transport ships, their bows encased in launch tubes angled at forty-five degrees.

"One of our transports will take you directly to the Tezcatilpoca genetics site," the younger male explains. "May God's highest light shine upon you both."

"Let's not keep my father waiting any longer." Jacob climbs into the two-seat pod, a flat, triangular-shaped vessel, twenty feet long from the tip of its bulbous nose cone to the end of its propulsion device.

Dominique straps herself into the seat next to him.

The entry of the vessel reseals, activating the ship's controls. A forward screen switches on, presenting them with an exterior image.

Stars and the blackness of space loom beyond the tunnel-like launch tube.

Docking clamps release. The engine activates, its deep thrum causing Dominique's skin to tingle.

Expelling a blast of energy, the transport accelerates through the launch tube, leaping into space. They pass high over the lunar base and the barren surface of the moonscape until the entire forward screen is filled with the silvery red world of *Xibalba*.

There is no sign of the *Balam*.

Dominique's heart pounds with trepidation as she stares at the surface of the alien world. *He's down there somewhere, suffering from an eternity of mental anguish. Will he recognize me? Is his mind even capable of a sane thought?*

WARNING: ENTERING PLANET'S ATMOSPHERE.

The transport plunges through dark magenta atmospheric storm clouds. Moss-covered volcanic rock appears beneath the overcast sky. In the distance is a continent-sized mass floating several hundred feet in the air.

"New Eden," Jacob says. "The habitat abandoned by the original transhuman culture."

"Incredible . . ." Dominique whispers. "But who were these transhumans? What happened to them?"

"I don't know."

Coming into view on the shadowed horizon is a silvery breeding pond the size of Florida's Lake Okeechobee. The transport follows the artificial shoreline for several minutes, then lands next to an arena-sized complex.

The domed roof of the facility has been shattered, destroyed long ago by a tremendous force.

Jacob turns to his mother. "I can handle this. Stay here where it's safe."

She unbuckles her harness. "I'm coming with you."

"Fine. At least plug your air hose into your nostrils and set your regulator. Remember, there's no oxygen on *Xibalba*, just carbon dioxide."

Breathers in place, they exit the vessel and head for the lake's edge. Jacob points to the domed facility on their right. "The posthumans' genetics lab."

"Yes, but what happened to it?"

"I don't know, but I get the feeling there's a lot the Guardian prefer we didn't know." Jacob stops at the silvery shoreline and closes his eyes.

Several minutes pass, and then, a mile out, the once-tranquil surface begins to froth.

Dominique watches an enormous wake build, rising higher as it moves inland.

"Okay, you handle it." She hurries back to the pod as the head of a monstrous alien being emerges, its viperous head dripping silvery ooze as it looms thirty feet over Jacob.

The genetically enhanced biological resembles a monstrous alien serpent, the creature's girth as wide as a train, its skull as large as the mixer on a cement truck. The beast regards Jacob with two of its cybernetic eyes—vertical slits of gold, surrounded by incandescent crimson corneas.

A thunderous snort causes Jacob to jump backward as the serpent expels a stench-laden breath through its synthetic nostrils. The frightening jowls part, revealing rows of ebony, scalpel-sharp teeth.

Jacob returns the creature's gaze, refusing to yield. A surreal moment passes as man and beast contemplate one another—

—and an overwhelming sense of déjà vu washes over Jacob's brain.

The suddenly docile creature lowers its head to the ground, keeping its right eye focused on the twin.

Jacob stands. He steps forward, placing both palms against the creature's oily, scalelike emerald green feathers, registering the being's deep, intense reverberations of breath—

—as a white haze envelops his mind . . .

Jacob's consciousness soars across time and space.

He remote-views the Nile River.

Moves inside the hidden chambers of the Great Pyramid of Giza.

Enters the Queen's Chamber.

Gazes up through a viewing shaft, its thirty-nine-degree angle aimed precisely at the brightest star in the evening sky . . . Sirius.

"Jake!"

The sudden intrusion startles him. He opens his eyes, his ears buzzing with energy.

To his surprise, he is lying on his back. His mother is by his side, the alien sky now filled with stars, the red supergiant directly overhead.

The great head of the alien serpent remains onshore, the rest of its 110-foot-long body still submerged in the exotic silvery liquid.

"Jake, what happened? You've been unconscious for hours. Are you okay?"

He sits up, still in a daze. Dominique notices that his entire body is trembling.

"My God . . ." He stares at the creature, tears forming in his azure blue eyes.

"Jake? What is it?"

"Those bastards . . . those manipulating *fubishitting* sons of bitches . . . they lied to us."

"Who lied? The Guardian?"

"Yes. Everything they told my father about *Xibalba*, everything they programmed into the *Balam*'s astrology charts ... it was all one big calculated lie. This planet isn't in the Orion Belt, and that red giant out there isn't Betelguese ... it's Sirius. And that white dwarf, it's Sirius-B!"

"What's the difference?"

"Don't you get it, Mother, we're not hundreds of light-years from Earth, we're on Earth!"

"What?"

"*Xibalba is* Earth ... only Earth hundreds of thousands ... maybe millions of years in our future!"

"No ... Jake how can that be? Look at the red sky—"

"The atmosphere's changed, the dust particles scattering light differently."

"But there are no oceans."

"They must have evaporated. Maybe it was the loss of the ozone layer, maybe even a massive greenhouse effect. The seas could still be frozen beneath the planet's surface ... same thing happened on Mars." He stands, then reaches out to touch the serpent. "And these poor creatures ... do you know what they once were?"

She shakes her head, still in shock.

"They were whales, mother, whales that were cloned and genetically altered to serve their posthuman masters."

"I ... I don't understand."

"Toothed whales evolved the ability to echolocate. The posthumans used this ability to tap into the nexus. They enslaved the whales ... altered their genetic pattern, then rewired the poor beasts with cybernetic implants. The mammal's ability to communicate in harmonics enabled the posthumans beyond the nexus into the spiritual realm."

Dominique rubs at her temple. "Jake, if this is Earth, then who were the transhumans and posthumans?"

"They're us. They're what happens to *Homo sapiens* in a million years. They're the ones who built the floating city and this genetics lab and sea." He spreads his arms out. "Take a good look around you, Mother, this is the future of the late, great planet Earth."

"One future," she reminds him. "If the caldera triggered this, then maybe the Guardian can stop it."

He nods. "Father said only a Hunahpu could prevent the second cataclysm."

Dominique stares at the beast, seeing it as if for the first time. "The creature seems to know you."

"It accessed my mind . . . my memories back on Earth. It knows I mean it no harm. It's here to take us to Mick." Jacob helps her to her feet. "Don't be scared."

"I am scared; just do what you have to do."

He nods, then closes his eyes, pushing his mind to enter the nexus, allowing him to communicate with the beast.

Dominique's heart skips a beat as the viper's head stirs, its gaping jaws hyperextending open before them, exposing hideous ebony fangs, surrounded by hundreds of needle-sharp teeth.

And then a second viperous head appears, identical but smaller, jutting outward telescopically to protrude from the mouth of the first.

Jacob and his mother step back as a third and final head pushes out from the mouth of the second, all three jaws locking in place.

Rotating inside the orifice is a cylinder of energy, a cosmic conduit of space-time, running from the serpent's outstretched jaws and through its torso, down into the silvery waters of the artificial lagoon.

Hand in hand, Jacob and Dominique step over the bottom rows of teeth, entering the serpent's mouth.

The creature's jaws close behind them, the third head retracting into the mouth of the second, leaving them in absolute darkness.

And then a white fog appears and Jacob hears the unified thoughts of the Guardian collective.

JACOB, FULFILL YOUR DESTINY.

The fog seems to come alive, shimmering, as it draws in upon itself—

—materializing into a sword.

Jacob grasps the double-edged three-foot-long blade by its hilt. "Just like in my dreams."

Dominique registers a nauseating sensation of something tugging at her internal organs, as if her intestines are being unraveled. She squeezes her eyes shut, as the funnel of energy seems to suddenly suck them forward, though they are not actually moving.

Sensing the light, she reopens her eyes.

The squeamish feeling is gone. They are no longer in the serpent's mouth.

Jacob and Dominique find themselves standing in an arena, a replica of an ancient Mayan Ball Court. The I-shaped field is covered in a sandy lead gray silicon soil, the long, parallel east and western walls composed of metal plates, giving the complex a gloomy, futuristic industrial effect.

The alien sky is a molten vermilion, obscured by choking charcoal gray clouds, like smoke from a petroleum inferno. As their watering eyes adjust to the tremendous 120-degree Fahrenheit heat, they notice it is not a sky, but a simmering subterranean ceiling, located a good mile over-head.

To their right, situated atop the forty-foot-high eastern wall, twelve feet above the giant steel vertically oriented goal ring, is a small temple. Seated upon a throne that overlooks the playing field is a tall human with elongated head, the leader of Lilith's band of sadistic killers.

The transhuman's flesh is covered in gray silicon dust, his face concealed behind the mask of a gaping serpent's head. A trail of green feathers runs down his broad bare back.

The leader begins chanting in an ancient tongue, his words echoing throughout the steel, silicon-dusty arena.

Jacob turns, detecting movement at the far end of the enclosed ball court. The second mouth of the serpent beckons at the base of the Mayan structure known as the Temple of the Bearded Man.

Moving out from the open mouth and into the arena—a tribe of gray-skinned transhuman warriors.

Unlike the holographic combatants, Jacob knows these beings are quite real, very unpredictable, and far more dangerous. They are tall, each over seven feet, with elongated skulls and well-muscled bodies that exceed 260 pounds.

Jaundiced yellow eyes glow from behind their ceremonial death masks. Six-inch spikes cover their elbows and knees. The warriors carry a variety of weapons: steel spears and daggers, spiked balls on chains, and body armament featuring sharp claws fastened across the knuckles.

Snorting behind their ceremonial masks, they line up facing Jacob beneath the eastern goal, their leering eyes focusing on him.

Dominique inhales deeply through her nostril tubes and regulator, desperate to clear her head, hoping she will awaken from the nightmare.

Jacob scans the arena, all too aware that his mother is the chink in his armor. *I need to find a place to isolate her . . .*

From his perch, the masked leader raises a round object above his head.

The warriors howl, bellowing an animal-like scream.

The leader tosses the object into the arena.

Game ball . . .

The severed head strikes the hardened soil like a coconut, bounces twice, then rolls awkwardly before stopping at Dominique's feet.

She looks down and screams.

Jacob catches her as she faints.

The head is Mick's.

The warrior's hoot and holler, their bellowing laughs echoing throughout the metallic ball court.

Jacob stares at his father's head. "Jesus . . . no—"

Mick's eyes open, their rolling gaze maniacal. The mouth parts to speak. "Who is it? Who's out there?"

Jacob hears his voice say. "It's your son. Jacob."

"Jacob?" A deep wail rises from Mick's mouth.

Before the twin can react, two of the silicon-skinned warriors step forward. From behind their masks they expel a bloodcurdling bellow.

"No . . . no . . . no . . ." Jacob detaches the regulator from his shoulder harness and pops it in his mouth, breathing deeply. *Refocus! Remember the story of the Hero Twins. The Death God and his minions will try to fool you. This is not your father, it's an aberration . . . a ruse!"*

Using the top of his boot, Jacob flips the skull-ball several feet off the ground, then steps forward like a soccer goalie and kicks the head as far downfield as he can.

One of the warrior's gives chase. Another runs toward the twin and his mother.

Tossing Dominique over his shoulder, Jacob sprints to the far end of the eastern wall and the hidden stairwell he knows will lead him to the leader's temple. He ascends the narrow steps three at a time, the sword in his right hand.

Waiting for him at the summit is the serpent-masked leader, armed with a spiked ball and chain.

Jacob releases his mother, then bounds up the remaining steps.

The spiked ball hurtles downward.

Jacob avoids the blow, then lashes upward with the sword, severing the transhuman's arm just below the elbow.

The warrior cries out, staring at his amputated, simmering-hot limb in shock, never seeing the looping shimmer of blade that lops off his head.

Jacob kneels beside his mother. He shakes her awake, then spits out the breather so he can speak. "Mother, stay here!" Grabbing the sword, he bounds back down the narrow stairwell, returning the regulator to his mouth.

Six of the masked goons bull-rush him as he returns to the playing field.

Swinging the sword with both hands, Jacob feints a blow to the nearest man's head, then drops to one knee and takes a powerful baseball-style swing at an entanglement of gray silicon-covered knees. The razor-sharp edge of steel heats up as it tears through flesh and ligament like a flaming sickle, amputating several men's legs with the continuous blow.

Screams and gouts of bluish-tinged blood rent the air as warrior after warrior topples to the ground.

A steel ball hurtles toward Jacob's face. He ducks, allowing the chained object to spike the demonic mask of another warrior, the six-inch spur burying itself in one of the man's occipital bones.

Jacob spins around and leaps, launching a forward snap kick into the throat of an incoming attacker, barely avoiding the swipe of steel claws lashing through the smoldering, carbon-dioxide-laden air. He lands, parries a would-be stab in the heart with his sword, then sidethrust kicks the transhuman in his exposed Adam's apple, crushing the being's windpipe.

Six down, six to go . . .

The skull-ball whizzes past his head.

Jacob spins around and launches a backthrust kick, the

heel of his boot snapping his approaching enemy's head backward, dislocating the man's cervical spine.

The ball . . . don't forget the game!

Jacob races after the skull-ball, overtaking two more warriors, who are batting it between them as they dribble it toward the eastern goal.

One of the warriors wheels around to fend off Jacob's attack as his teammate prepares to shoot.

Jacob leaps, using his momentum to launch a double–snap kick, the toes of his boots striking the startled warrior in the solar plexus. He lands, then glances up in time to see the skull-ball bank off the eastern wall—

—nearly slipping through the donut-shaped goal.

In one motion, the shooter turns, throwing a needle-sharp dagger at Jacob. The white-haired twin, caught off guard, staggers backward as the poison blade strikes his environmental suit just above the heart.

No blood. You got lucky, the blade didn't penetrate. Don't be so careless!

Angry with himself, Jacob yanks out the blade and hurls it at his would-be killer like a fastball. The knife strikes deep, puncturing his enemy's abdomen clear up to the handle.

The transhuman grunts, then drops to his knees, his stomach drenched in blue blood.

"Ja—cob!"

Jacob looks up. *Fubitch . . .*

Dominique is being forced to retreat over the edge of the eastern wall as the remaining three warriors, now in the temple, stab at her from above with their spears. She lets go, dropping twelve feet before grabbing on to the donut-shaped goal.

Jacob runs to the base of the eastern wall and drops his sword. "Mother, jump."

She looks down and jumps, her son catching her in both arms.

"You okay?"

She nods, struggling to catch her breath.

Jacob senses the three warriors hurrying down the stairwell. "Go get the skull."

She shakes her head. "I can't."

"It's not Mick's head, mother. Now get it—quickly."

She hurries off, ignoring the moans of her son's dying victims, as she steps over severed body parts.

Jacob turns to face his remaining enemies, finishing them off with a dozen quick slashes of his sizzling sword.

Dominique returns with the skull. It is elongated, the face bruised and bleeding, but it is not Michael Gabriel.

It is the face of a child.

Disgusted, Jacob dropkicks it at the western goal. The skull sails through the vertical hoop, the successful shot triggering a hidden mechanism within the goal.

A wave of nausea returns as the open jowls of the serpent's second mouth inhales Jacob and his mother into its vortex, transporting them into another realm.

Opening their eyes, they find themselves standing at the base of a narrow chasm, which cuts a winding passage through an imposing jagged mountainside.

Grabbing his mother by her arm, Jacob leads her down the Dark Road to *Xibalba*.

■ ■ ■ ■ ■ ■ ■ ■ ■ ■ ■ ■ ■ ■ ■

39

■ ■ ■ ■ ■ ■ ■ ■ ■ ■ ■ ■ ■ ■ ■

Jake, where are we?"

"The Mayans called this *Xibalba Be*—the Black Road to the Underworld. I suspect we're still on Earth, somewhere underground."

Slipping the blade of his sword between his belt and exoskeleton, he takes Dominique by the hand and leads her into the ravine. The eight-foot-wide passage snakes between the towering vertical cliff walls, the mountain faces so straight and high they nearly obliterate the lavalike scarlet ceiling percolating above their heads.

Whiffs of dense smoke cause the shadows to dance. The gray limestone rock face drips with heavy humidity. The lead-colored soil is as moist as wet sand, causing their feet to sink deeper with each step. A high-pitched wind whistles through the ravine, depositing a fine gray mist on their exposed faces and environmental suits.

Jacob pauses. Looks up.

The sound of fluttering wings echoes through the chasm.

Dominique tightens her grip on his hand. Points ahead.

Seated on the ground, its back against the canyon wall, is a humanoid.

It is a transhuman—a female. Her shaved, elongated skull sports a jaguar-hide tattoo that serves as hair. She is naked, save for a thin, tattered cloth that barely covers her exquisite torso. Her right side, exposed to the wind, is slick with an oily gray residue.

The woman is rocking back and forth, her dark, frightened eyes purplish red from crying.

They approach, Jacob's hand on the hilt of his sword.

Dominique kneels by the woman, her motherly instincts taking over.

"Mother, don't!" He grabs her arm, dragging her back.

"Jake, have some compassion. Can't you see she's terrified?"

"We don't know who she is or what she is."

The sound of flapping wings grows louder, echoing like old-time machine-gun fire in the narrow ravine.

The female hears it too. Panicking, she jumps to her feet and races through the chasm.

Dominique glances at her son, then chases after the woman.

"Mother, wait—"

Jacob starts after her, but is forced to stop, unable to run with the bulky sword dangling at his hip. He withdraws it from his belt, then sprints with it through the twisting canyon.

The ravine ends, Dominique's footprints continuing on ahead. He hears the sound of a heavy surf. Remaining at the edge of the mountain, he wipes beads of gray moisture from his eyes, then searches for his mother.

The mountainous passage has opened to a swampy beach. Silver waves crash upon an unearthly shoreline, which is littered with seaweed-type residue and tall, dead, dust-infested palm trees.

His mother is up ahead, hiding in the crevice of a large rock formation. She points.

Lining the beachhead are tall wooden posts, as thick as telephone poles. Fastened to each pole by heavy steel chains shackled about their necks are dozens of transhuman females. Bloody purple claw marks scar their naked, bruised bodies.

The flapping sounds grow louder, approaching from somewhere above. The female prisoners cower behind their posts like frightened children.

And then Jacob sees him.

The dark figure of the Seraph-reincarnate circles like a hawk, soaring hundreds of feet above the beach. The being's torso is heavily muscled, his bizarre, twenty-foot wings protruding from his genetically altered spine and latissimus dorsi.

Devlin . . .

Jacob and Dominique remain motionless and out of sight.

The winged Seraph detects movement coming from beneath a mound of seaweed. It is the escaped female.

Pulling his wings back, he dive-bombs after her like a pelican tracking a fish.

The female tosses aside her camouflage and races back toward the refuge of the cliffs.

Jacob signals to his mother to stay put, then grips the sword in both hands.

Leveling out over the swampy beach, the Seraph swoops in from behind the terrified woman and lands on her back, pinning her forcefully against the silicon sand.

Trapped beneath the heavier predator, the female tries desperately to crawl away on hands and knees.

Devlin is simply too big and strong. Like an enraged lion subduing a zebra, he claws at the girl's back, tearing her clothing and skin with his razor-sharp talonlike fingernails until she stops struggling. Pinning her facedown with his left arm, he caresses her breasts with his free hand, then bites into her exposed buttocks with his fang-shaped incisors.

The female screams and hisses as the Seraph, who mounts her from behind to rape her—

—never noticing Jacob, whose steel sword slashes downward against his still-flapping wings.

The glancing blow slices the moving appendage as the ever-alert Devlin wheels around to face his enemy. An insane leer is pasted on his angelic face, his mouth dripping the girl's bluish blood. The sociopath's eyes blaze violet, his pupils, a scarlet red.

Welcome, Father. We've been expecting you.

The voice—telepathic. Very deep, almost hypnotic.

Father?

As the being leaps toward Jacob, the twin slips inside the nexus.

The crimson ceiling instantly brightens, the beating wings of the Seraph slowing to a crawl.

Pushing forward through waves of energy, the white-haired twin meets the attacking humanoid with his raised sword, this time aiming for the mutant's exposed head—

—ignoring the female transhuman, who is suddenly racing at him at ungodly speed.

Lilith!

The Succubus embeds her fingernails into the flesh of his back, while her son claws at Jacob's forearm, tearing tendons and muscle, forcing the twin to relinquish his weapon.

Jacob swoons, the toxin adhered to Lilith's fingernails quickly attacking his bloodstream.

The paralyzed twin collapses in the ankle-deep mire.

Lilith scans the swampy shoreline, her predatory senses sweeping the area. "Where's the other twin? Do you see him?"

"No. And I did not sense him enter the nexus."

"Hmm. Perhaps he's more cunning than his brother." She gazes at Jacob, then whispers in his ear, *"I've missed you, soul mate."*

Devlin looks down the beach to the canyon walls. "We're vulnerable here. Let's return to the portal with this one. The other twin is sure to follow."

He manipulates his injured wing, testing it. Satisfied, he allows his mother to wrap her arms around his neck, then he bends down and picks up Jacob, as if the twin were a small child.

Flapping his mighty wings, the Seraph rises away from the ground, heading north.

Dominique waits another five minutes before coming out from hiding. She is terrified and angry and suddenly all alone.

Just stay calm and think. She picks up Jacob's sword, carrying the heavy weapon in both hands.

The shackled women cry out to her in animal-like grunts, motioning to their chains.

One of the females, a brown-skinned transhuman with claw mark scars striping her breasts and back, opens her mouth, showing Dominique that she has no tongue.

Dominique points to the north. "Do you know where they took my son?"

The female nods, pointing inland. Looming in the distance is an ominous mountain, its craggy summit backlit by the subterranean world's fiery scarlet roof.

"If I free you, will you take me there?"

The abused female nods.

Dominique examines the steel shackle around her neck.

A moderate chop with the sword's ultratech edge and the chain is broken.

It takes Dominique another ten minutes to free the remaining prisoners.

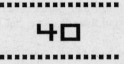

There are two colors in the subterranean world, both appearing in varying shades.

Gray is the color of death. It is the desolate plain Dominique and her transhuman companion have been walking on for hours, its solder gray, parched surface scarred with deep fissures and charcoal-tinged boulders. It is the brownish gray clouds rising from distant funeral pyres, smoldering like toxic smoke from a petroleum inferno. It is the muddied gray of the mountainside looming before them, its barren, clay-colored escarpments smooth and twisting, like cooled magma. It is the lead gray backs of the foot-long beetles that continuously scamper between their boots like restless vermin.

Red is the color of heat. It is the sliver of rose-colored horizon peeking between the mountain's summit and the roof of the subterranean habitat. It is the orange-red glow of embers twinkling like stars upon the cloud-covered ceiling.

Red is not the color of blood. Blood bleeds blue in this godforsaken carbon-dioxide habitat, appearing violet in the pinkish hue of everlasting twilight.

Violet is the shade of red Dominique sees every time she squeezes her eyes shut. Violet is the dull, aching, maddening pain that presses against the back of her eyeballs. It is her feet, throbbing inside her boots. It is her lower back, which still aches from a prolonged menstrual cycle. It is her overwrought nerves, which cringe at the perpetual squish—squish sound of recycled water being pumped by her leg muscles as she moves in her constricting environmental bodysuit.

But worse than the pain, worse than the colors of the Underworld, is the terror that gnaws at her brain, the anxiety of knowing her soul mate is close, but her son is in great danger.

They reach the base of the mountain. Dominique stares up at its twisting forty-degree incline and escarpments, seeing only violet.

The mute transhuman points.

"Guess it's not too bad," Dominique lies, straining to see the summit. "Almost looks like an extinct volcano."

Dozens of beetles scamper across the tops of her boots. "Go away!" She kicks at them, nearly losing her footing.

The transhuman starts up the slope.

Dominique follows, using the sword as a cane. *Jake's strong, he'll be okay. If they wanted him dead, they would have killed him back on the beach.*

Her thoughts turn to her other son.

At least Manny's safe . . .

And then she stops, tears welling in her eyes as the reality of her situation finally hits home. *Manny's not safe, Manny's dead! He died on this rotting hellhole millions of years ago, along with the rest of our godforsaken species.*

Leaning against a boulder, she sobs uncontrollably, choking into her regulator.

Her transhuman companion stops. Climbs down to her and takes her hand, squeezing it.

Have . . . faith.

The message, delivered telepathically, is but a faint whisper in Dominique's brain, but it speaks volumes.

Yes, she is marooned and desperate, but she is not alone. There is her other son, and maybe there is Mick.

And now—a friend.

If you have to die, go down fighting. Take that bitch Lilith with you!

Dominique stands.

The two women embrace, then continue climbing.

Hours pass.

The transhuman female reaches a plateau and stops climbing. Dominique joins her, the two humanoids staring at the challenge that lies before them.

Separating the plateau from the mountain's summit is a great crevasse, its sheer thousand-foot drop disappearing into blackness. Even at its narrowest point, the gaping slice is still a good twenty feet across.

The face of the mountain on their side of the fissure curves around to the left, but the geology is a sheer wall, impossible to maneuver around without equipment.

"Can't go up, can't go across, what the hell do we do now?"

The female points to a narrow ledge of rock, eight inches wide, which skirts the face of the mountainside as it curves around to their targeted destination.

"That ledge? That's way too narrow to walk on."

The female motions with her hands, indicating that they are not going to walk on it, they are going to lower themselves over the edge and make their way along the rock face, hand over hand.

Dominique breaks out in a sweat, causing the thermostat of her bodysuit to kick in, dropping its internal temperature fifteen degrees. "It's suicide. We'll never . . . I know, I know . . . have faith."

The transhuman leads her to the ledge. Points to her eyes, warning Dominique not to look down.

The long-skulled female lies down on her belly and rolls over the ledge, carefully lowering herself so that only her palms and the insides of her wrists are supporting the weight of her body.

Dominique bites nervously into the regulator's rubber

housing. She urinates into her environmental suit's bladder cache, waiting for her companion to move farther along the cliff face before she kneels.

Just do it. There are worse ways to die.

Shut up! You're not going to die, you're going to make it and find your family! Now get your ass over that ledge!

She lowers herself gingerly, the muscles in her arms shaking, her boots searching for unseen toeholds. Palm over palm, she begins making her way around the narrow outcrop of rock.

Keeping her wrists tight, groping for toeholds here and there, she finds herself actually making progress. *Right hand, left hand . . . right hand, left hand . . .*

She ignores the white-hot ligaments straining in her wrists, continuing her mantra.

Right hand, left hand . . . right hand, left hand . . . only another fifteen feet. Right hand, left . . . not so scary. Scuba diving in that cenote with Mick—now that was scary.

She pauses, noticing that her transhuman companion has stopped.

The female's eyes are looking up at the artificial sky, wide in terror—as if someone is scolding her telepathically.

How did you escape, Teresa? Did the other twin set you free?

Leave me be, witch!

Answer me, or I'll feast upon your parents.

The transhuman smiles. *Die in hell.* The female kicks away from the edge, falling . . . falling—

"Oh my God!" Dominique screams as the woman's body disappears into the shadows of the abyss.

An unearthly flash of white light blinks in the ravine, then disappears.

Dominique stares at the spot, hyperventilating into her mouthpiece. *What was that? What just happened?*

For a long moment she simply hangs on, her mind threatening to crash.

Then she remembers Jacob.

Okay, come on . . . gather your strength and finish this. Haul ass!

The fingertips of her right hand press into the rock, the muscles of her lower back and buttocks clenching, straining to shift her weight.

Right hand, left hand, right hand, left hand . . . eight feet . . . focus on the ledge . . . right hand, left hand, right hand, left hand . . . three feet . . . two feet—

In a burst of adrenaline and sheer will, Dominique forces her right boot onto the ledge above her head as she maintains her delicate balance . . . pushing the knee up, then her thigh—

—then her upper torso.

She rolls onto the flat expanse of rock, panting, crying, smiling, all the while, sucking air from her mouthpiece.

Just breathe . . .

In time she sits up. Regains her feet and follows the plateau to its steep incline—a two-hundred-foot-high ridge that loops around the entire expanse of summit, blocking her view.

Dominique is beyond exhaustion. Her joints ache, her hands and wrists are raw, and her leg and lower back muscles burn with each painful step.

Above her head, the pyroclastic ceiling percolates like lava.

Come on, stop thinking about it and climb.

Sucking great gulps of air, she drags herself up the gradient, crawling the last fifty feet on her belly until she finds herself peeking over the edge.

Dominique looks down.

She is perched on the lip of a volcano, its craterlike valley resting several hundred feet below.

Nestled in the mountainous basin like some Tibetan hideaway is a village.

The Village of the *Nephilim*.

It is urban pestilence, an architecture of chaos haphazardly erected in uneven rows of single-story, poorly constructed, dust-caked dwellings. It is a maze of gray, a neighborhood worse than the worst parts of the cardboard-and-aluminum shantytowns of Olongopo and Subic after the volcanic eruption in the Philippines.

Soot-covered abodes on soot-covered streets funnel to the far end of town and the shoreline of a vast lake, its surface enshrouded in thick mist.

Dominique stifles her breathing as the thick clouds part along the subterranean ceiling, revealing a monstrous object, erected on the near side of the lake. Carved from rock, immeasurably old, it stands as tall as a ten-story building, its upper half appearing polished, its details lost in the returning haze.

Somewhere in the distance a bell tolls, its baritone gongs echoing across the valley.

As if summoned, the shadowy gray figures of the multitudes bleed slowly out from their dwellings, making their way en masse to the lake's shoreline.

With a trembling hand, Dominique removes the smart-binoculars from her belt pack. She switches the viewer from day to night vision, then zooms in, focusing on the villagers, all of whom are covered in the same gray dust.

Something's happening. I've got to get down there . . .

The outskirts of the village is a swampy cesspool of silvery brown ooze, stagnant with humanlike feces, garbage, bones and the smoldering remains of ashen flesh. Twenty-inch scarab beetles feast upon the offering by the tens of thousands, their sharp mandibles creating a nerve-wracking *crunching* sound as they feed.

Sucking hard on her regulator, Dominique hurries through the knee-deep slime, making her way to more solid footing. The dusty soil beneath her feet is now a spongy surface saturated with the same brownish gray liquid of the swamp, ooze rising from the porous earth with each step.

She comes to the first quadrangle of claylike, window-less shanties. The rows of odd-shaped dwellings are listing in this unstable mire, their foundations sinking into stagnant sewage.

Dominique gags into her mouthpiece and readjusts her nose apparatus, the stench of her surroundings almost unbearable even through her breathing apparatus.

Composing herself, she makes her way to the end of a row, then peeks around a fractured wall.

The dust-choked streets appear deserted.

A fluttering sound causes her to look up. Perched on the roofs across the street are four owl-like creatures, each the size of a twelve-year-old human child. Their bulbous, featherless heads are caked in gray dust, their pupilless round eyes blinded by white cataracts. The folded wings, incapable of flight, are scaly, ending in sharp talons.

The mutant creatures are staring at her, gasping painful breaths through their deformed beaklike mouths.

What kind of evil creates such genetic mutations?

Dominique moves back into the shadows, contemplating. Her once-black environmental suit is already covered in gray dust. Grabbing handfuls of soil, she rubs more of the soot on her face and hair, camouflaging herself as best she can.

Satisfied, she moves down the grime-covered roadway, heading for a wider avenue that she prays will lead her to Jacob.

Dominique encounters the next villager as it hobbles out

of the doorless entry of a one-room shanty. The miserable wretch had probably been a male. The scowling being is walking on its hands, its lower torso having been severed below the waist. Massive pustulating blue scabs bleed through the gray cover of dust that coats its skin.

Topping off its painful deformities is a bowling-ball-sized violet-glowing orb that has been surgically embedded in the life-form's lower back.

The tortured being grunts as it straddle-walks on heavily callused knuckles, the ends of its tunic dragging along the dirt. A fine ebony mist snorts from its flared nostrils with each excruciating exhalation.

Fear and compassion fill Dominique's mind as she watches the life-form struggle with its artificial weight. She waits another moment, then hurries past him to a central thoroughfare.

It is an avenue of the undead, a procession of grunting, moaning, mutilated transhumans, all victims of amputation. Some of the beings lack legs, others arms. A phage-like bacteria festers their skin, slowly, agonizingly eating away at their flesh and bone.

The Nephilim . . .

As if their existence is not torturous enough, each transhuman has been fitted with a prosthetic orb that radiates in a variety of spectral hues. Reds and yellows, greens, blues, and violets. If there is a code behind the specific colors, Dominique cannot discern it.

Maneuvering around these pitiful beings, she makes her way to the front of the rank, the sounds of the gong growing louder.

The avenue opens to a congested gathering place along the lake's shoreline. Thousands of taller, more gangly bipeds push forward to join the mob. They are dressed in heavy soot-covered robes, their elongated skulls tucked inside hoods. Exposed flesh has long disappeared beneath adhering layers of mouse gray silicon, giving their faces a heavily pruned appearance. Neanderthal-like brows protect dark, deeply set eyes. Noses and surrounding cartilage are missing, leaving behind only open nasal passages. Lip-less mouths remain slack-jawed, exposing teeth caked with atmospheric dust and film.

Like cattle, the *Nephilim* push and prod each other, inching their way closer to the lake, following its shoreline to some unknown destination.

Avoiding the throng, Dominique hides behind the collapsed remains of a rectangular dwelling. She looks around nervously, taking in her surroundings, while the baritone gong continues to toll its bone-throbbing call.

The lake's silvery surface sparkles crimson, reflecting the emberlike ceiling overhead. But it is the towering object situated across the lake that now occupies Dominique's attention.

It is a statue . . . a statue of a monstrous humanoid. The face is demonic and frightening, highlighted by a wide, fanged mouth and aquiline nose. Huge goat horns, polished and ebony, are perched atop the being's elongated, pointed skull. Batlike wings, enormous and clawed at the tips, fold in behind the naked upper torso like a shawl. The icon's lower body is shaped like a goat's hindquarters, the long tail ending in a spike.

Dominique stares at the statue, transfixed. *It's Lucifer. They're worshiping the Devil.*

The statue casts an ominous shadow across the lake, its satanic gaze reflecting scarlet flames from the Underworld ceiling, the glowing embers twisting the mouth into an evil grin.

The bells stop tolling.

Dominique hurries to another dwelling, seeking a better view.

And now she sees where the *Nephilim* procession has assembled.

Along the far shoreline is an immense calabash tree, as old as time, as large as an African baobab. Its knotted, twisted trunk and bare branches are alabaster white, its spongy bark secretes a saplike ivory mucus.

At the base of the redwood-sized trunk stands a figure.

Lilith.

The Hunahpu queen is wearing a vermilion monk's robe, her hairless elongated skull and its bizarre jaguar tattoo concealed beneath the heavy hood.

As she speaks, her voice is amplified by the lake's natural acoustics.

"And it came to pass that our tyrant God, Yahweh, became so fearful and jealous of His own creations that He cast His most beautiful son, the archangel, Lucifer, into the depths of Hell. So selfish was our Creator that He banned His greatest creation, man, from the Garden of Eden. So egotistical was our Vengeful One that He sanctioned blood sacrifices among His most loyal followers. So unforgiving was He that He unleashed a great deluge and drowned His populace. So terrified of man's intelligence was our paranoid deity that He destroyed the Tower of Babel and scattered the survivors to the four winds, forcing them to speak in different tongues to stifle our ascension as a species, assuring our eventual self-destruction.

"'Thou Shall Not Kill,' commanded the Great Hypocrite, as He smote us like fish in a barrel and taught us to hate.

"But even the Great Hypocrite Himself could not stifle the love from our real father, our beautiful Morning Star, who reached out from Hell to instruct us. It is Lucifer who taught us how to taste the fruit of the vine. It is he who replaced abstinence with indulgence, ignorance with curiosity. It was Lucifer who liberated our spirits, encouraging our biological, spiritual, and intellectual ascent, and directed us toward the hidden forces of Nature. He is our salvation, and we are his, for the time has come to undo the wrongs of the past and release our father from his unholy bonds."

The crowd stomps and grunts, their rants causing the porous soil to flood. Across the street, the four owls continue staring, gasping great wheezes of breath.

Dominique fingers the sword, her arms trembling.

Lilith waits until her legion quiets. "And now, Yahweh

has sent another messenger of pain. But fear not, for the arrival of this Hunahpu shall not cause you more despair. Devlin, your true savior, shall use the Hunahpu's powers to unseal the Gates of Hell, releasing our father, the archangel, Lucifer!"

Wild stomping and grunts, the crowd trampling one another as it tries to move closer.

Lilith motions for silence. "Patience. The blessed resurrection shall be upon you soon enough. Until then, you may take one revolution around Lucifer's light before returning to your dwellings."

Dominique watches, dumbfounded, as the procession of the tortured circle slowly around the glowing alabaster tree, their colorful orbs absorbing its energy, glowing brighter as if suckling in its warmth, feeding off the tree's light.

And then the beings depart, grunting and shoving one another, the bipeds jostling the slower amputees as they return to the village.

Remaining hidden, Dominique uses the smart-binoculars to zoom in upon another object, this one anchored in close proximity to one of the tree's dangling lower limbs.

It is a wooden cross, supporting a crucified figure.

The head is obscured in a crown of thorns, the blood bleeding blue.

Jacob . . .

Dominique waits until the streets are deserted, then waits ten minutes more.

Moving out from hiding, she hurries down the avenue to the lake, slipping and sliding in the gray mire.

She steals a quick glance to her left. The smooth, quicksilver surface of the lake sparkles crimson, reflecting the ceiling embers high overhead.

Must hurry . . . before the demon sentry in Jacob's holographic program appears.

She jogs faster, adrenaline and fear distracting her brain from the physical pain, the double-edged sword gripped firmly in both hands.

Twenty years of existence, twenty years of nightmares. For six years she has watched her son prepare for war within this same hellish environment. But this is no holographic program, and she is not Jacob.

God, please let him still be alive.

She races past the alabaster tree, hurrying to the cross and its unconscious crucified victim.

"Jake? Jacob, honey, it's me!" She reaches the wooden cross's base, gazing up at its crucified figure—

—who slowly opens his iridescent eyes, a smile appearing on his angelic face.

Dominique's jaw drops. "Devlin . . ."

The Seraph spreads its wings, then leaps off the cross, his feet pouncing on Dominique's chest, his talonlike toenails puncturing her environmental suit.

And then his wings stop flapping, and he leans in closer, staring at her, his dark expression quizzical. "You're not

Immanuel?" He straddles her chest and sniffs her neck, his nostrils inhaling her scent. "First-Mother! Where is your other son? Tell me now, or I'll kill Jacob."

"I'll tell you . . . but first . . . I want to see him!"

Devlin's wings beat the air, lifting him off Dominique's chest. Regaining his feet, he pulls her up by the hair, then drags her toward the calabash tree.

Jacob is on his back, his throat and limbs pinned beneath the tree's thickly knotted alabaster roots.

"Speak now, or he dies."

"Manny never made the voyage. I took his place."

Devlin's eyes blaze violet. "Impossible."

"It . . . it's true."

"*Arrgggghh!*" Devlin clubs her in the back of the head, sending her crumpling to the oily ground—unconscious.

The Seraph closes his eyes, allowing his mind to slip inside the nexus. Lilith is waiting for his consciousness within the dense white haze.

Immanuel is not here, Mother. The twins have altered the past!

It doesn't matter, as long as the portal to Hell is unsealed and Lucifer is resurrected.

But it takes the presence of both Hunahpu twins to unseal it.

You forget, we still have One Hunaphu. His presence, combined with Jacob's, will provide all the energy needed to open the gate.

Yes, but we cannot tap into his energy field while he remains within his protected domain.

This time he'll leave. We'll lure him out using his loved ones.

The pain jerks Dominique awake as Devlin drags her by the hair toward the luminescent white tree.

The Seraph stands before the immense trunk, flapping

his wings. "Open your eyes, One Hunahpu. I want you to gaze upon the face of your beloved soul mate as I violate her before your God!"

The being punches Dominique across the back of her shoulder blades, the crushing blow dropping her to the ground.

She feels the Seraph's talons shred the remains of her environmental suit down the back, then screams through her regulator as he pulls her pants down, exposing her bare buttocks.

She gags as powerful hands lift her hips to his naked groin.

"Unseal the portal, One Hunahpu, or I swear to Lucifer, I'll rape and torture her every minute of eternity!"

Two pinpoints of aqua blue appear in the gooey white sap, the outline of a face revealing itself just beneath the surface of the calabash bark.

Ripples appear on the lake, and the surface begins undulating, as if something large is disturbing the depths.

Devlin stares at the exotic liquid. *It's happening. The portal's opening!*

Jacob opens his eyes.

The subterranean ceiling is alive with flames that leap away from the broiling embers like solar flares. He attempts to sit up but finds a great weight pressing against his throat, more resistance binding his upper torso and limbs to the ground.

He hears his mother's cries. Feels his father's presence.

Closing his eyes, he slips into the nexus.

Jacob Gabriel's mind enters the frigid white mist and he is afraid.

It's been an eternity, my love. Have you missed me?

The haunting whisper tickles his ear. He can smell the

jasmine, then he sees her eyes, radiating a bright Hunahpu blue.

The lithe form moves out from the mist, her swollen breasts pressing against the sheer fabric of a vermilion-colored negligee.

Her gaze is drawn to his right arm, which is still raw and bleeding from the last attack. *Come closer, cousin. Let me lick your wounds.*

Jacob backs away.

Still frightened?

Devlin . . . is the monster my son?

He is Lucifer's son.

It didn't have to be like this, Lilith.

Ah, but it did. Her irises simmer violet in the supernatural light. *I was born into Hell and I'll die here, not as its victim but as its conqueror. Abandoned by God, I turned to the only ones left who would embrace me, those of the lesser lights.*

They weren't real, Lilith. They were voices in your head.

You were a voice in my head, but I still loved you! And what did you do? You abandoned me in my hour of need, first when we were teens, then when you left on the Balam. *You helped sow the seeds of my corruption, now you can reap the harvest of your selfishness!*

Lilith's dark complexion pales to a ghostly white, the pupils of her azure eyes flaming to vermilion. The once-sensuous mouth deforms, twisting . . . distorting into a hideous vertical orifice. The purple labia-like lips widen, the grotesque grin chilling Jacob's blood.

Moving toward him, the she-demon allows the straps of her nightgown to fall, then she steps out of the garment, exposing her vile sex.

Jacob swoons, unable to focus, the nexus whirling in his head.

She leaps for him, driving him backward as if he were struck by a sledgehammer. Straddling his chest, she claws at the remains of his body armor as he struggles to regain his breath, the slit of her hideous mouth pressing closer to his face, revealing multiple rows of tiny, razor-sharp black teeth.

Jacob dry heaves at her sulfuric breath. He grabs her throat with his right hand, attempting to keep her groping face away, while his free hand fights the claw at his groin, frantically attempting to prevent the rape.

From his isolated isle of calm, the consciousness that is Michael Gabriel feels the sudden disturbance within the nexus. A sense of dread overwhelms him as he registers wakes of energy and senses the struggle so close to his protected domain.

Devlin abandons Dominique, moving as if in a trance toward the shoreline of the lake, whose waters now radiate an emerald tinge. "Hear me, Father. Send forth your demon sentry. Empty the pit of Babylon and reveal the Gates of Hell, so that I might release thee!"

Dominique crawls toward Jacob, distancing herself from the Seraph. "Jake? Jake, wake up!"

Jacob is pinned beneath the thick roots of the calabash tree, thrashing wildly, as if in the throes of a horrible nightmare.

The sound of a heavy gong tolls in the distance.

The village of the Fallen Ones empties, its members slowly making their way to the shoreline of the metamorphosing lake.

Jacob's mind screams as he struggles in vain to keep the Succubus at bay.

Lilith's face is hideous, taking on the proportion of a Gorgon. Amoeba-like mealworms crawl from porous openings along her flesh, releasing a putrid secretion and inhuman pheromones.

Jacob flings his head from side to side, gagging at the stench. Physically outmatched, mentally exhausted, pinned to the earth, he finds himself overwhelmed by a presence whose sheer force of will threatens to tear his own consciousness apart.

A bloodcurdling scream bellows from his throat as a scalding-hot mucus drips from the Abomination's naked loins.

Let me die, please God, I'd rather die—

Jacob cannot turn away as the Succubus increases her chokehold, a thousand icy pinpricks puncturing the fabric of his existence as he somersaults within her sulfuric lather, every cell in his body screaming for mercy.

And then he glimpses a shadowy figure appear from the hazy periphery, moving toward them through shimmering phase disturbances.

Father . . .

Michael Gabriel grabs the Abomination by her throat and flings the startled Succubus into the peripheral mist and out of the nexus.

Jacob crawls on his hands and knees into his father's warming embrace.

The two exhausted Gabriels hold each other, feeding off each other's energy as they stare into the haze, waiting for the she-devil to return.

Father . . . we have to leave the nexus.

I can't son. Not until the Nephilim have been freed."

A baritone growl.

Two pinpoints of scarlet mark her eyes, and the demon reappears . . . smiling her wicked vertical slit of a smile.

One Hunahpu . . . finally lured out of your cage. You and your son's aura will allow Devlin to wedge open the Gates of Hell.

She disappears into the haze.

Jacob feels ill, as if he has just stepped off a precipice.

Dad, what does she mean? Is Lucifer really coming?

Mick whispers into his son's consciousness, There is no Lucifer, Jacob, there is no Hell.

But evil—

The Devil is man's creation, son, not God's. Evil is the human residue of free choice. Hell is a self-imposed prison in the spiritual realm. This purgatory . . . none of it is real, it was all created from the demented subconscious of Devlin Mabus and the tortured minds of the Nephilim. My own anger, my own self-loathing imprisoned my tainted soul within its walls . . . until I felt your love. But I chose to stay . . . to help the Nephilim. To allow them to bathe in my warmth.

Then I must kill Devlin and Lilith.

You can't, Jacob. They're already dead.

What?

I killed them long ago, back in 2012, when they attempted to use Tezcatilpoca to return to Earth. I entered the serpent's nexus to greet them. They tried to trick me, but I saw through their ruse and killed both of them.

But—

God will not allow evil to enter His spiritual domain. So angry at God was Lilith that she refused to accept His terms. She and Devlin created their own netherworld, entrapping the confused, guilt-ridden souls of the Nephilim within its borders. Here, they can coerce and torture them, keeping them clear of God's embracing light while Devlin, using his pure Hunahpu lineage, feeds off their energy to forge his own version of Hell.

Why are the Nephilim so filled with guilt?

Because they survived Earth's holocaust when so many others died. It is my aura that soothes their souls, just as you soothed mine. Yours was a beacon of love . . . and love is God's light. Lilith dampens this light, feeding it to the Nephilim in small morsels, crediting its energy to Lucifer so as to keep them under control.

Then the Nephilim . . . they're dead as well?

Yes. They perished long ago, when they attempted to cross over into the spiritual realm.

Do they even know they're dead?

No. Neither does Devlin or his mother. They're absolutely convinced they're on a mission to resurrect Lucifer. Now, only the truth shall set them free.

But why . . . why are Devlin and Lilith so convinced they can open up the Gates of Hell?

Devlin can feel an energy surge coming, but it is not our combined presence in this purgatory that he feels.

The supernova?

Yes. Devlin's Hunahpu abilities allow him to tap into these forces. Even now, his mind is channeling energy, his subconscious giving life to a demon sentry.

Father, what happens when Sirius goes supernova?

Energy levels will spike, and Devlin's consciousness will give birth to Lucifer—at least his concept of Lucifer—created from the fabric of his own wounded mind.

Then this whole thing . . . it could actually become a self-fulfilling prophecy?

Not could, Jacob. Remember, humanity is stuck in a time loop. The deed has already happened before.

Are you saying man's concept of the Devil came from the future?

Looping back into the past . . . a frightening paradox. With each journey through the wormhole, the equation becomes more muddied, and mankind drifts farther from God.

Then the past . . . it will repeat itself again?

The moment the Guardian reenter the wormhole, as they are preparing to do even now. Once more, man's future will deliver the Devil into man's Garden of Eden.

Dad . . . this is all my fault . . . my selfishness pushed Lilith away, my moment of weakness gave Devlin life.

It's not your fault. Like me, you were simply a victim of circumstance.

So was Lilith. So were Manny and Evelyn, and the billions who perished back on old Earth. Dad, I have to stop this insanity . . . I have to end this once and for all!

How?

By defeating Devlin. By saving the Nephilim.

You can't defeat Devlin alone, and I cannot leave the nexus to help you.

There's another way I can succeed, but I need your help. Can you distract Lilith . . . keep her away from me?

I'll try. But the sentry, it would take both of us to—

I'll handle the sentry, you worry about Lilith.

Devlin stands before the lake's edge, his batlike wings twitching at his sides.

The silvery waters churn, then swirl, pulling in a powerful counterclockwise vortex. Within seconds, the once-placid liquid has become a raging whirlpool, its eye draining, inhaling the contents of the maelstrom to reveal—

—a massive orifice . . . the third mouth of the serpent.

"It's the portal, the portal into Hell!"

Devlin's subconscious reaches across dimensions of time and space, tapping into the chaotic energy of the red supergiant, unleashing a monstrous ball of crimson flame, which belches upward from the serpent's hyperextended jaws. The expulsion of energy causes the shoreline to rumble beneath Devlin's feet, sending the frightened *Nephilim* bowing in fear.

The lining of the serpent's throat radiates an emerald green hue as it slowly morphs into a rotating funnel of energy.

Father and son link minds, summoning Lilith, whose hideous presence reappears along the periphery of the mist.

I love you, Father.

I love you too, son. Now go.

Jacob's mind slips out of the nexus.

Michael Gabriel turns to face his eternal enemy. *It's you and me now, cousin. My son has given me his strength . . .*

*and I promise you that none of those who were born in the
light, begotten in the light, will ever be yours!"*

Jacob opens his eyes.

He is lying on his back, the binding roots of the calabash
tree having loosened around his neck and limbs. He pulls
himself out from under the thick bonds and sits up, transfixed by the unearthly emerald light pouring out of the
fifth-dimensional pit.

The porous ground oozes as Devlin's followers dance
and jump along the shoreline.

Rising out of the orifice, dripping globs of silvery ooze,
is Devlin's demonic biped, the one he has fought countless
times in the holograph suite, the one who has tortured him
in his childhood dreams. Powerful limbs, heavily segmented and smooth, propel its angular, heavily muscled
body across the lake's receding waters.

Devlin greets the sentry his own subconscious mind has
created, directing it to the calabash tree. "Slay them. Slay
them all!"

The silicon demon trudges up onshore, its powerful segmented arms lashing out, its scalpel-like fingers slicing
limbs and torsos of the scattering *Nephilim*.

The ash-coated beings cry out, blue-tinted plasma gushing from their wounds. Panicking, the throng pushes one
another aside, desperate to move out of harm's way.

"Jake!" Dominique rushes over, handing him the sword.
"Are you all right? Where's Mick?"

"Guarding the nexus." For the first time in fourteen
years, he embraces her tightly. "I love you, Mom. I'm so
sorry. All these years . . . I never showed you the love you
gave me."

"Shh . . . I love you."

"I love you, too." Tears stream from his eyes. "Stay
back . . . stay close to the tree."

"Jake, what are you going to do?"

"Fulfill my destiny."

Dominique starts to say something, then gags, the noxious fumes of Devlin's sentry causing her mucous membranes to sizzle. She cowers behind the alabaster tree, pressing the seal of her nostril hoses tighter.

The demon faces Jacob, its two pupilless eyes, blazing burned yellow, staring right through him. The cruel slit seems to smile as if in triumph, allowing a black goo to dribble from its anthropomorphic mouth.

The being's poison-tipped sickleshaped claws slice the air, warning Jacob away from the calabash tree. Jacob tightens his grip on the sword.

Suddenly a gray blur—moving at him with unfathomable quickness—as the creature launches its attack.

Jacob ducks—the demon's razored claws whistling past his scalp, as the Hunahpu warrior rolls forward and whips his sword around and down, slicing through the back of one of the being's thickly muscled legs.

The creature cries out, swearing in an incomprehensible language.

Jacob regrips the sword in both hands. For over a decade he has fought a holographic simulation of this being within the nexus. Now, every instinct in his body tells him to remain free of the higher dimension.

The demon circles slowly, biding its time. Mustard yellow ooze gushes from its wounded leg as it plans its next bull rush.

Another blur of gray—the being's bladed fingertips slashing through the carbon-dioxide-heavy air.

Jacob parries the blow with the blade of his sword, then, executing a flawless pirouette, he whirls around and hacks through the being's left arm, just above the elbow.

The wounded demon howls in its native tongue, cowering off-balance as the Hunahpu launches his own attack, his sword cutting the air in blurring waves of unyielding figure eights, the sizzling double blade hacking through silicon flesh, the mustard yellow pus spraying both combatants as Jacob mercilessly shreds torso and limb.

A flutter of wings, followed by a warning shout from Dominique.

Jacob wheels about and drops, stabbing upward, catching Devlin in the abdomen as the Seraph assails him from above.

Devlin flies off, landing awkwardly several feet from the edge of the glowing pit, clutching his ruptured flank.

"Jake!" Dominique points.

Blue-tinged blood is gushing from beneath his body armor along the left side of his rib cage, the sentry's talons having shredded flesh and muscle.

"Stay back!" Jacob sucks deep lungfuls of air from his mouthpiece, trying in vain to fight off the effects of the poison. He is lathered in blood and sweat and yellow phlegm, his muscles trembling.

Eyeing Devlin, Jacob turns to the mutilated sentry groveling by his feet. Bellowing a guttural warrior's cry, the Hunahpu raises his sword and, with a mighty two-handed downward chop, cuts off the demon's hideous head.

Devlin snarls by the edge of the pit but does not attack.

The frightened *Nephilim* continue to inch toward the calabash tree by the thousands.

Jacob drops to his knees, Dominique catching him as he collapses. "Jake, no . . . oh God, please—" She clutches his dying form to her bosom. "Jake, don't leave me."

Unable to speak, he points feebly to the trunk of the alabaster tree.

Michael Gabriel's mind is drowning in an abyss of evil, the Abomination's scarlet eyes dragging him deeper into her icy soul. Her whisper echoes into his consciousness. *The battle is over, cousin. I shall drain your life force, then carry First-Mother's carcass over Hell's threshold.*

An eternity of pent-up emotions explodes from the depths of Mick's crumbling being, piercing the walls of his protective domain—"Dominique!"

* * *

The whisper of her name reverberates in her mind like a tuning fork.

Jacob rasps, choking on his own blood. "Free him."

She lays her son's head down gently and stands. Grips his sword in both hands. Staggers to the calabash tree, its glow fading fast—

—and thrusts the blade into the trunk with all her might.

The Siren's scream echoes in Mick's mind, and suddenly the haze lifts.

The Succubus is clutching her side where a stream of black ooze sprays outward like oil. She wheels around, her demonic vermilion eyes spewing hatred at Mick.

No! Impossible!

Michael Gabriel smiles triumphantly. *Never underestimate the power of love.*

Another wound bursts open, this one in her throat. She flops on her back, gagging on her own excrement—

—as an eternity of shackles are stripped from Mick's being.

The heavenly glow of the calabash tree increases its brilliance as white bark melts into gobs of mucuslike goo.

Thrashing about within this rapidly liquefying mound are two figures. One is Lilith, her pale flesh gushing an oily excrement; the second is Michael Gabriel, his torso held from behind, the Succubus's fingernails digging into his back.

"Get off my man, bitch!" Dominique lashes downward with the sword, severing Lilith's arms at the elbows.

Devlin circles overhead, but refuses to get nearer to the painfully brightening light.

Dominique drags Mick's lifeless form from the tarry ooze. "Jake, he's not breathing!" She removes her mouthpiece and forces it past her soul mate's blue lips and into his mouth.

"Come on, Mick—breathe!" She shakes him, then starts mouth to mouth, but is unable to resuscitate him.

"Oh God, no . . . not after all this." Removing a pony bottle of air from her exoskeleton, she straps it over Mick's face, then begins CPR—

—as a second white light appears at her back, its unearthly glow warming her skin.

Dominique turns. Her jaw drops open, releasing the regulator. "Jacob?"

The brilliant light-force that is Jacob Gabriel rises from his deceased physical form, casting a heavenly glow throughout the spiritual dimension.

En masse, the *Nephilim* gravitate toward the source.

"Like moths to a flame . . ." Dominique whispers.

The energy from Jacob's soul bathes their skin, miraculously washing away the gray soot, revitalizing their flesh. Limbs are restored, the torturous orbs dropping from their rejuvenated bodies.

Dominique's mind is in a daze. And then Evelyn Strongin's words, spoken so long ago, are whispered into her consciousness.

There is a Hell, Dominique, but it is not a real place. Those who enter the afterlife possessing negative energy reside in their own self-imposed Hell. Judgment, blame, and guilt can distort or destroy one's own sense of self. Unless we allow love to purify the darkness of our souls, Hell can be a very forbidding place.

"Love . . ."

Tears of joy pour from Dominique's eyes as, one by one, the lost souls of New Eden's colonists, held so long within their self-imposed purgatory of guilt and shame—smile . . . then disappear in a blink of heavenly white light.

Devlin hovers above the melee, flapping his wings, screeching at the top of his lungs. "No! Get away from him! Leave him be!"

The remaining *Nephilim* push in tighter, desperate to embrace their newfound savior.

And then they are gone, all but Jacob, who moves toward her, bathing her in his loving light.

The alabaster ooze from the calabash tree melts like snow as it is kissed by Jacob's angelic glow, restoring Lilith's earthly beauty, healing her wounds.

Jacob kneels by Lilith. Touches her face.

Lilith opens her eyes, now filled with a childlike innocence. She looks up at Jacob and smiles.

Jacob takes Lilith's hand, then turns to his mother. He points to Mick, who is now breathing on his own. "Be happy."

Dominique chokes on the lump in her throat. "I love you."

Jacob smiles. And then he and Lilith are gone.

Mick groans.

Dominique rushes to his side. She strokes his thick mane of silver-gray hair and stares into his brilliant, azure blue eyes, recognizing the look of schizophrenia. "My poor baby, what did they do to you?"

The Underworld rumbles like thunder. Crimson flames shoot out from the serpent's open mouth, an emerald eruption of energy still pouring from the fifth-dimensional conduit. The subterranean ceiling is fragmenting, exposing curtains of brilliant white light.

Devlin snarls at her from the edge of the pit. Spreading his wings, he dives into the maelstrom.

And then everything is gone.

Dominique finds herself kneeling by the edge of the artificial lake, back on the planet's surface. Hurricane-force winds howl in her ears, threatening to swoop her up into its vortex. She looks around, blinded by volcanic dust.

Mick is lying by her side, the Guardian's transport pod rocking twenty feet behind them.

Stooping painfully, she positions Mick's arm across her

shoulder and half carries, half drags him to the spacecraft. She pulls him inside. Seals the hatch.

"Computer, get us on board the Guardian's transport as fast as you can!"

The pod struggles to lift against the monstrous currents of air and debris.

Dominique holds on, unable to think through the insanity of the moment as they are inhaled within the hurricane's vortex. She squeezes her eyes shut, memories flashing in her mind as the space vehicle whips around the eye wall of the storm as if caught in a washing machine.

Flash: She is back in the Miami mental asylum, sitting before her new director, Antonio Foletta, discussing her new patient.

"Why was Mr. Gabriel incarcerated?"

"Mick lost it during his father's lecture. The court diagnosed him paranoid schizophrenic and sentenced him to the Massachusetts State Mental Facility, where I served as his clinical psychiatrist."

"Same kind of delusions as his father?"

"And the mother. Archaeologists Julius and Maria Gabriel were convinced that some terrible calamity is going to wipe mankind off the face of the planet. Mick also suffers from the usual paranoid delusions of persecution, most of it brought about by his father's death and his own incarceration. Claims that a government conspiracy has kept him locked up all these years. In Mick Gabriel's mind, he's the ultimate victim, an innocent man attempting to save the world . . .

Flash: Her first visit with Mick. The handsome paranoid schizophrenic with the ebony eyes moves closer, inhaling her scent. *"I swear on my mother's soul that I won't harm you."*

Flash: She is in the Gulf of Mexico, on a boat with Mick, after helping him escape. *"Mick . . . back in the asylum when you asked me if I believed in evil. What did you mean by that?"*

"I also asked you if you believe in God . . . if you believed in a higher power."

"I believe someone watches over us, touching our souls on some higher plain of existence. I'm sure part of me believes that because I need to believe it, because it's comforting. What do you think?"

"I believe we possess a spiritual energy, which exists on a different dimension. I believe a higher power exists on that level, one we can only access when we die."

"I don't think I ever heard heaven described quite like that. What about evil?"

"Every Ying has its Yang."

"Are you saying you believe in the devil?"

"The devil, Satan, Beelzebub, Lucifer, what's in a name?"

Flash: Back in Chichén Itzá, on the winter solstice of 2012, the prophesied day of doom. Ennis Chaney grips her by her wrist, refusing to let go, as Mick walks purposefully toward the dead alien serpent's open mouth—the entrance into the nexus.

"Let me go! Mick, what are you doing—"

"I'm sorry, Dominique. I love you—"

He steps over the bottom rows of teeth and enters the serpent's mouth . . . leaving her forever—

Forever . . .

"I love you Dominique . . ."

Forever . . .

"Ma . . . thank you. I love you."

"I love you, too, Manny."

Forever . . .

"Be happy."

Forever . . .

Her eyes flash open as she screams, "Jacob!"

The transport ship leaps clear of the olive green whirlwind, climbs into the atmosphere, and races into space.

Mick's eyes flash open as he regains consciousness. "No . . . no!"

Dominique grabs hold of him as the pod rockets higher. "Shh . . . it's okay—"

"No! I am One Hunahpu! I am One Hunahpu!"

"Mick, it's me, it's Dominique—"

"Abomination . . . trying to kill me . . . seeping into my mind . . . I am One Hunahpu . . . I am in control . . . I control my mind, not the Abomination." He tears at his hair. "Oh, God, oh, God! Oh, God! Oh, God! Oh, God—"

Dominique struggles to restrain him as invisible hands guide the ship toward the potato-shaped moon.

Mick thrashes wildly, his madness like a raging tsunami. "My mind . . . a safe haven. My mind . . . protects me . . . a cave. Oh, God, let me die! I want to die! Let me die, let me die—"

The moon-shaped vessel appears in the view screen, an immense eighteen-mile-long, twelve-mile-wide iridium transport ship, its hull pockmarked by indentations and one very massive crater-sized dent.

"Abomination! Abomination! I will focus on the cave walls and not the exit and the Abomination cannot harm me!"

"Mick, stop, it's me! It's Dominique!"

A tractor beam grabs hold of the pod, guiding it inside a landing bay.

The craft stops with a jolt. The pod's hatch pops open, revealing the three Guardian elders.

Mick is screaming, tearing at his harness.

The female Guardian reaches inside the pod and touches her palm to his forehead. "Sleep."

Mick's eyes roll upward, and he passes out.

The younger male grabs his wrist, effortlessly lifting him out of the ship, hoisting his inert body over his shoulder as if carrying a small child.

The female reaches inside the pod to assist Dominique.

She pushes the female's hand away. "You lied to us. Why didn't you tell us this was Earth? Why didn't you tell us the *Nephilim* were dead?"

The female offers her a motherly look . . . as she touches her forehead.

Dominique blacks out.

* * *

An azure lagoon, surrounded by a lush tropical jungle. A cool breeze stirs the palm fronds.

Dominique climbs onto the foam cushion, lies back, and floats.

"Dominique? Dominique, dear, it's time to wake up."

She opens her eyes, staring into the female's face. "Where—"

"Safe. On the transport."

Dominique sits up, feeling light-headed. The female Guardian helps her off a free-floating medical table, then points to a solid wall.

A viewport projects upon the metallic surface. The image reveals they are traveling in outer space, the silvery red world growing smaller in the distance.

Jake . . .

Dominique turns to the female. "Jacob is dead. Why did he have to die? To save a bunch of evil people?"

"The *Nephilim* were not evil, my dear, they were lost lambs, led astray. It was God's will that they be saved. Jacob's sacrifice saved his own soul and theirs."

"And Devlin?"

"That, I cannot say."

Dominique rubs her eyes, thinking about everything. "So what happens now?"

"The Earth we knew is long gone. By returning through the wormhole and into the past, we may yet be able to prevent the holocaust that destroys human civilization."

The female's attention turns inward as she listens to an incoming telepathic message. "Come. Michael needs you."

Dominique follows her through a short corridor into the main compartment of the transhumans' transport ship. She looks around, incredulous.

There are close to a million of them—eight-foot-high cryogenic pods, set in countless rows on multiple levels throughout the eighteen-mile-long vessel.

Dominique peers inside the frosted glass at the gangly being inside. "The posthumans?"

The female nods. "Their souls are finally at peace."

She leads Dominique to an immense vaultlike door at the very core of the ship. At the female's telepathic command, the door swings open, revealing the interior of a spherical chamber.

The two women enter. "This chamber is a secured pod, its power source and life-support systems independent of the rest of the ship. Its walls create white noise which serves to shield its occupants from telepathic communication, in essence, rendering it a quiet zone."

At the center of the chamber are two drained cryogenic pods. A myriad of hoses and wires run from each machine into the floor, linking the pod to a series of enigmatic devices lining one wall of the room.

Harnessed within one of these cryogenic glass chambers is Michael Gabriel. He is unconscious and naked. The elder male Guardian hovers over him, securing a series of star-shaped electrodes to points along his scalp, crown, forehead, solar plexus, heart, sacrum, and feet.

Dominique moves closer. "What are you doing to him?"

"The experience of fighting off the Abomination for so long has damaged One Hunahpu's mind. The only way to restore his sanity is to rebuild his memories."

The female takes Dominique's hand. "The posthumans' technology gives us the ability to manipulate Michael's mind, to place him into soothing, safe, virtual-environments that will allow us to nurture him back to sanity. But the therapy requires a hands-on guide, someone who knows One Hunahpu intimately . . . someone he trusts."

Dominique stares at the empty cryogenic pod. "What do I have to do?"

The male Guardian speaks. "We'll place both of you under a light anesthetic, then link your mind to One Hunahpu's using the posthumans' virtual-reality device. Your consciousness will maintain complete control over the device, giving you access into One Hunahpu's thoughts, allowing you to guide him through his rehabilitation."

"Why the anesthetic?"

The male gazes at her with his piercing blue eyes. "The VR device will not activate until you enter REM sleep. The anesthetic assists in this endeavor. Since it will take many sessions before One Hunahpu begins to show progress. I suggest we begin the first therapy sessions immediately."

"Therapy." Dominique laughs nervously. "That's how the two of us met."

The female smiles. "He loves you, my dear. The therapy will not only heal his damaged mind, it will allow the two of you to be together. Once inside the pod, you will not be able to distinguish your shared virtual existence from the real world."

Dominique is beyond exhaustion, her body in constant pain. "I think I could use a break from the real world."

"Remove your clothing."

She strips down, then allows the male to assist her into the pod. He connects the seven neural chakra links, then attaches a dime-sized anaesthetic patch to the back of her neck. "This will help you to sleep."

Dominique tastes a metallic bitterness in the back of her throat. She looks up at the Guardian elder, swallowing hard. "I'm cold."

"You'll feel comfortable in a few moments."

The female leans over her and smiles. "Pleasant dreams, my dear . . .

My dear . . .

My dear . . .

My dear . . .

The male checks Dominique's vital signs. *She's stable. We must hurry, before the star goes supernova.*

The male Guardian quickly connects a tracheal tube, intravenous tubes, and elimination hoses to Mick and Dominique while the female fits plugs into Dominique's nostrils and ear canals. *Is cryogenic suspension really necessary?*

This was all discussed. One Hunahpu's mind is in chaos, but it is still quite powerful, and it still has access to the nexus. If left unbridled, it could potentially affect the ship's trajectory through the wormhole. Placing him in cryogenic suspension is the only way we can shield his mind from the higher dimensions.

I was referring to First-Mother. I don't like lying to her.

She would have fought us if we revealed everything. She would have delayed the therapy, potentially risking One Hunahpu's life.

I disagree.

As is your right. Computer, seal both pods. Begin preservation process.

A clear gel-like liquid flows out the bottom of each pod, lifting the two inert bodies as it rises to fill the tank. The Plexiglas frosts, then crystallizes.

The male elder enters the ship's control room, his mind instantly updated telepathically with multiple status reports from the four Guardian elders inside.

The Balam?

Long gone. It disappeared through the wormhole hours ago.

Most distressing.

Is it possible that One Hunahpu is controlling it?

Impossible to say. The origins of the Balam remain a mystery.

Preparing to enter wormhole.

Appearing on the forward viewport is the wormhole's glowing emerald green orifice, beckoning them in.

The mammoth oblong transport ship accelerates, entering the time-space conduit.

A moment later, Sirius-B goes supernova, the titanic explosion rattling time and space with the energy of 100 million suns.

A male voice . . . his screams echoing in the dank, dungeonlike basement.

Dominique's consciousness moves through the antiquated concrete-block corridor of the Massachusetts asylum, following the guttural sounds to a row of cell doors. She stops at a cell marked SOLITARY CONFINEMENT. Tries the door.

Locked.

Remember, you're in control.

"Open, please."

The bolt unlocks, the door swinging open.

Inside is an eight-foot by-ten-foot cell, its bare cement floor and walls damp with mildew. A broken toilet and sink. A bare bulb, no windows.

Scratched into the far wall is a map of the world, a half dozen points X'd off in dried blood.

Mick is curled up on a wafer-thin mattress on the floor. He turns and gazes up at her, his ebony eyes so dark, it is difficult to tell where the irises begin.

"Who . . . who are you?"

She smiles. "A friend."

Mick sits up. "Dr. Foletta won't let me have visitors."

"Dr. Foletta's been transferred. I'm in charge now." She holds out her hand. "My name's Dominique, and I'm here to help you."

The transport soars through the wormhole like a pebble flowing through a garden hose, the effects of the supernova twisting and turning the currents of energy, until the massive spaceship is forcibly spit out the other side.

The blackness of space returns.

They soar toward a yellow sun and familiar star patterns. Up ahead, a bright blue world.

Home.

The asteroid-sized transport slows, establishing orbit around the watery planet.

The elder male Guardian paces the conn, his transhuman blood simmering. *What happened? Every calculation was accounted for!*

Apparently not every calculation. The younger male Guardian's telepathy burns in his superior's mind. *The* Balam *entered the wormhole before us. Its presence apparently altered the wormhole's trajectory.*

The female, positioned within a comm link station, opens her eyes. *Cartography confirms we overshot both third and fourth dimensional coordinates.* She activates the viewport, the image of the blue world they are orbiting appearing below. *The planet we are now orbiting is not Earth, it is Mars. Ancient Mars. The computer positively identified the planet's moon as Deimos.*

Mars has two moons, not one. Where's Phobos?

I believe we are Phobos.

The elder male stares hard at her. *How far into our past have we traveled?*

She looks up at him. *The time period equates to 127 million years before the time of Osiris.*

And the wormhole?

Gone. We are stranded in this time period.

Warning lights and a telepathic siren blare throughout the vessel.

WARNING: TACHYON DRIVE OVERHEATING. PRIMARY AND BACKUP COOLING SYSTEMS OFF-LINE. EXPLOSION IMMINENT.

The female works her control. *The ship's engines have seized, so have our shields!*

The gargantuan internal explosion violates the hull, igniting a flash fire that races through the vessel, consuming everything in its path. Sections of infrastructure melt and collapse, the Guardian crying out in agony as the intense heat bursts their hairless elongated skulls into flames, melting their eyeballs, peeling their charred skin away from their bones.

Steam fills the corridors as rows of cryogenic pods begin to melt. Glass fractures, a river of gel pouring from the shattered vessels, percolating along the gridded floor.

It is over almost as quickly as it began. Within seconds, the vacuum of space inhales the ship's air supply, dousing the flames, leaving death and destruction in its wake.

The damaged iridium-and-iron satellite continues orbiting Mars, its interior hull now lifeless—

—save for two isolated souls.

An azure lagoon, surrounded by lush tropical foliage. A cool breeze stirs the palm fronds.

Dominique lies naked on the cool pink sand, watching in delight as Mick climbs to the top of a twenty-two-foot waterfall.

"Dom, watch!"

"I'm watching, but you'd better hold on to your you-know-what."

With boyish charm, Mick leaps from the rock, executing an awkward one-and-a-half gainer.

Dominique waits until he surfaces before applauding. "That was really . . . awful."

"Thank you." He swims closer, his bronze body as naked as hers. "Come here."

She enters the lagoon, wading in the shallows and into his arms.

"Do you know how much I've missed you," he whispers.

"Yes."

They embrace—Adam and Eve in Eden—the only two souls in the world, oblivious and carefree in their own uninterrupted eternity of happiness—

—until that fateful day when a serpent shall again reenter their garden.

DECEMBER 27, 2033
CAMBRIDGE ARCHAEOLOGY DEPARTMENT

The American strides purposefully down the empty corridor, the sound of his footsteps picked up by the acoustic monitors, activating the holographic guard image at the security checkpoint. "Good evening, sir. Authorization, please?"

The American holds up his forged passport and palm. The infrared beam scans his ID tab.

Two floors up, the information is instantly sent to the Cambridge Archaeology Department. A moment later, an older gentleman's face appears in place of the guard's. "You came fast, Professor Rosen."

"I happened to be in the country. When were the papers found?"

"Two days ago. Construction workers discovered the vault when they started tearing down the old library. None of the department heads remembered it being there. Must've been built back in the early 1940s."

"The papers . . . may I have them, please? I'm in a bit of a hurry."

"Who isn't these days? Give me a few moments."

The American watches the digital clock. Wipes perspiration from his brow.

Minutes pass like hours.

Finally, the elderly British professor appears in person, a rusted metallic lockbox in his hand. "Everything's inside, Professor Rosen, just like we found it. Not sure why you'd even want it, to be honest. Gave us all a good chuckle when we read it."

The American takes the box, stifling his excitement. He opens it, removing the dust-covered text:

■■■■■■■■■■■■■■

THE FINAL PAPERS
OF JULIUS GABRIEL

■■■■■■■■■■■■■

Secured within the vault of
Cambridge University
AUGUST 21, 2001

The azure blue eyes glisten behind the hazel contacts, the dark-haired American forcing a smile. "Yes, I'm sure we'll all have a good laugh at this back in the States."

"What part of the States you from?"

"Uh, Florida."

"Really? The missus and I are heading there next month. Just booked passage on the space plane—our first trip. Twentieth anniversary and all. Ever been up?"

"Not yet."

"Took us four years just to get tickets. You ought to book as soon as you can. By the way, you can keep those papers. Nobody 'round here seems to give a *bluck* about them."

Bluck? Bloody fuck . . . Damn British string slang.

The American waves, then turns and leaves. He exits the building and climbs in the back of a waiting cab.

The large African-American in the front seat glances up at the rearview mirror. "So?"

Immanuel Gabriel holds up the lockbox containing his paternal grandfather's papers.

The bodyguard turns to his Caucasian companion. "Get us outta here, Salt, before the wicked witch figures out we just stole her broom."

The cab turns into traffic, accelerating into the night.

THE END OF *RESURRECTION*

Available now
Part III of the DOMAIN TRILOGY:

PHOBOS

For a Sneak Peek
Click on www. SteveAlten.com